To Missy!
Thank you so m.
Please Enjoy!

Also by Richard F. Welch and Vallorie Neal Wood

Dorowski Bridge

Bitter Wine

Knight's Gambit

The Murder of Belle Starr (a screenplay)

Vallorie Neal Wood

In The Shadow
Of Mountains

RICHARD F. WELCH

&

VALLORIE NEAL WOOD

ISBN-13: 9798526960441
Imprint: Independently published

DEDICATION

To my wife, Jill Williams, who has guided and inspired me all these years

To my husband, Wayne Wood, whose spirit is still with me and still encourages me daily

ACKNOWLEDGMENTS

This is the result of a collaboration that began more than thirty years ago at Kennesaw State University. Over those years, we have attempted to provide readers with action, suspense and mystery across many countries, using characters with real faults and real needs.

PROLOGUE

Keely Greer loved the morning just before the sun ascended above the spit of land that jutted into the Mediterranean Sea, sheltering the broad sweeping beach of Tangier. The serenity of the white sand and the blue waters still bathed in shadowy light made her morning run sweeter. Particles of salt carried on shore by the constant breeze kissed her lips, as she crested the hill where the Medina of Tangier looked down on the Mediterranean.

Running connected her to the earth, the sun, and the sky, as she desperately searched to regain her sense of self. Every stride crushed memories she needed to exorcise. The five-mile ritual each morning didn't exhaust her; she had always pushed her body hard, muscles burning. Now it was penance for her sins.

She had come to Tangier to escape her past; to free herself of guilt and anguish caused by the last few months. In spite of her efforts, the memories still haunted her. But on mornings like this, the fresh air filled her lungs as her skin absorbed the sun's rays. She breathed in the brackish air and exhaled as she ran, focused on the here and now. 'Redemption in progress,' she whispered. She ran harder and faster, the soles of her feet punishing the ground.

Keely was not the kind of woman who would stand out in a crowd, although she knew she was not ordinary. The well-defined muscles of her arms and legs hinted at years of intense physical training. Her skin was the color of cafe au lait-- passed down from her Sicilian mother. In the Moroccan sun, it had burnished to a glowing bronze. If someone didn't look too closely, she could easily be mistaken for the Moroccan girls who sauntered through the Medina, the bazaar at the center of the old city and center of activity in Tangier. Those girls were a stark contrast to the tall German tourists whose height, shock of blond hair and pale skin perpetually pink from the North African sun marked them as 'foreigners.'

Chestnut eyes dominated Keely's oval face, several shades lighter than her dark-brown hair in uncontrollably tight curls. Now she wore short hair, a symbolic gesture of letting go of the past. She had always been quick to smile; she could often see the humor in most situations. Smiles came less often now.

She reached the beach on her morning run and turned to admire the beauty of the Medina clustered on the hillside overlooking the harbor. Tangier is the point in North Africa closest to Europe. By the 14th century, it had become a major port of call for traders. For three hundred years, the Spanish, Portuguese, and British fought over ownership with the British besting the others, creating a hodgepodge of Colonial, Moorish, and European architecture. Shops jammed the narrow zigzag streets. Bright blue doorways and windowsills punctuated the whitewashed Medina. At first, Keely had thought these were Arabic affectations, but learned that Moroccans believed the bright colors dissuaded mosquitoes from entering their houses.

Below the Medina, and running in a sweeping arc to the east, a raised stone pedestrian walkway divided the Avenue Mohammed VI. Cheap tourist hotels and sidewalk cafes huddled around the entrance of the port. Further east along the wide Esplanade, the classier hotels overlooked a wide, white beach. At the far end were the newest hotels with fancy restaurants and a casino. Keely never visited them.

Behind the hotels, the land sloped up, crowded with new high-rise office buildings, few occupied and many only half finished. She had asked a waiter about the construction. He winked, looked around, and whispered, "Drugs." Apparently, laundered drug money fueled the building boom. Beyond this commercial district, houses had been built along a ridge that enclosed the city proper. They reminded Keely of the expensive homes perched along the California coast, although much smaller.

2

Keely spent her days and nights alone--she wanted it that way. Her first week in Tangier, she stayed at one of the smaller seaside hotels, not sure how long she would be there, but not wanting to attract undue attention. Finally concluding she had nowhere else to go, she sought something more permanent and private.

Her apartment was in a cluster of buildings just outside the eastern portal to the Medina.

At first, she thought the noise from the bazaar would be bothersome, but she discovered that most shops closed by seven, after which an almost unnatural quiet fell over the area. After nearly a month, her apartment remained devoid of personal trappings, as it had been when she moved in. Its monastic severity helped her focus on an uncertain future. The friendliness of her Moroccan neighbors surprised her. Shop owners aggressively cajoled tourists into buying overpriced trinkets, but once they discovered she was a 'local,' they seemed to respect her privacy.

Most mornings, her route provided the solitude she craved. Some mornings, she encountered old men shuffling along, glancing her way with toothless smiles and waves. She saw few women out early, assuming most must be tending babies or in the shops. Sometimes young men who had spent the night drinking in one of the clubs in the newer part of the city would catcall after her.

One morning, a group of young toughs blocked her way. The most brazen of the bunch stepped forward, his arms reaching out and motioning her closer-- his smile anything but amiable. Keely stopped and waited. When the young man reached for her arm, her hand shot forward, grabbing his wrist and twisting it in a decidedly direction. Before the others could react, he had fallen to his knees screeching in pain. Keely lessened her grip a bit and leaned down.

"*Tu devrais avoir honte*," she whispered. "Allah will not smile on you."

Such encounters were few.

Keely shared her daily ritual with the fishermen in rickety skiffs two hundred yards off shore soundlessly pulling in their nets. Today appeared to be a good catch, she thought, as they heaved their prize into the boats. Her mouth watered at the prospect of a good meal at her favorite restaurant later in the evening. She passed tourists-- mostly Brits and Germans-- working off a hard night of drinking. Up the side streets, children with tiny Mickey Mouse backpacks sleepily headed off to school. Keely watched it all, disconnected. She shared her world with no one, by choice. She maintained a steady pace, each stride carrying her further down the beach.

She looked at the rolling, barren hills, so different from the mountains where she grew up. In the shadow of those mountains, she forged a moral fiber that grounded her. She thought herself strong, loyal, and sensible. In the shadow of other mountains she tried to forget she lost herself. Could she recapture that other lifetime? Before she had crossed the line.

PART ONE

CHAPTER ONE

She heard her name called in the distance. It was probably her father, but the dry, mountain-chilled air was too intoxicating. She ignored him and continued to run. A sudden zephyr kicked up a cloud of dust and obscured her view of the mountains that formed the backdrop of Cortez, Colorado, which sat in a valley formed by the Sleeping Ute Mountain to the West and Mesa Verde to the South. On very clear days, Keely could just make out snow-capped Mt. Wilson to the north, the tallest peak in the Southwestern corner of Colorado. Thousands of tourists passed through Cortez on their way to the Anasazi cliff dwellings at Mesa Verde; many stayed a day or two longer for the natural hot springs around the city. Cortez was a sleepy community whose most famous native son-- the Sundance Kid-- had grown up there before becoming a notorious bank robber. Keely had been away from Cortez long enough to understand how comforting a small town could be.

Running was a morning ritual, less for her body than for her mind. It was time without thought. The pounding of her feet on the tarmac, the jolt that traveled up her legs, the altitude searing her lungs blocked out all other thoughts. Not that she had much to agonize over.

She heard her father call again, this time more insistent. To the outside world, Jim Greer was a gruff, no-nonsense Irishman, but his daughter knew he was mostly hot air. His blood pressure problems were of his own making, worrying too much about his business and his children. He loved both equally.

As a young man, he wanted to make the military his career and joined the Air Force shortly after finishing high school. It was the tail end of Vietnam, but he was sent as a crew chief for a C-123, flying between Tan Son Nhut Air Base in Saigon to posts up country. With two weeks left before he rotated back to the States, Jim was on a routine hop to a firebase close to the DMZ. The plane was on the final approach when it took ground fire. It was just small arms, but the rounds pierced the thin metal sheathing and caught Jim just above the knee. It all happened so fast that he was unaware he had been hit until he tried to stand and collapsed. Blood soaked his flight suit from mid-thigh down.

Back in Saigon, the Army doctor explained that the round had shattered his kneecap. His military career was over. Discharged, he was given a small monthly disability pension. Back in the States, he went to flight school, got his commercial pilot's license, and bought his first single-engine plane. He had spent time at Peterson AFB in Colorado Springs and had fallen in love with southern Colorado. He talked his wife into moving to Cortez where he opened an air taxi service. He started with a Cessna 120 that had seen better days and built a business ferrying hunters into the backwoods and transporting equipment and supplies throughout the four corners area. Their three children were born in the shadow of the mountains.

The high-altitude constricted Keely's lungs as she sucked in the cold mountain air. Rounding the far end of the runway her father's company shared with several other private air services, she could make out her father standing at the door of his office, hands on his hips. Her legs worked hard against the packed earth next to the runway. She watched her dad return inside. She stopped and turned to see the Sleeping Ute that rose from the flat plain several miles to the west. The mountain was smooth and rounded, like a naked female body in recline. The sun shone brightly on the crests while the valley below was still shrouded in dawn's half-light.

She hadn't realized how much she missed the mountains until she had come home six months earlier. It brought back welcomed memories of her childhood. There had been the long summer afternoons when Keely and her mother would sit on an old wooden swing her father had attached to the low branch of a tree in the backyard. They would talk until they no longer saw the mountains under a faded sun. Meghan Greer would absently stroke Keely's hair as she spoke of the simple things of life. She spoke of her hopes and dreams for her children. They weren't materialistic things. Hope, happiness, doing good for others... these were the achievements she saw as most worthy. Keely knew her view of the world came from her mother.

Growing up with two brothers, and in a neighborhood where the boys outnumbered the girls, Keely often found herself in battle, many of them physical. Her mother wanted her daughter to act more like a girl, and worried that she was turning into a tomboy. Her father agreed and arranged for piano lessons twice a week. They didn't help.

Keely had been fourteen when her mother died of breast cancer. It had come quickly, and her mother had remained optimistic until the end. In her final days, she had Keely promise to look after her father and brothers.

"They're good people," her mother had said, "but they need a woman's touch." It was the first time her mother had referred to Keely as a woman.

The day of her mother's funeral, Keely found her father sitting on the wooden swing. As she approached, she could tell he was crying. Quietly sitting beside her, she began to cry as well and as the sun sank below the mountains, their sorrow forged an unspoken bond that continued into her adulthood.

Jim Greer tried to be both father and mother, although Keely and her brothers thought him too strict and demanding. While their friends were off swimming and fishing, he had them work long hours cleaning and washing airplanes or doing paperwork he didn't want to pay a secretary to do.

Without her mother, Keely felt adrift. Though her father and brothers were capable of taking care of themselves, Keely honored her mother's wishes, cooking and cleaning while keeping up with her schoolwork. She did it conscientiously because deep inside, Keely knew this is what her mother wanted. Years later she realized it had also been her way to keep her mother's memory alive.

When Keely graduated from high school, she had no set plan. Her father wanted her to go to college in Fort Collins where he could keep an eye on her. Keely wasn't even sure she wanted to go to college, but her father had insisted. She decided to attend college at the University of Colorado in Boulder. At first, her father objected, but he knew that once Keely had something in her head, he was not going to change it.

The University was massive, dominating the smaller community that had grown up around it. It was not made for a girl from a small town. Very quickly, she felt herself slipping below the surface of campus life, unseen and uninterested. She hadn't declared a major because she had no clue what she wanted to do. Her freshman classes left her cold and her social life consisted of sitting in her dorm room reading trashy novels.

In her second semester, she was thinking of dropping out and returning to Cortez when she met Maggie. Maggie Mavoni was everything Keely was not-- blonde, bouncy, flighty and girly. They met in an art appreciation class when they were assigned to do a project on Durer, a painter neither had ever heard of.

Maggie was a sophomore and they hit it off from day one. Maggie appreciated Keely's sarcasm; Keely appreciated Maggie's outgoing nature. Maggie dragged her to clubs and parties, and soon the thought of leaving school faded. By her sophomore year, Keely felt more connected to school.

The one incongruity in Maggie's girly makeup was that she was a killer soccer player. Keely had been a sweeper for her high school's soccer team, but never thought about playing in college. She had played in pick-up games for exercise at college when Maggie dared her to try out for school's team. She surprised herself by making the practice squad, and after two of the team's forwards were red-shirted early in the season, Keely was moved to second string.

Although she never got a scholarship, she impressed the coach with her speed and brains.

In her junior year, a teammate took her to a meeting of the Air Force ROTC. Keely had finally decided on a major -- psychology -- only because she liked the names of the courses. She still had no clear vision of life after college. The Air Force intrigued her; especially when she found out she could officially earn her pilot's license and might even become an Air Force pilot. She had been around airplanes from the time she could walk. By the time she was a senior in high school, she could take apart an engine and had logged 150 hours of flying time, although she had never bothered to test for her license. Without consulting her father, she signed up.

He surprised her when she finally told him. "Sounds like a good deal."

ROTC gave her a new circle of friends, but she continued to play soccer. She and Maggie got a small apartment off campus. Maggie was now a communication major with visions of anchoring on CNN. When she graduated, she accepted a job with a station in Wichita, but she and Keely continued to talk on the phone and visit on weekends.

After graduation, Keely was commissioned a second lieutenant. She had signed up for flight school, but the Air Force had different ideas and assigned her to Air Intelligence School instead. Disappointed, she was at least comforted by the fact that the school was at Lowry Air Force Base in Denver.

Keely found the training much more interesting than she expected. Her instructors were pleased how she put in the long hours necessary to pull together bits of information from many different sources. She also excelled at photo interpretation--identifying objects on the ground from aerial reconnaissance. She figured it was from spending so many hours in small airplanes.

She applied for embassy duty just before she finished training, but ended up being assigned to a fighter wing at Mildenhall AFB in England as an intelligence officer. The job was simple-- briefing pilots and the base commander on weekly intelligence digests sent from the States. Her weekends were free, which allowed her to travel extensively. She had a boyfriend in high school and dated some in college, but never found anyone with whom she wanted something more intense. In England, she didn't want to get romantically involved with anyone, although there had been a sergeant from Arkansas-- sweet, attentive and, in his own way, romantic. When he rotated back to the states, they parted as friends.

After three years, she was reassigned to Offutt Air Force Base in Omaha, Nebraska, headquarters of SAC. The place was a zoo. There were so many generals running around, a newly promoted first lieutenant was lost in a sea of brass. One of her duties was attending mandatory social functions, which meant standing around for several hours with watered-down drinks and barely edible appetizers. Keely had no reason to be at such functions but knew that the young female officers on base were trotted out for 'window dressing.'

On one particular occasion, she was required to attend a reception for a group of British Air Force officers who were at Offutt for training. They looked so casually proper next to their American counterparts, Keely almost felt sorry for her generals. She smiled, scanning hors d'oeuvre trays.

"I thought they look cool, too."

Keely turned to the man on the other side of the buffet table. "The hors d'oeuvre or the Brits?"

He glanced past her toward the British uniforms in the room. "Them. Neat looking bunch of guys."

Keely nodded. "Makes us look like a bunch of movie ushers."

He came around the table and extended his hand. "David Fuller. You're over in planning, right?"

He was handsome, although it was obvious he thought he was much better looking than he was. She noted his captain bars and the two rows of brightly colored ribbons above his left jacket pocket: the usual wing commendations and a marksmanship ribbon. Hard to garner impressive medals in peacetime. She also noted the wings on his right pocket. A pilot.

She accepted his handshake. "Keely Greer."

"Nice to meet you. I'm the chauffeur."

"The what?"

"I fly the big wigs home for the holidays."

They both smiled. David turned to look at the circulating British. "They should be leaving in about half hour. You have any plans after this?"

David seemed no different than the other young officers she had met, but he seemed harmless enough and she had been feeling particularly lonely in the last few months.

"Television. TV dinner."

"Sounds disgusting." He picked up a limp shrimp. "How about some real food later?"

It took them almost an hour to slip out of the reception, stop at the Bachelor Officers Quarters for Keely to change into civvies, then to David's apartment. Keely surveyed the place while David changed.

It was typically male, a few photos on the wall featuring David and friends beside various aircraft. There were a couple of baseball trophies from college on a bookshelf alongside what appeared to be family photos. The furniture was expensive, but not very stylish. When he emerged, he looked a lot less pretentious in jeans and a sweatshirt.

They headed into Omaha, and drove to the district adjacent to the University, one of the few sections of town that had coffee shops and small jazz clubs. They parked and strolled down the street, merging with the stream of college kids. David steered her to a small club filled with smoke and passable jazz played by a student trio.

After two glasses of wine and a plate of nachos, David shifted his attention from the music to Keely. "How long you been at Awful Offutt?"

"Long enough to have me pounding on CPBO's door every day begging for a transfer. Actually, I only have about six months left, and I guess this is as good a place as any to wait out my hitch."

"One and done? For some reason, I pegged you as career."

Keely didn't know whether to be flattered or offended. Instead, she ignored the comment. "Well, I haven't made up my mind yet. There's really nothing keeping me in, but there's nothing on the outside that's calling to me."

"No 'steady beau' waiting patiently back home?"

"Never got around to one, I guess. The guys in my town ride around in pick-ups and think hunting is the height of culture."

"And nobody around here?"

Keely was a bit annoyed by his obvious attempt to find out his chances with her.

"Nope. No boyfriend… or girlfriend."

David blushed and she stifled a chuckle. They sipped their drinks for a few more minutes, then David smiled, almost bashfully, before he spoke. "It's just that… you don't seem the type who likes to be alone."

Keely nearly laughed, wondering how he'd come up with that. She managed to keep a straight face. "I guess it mostly depends on the company."

10

David grinned after a bit. "Hey, I know this quiet place we could check out tomorrow.

What do you say?"

Their relationship developed slowly; Keely reluctant to start anything serious. He was the youngest son of what he called a "Texas farmer." Keely found out that the 'farm' actually covered 10,000 acres in east Texas. Another 10,000 acres located in west Texas, and a small but very lucrative natural gas field in Oklahoma summed it up: David was rich. His older brothers had followed their father into the family business, but David had always been a rebel. He fell in love with flying as a teenager and talked his father into getting him an appointment to the Air Force Academy. After a mediocre college career, David went to flight school and then fighter training. He was a hot dog, but that was expected of fighter pilots.

His good looks, pilot wings, and endless cash got him lots of girls, but he had trouble maintaining relationships for very long -- because of the kind of girls he seemed to attract and because he lost interest quickly. While in advanced fighter training, he was almost court-martialed for sleeping with a general's sixteen-year-old daughter who looked twenty-one. His father's political clout was the only thing that saved him, but he was forced to leave fighter training and was relegated to flying C-21s.

As time for Keely's reenlistment drew near, David talked about the advantages of re- enlisting, but Keely knew it was because he was too comfortable having her around. After assessing what she could do in civilian life, she realized she had no real options. Going back and working for her father would feel like going back to being a kid. She wasn't sure she wanted something more permanent to develop with David. Was it convenience or commitment?

Nonetheless, with a lack of alternatives, she signed up for another four years.

She was promised another two years at Offutt, which was fine. She and David had settled into a comfortable relationship. On her twenty-seventh birthday, David gave her a three-carat diamond. He said it was a pre-engagement ring.

David had taken Keely to Texas and introduced her to his family as a 'friend.' His parents weren't fooled, nor were they happy. They had nothing specifically against Keely, but David was expected to marry into Texas aristocracy-- not get hooked up with some girl from Cortez, Colorado. David never took Keely back to his parents' home, and that suited Keely just fine.

Three months into their 'engagement,' Keely received orders for NATO headquarters in Brussels. David was less upset by the news than Keely expected. He just shrugged and mumbled something about a long-distance romance. At the airport, David kissed Keely perfunctorily and promised that he would fly over at the first opportunity.

Neither wrote much; it just wasn't their style. Phone conversations were short and filled with mundane chitchat. Keely was in Brussels four months before David paid his first visit. She met him at the airport, and her first impression was that he'd rather not be there. On the way to her apartment, the silence had been very awkward as Keely fumed. She hadn't asked him to come, it had been his idea.

But by the time they arrived at her front door, she had decided she'd give him the benefit of the doubt. Maybe she was reading his disposition all wrong. Once inside, David sat brooding on the couch. Finally, Keely demanded he tell her what the problem was. He confessed that his parents had coerced him into an engagement with the daughter of a rich Texas family -- they said it was this girl or his parents would cut him off.

Keely realized she was more upset David hadn't stood up to his family than at the thought of losing him. She walked to the small refrigerator in the kitchen, returned with two beers, and handed one to David. She toasted him.

"Well, hope you'll both be happy."

He looked like a dog that'd just been whipped. "You gotta understand. We're talking big money here. What was I going to do?"

Keely finished her beer. "Hey, listen, David, don't worry about it. They're probably saving us the cost of a messy divorce, anyway."

She took off the pre-engagement ring. "Better take this back." At first, he hesitated, then took it. "If you insist."

He looked around the small room, took a sip of his beer and shifted uncomfortably on the couch. "Look, Keely. Like I said, this marriage is really just a business arrangement. Maybe you and I could, you know…."

Keely knew. She put him on next flight back to the States.

Although David was out of the picture, she still had two years left in her tour. She threw herself into her work. To her surprise, she began to enjoy herself, working primarily as an analyst for NATO command. When her commanding officer recommended her for captain, she was flattered. But when her tour was up, she resigned her commission. She had had enough of uniforms.

Her father suggested she come home to Cortez. It would afford her the time to think about a career outside the Air Force and help focus her future.

Keely finished her morning jog and sauntered into her father's office. He sat behind his desk with a coffee cup in one hand and newspaper in the other and glanced up as she took a bottle of water out of a cooler beside the front door. She flopped into an overstuffed armchair, leaned her head back and closed her eyes.

"Damn, girl. Didn't you hear me hollering?"

"I figured if it was important, you'd come get me." She sat up, opened the bottle, and drank deeply.

"It was important," he grumbled." I may need you later if that bum McCallen doesn't show. So, get cleaned up."

There was a shower in the back of the building, and Keely kept a flight suit in her locker so she could change after her run. Although not officially on her dad's payroll, she logged fifty flying hours a month. Her father had paid her off the books, not much but enough. She hadn't expected to get rich if she lived at home. She glanced up at her father, noticing for the first time how grey his hair was turning.

"What's got you all steamed up?"

"I told you-- McCallen's late and I need somebody to run up to Fort Collins to pick up cargo."

"No problem, Dad. If he doesn't make it, I'll go. Don't let it get to you. You should take up walking."

"I should just fire McCallen and get me a pilot that can be on time. That guy doesn't even have the courtesy to call in when he's gonna be late. Thinks nothing of leaving me high and dry."

Keely drank down some of the water. "Yeah, Dad, that's what I'd do.'"

Her dad grimaced as he gruffly put down his newspaper. "You'd do what?"

"Fire his ass."

He opened the top drawer, rummaging through. "Don't make jokes. I'm trying to run a business here."

The opening of the front door interrupted him; he looked up. A man who appeared to be in his forties entered tentatively, glancing about as though he wasn't sure he was in the right place. His tan looked as though it came from lounging around some pool. His disheveled short black hair was peppered with gray at the temples. His eyes were a pale blue and he had the look of a mischievous schoolboy.

Jim Greer walked over to the counter. "Morning. Can I help you?"

"Good morning." The man's accent was British. "Perhaps you can. Name is Swift. Jonathan Swift."

He was ruggedly handsome but seemed not to realize it. He was dressed in expensive slacks and leather jacket, not the typical customer for their air taxi service.

"Seems I missed my flight to Denver this morning, which means I also missed my connection to Las Vegas. Need to get there in a bit of a hurry. I assume you have charters."

"Going for a day at the tables?"

Jonathan smiled. "Just business, I'm afraid. Actually, I will only need a one-way ride." "Well, let me see what we have."

Keely hadn't moved from the armchair, her feet propped up on the cooler. The man glanced in her direction with only the slightest curiosity. He gave her a half smile and turned back to her father. Keely wondered what would bring a dandy like him to Cortez.

The air of quiet confidence about him made her think life had tossed him about, but he had thrived. She noticed a bit of a limp as he moved to the counter, as though his knee was giving him a bit of pain. He seemed to move to avoid calling attention to it. Her father's voice distracted her.

"It could be a while. One of my pilots has a trip already booked and I have to run some fishermen back up to Denver this afternoon."

Standing up, Keely walked over to the counter. "Las Vegas? Take about three hours. We don't fly jets, I'm afraid."

Her father eyed her. "Don't you have somewhere to go?" He turned toward the Englishman. "My daughter. I can't keep her from hanging around here."

She ignored her father. "You said you were in a hurry, right?"

Jonathan looked from one to the other, his expression apologetic. "Well, yes. I have an appointment I really can't miss. Are you a pilot?"

Keely's father's displeasure echoed in his voice. "Fort Collins, remember?"

"I can do both. Why waste the gas?"

Jonathan looked from Keely to her father. "I don't want to cause any problems."

She looked at Jonathan. "You won't." She turned to her father. "Get me air clearance, Dad. I'll get the plane fueled, and I'll swing back through Fort Collins." She turned back to the man. "Pay my father and meet me outside." With that, she headed for the shower area to change.

They had been airborne for half an hour. He had said nothing since he had buckled himself in and they had taken off. The flight was smooth and easy, but she felt she was making him nervous. She glanced over to check on him, and noticed his eyes fixed on the name patch "GREER" on the flight jacket she wore. He met her look.

Your father was in the Air Force?"

"Yeah, he was. But this isn't his. It's mine."

His eyebrow rose slightly, but he said nothing. She smiled at his surprise. "Seen any Lilliputians, lately?"

14

His looked indicated he had been asked that before. "Sorry. Didn't your parents know you'd get kidded when they named you?"

"Actually, Jonathan Swift-- the original one-- was my great, great, great grandfather.

I'm actually Jonathan Swift the fourth, although that sounds pretentious. I went by 'John' in public school, but realized Jonathan just suited my personality better. More elegant. Has more style, don't you agree?"

"Sure."

Keely turned her attention to the instruments. They rode in silence for several minutes, Swift glancing at the ground periodically. Keely didn't know if he was accustomed to flying with female pilots.

"Worried about my flying skills, Mr. Swift?"

He looked at her and smiled. "Hardly. And please, Jonathan."

"Just making sure. Some guys are afraid to fly with a woman pilot."

"You seem to know what you're doing. Otherwise, I doubt seriously your father would have allowed you to fly me."

"You're right about that."

"Do you mind if I ask, do you always get your way with your father?"

Keely glanced over at him before she checked the altimeter. "Usually."

He laughed and looked away from her, closing his eyes for a second.

Keely glanced at him. "What kind of business are you in, may I ask?"

He studied her for a second. "I collect things."

"A collector? Must be good business. What sort of things do you... collect?"

"Various items. Not really all that interesting."

"Something in Vegas you just have to have? Is that why the rush?"

He looked over at her, then back to the front window. "I assume your chat is part of the in-flight service?"

Keely felt her cheeks get hot. "Just curious how fast you need to get there."

"Get us there, and I'll be fine."

A quarter of an hour passed in subdued silence. This man had a way of turning his charm on and off. That irritated her for some reason, though she had no right to make any sort of assumptions about him. 'Just be civil,' she thought.

Finally, he broke the silence. "When did you learn to fly?"

Keely glanced at him to read his expression; was he trying to compensate for being a pompous jerk earlier.

"Dad started teaching me when I was old enough to sit on his knee and look out the window, me and my brothers. We had to work at the airfield when we were kids. But I didn't get my license until I was in the Air Force."

Jonathan's eyes traveled over her flight suit. "You don't seem the service type."

Keely laughed. "What 'type' is that?"

He laughed, too. "I didn't mean to infer anything negative. I was about to say you didn't look old enough."

"I assume your inquisitiveness is part of your in-flight banter."

Jonathan laughed again, touching two fingers to his forehead and saluted. "Touché."

"Two tours. I left as a captain."

"No doubt one of their best pilots."

"I wasn't a flier-- I worked as an intelligence officer."

He didn't answer, but when she glanced over, his fixed smile hid his pensiveness.

Keely had flown the route to Las Vegas many times, following the Arizona-Utah border, turning southwest after spotting the Grand Canyon out the left side of airplane. Passing over Page, Arizona, she made radio contact with a controller who was a friend of her father. He had a message waiting for her-- *call home.* Keely laughed, then looked at Jonathan.

"I usually get my way, but my father always has to get the last word."

"He wasn't happy that you volunteered to fly me?"

"No, he wasn't."

"Well, I can only apologize." He chuckled.

"My dad still sees me as a little girl. Nothing I can do about that. But he knows I'm capable of flying anywhere. Plus, my dad installed a button that will launch somebody in your seat right through the roof."

"Hmmm. How James Bondesque."

Keely laughed as she checked the altitude then checked the ground for landmarks. "I promise, you're in no danger,"

Jonathan said, leaning toward her slightly. "I'm glad."

She started to reply, but a sound from one of the engines grabbed her attention; something she wasn't pleased to hear. Jonathan heard it too and looked out his side window.

"Did you know your right propeller seems to be slowing?"

She tightened up on the controls, but not out of alarm. "I know. But don't worry."

He casually glanced at her. "Oh, I'm not worried. At least it isn't on fire."

"There you go, look on the bright side. But really, don't worry. It's done this before."

His look lingered on the propeller. "Before, huh?"

16

"I thought our mechanic had fixed it." She caught his concerned glance, and she smiled her best, reassuring smile. "Really. It'll be okay. We're not far from Vegas. And we're not over water. Another blessing."

Jonathan didn't seem convinced as he watched the altitude indicator begin to drop. "Well, Captain, you're the pilot."

Keely didn't answer, concentrating on the controls as they became sluggish. She knew she wasn't making it to Las Vegas Municipal Airport and quickly calculated her alternatives, a good place to put the plane down safely. She eased the airplane to the north and looked over at Jonathan.

"I'm really sorry. We'll have to make a slight detour. Just relax. Everything's fine. We're just a bit east of Vegas, but I would rather be safe than sorry. There's a landing strip in Overton, Nevada, about a forty-minute drive from Las Vegas. I'll arrange for ground transportation…and of course, we'll refund your ticket and pay for the transportation to Vegas."

Jonathan did not seem shaken. "Do what you think is best." He checked his wristwatch. "I should still be able to make my appointment."

Keely radioed the air controller at the small runway outside Overton at the headwaters of Lake Mead where she had landed a number of times. They could be there in less than ten minutes. She asked the controller to have a car waiting. When they were over the field, the tower's radio operator informed Keely the runway was clear for landing. She brought the plane limping into the Overton airfield. Keely taxied to the small building that functioned as the terminal. When the good engine was shut down, Jonathan and Keely climbed out, and she examined the engine. Streaks of oil splattered the underside.

"Damn. This will take a couple of hours." She turned to Jonathan. "Sorry about this. Mountain Airways is usually more dependable."

Jonathan smiled and moved closer to her. "And I suppose you're going to tell me you will fix the plane as well."

"Well, actually I could, but the ground crew here is pretty good. I'll let them handle it."

Keely walked ahead of him; Jonathan lingered back a moment glancing from her to the plane and back. He followed her finally into the terminal. Keely talked with the mechanic, arranging for the repairs. When she finished, she walked Jonathan outside to the waiting taxi and handed the driver three twenties. They shook hands; Jonathan held her hand a few seconds longer than necessary.

"Thank you for an… interesting ride. Perhaps I could call on you again. For transportation."

Keely withdrew her hand and gave him an exaggerated British salute, palm out. "Glad to be of service."

She watched the taxi pulled away from the terminal, intrigued by the man. There had been something unnerving about him. He seemed too self-assured, too self-contained, but he had intrigued her. It was not attraction as much as curiosity. She wanted to know more about him, but wasn't sure she wanted to spend more time with him. The feeling surprised her, as she turned back to the terminal.

'Doesn't matter,' she said under her breath, "I'll never see him again."

CHAPTER TWO

Keely sat alone in her father's office, watching the first rays of early-morning sunlight creep across the airfield. Her father had a six a.m. charter, and Keely had promised to mind the store until he returned. Keely hadn't been in the air for over a week. She was about to close up and head home for breakfast when the phone rang.

"Mountain Airways."

"Keely. I was hoping you were there."

Keely immediately recognized the voice of the strange Brit she had flown almost to Vegas three weeks earlier. "Hello, Jonathan. I take it you got to Vegas in one piece."

"Never missed a beat, thanks. Anyway, I'm calling to see if you may be available for another charter."

"When?"

"Well, today if that's possible."

Keely hesitated. She knew her father would not want her to take a flight without clearing it with him. But he had just leased a Cessna Skyhawk SP, and she was dying to take it up.

"I'm glad you weren't frightened by your last visit there. What's the job?"

"I don't scare easily. How long would it take you to get to Overton and back?" Keely believed he didn't. "From Overton to Cortez?"

"Yes." There had been the slightest hesitation that made Keely wary, but she dismissed it. "Fine. I don't see any problem," she said.

"Splendid. Shall we say Overton at one thirty?"

After they hung up, Keely sat for several minutes wondering about this strange Englishman. She hadn't been able to shake the feeling he would somehow be back. But she wasn't sure how she felt about that. It wasn't necessarily an attraction; it was more curiosity. He never explained what his business was, but she got the sense it was as straight-forward as he had made it sound.

She picked up the phone and dialed the tower to get clearance and log her flight plan.

When the plane touched down at Overton, Keely was fifteen minutes early. The Skyhawk cruised at 160 miles per hour, so the trip took just under three hours with favorable tail winds. Keely taxied to the terminal and went into the service office to arrange for refueling.

She had radioed her father about the flight, and but his gruff tone told her he was not happy.

"That damn Englishman? I don't have a good feeling about him. He's bad luck. Besides, I need you in the office."

"Dad, you need an answering machine. Someone can't sit in there all the time. Besides, this is my chance with the Skyhawk. And we get paid for it."

Her father paused for a long time. "Damn girl, why can't you be like your brothers and listen to me."

"Thanks Dad."

At precisely one-thirty, a taxi pulled up outside the service office, and a balding man in his late fifties stepped from the vehicle, looking lost and frightened. His clothes were new, cheap, but ill fitting, as though he had just run into Wal-Mart and grabbed the first thing he found. He nervously brushed a fringe of gray, unkempt hair over his ears; a medieval monk lost in the desert. His eyes flicked about, as though he expected someone to jump out at him at any minute. He stood by the door as the driver unloaded two large suitcases from the trunk. As Keely watched the man, one of the attendants approached.

"Keely? Phone call."

Keely expected to hear her father's voice and practiced her defense on her way to answer the call. She went to the desk and picked up the receiver, still watching the older man who had moved into the shade of the terminal's overhang but had not made a move to come inside. She was curious why he had not paid the driver, who had driven off after depositing the man's luggage on the sidewalk. She turned her attention to the phone.

Jonathan's voice, instead, surprised her. "Don't tell me you've taken flight without your father's knowledge?"

"Jonathan, where are you?"

"A slight change of plans, I'm afraid. I won't be flying with you today."

A mixture of disappointment and anger churned inside her. "You mean I flew all the way over here…."

"You didn't let me finish. If you look outside, there should be an older gentleman looking terribly lost. He's your passenger."

Keely swallowed several choice replies popping into her head. She knew Jonathan was strange, but this was a bit much. She looked out the window at the man. "Yeah. I see the guy. I take it, you're not coming along?"

"'Fraid not, but I will meet you."

The irritation was more than obvious in her voice. "Is this some kind of game?" Keely toned down her voice. "I'm sorry. I don't like games."

"I assure you, it's all quite… innocent. I just need you to transport my friend back here."

She did not like his use of the word 'innocent' and she did not like the idea of being played. She noticed how uncomfortable the older man was waiting outside. She wanted to walk away, but after all, she was here already. "So where am I taking him to?"

"Cortez. I'll meet you there."

"Fine. We'll be in Cortez by five."

She went to slam the receiver down, but Jonathan had one more thing to say.

"Oh, one last thing. Mr. Smith-- that's my friend's name--has a package for you. Please open it before you take off."

Jonathan hung up before she could respond. Tension knotted her neck. Her hot temper burned her cheeks, but she had made a deal. She replaced the receiver and walked to the front of the terminal. When she stepped outside, the desert air had heated up and the perspiration had already stained the man's collar.

She approached him, smiling. "Hi, I'm Keely. Jonathan sent me."

The older man gave the smallest of smiles, though he seemed petrified. He looked around furtively and leaned in. When he spoke, his stale breath smelled of cigarettes and garlic. "Mr. Swift said you were pretty."

The man had a strong Arabic accent, which went right along with the Nevada desert. His skin was dark and his hair almost gray but full. His eyes were watery and faded. She guessed he had spent years squinting at a computer terminal. His skin was mottled, tracing a map across his neck. Keely tried to keep a friendly smile although the knot in her neck was killing her. She reached for his bags and motioned for him to follow her.

It took only ten minutes to load the luggage, log her flight plan, get tower clearance and taxi to the end of the runway. Mr. Jones sat strapped into the seat, his eyes racing around the cabin like a rabbit caught in a trap. He clutched a battered briefcase against his chest as though it was a talisman. Keely could tell he had never flown in a small plane before and turned to him with her best assuring smile.

"Don't worry. This plane is as safe as the biggest jets. Maybe safer. Besides, you'll get a much better view of the ground." Keely had almost forgotten Jonathan's last words. "Mr. Swift said you had a package for me?"

The man looked as though he was about to lose his lunch, but he opened his case and withdrew a small manila envelope. She opened it. Inside were seven $100 bills, a thin cell phone, and a note. She folded the money and slipped it into her flight jacket, laid the phone on the floor between them and opened the note.

It read: 'Thanks for putting up with this inconvenience. The phone is in case you need to contact me. I am on speed dial No. 1. If you would be so kind as to turn the phone on before you depart.' Simply signed 'J'.

Keely grudgingly turned the phone on and then turned her attention back to the flight.

Fifteen minutes into their flight, Keely checked on her passenger, who had sat quietly peering with utter fascination out the window. The engines were loud, making conversation difficult, but not impossible.

"Everything all right?"

Smith reluctantly turned his attention to Keely. "Oh yes. Yes. So beautiful down there. It reminds me." He stopped in mid-sentence as though realizing he had said too much.

From his clothes and sloppy haircut, he was not a VIP. And with that accent, his name couldn't possibly be 'Smith.' It was none of her business, but once airborne the plane practically flew itself.

"Is this your first trip out West, Mr. Smith?"

Smith nodded, looking unsure about answering her question. Keely almost jumped out of her skin when the cell phone rang. She let it ring three times before reaching for it. The look of fear returned to 'Mr. Smith's' face. She pushed 'on' and held the phone to her ear.

"Keely, glad you read my note." Jonathan's voice was strangely comforting. "How is our Mr. Smith getting on?"

Keely looked at Smith, who stared straight ahead, his face even paler than before. His knuckles strained against the briefcase.

"Not a seasoned traveler, is he?" Keely said quietly into the phone.

Jonathan chuckled. "Probably not. Anyway, I have one more favor to ask."

Keely's irritation flared quicker than before. She felt at a disadvantage and she didn't like that. "What?" She hoped her impatience came through in her voice.

Jonathan apparently ignored it. "There's been a slight change of plans. Instead of Cortez, could you touch down in Kayenta?"

Kayenta was in eastern Arizona, about an hour out of Cortez. She had passed the town a couple of times by car on her way to Phoenix. There was nothing there.

"Look, I already filed my flight plan for Cortez. The FAA is really not happy with people who change plans."

For the first time, she sensed Jonathan was not comfortable, and his voice took on a different tone, much more business-like. "I understand Keely, but this is absolutely necessary. Believe me, I wouldn't ask if there was any other option."

Against her better judgment, Keely agreed, silently convincing herself that it was no big deal. Jonathan said he would meet them at a small field just to the southwest of the town along Highway 160. He also explained there was no tower, so she'd have to come in on her own.

She flew on for a half an hour in silence. With each passing minute, she became more intrigued by Jonathan's business. She ruled out smuggling. Her passenger hardly looked the type. She wanted to grill him, but seeing that his nerves were already frayed, she wouldn't get much out of him. Besides, she was more interested in Jonathan.

There was an aeronautical map of the four corners region in the back and she asked Mr. Smith to find it. He fumbled around for a bit and held up the folded map sheepishly. "Is this it?"

Keely couldn't help but smile at the nervous man. "Open it up and try to find a town called Cortez."

Mr. Smith worked with the map, but it was obvious he had never seen this type of map before.

"Look, fold the map in half with the printed side out." He followed her directions. "Now, fold it in half again, but in the other direction." The simple task seemed to ease his nervousness.

She glanced over to see how he was holding the map. "Good. Now, look up in the right-hand corner of the map for a city named Cortez. I've got it circled in red." He found it, beaming as he looked up, his pudgy finger marking the spot.

"Great. Now, slowly move your finger down and to the right about four inches… ten centimeters." Again, he followed her instructions, slowly moving his finger across the map. "You are looking for a small town named Kayenta. K-A-Y-E-N-T-A."

When he found it, he smiled broadly. "Here?"

He kept his finger on the spot until she had taken the map. She studied the area. Indeed, there was a small runway just outside the town. She noted the runway's orientation and surrounding landmarks.

Keely touched down just after three p.m. There was an abandoned shed to one side and beside it sat a van, Jonathan casually leaning against it. Keely taxied to a spot adjacent to the van. She cut the engine and climbed out as Jonathan stepped forward. Another man sat in the van, its engine running. She walked to the passenger side of the airplane and helped Mr. Smith down. She smiled, seeing how very happy he was to be back on the ground.

Jonathan reached them, shook Mr. Smith's hand and turned to Keely. "I really must thank you for this highly unusual stopover."

Keely wanted to come back with something sarcastic but decided against it. They unloaded Mr. Smith's luggage and Keely stayed by the airplane while Jonathan walked the man to the waiting van. Just before Mr. Smith stepped in, he turned in her direction, smiled and gave a small wave. Keely watched the van pull away leaving Jonathan behind.

He walked back to her. "Thank you again, and if you don't mind, I'm returning to Cortez with you."

Keely wanted to tell him he could walk back, but only motioned to the passenger side.

They did not speak for the twenty-minute flight to Cortez, but as they taxied toward the hangar, a smile spread across his face.

"I would like to apologize for this highly unusual flight and would like to treat you to dinner tomorrow evening."

The whole day had been 'unusual,' but there had also been something about it that, deep down, had energized her. It was obvious Jonathan wasn't what he seemed, but she sensed that he was one of the good guys. She didn't know how she knew; she just did.

"Fine. Since you don't have a car, I'll pick you up. At--?"

"The Cortez Inn. On East Main, I believe."

The restaurant was crowded and boisterous. It was the best and most authentic, Mexican restaurant in the city. Keely and Jonathan made their way through the tightly packed tables to a spot toward the back. Keely greeted a number of patrons before they reached their table. A comely waitress in jeans and T-shirt reached them before they had settled in their seats.

"Hi, Keely. Collin home tonight?"

Keely smiled sweetly at the girl and shrugged. "Actually, I think he decided not to come home this weekend. Can you get us two Coronas?"

The girl looked disappointed but waltzed away and Swift followed her with his eyes. "Lovely girl."

Keely sensed he was baiting her. "Yeah. She's got the hots for my brother. But he's not interested. Of course, in a town like this, pairing up isn't always that easy. Not a whole lot to choose from."

He turned his attention back to her. "How about you?"

She felt a flush rising in her neck. "I'm not looking. Been there, done that, got the T- shirt," wishing immediately she had not been so glib. "I'm not looking for any relationships right now. And," she laughed, wondering why she had to explain in the first place, "it's really none of your business." She immediately wished she hadn't said that either.

The waitress arrived with their beers before he could respond, and took their orders, Jonathan deferring to Keely to make the selection. When the girl left, Jonathan looked at Keely for a long moment with an inscrutable expression that made Keely slightly uncomfortable. She was relieved when he broke the silence.

"I must confess this dinner is more than just an apology." "You're just full of surprises, aren't you?"

"Actually, occupational hazard."

"Yeah, that reminds me. What do you do? You some kind of travel agent for little old guys from the Middle East?"

Jonathan smiled broadly. "Syria, actually. Nice try though."

He brought his beer to his lips, never taking his eyes off her. The look was innocent enough, although Keely felt there was more to it. There was an impenetrable, unnerving look to his eyes. He put down his beer.

"I was quite impressed how you handled yourself... yesterday and several weeks ago." He hesitated; she wondered where his idle conversation was going. "I was wondering how attached you are to your present position."

Keely shrugged, totally baffled. "My present situation? What are you babbling about?"

Jonathan smiled and removed a piece of paper from his jacket. He unfolded it and began to read: "Greer, Keely A. Honorable discharge as an O-3 in 2014. Two tours in England, one in Omaha and finished in Brussels." He looked up. "Not bad duty." He continued to read. "Worked as a 14N3 in planning and analysis. Assorted commendations and recommendations. Top secret clearance. Speaks conversational French, passable German. Not married."

He laid the paper on the table and looked at her with expressionless eyes. Keely was stunned, angry, and embarrassed all at the same time. She was also a bit frightened. She didn't like the idea of a stranger prying into her life.

"Where'd you get that? And why?"

"Let's just say I have friends in high places. As to why, well, it has to do with my business."

He reached into his pocket and brought out a business card, sliding it casually across the table. Keely picked it up. It was simple, but elegant. Centered on the card was the name 'Jonathan Swift.' Below it was two lines: 'Senior Consultant' and 'Swift Enterprises, Limited.' In the lower left-hand corner was a telephone number with a British international code and an email address. She looked back at him.

"Swift Enterprises. Never heard of it."

Jonathan smiled as he folded her biography and returned it to his pocket. "Don't expect you would have. We don't do a lot of advertising."

"And you're telling me this because--?"

"Keely, how would you like to come to work for me?"

She sat for almost two minutes sipping on her Corona and watching the man across from her, unsure how to react to Jonathan's offer. He intrigued her; especially wondering how this Englishman could have gotten so much information about her so quickly. The initial shock passed, she wanted to be offended, but strangely, she wasn't.

Jonathan sipped his beer as well, a slight grin on his face, as though amused by Keely's consternation.

Finally, Keely responded. "And where exactly is this company? What kind of business? What kind of revenue? And just how . . . legal is this business of yours?"

Swift smiled. He leaned in, his fingers absently pulling at the bottle's label. "Swift Enterprises is a service provider for certain government agencies here and other places. We handle situations from which our clients would like to maintain a certain amount of distance. In return, they pay Swift a handsome fee."

He had piqued Keely's interest, but it sounded like something out of a spy novel. "Are these services legitimate?"

Jonathan stared at the ceiling as though searching for the correct terminology.

"Within certain parameters. Of course, there are circumstances when rules do get a bit bent."

"What kind of circumstances?"

"Well, each situation is unique and requires… unique responses. We make decisions based on circumstance. Most of our contracts are rather mundane."

"Sort of like with Mr. Smith?"

"Precisely."

"And the ones where the rules get bent?"

He chose his words carefully. "I won't mislead you. There is a certain amount of risk involved with some of our assignments, but we take every precaution to avoid trouble. Besides, after the way you landed that plane a few weeks ago, I'm surprised you would be concerned."

26

"Helps in the decision-making process. These risks? Can you be a bit more specific?"

"Of course. The risks are usually connected with discovery by local authorities not privy to our contract. We are, after all, taking on sensitive work that our clients do not want broadcast far and wide. Since we have contacts in very high places in most of the countries where we work, the risk usually entails a few uncomfortable hours at a local constabulary office. In other countries, we play it by ear."

Keely didn't respond.

He continued. "Most of our work is in Europe, although we are not limited to that area. I would expect you would have to relocate to England. You did say there were no ties to keep you here?"

It was all coming at Keely too quickly. It sounded too good to be true, but Swift made it sound tempting. The fact he could get her service record so quickly showed that he did indeed had friends in high places. Still, she wasn't convinced.

"Sounds like a big decision. And still not convinced you are telling me everything."

He looked hurt. "I was hoping you would be intrigued."

"I haven't said no."

The waitress interrupted, placing their meals on the table. With a look of delight, Jonathan went to work immediately on his combination platter, but Keely was no longer interested in food. After several minutes, Jonathan noticed she wasn't eating.

"I'm sorry. Is something wrong with your dinner? Mine's marvelous."

Keely had finished her beer and had motioned for two more, which now arrived. She took a long pull from the new bottle before she spoke.

"So basically, what you're saying is that your company does some sort of spook work that no one wants to own up to. And what would be my job?"

Jonathan placed his fork precisely on his plate and wiped his mouth gently with his napkin. "First, there would be a certain amount of training involved, but from all indications, that should be no problem." He patted his pocket where he'd slipped her biography. "And, of course, a more thorough background check."

Keely leaned back. "Seems you have more than enough already. What else do you need to know?"

Jonathan smiled. "There's the matter of financial encumbrances, law enforcement records. Any unusual skeletons hiding in your closet. The usual.
"

Keely knew that working in sensitive areas as he had described required someone with a clean background. She just wasn't sure why he wanted her for the job.

"So why me?"

Jonathan smiled. "Actually, happenstance. Let's just say you impressed me in a number of ways. It started with your calm presence of mind on our first flight-- an important ingredient in any situation. When I returned home, I made a few inquiries. What I found out intrigued me. Then, my work with Mr. Smith took an unexpected turn and I needed to move him out of Las Vegas. I should confess that your little sojourn with Mr. Smith was a bit of a test." He folded his hands in front of him. "And, of course, you passed admirably. As to why you, it's because I have considered for some time that my company needs a female operative."

Keely eyed him suspiciously. "Wait, I would be the first woman?"

"No, no. Our office manager is definitely female and quite the task master. But she is not interested in field work. More comfortable behind a computer."

"So I would be bait. Or a hooker."

Jonathan laughed. "I can assure you that has nothing to do with it. With all due respect, I took into consideration your physical attributes. Your height and physique, your hair and facial features would probably allow you to go unnoticed in a crowd anywhere."

Keely leaned back, retreating from his less-than-flattering assessment. Of course, she knew the best operatives were those who did not stand out, who were -- unnoticeable. She had never thought of herself as exceptionally attractive, but he made her sound like a plain Jane. "Thanks."

He quickly put up his hand. "I don't mean to imply that you're less than attractive. I was thinking more that in certain countries-- particularly in the Mediterranean-- you could easily pass as a local, which ultimately helps you to be 'invisible' if necessary. Also, because you are so youthful looking, you could pass as a college student. Also, a great asset."

"That still doesn't explain why me."

Again, Keely felt Jonathan was not comfortable answering that question, but he pressed on. "I can assure you, I pride myself in being a great judge of character. And as I said, I have come to realize that we need a female field operative. As for you specifically, it is simply a case of the right person in the right place at the right time. I would like to offer you a position."

The thought of doing something intriguing and potentially rewarding was appealing, but it all seemed to be coming at her too quickly. "What if I don't work out?"

"We will draw up an employment contract that allows you to leave any time you wish. And if you decide this is not for you, you would still receive one year's compensation."

"I'm still not saying yes, but you still haven't explaining exactly what I would be doing?"

Jonathan picked up his fork again and brushed it across the plate, a few morsels left.

"Let's use Mr. Smith as an example. He is-- was-- a low-level bureaucrat in his country's intelligence agency. Actually, just a lowly accountant, but he knew where all the money came from and went to. He got word to a member of British intelligence that he was frightened what was happening in Syria and wanted to leave. Although England has strained relations with Mr. Smith's country, it felt uncomfortable helping him leave. But the information he could provide was very tempting. That's where Swift Enterprises entered the picture. We facilitated his departure, arranged for his transportation to the States, and have secured him a pleasant and secluded residence."

Keely narrowed her eyes. "Seems simple enough."

Jonathan nodded his head. "And for our services, we received fifty thousand dollars." He toasted her with his beer. "Plus expenses, such as airfare."

Keely felt her mouth drop open despite herself. "Fifty...."

Jonathan smiled. "Now, this was a particularly advantageous contract, but not an unusual one. I would venture to say that in your first year, you could expect to make two hundred fifty thousand dollars."

Keely's military pay had been modest at best but had been plenty for her needs. She had a nice little savings account and with what her father paid her and the fact she lived at home, expenses were negligible. This offer was too good to ignore. Her first thought was to jump at the chance, but there was a nagging concern that an offer too good to be true, probably isn't. She stared at Swift. He seemed honest, if a bit pretentious. And he did have her service record.

"You've said 'us' a lot. Just how many other people work for Swift Enterprises?"

He toyed with his food for a second, then looked at her sheepishly. "Perhaps I misused the imperial 'we.' Actually, at the moment, there's just myself and our office manager. I do use contractors on occasion, but I think it is time to . . . expand."

"I'd be one of only three employees at 'Swift'?"

"There have been a number of assignments I've had to pass on because I did not have a female operative. To be honest, most good female contractors are kept busy by the big players."

"How long do I have to decide?"

"Take as long as you like, as long as I can have an answer by next week."

She didn't sleep much after dropping Jonathan off at his hotel. She had driven up into the mountains, stopping at an overlook with Cortez spread out below her. She had been happy coming back home, but she had always known that someday she would want to move on. Her dad liked having her around, but there really wasn't enough business to keep both of them occupied. But could she really allow herself to be talked into something that seemed so unrealistic? Swift was real enough, but she was still leery about making such a big commitment.

The next day, she called a friend stationed at the Pentagon. Lorie Monroe had shared Keely's office at Offutt. Lorie sang at a local country and western bar at night, her sweet voice calming even the most hardened cowboy. Keely tracked her down and asked her to check on Jonathan Swift. Lorie called back two hours later.

"Man, this Swift guy has a lot of clout. I talked with somebody I know over at NSA. She said he's a real big shot; that when he calls, people answer the phone. But that's all I can tell you. Get this, there's a big, fat 'No Access' on his file."

She then called Maggie, now with CNN in London. Maggie made some inquiries and came back with the same report Keely had gotten from Lorie. Keely called Swift and invited him for lunch at Bob's Drive In.

Once they were seated and had received their burgers, Keely took a sip from her soda. "I'm still curious about one thing. You said you were the only operative. Is there some reason you haven't hired anybody else before now?"

Jonathan took a moment before he answered. "I have always felt that the fewer people involved, the less chance of complications. But lately, I've wanted someone to bounce ideas off. Someone who could be more creative in fulfilling our clients' needs. And, of course, I felt a female operative could access places I could not."

"Maybe you need a nanny."

Jonathan frowned. "I believe you are reading too much into this. With you at Swift, we-- I can expand our services." He seemed to hesitate. "There is one other item I may have neglected to mention."

"Here it comes."

He cleared his throat, then looked at her across the table. "This isn't a 'stay in the office' kind of job. Most of our contracts take me to various places around the world. We may be traveling together, in close quarters. Would that present a problem for you?"

She smiled. "Not for me. You?"

"Not at all."

She sat quietly for several minutes, staring at her French fries. Finally, she looked at him. "I'm still not one-hundred percent sold on all this, but as long as I can always walk away, I guess I can give it a try."

Jonathan smiled. "I am delighted. I think we will make a fine team."

"I'll need time to take care of some things before I come to England. Please let me know how much you will need to transition to England, and I will make arrangement. Rhonda, that's our office manager, will be in touch to arrange air."

He nodded. "Take as much time as you need. That is, as long as I can be sure you will come."

Jonathan remained in Cortez for a few days, during which time, he gave her a cashier's check for $5,000 for 'moving expenses.' Before he left, they had dinner one last time. Over cocktails, Keely broached a subject that had been preying on her mind since she had met him.

"So exactly how did you get into this business?"

Reluctantly at first, Jonathan began to explain.

He had been an officer in the Special Air Service, Britain's ultra-secret military Special Forces that had its roots in World War II and Korea. In the last ten years, the S.A.S. was deployed to hunt down and eliminate terrorists-- actual and potential--with impunity. They were also used in hostage situations and as extraction teams when British subjects were threatened anywhere in the world. They operated outside the normal military chain of command; few questions were asked or answered concerning their activities.

Jonathan had been with the S.A.S. for almost ten years when he was part of a team sent to Malta to 'neutralize' a Libyan who had been implicated in a series of bombing that had killed three British tourists in Egypt. They snatched the man from the streets of Valletta with relative ease and drove him to the virtually uninhabited western tip of the island. The man begged to pray before he died, and Jonathan let him walk several paces away. As the man knelt in prayer, Jonathan watched impatiently, not sure how long the road, which snaked back toward the populated areas of the island, would remain empty.

Without warning, the man jumped to his feet and ran toward the rocky cliffs above the sea. Jonathan, taken by surprise, instinctively gave chase. He had almost reached the Libyan, when the man stopped suddenly and whirled to face Jonathan. He caught Jonathan in the chest with a forearm, and Jonathan's pistol skidded along the rocks. The man dove for the weapon and fired blindly in Jonathan's direction. He only managed one shot before Jonathan's team emptied their weapons into him. Unfortunately, the bullet the man had fired shattered Jonathan's knee.

After extensive surgery and painful therapy, Jonathan was able to walk with only the slightest limp. But his days in the field with the S.A.S. were over. They offered him a desk job, but he laughed that off. He was not the desk type. Even though he was given full military disability, Jonathan was restless. But his skills were not marketable in the normal sense. After a year of inactivity, a friend at MI-6, Britain's equivalent of the CIA, called to ask if Jonathan would be interested in a temporary job. It was surveillance, which MI-6 was reluctant to undertake because of the potential political embarrassment it might cause if anyone found out they were looking. Jonathan accepted the contract.

The job was simple and over in less than a fortnight. Jonathan was paid the equivalent of a year's Army salary for the work. And Swift Enterprises was born.

The word went out to the intelligence community that he was available to undertake tasks that intelligence organizations would or could not do. Soon, his reputation spread to the Americans, the Israelis and other NATO countries, and he had more work than he could handle. He periodically subcontracted work to others: usually former intelligence agents who, because of injury or age, were no longer active. Swift Enterprises had been in business almost six years.

Keely got all of her affairs in order; she had accrued few possessions and fewer bills. Her biggest problem was her father, dead set against her running off with some 'foreigner.'

He fumed for a day or two before confronting her.

"You don't know what you're getting into with this guy."

"Dad, I had him checked out. Maggie says he's legit and well connected in London. Besides, you saw the contract. You even had Tim look it over." Tim Hollerand had been the family's lawyer for years. "Tim says I can get out of it any time I want and there's even a clause that says Swift has to pay a year's salary regardless."

None of that satisfied Jim. "Look, there might be danger in this. You just don't know. How can I send you off with that hanging over my head?"

Keely walked over to where he was sitting and sat on the arm of the chair. "Look, you raised me to be smart. I'm not going to take chances. You've got to trust me on this." She wasn't sure whether she was trying to convince her father or herself.

He tried to be cheerful for her sake, but he remained opposed to her going. A week later, he halfhearted flew her to Denver for the first leg of her trip to England.

At the drop-off, he hugged her. "Home's always here."

CHAPTER THREE

Keely landed at Heathrow Airport, something she'd done a number of times, and made her way to customs. The flight had been uneventful. The only difference from her other trips was this time she was in Club World class.

Her seatmate was an older man, who explained he was a litigation lawyer with a large firm in Pittsburgh heading to London for a deposition. When he asked Keely what was taking her to England, she hesitated. Jonathan had not said to keep Swift Enterprises confidential, but she guessed he wouldn't want his work broadcast.

Instead, she told her seatmate she was interviewing for a job with a financial firm in Birmingham. She found lying came easy-- maybe too easy.

"Besides," she said motioning around the cabin, "how often do you get the royal treatment for a job interview?"

As the flight continued, however, she wondered just how much she would be asked to bend the truth in this job, and if she had ethical concerns that would inhibit her.

She knew from experience that customs at Heathrow would be exhaustive. Standing in the mass of passengers in baggage claim, she assumed Jonathan would be waiting on the other side of passport control. When her bags finally appeared, she loaded the pieces onto the trolley she had commandeered and headed for customs.

Jonathan had faxed her a temporary work permit two days after he had returned to England; a feat that re-enforced her impression that he was indeed well connected. The customs official took his time examining her passport and papers. He paused at the pages that had stamps from previous entries into England during her Air Force tour.

Keely wondered if her impression of Jonathan's pull was misplaced, but the official finally stamped her passport and welcomed her back to England. She finally exited into the sprawling terminal.

A crush of people waited along the ropes to welcome passengers, and Keely was surprised when she saw a young woman with unnaturally bright red hair holding a sign bearing her name. The girl smiled and waved when Keely looked in her direction. Keely made her way to the girl, who appeared to be in her early twenties, quite attractive, but wearing what looked like an outfit from the sixties. When Keely reached her, the girl hugged her.

"Keely, what a real pleasure. Jonathan described you perfectly, although he didn't say how pretty you are."

Her accent was Midlands, although she obviously was working to hide it. Keely smiled. "Where's Jonathan?"

"Oh, he said to tell you he was sorry for not being here in person, but he was called away on business. I'm Rhonda, Jonathan's assistant. Actually, more like Jane-of-all trades, if you know what I mean. He'll be back in a few days. Asked me to fetch you and get you settled. That's all your luggage?"

Keely masked her disappointment. "Not really a clothes horse."

Rhonda reached for a suitcase to carry, then pointed toward the street. Keely picked up a suitcase and hurried to keep up with Rhonda, dodging other arriving passengers.

"Are we going far?" Keely called to Rhonda.

"About twenty miles north of London proper… about a forty-minute drive from Heathrow." Rhonda continued toward the exit.

Outside, Rhonda led the way to a Land Rover in the reserved parking area. As she opened the rear door, Keely noted the license plate's diplomatic sticker. Rhonda followed Keely's look and smiled.

"Jonathan hates looking for parking spots."

Once the luggage was stored and both of them buckled in, Rhonda maneuvered the vehicle out of the airport and headed north on the M25. Keely had no idea where they were. She had been stationed at Mildenhall Air Base, 100 miles northeast of London, and on the rare occasions when she had come into the city, she had taken the train.

Keely looked at the young woman, whose fingers tightly gripped the steering wheel as she kept the car in its proper lane, a bit intimidated by other cars weaving in and out of traffic. "Jonathan never did tell me exactly where the office was located. I just assumed it was somewhere in the city."

The girl smiled through her nervousness, but never took her eyes of the road. "Actually, we're in a little town called St. Albans. The train can get you to Victoria Station in less than an hour."

Keely scratched her forehead, bewildered. "St. Albans?"

Rhonda chanced a look at Keely and smiled sweetly. "That's where Jonathan grew up.

His family has a lovely place just off a park there. Jonathan has the office set up above the living quarters."

"So, we're in Jonathan's home?"

Rhonda giggled. "Don't worry, luv. We're chummy, but not that chummy. Jonathan has taken a flat for you on the other side of the park. Quite lovely and modern, although small. Two blocks from the train station. You can walk anywhere in the city in less than twenty minutes. Can get to High Street in ten. All the services you need--grocers, public house, chip house are just 'around the corner."

"And you?"

Rhonda understood the question. "Live with me'mom close on to High Street. Been there my whole life except for university."

Keely looked at her and could tell Rhonda was used to that reaction. "University of Surrey for a diploma in Political Studies. Quite fun."

Keely felt embarrassed. She decided she better be careful about snap judgments. Rhonda sensed her embarrassment and smiled.

"You'll get used to St. Albans; it's a great place because it's not too big. Jonathan has also rented you an auto--small one. He said you had lived here before, so you're familiar with the roads."

Keely didn't want to admit that she had always been scared to death of driving in England. It was good that the airbase had been out in the boonies. She had never attempted to drive in London. She sat back and watched the rolling hills of the western edges of the London suburbs.

When Jonathan had talked about the company, she imagined his office was in crowded and noisy London. The thoughts of living in a large city had helped her decide to take Jonathan's offer. She enjoyed the bustle of big cities, though she was basically a small-town girl at heart.

Soon, Rhonda exited the M25 into the sparsely populated countryside. Rounding a wooded hill, Keely got her first sight of St. Albans. It was like the small English towns she remembered. Quaint brick homes set haphazardly among rolling hills, church steeples rising above the houses. Closer to the town, stores crowded winding avenues. Buildings centuries old leaned precariously against one another. They passed rows of tiny shops, many with shopkeepers lounging outside talking with passersby.

They crossed over a bridge, passed the tiny train station, and pulled into a cluster of incongruously stylish apartments. There were four buildings surrounding the parking area. Rhonda pulled into an empty space and shut off the engine.

"Welcome home."

They climbed the open-air stairs to the second floor of the building on the north side of the parking lot. There were only two doors on the landing and Rhonda put down Keely's suitcase while she fished in her purse for a key. Once inside the apartment, she led Keely into the small living room and opened the curtains to a miniature balcony just big enough for two people to stand.

Keely could see a cluster of trees over the roofs of adjacent houses. She walked to the sliding doors and opened them, the damp, cool mid-morning air carried in on a brisk breeze. Keely suddenly felt very comfortable in this place.

Rhonda took her on a tour of the apartment, such as it was. There were two bedrooms, one not much bigger than a closet. Keely noted that a desk with a laptop computer dominated the space. A galley kitchen opened into the combined living-dining area and a small bathroom off the larger bedroom. And that was it. Keely had had better apartments, but the place was clean and new—what else could she need.

Rhonda stood in the hallway as if wondering what to do next. Keely walked to her and gave her a hug.

"Thank you, Rhonda. For the ride and for helping me. You're sweet."

Rhonda blushed. "Well, shall I leave you to unpack or…."

"You saw how little I have. I can do that later. How about showing me around the city."

Rhonda giggled with an infectious laugh. "Hardly a city, luv, but we try."

They walked for two hours, Rhonda showing her the best shops, where there was good take-out Chinese and Indian food, where the post and telephone offices were. St. Albans was bigger than Cortez, although not as spread out. There were a number of lovely clothing shops and pubs on almost every corner. Rhonda explained everyone had his or her favorite, rarely visiting any other. The town sat adjacent to a magnificent cathedral, whose grounds spilled down to some of the oldest known Roman ruins in England.

Keely placed a call to her father from the telephone exchange even though it was four a.m. in Cortez. He answered on the first ring. Keely told him her flight had been great and explained, briefly, where she was and that she would call later to give him her new phone number.

The two women found themselves near the St. Albans Cathedral close to teatime, and Rhonda suggested supper at a pub sitting across from the Roman ruins. As they passed through its lop-sided and cramped entrance, Rhonda proudly pointed out that it was oldest pub in England. The two talked for a long time, Keely enchanted by Rhonda's animated chatter.

Rhonda had worked with Jonathan for two years, having taken the job right out of University. The work was not particularly difficult, but Jonathan had impressed on her the importance of maintaining the highest level of confidentiality. Jonathan was gone at least two weeks a month, which meant Rhonda spent most of her days answering a few calls, handling correspondence, and reading trashy romance novels. Jonathan had installed an imposing computer system, but it took Rhonda to show him how to get the most out of it. She was a natural with technology and Jonathan never made a purchase without first consulting her. She spent a considerable amount of time doing research that required hours on the Internet, something at which she also excelled.

It was early evening when the two finally made their way back to Keely's apartment, their arms filled with packages from various shops to stock Keely's kitchen. The long flight, even in business class, had finally caught up with Keely, and she told Rhonda she had to lie down or she would fall down. As Rhonda was leaving, Keely hugged her again.

"I think this will be grand fun, don't you?"

Rhonda smiled her best little girl smile. "Oh, I am so happy we'll be working together.

It's quite nice to have another body around-- especially another girl. I'll come around tomorrow morning and take you to the office. Actually, you can almost see it from your balcony. It's just on the other side of those trees."

The next morning, Rhonda arrived promptly at eight. Keely had been awake for several hours. She knew her body would not adjust to the time change for several days, but she felt rested and ready to get to work. Rhonda bounded into the apartment. If possible, she was more effervescent than she had been the day before.

"Right, have you had your morning coffee?"

Keely was working on her fourth cup and held it up to show Rhonda. The younger woman seemed crest-fallen.

"I wanted to take you to my favorite breakfast spot."

Keely put down the cup walked to the door, took her coat off the hook, and looked at Rhonda. "What are you waiting for?"

After a fortifying English breakfast of eggs, baked beans, bangers and bread and jam, the two walked to Swift's house. It was a lovely fieldstone home tucked in among the trees overlooking a tiny park. The vacant street seemed to meander out of sight through the foliage. In front was a lovely English garden and hedgerows twenty yards on either side of the house, separated the adjacent houses, ensuring privacy. The house itself looked at least 150 years old but appeared in immaculate condition. Keely had no clue what housing prices were like here, but she figured this place had to be worth a small fortune.

Rhonda pulled the car onto a cinder drive, circled the house and parked beside a two-car garage. She exited the car and pointed at the back door, which appeared to be made of heavy oak reinforced with ornate iron scrollwork.

"Usually, we go in the back, but today, you need the full effect." Rhonda led the way to the front door. It was ornate, with scroll works accenting the dark oak.

Inside, a hallway ran from the entrance to the back of the house. To the right was a formal sitting room crowded with a collection of overstuffed Victorian furniture. To the left were closed pocket doors. Rhonda motioned to them.

"Jonathan's quarters. Used to be a proper English home, but Jonathan had it reworked." She motioned to the sitting room. "Beyond that is a dining room and kitchen in back. Jonathan just has a bedroom, library, and bath."

Keely gave Rhonda a questioning look. The girl smiled. "Don't be naughty."

Keely followed Rhonda up a flight of the stairs with an intricate balustrade of dark, polished wood. At the stop of the stairs, there was a small landing and another antiques door, the only incongruity was a keypad, on which entered a seven-digit code. "I'll get you the numbers. You'll find out, Jonathan likes secrecy."

Walking through the door was like stepping from the 19th century into the 21st. The room ran the width and length of the house. Frosted windows long both sides allowed in light. Its whitewashed walls were covered with large maps of Europe, Asia, Africa, and the Middle East. There were three steel desks, two of which had imposing computers to one side. In the back, was a glass enclosure filled with electronics, several copiers, and what looked like Teletype machines.

Rhonda turned around and smiled when she noticed Keely's awe of the enclosure. "The boss used to have all his gadgets out in the open, but I kept whining about all the noise until he built that."

She led Keely to the desk that had the least amount of clutter on it and a computer docking station.

"This will be yours. Your laptop fits into that gizmo and is wireless, both here and in your apartment. Jonathan asked that I get you up to speed on our current projects."

The girl's demeanor shifted effortlessly from casual to business. "Those red notebooks have the organizational charts of each of the agencies with which we do business. You also have summaries of our most recent projects in those blue notebooks. You can access the complete files on your computer at home, encrypted of course. There's a laptop for you at your apartment, which means you can work from home if you like, but Jonathan prefers we not access our files away from the office."

Keely looked at the notebooks. "So why the notebooks?"

Rhonda giggled. "I like real paper."

Keely's impression of Rhonda made it obvious why Jonathan had her as his assistant. She had Keely drag another chair closer and have a seat beside her. With a few keystrokes Rhonda was into the system.

"You'll want to set up your own passwords but be a luv and let me know. Not that I'll peek into your files, but Jonathan is always forgetting his and I have to help him in."

She showed Keely how to work her way through the computer system, including setting up her own access codes.

The remainder of the morning was spent reviewing files, becoming comfortable with the computer system, and generally settling in. Rhonda had gone downstairs after Keely had begun reviewing the notebooks, only to return with a tray carrying a silver coffee service and a plate of scones with lemon curd on the side.

"I noticed this morning you were having coffee. But you might prefer a cup of tea with these. Me'mom makes the scones for us. They're lovely."

Keely tackled the projects first. They were a grab bag of work, mostly surveillance or collecting secondary-source intelligence. As she read, her admiration for Jonathan's business sense grew. He seemed to pick jobs that were tricky without being dangerous. She knew from her years in the Air Force that the best intelligence was tediously collected from a number of sources, usually by pouring through data, but she had imagined that an independent contractor would be called on for more hairy jobs. That didn't seem to be the case. She had thought that a former S.A.S. officer would lean more toward the dagger rather than the cloak.

By mid-afternoon she had worked her way through the blue notebooks. She began on the red ones just as Rhonda returned with sliced meats and cheeses, hard-boiled eggs, thick-sliced bread. And tea. Rhonda looked a bit sheepish.

"I'm sorry, I forgot to ask what you preferred for lunch. Just mucked up a collection of what was in the frig. If you'd like something else...."

Keely held up her hands. "Actually, I'm not a big lunch eater. Maybe just coffee."

By five, Keely had finished both stacks of notebooks and had familiarized herself with the computer system. She had also sent off emails with her new address to her father, her brothers and to Maggie, suggesting they get together soon in London. She was impressed with the structure of the computer system. There was an internal system used, apparently for work. The hard drive had been partitioned in such a way that she could switch to a secondary system that seemed to allow free access to the Internet. When she asked Rhonda, the girl smiled.

"When I devised the system, I wanted a secure intranet that couldn't be hacked. But we also needed ready access to the world. I devised a system through a mainframe that allows us to switch back and forth without allowing hackers access."

Rhonda had stayed in perpetual motion--faxing, making copies, and making phone calls. The only time she sat still for more than five minutes was when she was online. She had asked Keely if she would like to help her locate background information on Muslim sub-sects in Yemen other than Sunni and Shi'ia. Keely's confusion brought an explanation from Rhonda.

"During down times, I have a list of 'research projects' that I do. We keep extensive files on lots of things--the best restaurant in Kuala Lumpur, a nice but private hotel in Greenland, all kinds of info on airlines and how to get tickets quickly. I also update files on major political issues and hotspots."

With each passing minute, Keely was coming to realize just how important Rhonda was, and the diversity of each mission of Swift Enterprises. She rolled her chair next to the redhead. Rhonda's fingers flew over the keys, and web pages barely had time to compose before she was off in a new direction.

Periodically, she would hit the print button, and just as quickly be off in a new direction before the laser printer began to spew paper. Keely watched the screen and Rhonda and saw the fascination of a young child on the girl's face. This was a real adventure for her.

The sky outside the window was darkening, both because of clouds that had moved in during the day and because it was close to 6 p.m. Rhonda had finally begun to wind down and Keely's eyes burned from hours of staring at the computer screen. Jonathan had not shown up or called, but Rhonda seemed unconcerned, so Keely assumed this was business as usual. Finally, Rhonda leaned back in her chair and stretched like a kitten finished with her nap.

"Well, my eyes have gone all woggly. The day's done for me."

She stood and perched on the desk. "What do you think of our little office?"

Keely smiled up at the girl. "Feel like I'm back in school, but it is very interesting, if a bit overwhelming."

Rhonda was satisfied. "Great. And now you will come have dinner with me and me'mom. No sense spending the night alone."

Jonathan did not show up for three more days. He provided no explanation why he had not called, nor did Rhonda ask. Keely figured the less said about his movements, the better. He greeted Keely grandly, asking her how she liked her apartment, the office, St. Albans. She went a bit overboard in her enthusiasm, but most of it was real.

"But… there is one thing you didn't tell me about."

Jonathan looked concerned. "What?"

"Rhonda, and what a treasure she is."

Rhonda, head buried in her computer, beamed. Jonathan smiled.

"Yes, she's quite special. Don't think I could survive without her."

Rhonda never looked up from her computer. "You wouldn't."

Jonathan ignored her. "Now, what say the three of us go to my club for dinner? Of course, we'll all have to change."

Jonathan's club turned out to be a modern mansion just outside town called the Centurion Club. A doorman greeted them upon arrival, and the three walked past a solicitous Maitre d' into a chandeliered hallway that looked like a movie set. Keely felt conspicuous when she spied several women in cocktail dresses. Her basic black dress seemed frumpy in this setting.

Rhonda, on the other hand, seemed perfectly at ease, even though her outfit was outlandish compared to any crowd. Jonathan dressed in a suit and tie seemed not to care about either of their styles. They made their way through the reception area to a circular dining room overlooking a golf course.

Throughout dinner, Jonathan regaled them with stories from his days growing up in St. Albans. He had attended a boarding school called Caldicott, then Eton and finally Cambridge, majoring in history. Keely wasn't sure how much was true and how much fiction, but if Jonathan had been involved in half the adventures he spun, he had certainly had an exciting childhood.

Over drinks after a bounteous, if bland, dinner, Keely thought she should impress Jonathan with the studying she had been doing.

"I was kind of surprised by the project files I was reading. Kind of mundane stuff. Very little cloak and dagger."

Rhonda looked a bit uncomfortable, but Jonathan smiled. Apparently, talk of work was supposed to be reserved for the office.

"Actually, our work is rather mundane." Jonathan lowered his voice. "You see, we are solicited more for our anonymity than for our daggering."

Keely shifted in her seat, feeling the sting of a reprimand in his wording. Jonathan laughed patronizingly.

41

"Our clients turn to us because they need information, they are uncomfortable seeking themselves. Agency directors want deniability. When questioned by members of Parliament or a Senate sub-committee, they want to say with all honesty, 'my department never actively gathered intelligence on Person X.' Now, if such information should make its way to their desks via some third party, well, they could hardly ignore it. We provide a service for which we are paid handsomely. Countries and companies need to know things, but sometimes gathering that information can be an embarrassment. That's where Swift comes in."

Keely thought for a moment. "Oh. More like glorified private detectives?"

Jonathan's loud laughter brought disapproving glances from patrons at the next table. "Yes, my dear, I guess you could say that. Let me add, our work is usually much safer, and much more lucrative. And we don't follow cheating husbands or wives." He stood, signaling dinner was over. "But it is late, and tomorrow you begin your training in earnest. So, it's back to home and bed."

Despite Jonathan's explanation of the kind of work they did, Keely's training also took a decidedly martial turn. Over the next two months, Jonathan established a grueling training regimen that began with mornings spent pouring over data and material drawn from a wide variety of sources.

After a light lunch, she spent two hours with language coaches, first French then Spanish and German. Jonathan would later add Japanese and Arabic, but he didn't expect more than a passing knowledge of these languages, enough to get through airports and order dinner.

Around three every afternoon, Jonathan would drive her to a shooting range some distance from St. Albans. There, he would spend two hours familiarizing her with various types of small arms. Keely had been around weapons her whole life. Her father and brothers had done their share of hunting, although she never could see the excitement of tracking down a defenseless animal and pumping it full of holes.

In the Air Force, she had qualified each year with standard military issue side arms. That entailed going to a range, firing two dozen rounds at a silhouette and being chided by a grizzled staff sergeant for not hitting in a tight pattern. Because of her field, she was also expected to qualify with an M-16.

Jonathan was more patient, but more thorough in his training. She started with side arms- revolvers and automatics that were standard issue for various NATO forces. Jonathan showed her how to fire two-handed with the weapon held chest high; not sighting down the barrel but sensing the target and the path the bullet had to take.

"You need to accustom your hands and arm muscles to the weight of the weapon, and the recoil it produces."

42

Keely fired almost three hundred rounds with each weapon before she could hit the bullseye. Jonathan explained technical aspects of the weapons as she trained, including how to clear misfires and how to disassemble the weapon. Keely could only move on to the next weapon when she could place eight rounds in a circle the size of a dinner plate twenty-five yards away in under thirty seconds.

Once she had mastered a dozen or so pistols, they moved on to long rifles, again working through the standard issues of several armies. By this time, her marksmanship had greatly improved, so Jonathan had her work on speed and distance. He would not proceed to the next weapon until she could place a dozen rounds in the silhouette at a hundred yards.

One afternoon as they left the shooting range, she asked, "Why all this weapon training. Thought you said we don't take dangerous jobs?"

Jonathan's slowed his pace until he came to a standstill and looked around at her, his arms folded behind his back. Keely almost swore she saw a hint of guilt in his eyes.

"We often don't always know the true situation till we arrive. And I believe it is best to be prepared for any contingency."

"Makes sense. But makes me wonder how dangerous jobs like your Mr. Smith could be."

Jonathan looked at her. "If we're not willing to train for the worst, the worst might kill us."

His sudden seriousness stopped Keely. "For the record, I happen to like this job. But I need to know what's ahead. Tell me and we'll get along fine."

Jonathan immediately laughed and then looked at her with a new appreciation. "Just continue to train and you will work out just fine."

The last hour of the day was spent in the basement gym at Swifthouse-- as she had begun to call Jonathan's home-- with Mr. Che. The elderly Asian gentleman had been a martial arts instructor for the S.A.S. since shortly after it began operations in Northern Ireland. Now in his seventies, he still had the suppleness of a twenty-year-old. He had belts in more forms of martial arts than Keely knew existed, but his favorite was Shaolin. It was the combat form of T'ai Chi Ch'uan, the Chinese Zen exercise practiced by millions young and old.

Mr. Che first taught Keely the movements that comprise T'ai Chi, and each day they would spend twenty minutes dancing slowly through these movements. Afterwards, he would show Keely how the moves, which were performed with almost excruciating slowness in T'ai Chi, transformed into lethal blocks and strikes when sped up.

43

Keely had always prided herself on her physical fitness, but she found the combination of T'ai Chi and Shaolin sapped every ounce of energy. After training, she would drag herself back to her apartment, stand beneath a scalding stream of water in her shower and fall into bed, sometimes not moving until the next morning.

Jonathan said training in martial arts and weapons helped sharpen her concentration. Indeed, the combination of data analysis, language training, target practice, and Mr. Che seemed to heighten her ability to bring disparate ideas together quickly. As her training progressed, Keely also felt her body change. It was as though every muscle had been awakened, toned, smoothed.

On the weekends, Rhonda and Keely would head into London. Rhonda introduced Keely to all the places where young people hung out--particularly the artsy crowd. Keely had hoped to spend time with Maggie in London, but the newswoman bounced around Europe so much that they were only able to connect once or twice in the first two months Keely was in England.

When they met, Maggie wanted to know all about her new job. Knowing Jonathan's penchant for secrecy, Keely felt uncomfortable explaining exactly what she was doing, but Maggie seemed to understand.

Keely had become very close to Rhonda and although she missed her old friend, her new friend was a wonderful substitute. On their weekend excursions to London, they would inevitably find themselves in some West End pub by mid-afternoon, commenting on the overstuffed young dandies who looked as though they still had on their starched collars, even in casual clothes. One afternoon, as a slight drizzle poured outside, the two sat quietly in a corner booth watching the world rush by outside.

"Rhonda, I've been meaning to ask you for some time. You never talk about a boyfriend. Do you, you know, have a crush on Jonathan?"

Rhonda giggled into her pint of beer. "Actually, no. He's not really my type."

"Oh, really. Who is?"

Rhonda giggled more. " Actually, your friend Maggie."

Keely was at first confused, then realized what the girl meant. She had several friends in the service who she knew were lesbians, although until recently, they could never admit it. She smiled. "Well, don't know about Maggie, but I'll keep my eyes open."

They both laughed.

Rhonda looked around the bar, populated mostly with young men. "Bit tough in St. Albans, actually. Not many girls who like girls there. I thought about moving to London, but my sex drive was not as strong as my love for St. Albans and me'mom and all."

Keely patted Rhonda's hand and smiled. "Well, kiddo, I think any girl would be crazy not to fall for you."

Rhonda smiled, squeezed Keely's hand and withdrew hers to raise her mug. "Here's to true love."

They clinked mugs and drank. After a moment, Rhonda looked at Keely.

"So now you know about my love life--how 'bout yours? You've been here couple months now and no dates as far as I know."

Keely hadn't even thought about dating since arriving in England, mostly because of the exhausting schedule at her new job, but also because there were very few opportunities for her to meet any men even if she had been interested.

"Guess I'm caught up in the work. Haven't really had chances to meet anybody."

Rhonda had a twinkle in her eye. "What about Jonathan? He's your type, isn't he?"

Keely didn't know how to answer. She had often caught herself lost in the depth of Jonathan's steel blue eyes. But she had attributed her reaction to his disarming personality. Jonathan was unlike any man she had known. It was not just his S.A.S. swagger. Something about him was both captivating and intimidating. She also felt there was something just below the surface that made him worrisome.

"Jonathan is handsome and all, but he's too intense for my taste. Besides, I kind of swore off men for a while after my last relationship. Not that I'm off men completely."

Rhonda giggled. "Not to worry love. I don't go where I'm not wanted, if you know what I mean."

After another month, Jonathan began to take Keely to London on weekends, but not for sightseeing. Jonathan taught her how to conduct surveillance, how to follow a target without being seen, how to discreetly inquire about someone without raising suspicion. Although Keely had been through the Air Force's intelligence school and had worked in the field for eight years, she had no training like this. She enjoyed the 'spy-game' quality of the outings. Jonathan would randomly pick someone on the street and Keely would have to follow, sometimes for blocks. As she learned to follow, Keely noticed that her attention to details became more acute. She found herself capable of discerning small changes in someone's movements that indicated a change in pace or direction. She could describe how someone was dressed with only a quick glance.

Jonathan commented several times how pleased he was with her development. In the same breath, he would reprimand her for the simplest detail she had missed, but in a tone that was professional. He seemed to genuinely care that she learned these skills.

45

The winds of autumn had blown heavier rains across the English countryside. And along with them, a chilling cold that could barely be staved off by the heaviest of sweaters. While Keely's training continued, she began to wonder where all this was leading. Although she was enjoying herself, she felt guilty for not earning her keep. The rains had limited weapons training, but Mr. Che continued to appear every afternoon.

After a particularly grueling session with fighting sticks, during which Keely received her fair share of raps on shins and knuckles, she struggled up the stairs to the second floor to fetch her purse and head for home.

Rhonda sat at her desk, earphones tightly gripping her head, swaying to a rhythm just barely audible. Jonathan sat at his desk, feet propped up, a stack of folders scattered in front of him.

"Well, Mr. Che has beaten the shit out of me again, so I guess I'll just head home."

Jonathan looked up and smiled. "He's rather spry for an old gentleman, isn't he?"

Keely grimaced, "Yeah. Spry. Anyway, I'll see you tomorrow."

"Take this with you." Jonathan sat up and rummaged through the files on his desk, withdrawing one with a rather large sheaf of papers inside. "You'll need to study up."

Keely walked over and took the folder. Jonathan had never asked her to take work home before. She looked at him questioningly.

"That is your first assignment. You leave for Germany next Monday."

The bells in the cathedral on the edge of Dusseldorf's old city rang shrilly in the chilled morning air. The sun streamed through the bedroom window and Keely stirred. As her eyes struggled open, she wished she had taken a room further from the church and its incessant bells. It was her fifth day in Dusseldorf. She was in a small pensionne, the Antares Dusseldorf Hotel Garni, comfortable, but not upscale. Jonathan preferred smaller hotels because it made him less conspicuous.

She had dreamt about Jonathan again-- something that had become all too common. She would be at her desk at Swifthouse. He would come in and lead her silently to his private quarters on the first floor. There, he would sit passively on the edge of the bed while Keely undressed and knelt before him. She would reach to touch his face, but he would pull away.

Instead, he would grab her hand and roughly guide it to his belt buckle, which she would begin to unfasten. And then she would awaken.

At first, it had disturbed her, but she attributed the dream to the endless hours they had spent together during her training. She couldn't help but be attracted to him--a strong person, demanding and challenging. Occasionally, it was Rhonda instead of Jonathan who led her to the bedroom. She didn't want to analyze that dream at all.

Keely stretched and threw back the covers. She walked to the window and pulled back the sheers. The pre-dawn light washed the narrow streets of this city along the Rhine to pale sepia. In the distance, she could just make out the ultra-modern parliament building perched on the east river bank-- more glass than steel. For some reason, it fit in nicely with the weathered stone buildings of the old town. A far cry from Cortez, Colorado.

The folder Jonathan had given her contained a dossier on a member of the Rhineland-Westfalia *Landesregierung*; a legislator who was suspected of funneling money to right-wing extremists, including ultra-nationalists who were tied to a series of killing among the refugees flooding all of Europe from Syria and Iraq. Although there was concern among most Germans about the influx of refugees, these ultra-nationalists had taken on a frightening aggression.

The legislator, a roly-poly man in his mid-sixties named August Scheider, was a minor, but influential, member of the minority conservative party in this otherwise liberal part of Germany. He had been a successful businessman before entering politics, having taken over his grandfather's manufacturing firm despite the company's ties to the Nazis during World War II.

With his financial success came political pull, and he converted that into an elected position after he retired. The *Bundesnachrichtendienst*, Germany's Federal Intelligence Service, was concerned that if word leaked out that Herr Scheider was being investigated for ties to the ultra-nationalists, the conservatives would howl. So Swift Enterprises was hired to investigate.

Keely had taken a room in a small hotel across from the apartment Scheider kept in the city. He only visited his palatial estate outside Reidt on weekends. Keely had established a routine of rising early, jogging along the Rhine for several miles and returning for a breakfast of Kaiser rolls and coffee in the first-floor dining room in the hotel--all before seven a.m. She always chose a table that provided a view of Scheider's front door. With Prussian precision, Herr Scheider would appear precisely at eight. He was not hard to miss. His cropped hair looked like he could balance a tray on his head. His piggish pink face swallowed his eyes and was accented by a thin moustache above blubbery lips. He waddled as he walked, which made his pace tortuous, but facilitated shadowing him.

She had talked with shopkeepers on the block, posing as an American graduate student who had come to Dusseldorf to study the legislative process of the *Landesregierung*. Most people in this cosmopolitan city spoke passable English, so stumbling through a conversation in English with minimal German allowed her to ask questions that might otherwise be suspicious, even though her German had become quite proficient. When she asked about the legislators of the *Landesregierung,* the manager of her pensionne was quick to point out that an eminent politician lived in that very block, and even offered to introduce her, which she declined, saying she didn't want to bother such an important man.

The job was almost too simple. She followed Scheider whenever he ventured outside his apartment and noted any visitors. His routine was agonizingly predictable. At eight a.m., he walked three blocks from his apartment to a small restaurant, where he ate breakfast alone. At nine a.m., he took a taxi to the *Landesregierung*, where he remained until five. Then he retraced his route, going to the same restaurant for dinner again alone, returning to his apartment by seven p.m.

From what she could tell, he led an almost monastic life. There seemed to be no visitors, and since he was a widower with grown children who lived some distance away, there was little social contact.

However, on her third morning of surveillance, a young man who did not look like a tenant emerged from Scheider's apartment building shortly before Scheider. Dressed in leather pants and woolen jacket, he looked to be in his late teens or early twenties, with a thin goatee and the gaunt look of someone on drugs. He had his long straggly hair haphazardly tucked up under a wool cap.. Keely snapped several pictures. The young man looked about furtively and then walked off at a quick pace. Scheider appeared moments later, much more hurried than usual, and walked in the opposite direction. Keely noted the detail in her log.

She walked across the street and looked at the names of the tenants, most listed as *Herr and Damen.*

Three days later, the same young man emerged from the building with the same furtive behavior, followed minutes later by Scheider. The coincidence was too great, and Keely decided to follow the young man instead of Scheider.

He walked rapidly, his head down, apparently in a hurry to get somewhere. They walked in tandem-- Keely a block behind on the opposite side of the street as Jonathan had trained her-- for more than a mile into a squalid part of town. The man turned into what appeared to be a club, and Keely continued past, noting the name-- Das Banger.

48

That evening, once Scheider was safely ensconced in his apartment, Keely made her way to the club, whose marquee was now garishly lighted with mismatched colored lights. Inside, it took some time for her eyes to adjust to the smoke-filled half-light. The room was small, dominated by a bar along one wall. There were a few tables scattered about and a small riser on which sat a stool and microphone stand.

Keely went to the bar and ordered a beer, disconcerted by the look of astonishment on the bartender's face. Sipping the beer, she glanced around the room and noticed few women present, and those there wore outlandish wigs and outdated cocktail dresses. It took only a moment to realize that those 'women' weren't women, and that Das Banger was a gay bar. She smiled to herself. So Scheider did have a secret, but it did not involve whack jobs. Maybe his apparent sexual preferences necessitated his secretive behavior given his position as conservative leader.

She spotted the young man huddled in the corner with an equally gaunt youth, the two pawing at each other as if they were in the backseat of a parked car.

Keely remained for another three days just to make sure. The youth came out of the apartment one more time before she decided to approach him. In the afternoon at a cafe near the bar, she walked up to him on the pretense of needing directions. Keely had purposely dressed provocatively; she did not wear a bra and her blouse unbuttoned almost to her waist. She tried hard to flirt with the young man, but to no avail. Even if she was not his type, she knew guys well enough to know she would have gotten some response from him if he had been straight. She had gotten nothing. She tried a different tact. She wasn't sure Jonathan would approve, but he told her to be inventive.

"I think we have a mutual friend," she said, a sly smile on her face. "Herr Scheider?"

The boy looked scared then defiant. "I know no one by that name."

Keely shook her head. "Really? He talks of you a lot. He says you are very… how did he say it… needy, especially in bed. But I think he is tired of you and wants something more," Keely rubbed one hand gently on her breast, "sexy."

The boy started to argue, but Keely leaned close to his ear. "How much does he pay you?"

The boy looked defeated. "One hundred Deutsche Marks a night."

She leaned back and withdrew three hundred DM from her purse. "I do not like competition. Please don't let me see you near our friend again. Or I will have some of my friends visiting you." She turned and walked away.

She called Jonathan and sketched out what she had done. He laughed and suggested they would share those with their client.

"Nice job. Come on home."

On the short flight back to England, Keely assessed her first assignment and determined that her job at Swift Enterprises was significantly more fun than she imagined. And perhaps the weapons training and her torturous lessons with Mr. Che were just what Jonathan had said-- a way to train the mind as well as the body. If all the assignments were like this, she had little to worry about. Life felt pretty good.

Over the next six months, Keely lost count of the number of roly-poly politicians and businessmen she watched, and the number of dead-ends she and Jonathan uncovered. She didn't want to admit it, but she liked it best when he showed up unexpectedly, which he did regularly at first. He claimed it was all part of her training. He needed to see her in action, to make sure she could handle herself. She didn't care what his reasons. It was a nice diversion from the tedium of surveillance.

The few times she uncovered something wrong, it tended to be some official skimming funds to pay for high-priced hookers or pay off gambling debts. Keely knew that good intelligence was a matter of elimination-- checking every possible behavior for an explanation, no matter how ludicrous. In the end, most activities that appeared "suspicious" were human foibles or inadequacies. Swift Enterprises made a considerable amount of money proving that problems did not exist.

Over lunch in the first-floor dining room, Keely had asked Jonathan if their work was always as boring. Keely looked forward to these casual lunches; to talk freely about work she could not share with others. But it wasn't only that.

She felt a kinship with Jonathan. Beneath his staid, British exterior, she had found warmth and a wry sense of humor that was refreshing and invigorating. He never treated her less than his equal. He never explained things unless she asked, constantly sought her perspective on contracts, willingly listened to her ramble on about trivial matters. It had evolved into a friendship based on work and mutual respect. If there was an attraction, it seemed to be purely professional.

Keely knew that Jonathan had women to his home on occasion. He was very discrete. They apparently arrived after work on Friday and were gone by Monday morning. Keely had stumbled across one when she went to the office on a Saturday. As Keely entered the back door, the woman was coming out of the kitchen. Both were startled.

The woman was a few years older than Keely, tall with a model's body. Although her make-up was perfect, as was her hair, she wore only a large T-shirt. Keely had smiled sheepishly and made her way to the office.

In a few minutes, Jonathan entered. "Sorry 'bout that. My friend didn't think anyone was about. Nor did I."

Keely retrieved what she had come for and smiled at Jonathan's discomfort. "Not to worry, I won't tell a soul. She's quite lovely."

Jonathan had no reply. She sensed that he was both embarrassed and a bit annoyed. Keely walked passed him, feeling his stare as she left the room.

At first, the encounter had amused Keely, especially Jonathan's discomfort. But she realized there had been a tinge of jealousy to the encounter. She couldn't tell if she was jealous because Jonathan had a woman-- and considering her looks, she didn't blame him-- or because another woman had invaded what she had grown to believe was her territory. There was also the fact that Jonathan had something she didn't. Rhonda had introduced Keely to a number of nice young guys in St. Albans. She had even dragged Keely to clubs in London where the boys were not near as sweet. But in the end, that was just it-- they were all boys to Keely.

Her assignment several months later topped all the other lackluster jobs, this time following a Scottish member of parliament, possibly the most boring person Keely could imagine. To debrief, Keely and Jonathan had repair to their favorite pub in St. Albans. She had already finished her first pint. She put down her mug and stared at Jonathan.

"Don't you find it odd that we make lots of money just to find out if somebody has been a bad boy?"

Jonathan gave her the smile he always used just before he lectured.

"My dear Captain. Surely, you were in the military long enough to realize that most of what appears to be 'malevolent' is actually just human frailty. People have this image of spies running around the world doing daring deeds, saving the planet from villains.

"Unfortunately, the reality is much less dramatic; the world is in far more danger from incompetence than from evil. I am not saying our world is not full of people out to do harm. There are plenty of them, and for them countries are more than willing to send in their forces with guns blazing. We are the ones who work in the gray areas. When countries are not sure something is lurking around the bend to do them harm. And when the problems are not so perilous-- when it is not a matter of life and death."

Keely had heard this speech before, and after almost a year with Swift, knew Jonathan was right. Their work was really like private detectives, only on a global level. They collected information, turned it over to the client and allowed the client to take the next step, if indeed a 'step' was warranted.

Jonathan was not yet through sermonizing. "As for the money, intelligence budgets are the last item cut, whether in government or business. Politicians and C.E.O.s don't worry about a few million here or there as long as they are not held accountable. The intelligence community has grown up with a silver spoon in its mouth. It can spend what it wants, when it wants, for whatever it wants without being concerned about some bureaucrat blowing the whistle. It's not our place to tell these folks they are wasting their money on foolhardy adventures. We do what we are contracted to do and nothing more, and we leave the soul searching to others."

She knew he was right, but there was something 'mercenary' about the whole situation that made her a bit uncomfortable. "It's just that I was brought up to fight for my country and its ideals-- you know, rally around the flag and all that."

Jonathan was patient. "You still have not learned that you no longer have a country. You are now a citizen of the world. There are lots of other people who are citizens of that same world-- journalists like your friend Maggie, for instance. And, of course, contractors like us. We all work for ourselves, not for countries. It may sound crass, but our allegiance is to the bottom line first. It doesn't mean we work for anyone. There are parameters, and I believe the countries we work with deserve to be supported. But my dear, this is the future, and you are now in it."

The thought unnerved Keely, and she started to say it was hard to accept this 'citizen of the world' bullshit. She had grown up thinking there was right and wrong. He made it sound as though 'right' was always subjective and situational. Everything he had just said rattled her beliefs. She had always thought of herself as American-- even served eight years in the military. Her roots went deep into the Cortez Mountains. Home and country were united there. Jonathan's idea of 'statelessness,' owing allegiance to no political entity was foreign to her. And yet, he was right. That is exactly what her life had become.

She had done jobs for governments and businesses in Germany, England, France, Belgium, America and Israel-- whoever had the money, whoever had the job. Of course, Jonathan was very particular about the assignments they took, working only for those he considered 'the good guys.' And she had appreciated the lack of fealty that went with being a mercenary. It kept nationalism from getting in the way of doing her job.

Something else that had bothered Keely, and she decided since Jonathan was in a talkative mood, she'd broached that subject as well.

"I've been here almost ten months now just desk work and trips to baby sit someone. But you made me train with all kinds of weapons-- and martial arts. Was that just for show?"

Jonathan's expression changed so dramatically that Keely couldn't finish her thought. He stared at his plate for a long time, fingers joined in front of his mouth. Finally, he looked at her.

"Keely, have you ever killed?"

Keely sat up straight and placed her hands on the table in front of her, bracing herself almost.

"Well, I used to hunt with my dad and brothers, but I didn't really enjoy it. I didn't mind handling the guns or shooting. I minded the killing. I mostly shot at branches."

Jonathan smiled as if questioning a small child. "No, what I meant was, have you ever killed a person."

"No. I haven't. I'm not looking to kill anyone, either."

He took a sip of his beer, sat it down and looked about them, then to her. "Then I wouldn't be too anxious for the experience." He leaned forward. "As for the training, fortunately, most of our contracts do not require us to worry about that. If and when that time comes however, I want you to be prepared. Listen to me carefully, to lack the skill-- to hesitate for even a second because you do not know how to defend yourself or are afraid to-- may cost you *your* life."

His intensity sent a chill down Keely's spine. She had grown up with spy movies-- with their rapid and random killings. She had even anticipated the possibility that her work at Swift might involve some danger. But she had never quite put it in the kill-or-be-killed context before.

"Do you think-- I mean, am I...?"

"I have watched you on the target range. You're competent. You also seem to have taken to martial arts with a passion."

Both were true. The speed with which Keely had acquired skill with both weapons and Shaolin had surprised her. She had always been physically active. But she had taken to both with a zeal that at times bordered on obsession. Perhaps it was the sense of power, the sense of control that attracted her to these violent arts. Perhaps it was the precision that both required.

"But you think I'm capable of actually using it in the field." She couldn't finish the thought.

Jonathan watched her for a long moment. "We will see. Sooner than you may like."

CHAPTER FOUR

Keely's chance to prove herself under fire came sooner than she expected. A few weeks after their conversation, Jonathan was approached by the French Directorate of Territorial Security to monitor a government clerk's involvement with a weapons' dealer. Jonathan thought about passing on the job because it could get hairy. Keely protested his decision.

"I have got to do one of these sooner or later, or there's no reason for me to stay."

Jonathan, seated at his desk, leaned back. "Is that an ultimatum?"

"No, just fact. Look, you said I'm ready, now let's test it in the field."

Jonathan hesitated for a long time then looked over to Rhonda, who had kept her head down, not wanting to get into the middle of it. "Rhonda, book Keely on the next flight to Paris. I'll follow in a day or two."

Rhonda had booked them into a pleasant pensionne one block from the Rodin Museum in the center of Paris, another example of Jonathan's preference of anonymity over comfort. When Jonathan arrived several days later, they had eaten a late supper in a Vietnamese restaurant in the same block and returned to Keely's room. Jonathan asked her to wait a minute, left and returned in a minute with a package, which he set on the small desk.

"Go ahead, open it."

Keely moved to the desk and unwrapped the package. Inside was a box, which she opened. A thin leather holster contained a Beretta Tomcat, a small semi-automatic; short, light but fired .32 caliber shells. Keely slipped the gun out of the holster, checked that the chamber and clip were empty and replaced it.

"Cute."

"But serviceable. The weapon is merely a safety measure, given the supposed connection this…" he referred to the dossier, "Monsieur Keci has with undesirables. Most likely, you will not need it. Consider it an insurance policy in case things get… dicey."

Keely was intrigued, both by the word 'dicey' and by Jonathan's obvious concern. "So exactly what do you call 'dicey'?"

Jonathan returned to the dossier for a moment, then looked at her.

"The Directorate seems to think our friend may not have the longest life expectancy. It wants to insure he stays alive for a while."

"And we're to make sure he does?" He nodded his head. "Precisely."

"That doesn't sound too dangerous, so why are you so concerned? Unless you don't think I can cut it."

"It's not so much that I feel you can't 'cut it' as I feel a sense of responsibility for you. After all, I was the one who talked you into joining Swift. But if you are truly going to be a partner, you should experience the whole gamut of work we do."

"I appreciate your concern. Really. But I can handle it." She thought for a moment, then flashed her best mischievous smile. "I had a good teacher."

That evening over drinks in his room, Jonathan reviewed the information he had received from in the Directorate. The clerk, Marc Keci, somehow had become entangled in an attempt to circumvent the NATO embargo on weapons sales to separatists still active in Chechnya. He was second-generation French; his parent having emigrated from Azerbaijan.

Although he was Muslim by birth, he did not practice his religion. But his Muslim roots were still strong enough to get him involved in a small group trying to get the Russians out of Chechnya. Although there was a tenuous peace accord in place, there was still a vibrant black market in weapons there. The West tended to look the other way when the arms were destined for forces attempting to keep the Russians busy.

Keci was the go-between for the separatists and an arms dealer in Marseilles. The connection was Keci's brother-in-law, who had escaped from Ossetia with his sister during the civil war with Georgia. The brother-in-law had returned, and now wanted Keci to assist in getting weapons.

Keci had no background in clandestine activities. His record with French authorities was clean; the reason he was able to get a clerk's job in the Ministry of Culture. His brother-in-law had given him the name of a gun dealer, and after considerable prodding from his wife he had made contact.

They had made three transactions, but Keci was on the verge of quitting. The time had come to shut down the operation, since the *Police Nationale* had kept him on a short leash.

Complicating the situation was the fact that a second gunrunner had begun to put pressure on Keci. He was known only as Kestrel, and the *Police Nationale* assumed he was somehow linked to the FSB-- Russia's reincarnation of the KGB.

Keely looked at Jonathan. "Kestrel?"

Jonathan smiled. "A kestrel is a type of falcon. Apparently, this one has a flare for the dramatic."

Kestrel had surfaced ten years earlier, marketing weapons acquired from the fragmented Soviet satellite states still desperate for hard Western currency. Security forces in a number of countries were looking for him. Kestrel had sold weapons to anybody who would buy-- usually to both sides, but the Chechens refused to deal with him. He was seen as an infidel. The police received information Kestrel planned to make an example of Keci to dissuade the competition.

Jonathan and Keely were to ensure that Keci made one last transfer of funds to the dealer.

The French would then put Keci out of business.

After reading the dossier, Keely was still confused. "Why don't the cops just pick Keci up? Why all the games?"

Jonathan assumed his professorial mode. "The police are afraid that if something happens to Keci, they will be blamed for not acting sooner. Particularly since they have had him under surveillance for some time. They also hope he leads them to a major arms dealer. Bait to catch a big fish."

"Sounds pretty cold to me." "*Real politik.*"

When Jonathan left her hotel room, Keely poured over Keci's file. He was in his forties, lived in the Saint Denis area of Paris, just north of Sacré Coeur. The picture in the file, obviously from his government identification card, showed a haggard face, heavily lined, but with black eyes that could have been piercing had there not been a veil of fear over them. He didn't seem to have many vices, except perhaps a penchant for expensive wines. His wife worked at a small ethnic grocery store in the same block as their apartment. They had no children. He seemed to be a man caught up in something he was neither suited for nor comfortable with.

She put down the file and picked up the automatic. She worked the slide and examined the chamber. Next, she removed the clip and loaded it with seven cartridges. She hesitated to replace the clip and instead laid both on the bed in front of her. She stared at the weapon for a long time wondering if she could actually use it.

The hours on the firing range now seemed unrelated to actually carrying the weapon and perhaps having to fire it at another human being. She shuddered and hoped that would not be a question she would have to answer any time soon.

Jonathan set up a surveillance schedule-- twelve hours on, twelve hours off. If Keci looked like he was on the move, they would follow. A bookstore/coffee shop provided a view of the front door to Keci's apartment house. Keely would station herself there before seven every morning. When he emerged, she would follow him through the Metro to his office. It was obvious by his slow pace that he was unaware he was being followed.

Keely sat across in a sidewalk cafe from the ministry where Keci worked. She was thankful that Parisian's thought nothing of a person sitting in a café most of the day. She had brought along a book, feeling that Keci would be pretty safe inside a government office. He left the building at noontime but walked less than a block to a patisserie. Keely followed. She waited five minutes before she sauntered in, playing the typical American tourist. She saw Keci out of the corner of her eye seated at a table in the rear of the restaurant. She sat near the door and ordered lunch.

In the later afternoon, Keci exited his ministry along with a stream of other bureaucrats heading home. Keely kept him in sight, paralleling his slow steps on the opposite side of the street. He was headed toward the Metro, and Keely thought she might lose him in the mass of humanity funneling below the streets. She hurried across the street and stayed less than five yards behind him. He didn't look back. The subway platform wasn't nearly as crowded as London's at day's end, so Keely was able to position herself close enough to Keci to protect him, but at a distance that wouldn't seem too obvious.

They rode in the same car for six stops, then Keci worked his way to the door. Keely exited only seconds after he did and reached the street in time to see him waiting for the light to change. They were only a block from his apartment.

It was close to eight in the evening when Jonathan walked up to Keely as she sat at a sidewalk table sipping Pernod. He took the seat opposite her.

"Everything seems to be quiet. I hope you passed a pleasant day?"

"Bor-ring."

"But think of the money you earned. And, the evening to enjoy."

Instead of leaving immediately, Keely stayed for dinner, watching with Jonathan, who proceeded to tell her about his day spent in the Louvre. It was close to ten before Jonathan encouraged her to head back to the pension.

"You will need rest after such an arduous day."

The phone beside her bed shocked her from sleep. The clock showed four a.m. It took a second or two for her to become oriented. She reached for the receiver. "Yes?"

Jonathan's voice brought her fully awake. "Keci is on the move. Meet me at Gare Nord.

Now."

She began to replace the receiver when she heard his voice again. "Keely. Better come prepared." Keely knew what he meant.

The train station was almost deserted at this hour. A few late revelers staggered home. A few workmen headed to early jobs. Jonathan met her at the main entrance, pulling her into the shadows. She had dressed in jeans and heavy sweater, her Beretta tucked inconspicuously in its holster at the small of her back.

"He's waiting on the far platform. It's the slow train south. He's not on the TVG. I assume he's going to meet his friends somewhere along the way. Is there a chance he may have seen you?"

Keely was offended by the inference that she had not been careful, but she realized that he was merely trying to decide how to keep Keci from being spooked. "I doubt it, but I really don't know."

"All right. I'll stay in the car with him. You stay one car away, preferably the car behind where he is sitting. Keep your eyes open. Once we've set out, move into the car with us, but only if you're sure he won't see you enter. Take a seat close to the door. Here." Jonathan handed her a copy of *Paris Match*. "Just in case he decides to wander about. If he leaves the car, let me follow, then you. Got all that?"

Keely nodded. On impulse, she leaned forward and gently kissed his cheek. He looked surprised. "That's for trusting in me. And for being a mother hen."

They waited until the last call for the train, and each entered through different doors. Jonathan followed through the door Keci had entered moments before, Keely one car behind. She worked her way forward and stole a glance through the glass of the sliding doors between the cars. She could see the top of Jonathan's head halfway up the car. She couldn't see Keci, but assumed he sat just a few seats ahead of Jonathan.

Keely turned back to her car. There were only three other passengers. A young sleepy couple clung to each other about halfway back, their worn backpacks wedged into the luggage rack above their heads. At the very back was an old woman in tattered clothing, a torn shopping bag at her feet, staring straight ahead. Keely fell into the seat closest to the door, feeling the butt of her pistol press against her flesh. She hadn't thought much in her bedroom as she had checked the clip of the weapon, chambered a round and made sure the safety was on. She had picked up two additional clips along with some money and her passport. She hadn't wanted to carry a purse. Sitting now, waiting for the train to pull out of the station, she could feel the adrenaline rushing through her system. She tried to control herself, but she was too keyed up to sit quietly. She practiced the breathing exercises her Tai Chi teacher had drilled into her, but they only took a slight edge off her excitement.

The train jolted to life, and Keely had to use every ounce of self-control to keep from jumping up and running through the doors. Instead, she focused on the images out the window as the train pulled out of the station and through the still sleeping Paris. The beautiful cluster of old buildings was even more resplendent in the pre-dawn light. Lamps twinkled on street corners.

Lights in windows gave definition to the avenues of quiet apartments.

Keely waited until they were beyond the city sprawl before she stood and ventured another look through the doors. Jonathan had not moved. She opened the door and stepped onto the connecting platform, the train cars swaying to alternating rhythms. She reached for the handle, checked through the glass one more time, then quickly opened the door and closed it just as quickly. Without looking, she slid into the first seat and moved to the window. She finally breathed.

Keely's palms began to sweat. Jonathan hadn't moved since she had entered the car more than an hour before. He had glanced back and indicated with his eyes that Keci was sitting on the same side of the car as she was. They were the sole occupants.

The train continued into the countryside and into the morning. There were several stops, and with each one, more people joined them in the car. Now, there were almost twenty other passengers. If there was trouble, she was afraid civilians would get hurt. She immediately realized that no one would try something in this crowd. Keci was still not visible.

Morning had broken clear and bright, but Keely was tired--in part by having been awakened so early, but more because she had sat so rigidly for so long. She tried to fight off fatigue by watching the countryside fly by. The villages and farms randomly dotting the rolling hills were every bit as picturesque as she would have imagined. It was as though the modern world had somehow skipped this part of France.

The conductor passed through, punching tickets. She watched carefully to identify the exact seat where Keci was sitting. She just barely recognized the top of his head as he handed the ticket to the conductor.

As the train neared a small station, Keely was unprepared when Keci hurriedly got to his feet and began working his way back toward her. She glanced outside at a sign that read Moulin. Keci carried a briefcase clutched to his chest, as though holding a priceless object. She had only a second to grab the magazine and open it before he passed. She couldn't tell whether he had noticed her or not, but when she looked over the edge of the magazine, she saw Jonathan moving quickly down the aisle. He paused for only a second and whispered to her, never taking his eyes off the door through which Keci had passed.

"I think he's getting off. Go out the other door but wait for my signal." He went through the door.

Keely got to her feet and moved in the opposite direction. She didn't know how long the train would be stopped but knew it couldn't be more than a few minutes. She reached the door and stepped onto the grilled landing between cars. She took two steps down the metal stairs and carefully looked onto the platform as the train came to a halt.

Keci left the train and moved rapidly away. Jonathan was already on the platform and turned to motion her to follow. Keely stepped down, started to follow, but instead walked to the opposite side of the platform and studied the schedule posted there. She chanced a look in the direction Keci had headed and saw him round the corner of the station. She sprinted to the entrance of the small station and saw that it had large double doors that opened on both sides of the building. She hurried to the doors and opened one, peering out. Keci was heading down the street away from the station. Jonathan had apparently stopped at the edge of the building to avoid being seen.

Keely quickly surveyed the street. Lined with small shops along a narrow sidewalk, the street appeared to run several blocks in both directions, dissected periodically by side streets. Although it was early, there were a number of people—mostly women—on the sidewalks. She moved out quickly, crossing the street and turning in Keci's direction. Jonathan motioned for her to move ahead.

Keci was a block and a half ahead, and although he had left the train in a hurry, he now slowed his pace and was almost casual as he strolled along. Keely kept a relaxed pace, looking at shop windows as though taking in the sights, all the while keeping Keci in her peripheral vision.

After two blocks, Keci stopped suddenly and stared into a shop window. After a moment's hesitation, he entered the building. Keely looked behind her and saw Jonathan had shadowed her twenty yards behind and on the opposite side of the street. Now he rushed forward. When he reached her, he was slightly winded.

"Looks like our boy has found what he was looking for."

They moved forward, Jonathan slipping his arm into hers as though a couple out for a morning stroll. As they approached the building, Jonathan stopped her and turned toward a store window filled with dusty antiques.

"I'm going to stroll by. You stay here. I'll signal you."

Before she could respond, he moved away. She stayed turned toward the window but could see him casually pass the storefront Keci had entered, glancing equally as casually in the window as he passed. He stopped a few yards beyond, apparently to examine yet another window. He looked back and made a circling motion with his hand. Keely nodded. She was to circle around the back of the building.

It sat in the middle of a block, so Keely had to backtrack until she got to the side street. She turned the corner, walked halfway up that block until she reached an alley that ran behind the stores. She glanced around and then, as inconspicuously as possible, began to work her way down the alley.

It was crowded with discarded boxes and refuse, the smell of rotting fruit strong. She had counted the storefronts and knew that the building Keci had entered was the fourth in the block. When she reached the third, she knelt down as though to tie her shoe laces. There was no movement in the alley. No sound. She stood and positioned herself so that she had a clear view of the back door of the building.

Time stood still, and Keely felt she must have waited for hours although it had been less than five minutes. She assumed the silence was a good sign but began to wonder whether she should return to the main street. What if Keci had come out and headed off? There was no way for Jonathan to let her know. She was about to head back to the side street when she heard the back door of the building being unlocked. She quickly ducked behind a pile of boxes just in time to avoid being seen by Keci, who peeked out, closed the door behind him and took off down the alley. Keely counted to five, then looked around the boxes. Keci had almost reached the far end of the alley.

Suddenly, a distinct ping filled the silence. Keely knew that sound. She had heard it many times at the practice range when she learned to fire her automatic fitted with a silencer.

Instinctively, her hand went for her gun. Keci must have heard the sound as well and had stopped but did not seem to understand its import. As best as she could determine, the shot had come from the side street ahead. If Keci continued to the street, he'd be a sitting duck. Keely jumped to her feet and sprinted toward Keci, the pistol held carefully behind her.

"Monsieur. Monsieur."

Keci stopped and spun around, a look of primal panic on his face. A second ping and a chunk of brick just above his head exploded. Keci spun back to the street. Keely was almost to him and called to him in French to get down.

He dropped to the ground just as another ping sounded and the brick wall shattered right where his head had been. She reached him and patted him gently on the back, then she swung her weapon in an arc covering the visible portion of the side street in front of them. There were three cars park along the far sidewalk, but none seemed occupied. She paused. Suddenly, she detected movement at the front of the first parked car. She sighted on the spot as an arm moved into view, unmistakably holding a gun.

Keely took a deep breath, then released half of it, and squeezed the trigger. The weapon recoiled only slightly, but Keely heard a moan and the arm was withdrawn. Keely didn't move. Her eyes were locked on the front of the car and she didn't see the head rising above the back until another ping and the sound of a bullet rushing past her ear. With deliberate care, she swung her shooting hand and fired three rounds in rapid succession. Whoever had fired had ducked back behind the car.

Seconds passed and she heard footsteps coming quickly in her direction. She kept her eyes and weapon trained on the front of the car. The footsteps stopped.

"Keely!"

Jonathan's voice. Keely released her breath, her arms aching from the tension of holding them so rigidly.

"Across the street. The first car."

Just then, the car started and screeched away before Keely could fire again. She lowered her weapon and finally looked down at Keci. His face was pressed against the dirty pavement, his hands over his head. She touched his arm.

"*Ils sont allés.*"

He didn't look up right away, still cowered on the ground. Jonathan rounded the corner, his weapon out of sight. He motioned for her to put hers away, then glanced around.

"Monsieur?"

Jonathan leaned closer and whispered something only Keci could hear, and he seemed to relax a little. Jonathan continued speaking in a soothing voice. He reached down and helped Keci to his feet, brushing off the front of his jacket. The little man seemed scared to death, and glanced back and forth between Jonathan and Keely, who smiled her most sympathetic smile. Jonathan straightened the man's tie and collar, telling him friends had sent them and questioning him about the delivery. Keci leaned toward Jonathan and smiled weakly. He told them he had already delivered the goods back in Paris. He was here to visit his brother's shop.

Jonathan told him to go to the local constabulary and explain that someone had been shooting at him. He handed Keci a piece of paper and told him to ask the police to call the number written on it and someone would help him get back to Paris safely.

Keci nodded to Jonathan, mumbled softly something only Jonathan could hear, then walked cautiously toward the other end of the alley. He looked back at them, and Jonathan waved merrily at him. He disappeared around the corner.

Keely looked confused and raised her hands as if to say, 'Why aren't we following?'

Jonathan turned and smiled, moving a strand of hair out of her face that had fallen in her eyes. "Seems Keci has been banking his commission with his brother. And since the funds have already changed hands, our job here is finished."

"Just like that? What about the clowns shooting at him?"

Jonathan didn't answer but sauntered into the street. He stopped where the car had been, then motioned her over. When she got to him, he pointed to the ground. There was a small, but distinct pool of blood. Jonathan smiled. "Guess Kestrel's boys didn't know the delivery had already been made, either. But I have a feeling your little Annie Oakley act made them realize Keci was no easy mark. Anyway, we've fulfilled our contract."

Keely felt relieved and frustrated. Did this mean they walk away from Keci? What if those guys tried again? Jonathan seemed to be reading her mind.

"Our job was to shadow him until the money was delivered. That's done. Our assignment is complete. That number I gave him was our contact in Paris. He'll get him back safely. Our friends at the Directorate will put the word on the street that Keci is no longer a 'target'. By the time our little man is back in Paris, Kestrel will know he missed his chance."

"It's as simple as that? This Kestrel will back off?"

"We're talking business here. Once a deal is blown, they can't be bothered with petty things like revenge. Not good business. Start doing that, and everybody will be shooting everybody else. Besides, haven't you had enough excitement for one day?"

Keely felt drained and extremely energized at the same time. She also believed she had come through Jonathan's 'test' with flying colors. She didn't freeze. She hadn't hesitated. She knew she had wounded the assailant, and she was surprised that she really didn't care. In fact, she a rush had gone through her when she had fired at the shooter.

Jonathan leaned forward and kissed her cheek. Before he could pull back, she turned her face slightly and kissed him on the lips. Not passionately, but long enough to let him know that it was more than just a friendly gesture. His eyebrows rose slightly, and he walked away.

Keely maintained her cool all the way back to St. Albans. The adrenaline rush had lasted most of the train trip back to Paris. Jonathan had gotten in touch with the Directorate, explained what had happened and told the man a full report would be forthcoming in a week. They left Paris immediately for London by train. Jonathan had been quiet on the return trip, but when they pulled into the driveway to Keely's apartment, he accepted her invitation for a quick drink.

Once inside, she took her bag into the bedroom as he fixed them both a whiskey. She changed into jogging pants and a T-shirt and joined him on the couch.

As she drank, she saw a wry, little smile spread across his face. "What?"

He finished his sip and set the glass on the coffee table. "Oh, nothing, really."

"Come on. That grin means something."

He seemed to enjoy toying with her. "It's just that you impressed me, Captain."

She leaned toward him. "Does this mean I've passed your test?"

He studied her for a moment, the smile remaining. "I liked the way you handled yourself. I'll feel better about sending you into similar situations in the future." The smile faded and he looked away for a moment.

When he turned back, he spoke precisely, choosing his words carefully. "But don't get too confident and think this is just a game. Those were real bullets you were firing at a live target."

She had to admit that the chase, the weapons, the thought of danger had all been more exciting than she had imagined. It was as though every nerve in her body had suddenly been awakened. On the train ride back, she had reflected on the rush firing on another human had given her, disquieted by how easy it had been.

"Is it always like that? The rush, I mean?"

Jonathan picked up his drink, studied the ice cube dissolving in the amber liquid, sipped again and finally looked at her. "Initially. Understand, the adrenaline always comes. And some in this business get hooked on it. After a while, it's like any other narcotic, but then need replaces pleasure."

Keely looked uncertain, but Jonathan reached over and gently touched her cheek. It was the first intimate touch that felt more than paternal. "But I don't think that will happen to you. And, yes. It is quite a rush."

Without thinking, Keely leaned over and kissed Jonathan, gently at first, but she became more insistent. Jonathan responded in kind, but she could feel him holding back. Keely leaned back, the blush rising in her neck.

"Sorry."

"Don't be. Perfectly normal. You're excited and just want to continue that excitement."

Keely didn't know whether to be insulted, embarrassed or angry. Instead, she moved closer and kissed him again, this time wrapping her arms around his neck. His right arm moved around her waist. His lips were surprisingly soft, and as they parted, she could feel the tip of his tongue. Her hand moved from his neck, down his arm to his thigh.

He pulled back but did not remove her hand. "Are you sure you won't regret this in the morning?"

She leaned in harder, forcing him on his back, her hand seeking out his belt buckle. "Shut up."

She did regret it the next morning. They had made love quickly, roughly. Then she lay in his arms for a long while, dozing fitfully. He left shortly after midnight. As he dressed, she was not sure what to say, or if she should say anything. She didn't have to. He did.

"Don't rush into the office tomorrow. But I will need a complete report within the next couple of days." He shrugged into his coat, leaned over and kissed her on the forehead. "Now, be a good girl and go to sleep."

As she nursed her coffee the next morning, Keely tried to assess what had happened the night before and Jonathan's rather cavalier attitude as he was leaving. What disturbed her most was that he had seemed as passionate as she had been yet tried to brush it off as typical after a 'hot' assignment. She had the feeling that, for him, it was more recreational than relational. She might have been more upset, except for the fact that she did not want a relationship with Jonathan Swift.

But they had crossed a line, and she wasn't sure how that would ultimately affect their working relationship. She finished her coffee, slipped into her bulkiest sweater and set out for Swift House.

Rhonda was already at her desk but jumped up and ran over to Keely as she entered, giving her a big hug. "Miss Bonnie Parker, I do believe. The boss says you did a good job."

Keely was slightly perturbed that Jonathan had told Rhonda about the shooting. He sat at his desk, the *London Times* open in front of him. As Rhonda yelped, he looked up and smiled his usual quirky smile. Business as usual.

Rhonda gushed with delight. "Only one shot sent the bad guys running. Jonathan says you were cool as a cucumber."

Apparently, Jonathan had been quite detailed in his description of events in France. She wondered if he had been as detailed about what happened when they got back to England. She looked from Jonathan to Rhonda.

"It wasn't all that dramatic. Hardly knew what was going on till it was over."

"Modest, aren't we. The way Jonathan described it, you were a real Emma Peel."

Keely made a face and shooed Rhonda back to her desk. "Watch it, my ego can't take all this praise."

She took her own seat, sorted through a small pile of mail, barely glancing at the contents, and then turned her attention to her report, carrying on as if nothing had happened. Half way through the morning, she glanced in Jonathan's direction, but he was engrossed in his computer. Perhaps last night had been an aberration, and now they were to pretend it didn't happen. Like the woman she encountered that morning--maybe it had been business as usual. So be it.

Over the next month, Keely went out on two more assignments, both in Germany, having to do with potential misappropriation of funds by defense contractors. The routine surveillance, interviewing and reviewing records was dull. Jonathan had not suggested she take a weapon. She didn't argue.

He had been more aloof, and it wasn't her imagination. They still had lunch together, but when it was just the two of them, he never mentioned that night. His behavior toward her turned even more professional and deferential.

Keely was very careful not to do anything that might be construed as flirtation. He wanted to bury it; she could do that. The balance they had achieved was enough, and now was not the time to make waves. But occasionally, he would catch her looking at him and she would blush.

It was early October, but the English weather apparently thought it was much later in the season. There was no snow yet, but freezing rain made Keely colder than the heaviest snow in Colorado. It was Friday, and she had not been on assignment in several weeks. There was little to do, except catch up on her reading and exercise.

Jonathan insisted she read the *London Times* and the *International Herald-Tribune Daily*. In addition, the company subscribed to dozens of economic and political journals, which she had to wade through each month. The reading was tedious, but Jonathan said that they had to be conversant with all aspects of international affairs. They often used current events to seek out potential clients.

Not that they were desperate for work. Jonathan had started her off with a salary of 50,000 pounds-- almost $80,000. In addition, she received small bonuses for each assignment, usually about two per cent of the contract. Because the company paid for her car and apartment, and the clients paid all expenses, she had been able to save close to $50,000 in the eight months she had worked for Swift Enterprises.

Jonathan had insisted she set up a numbered Swiss account, accessed through the Bank of England by way of funds transfers.

She thought it a bit cloak-and-dagger, but he pointed out that if and when she decided to quit, she didn't want to confront all the red tape of moving her money around. In addition, it saved her from tax liability. Keely had been surprised that he would talk about 'if and when.' She had never thought much beyond the next day. As far as she was concerned, her future was there.

On this particular morning, Keely walked into the office, shaking the rain off her coat. "Damn, it's cold. You British must have ice in your veins."

Rhonda carried a steaming cup of tea over to Keely's desk. "Just makes us want to jump in the sack more, luv."

Jonathan wasn't at his desk, but Keely didn't ask where he was. She picked up a copy of the *Economist*, dreading having to wade through stuffy prose about arcane and convoluted financial minutia.

A few minutes later, Jonathan walked in and hung his coat beside Keely's. He smiled at Rhonda and motioned Keely to follow him to his desk. Once seated, Jonathan handed her an envelope and motioned for her to sit down.

"How would you like to go to Switzerland for a few days?"

"What's the job?"

Just before the outbreak of World War II, a German banker named Hopler saw the futility of the war and moved his family to Zurich. But he kept up his relationship with many influential Nazi party members. For them, he created blind trusts into which they deposited funds siphoned from the government or stolen from the enemies of the Reich. After the war, many of those people took their money and ran. But some did not survive, with Hopler the executor of the trusts.

67

Now his grandson had taken control and started to move small amounts of money to other accounts, minuscule by Swiss banking standards-- a couple thousand Euros here and there. Those accounts had been traced to Neo-fascist movements in Europe--bands of skinheads who had been tied to dozens of murders of immigrants and other 'undesirables.' The head of the bank was very concerned and had contacted a friend in NATO who had sent him on to Jonathan.

"At first, the banker was going to fire the man, but our friend convinced him to wait and see if we could trace the money. I had a team tap his phones and Rhonda hacked his computers, but apparently his contacts are in person. For now, we are to find out who he is working with. The problem is, what he is doing is legal, if immoral. And the Swiss authorities do not appreciate people prying into the lives of their citizens, especially when that citizen is a banker with political connections. The bank's chief executive knows the P.R. nightmare if Hopler's activities come to light." Jonathan glanced at her. "Be ready to go by Monday."

As she stood to leave, Jonathan came around his desk. He laid his hand gently on her arm and looked at her with more concern than she had seen in a long time.

"You might want to get in a bit of practice on the range. This one could get a bit 'dicey'.

CHAPTER FIVE

Zurich, Switzerland, sits at the north end of the *Zurichsee*, a clear mountain lake that reflects the surrounding mountains. Although the largest city in Switzerland, it is small compared with other European capitals. Despite its bustling financial district, the city still has turn-of-the- century charm, its 19th century buildings unfazed by modern steel and glass. Keely had passed through Zurich but had never stopped long enough to marvel at the city's beauty.

Rhonda had made reservations at the Hotel Schweizerhof on the Bahnhof Platz, across from the train station. It sat not far from the upscale shopping and dining district, a surprise because Keely usually found herself tucked away in clean, but unimpressive lodgings on such trips. Of course, it was in walking distance of Hopler's bank.

When she had exited the international air terminal that morning, bright sunshine welcomed her, a refreshing change. It was unusually cool for Zurich with the temperature hovering in the low 40s. But unlike St. Albans, the air was dry and crisp. A pang of homesickness hit Keely, remembering the clean mountain air in Cortez.

She had been provided with a description and photograph of the banker. Jonathan had been circumspect about the details of the contract, saying only that Keely was to maintain a loose surveillance until the client decided what action to take.

Hopler worked for *Vontobel*, with branches in, among other places, London, Dubai, Berlin and Buenos Aires. Shortly after she checked into her hotel, she strolled over to *Weinbergstrasse*; Hopler's bank sat in the middle of the block. Had it not been for a discrete sign on the door, she would have missed it. She stepped into the silent lobby and walked to an information kiosk where a prim young woman sat staring intently at a computer screen.

"Guten Tag. I was wondering to whom I would speak if I wanted to open an account?"

The woman looked up and smiled perfunctorily. "Would this be a personal account or business account?" Her English was so practiced and meticulous, Keely felt like she was talking to an automaton.

"Personal."

The woman wrote something on a piece of stationary and slid it across to Keely. The handwriting was as meticulous as the voice. "Mr. Kunslrichs handles personal accounts for internationals. To the back, the elevator to the third floor. Give this to the receptionist."

Keely smiled and headed toward the single elevator. As she had hoped, there was a directory and she located 'Hopler.' He was also on the third floor. She feigned looking for something in her purse then gave a disgusted look and marched back to the kiosk. The woman looked up from her computer screen. Keely laughed, acting embarrassed.

"I'm such an idiot. Left all my banking stuff back at the hotel. What time does Mr. Kunslrichs leave in the evening?"

The woman seemed uninterested but knew her job. "The bank closes at three p.m."

Smiling, Keely shook her head. "Oh, so Mr. Kunslrichs leaves at three? Seems like a mighty short work day."

The woman was now irritated, but she had a job to do, even with an obnoxious American. "The officers work until five., madam." There was a definite chill to the last word.

"Oh, I didn't mean…" Keely turned to leave, then turned back. "Sorry to be such a pest, but is there a back door? I wanted to visit some shops on *Clausiusstrasse.*"

"I am sorry, there is only the front door."

Smiling and giving a little wave, Keely turned and walked out the front. She circled the block, sizing up the building. Apparently, there was an underground parking garage, but Jonathan's sources had said Hopler lived close to the bank, so he probably didn't drive. A uniformed guard armed with a sub-machine gun stood watch at a back door. Keely innocently approached; the guard touched the bill of his cap and stopped her.

"Ich bin traurig, madam. Diese Tür ist zur Öffentlichkeit geschlossen." Keely looked confused. "I'm sorry?"

The man gave the smallest of smiles. "I am sorry, madam. This entrance is closed to the public."

"Oh, sorry. Thank you."

She spent the rest of the day reconnoitering the surrounding area. Shops and cafés faced both the front and back doors. Keely assumed Hopler and the other workers used the back. At 4:45 p.m., Keely was seated in the window of a lovely café, sipping hot chocolate and thumbing through a travel guide of Zurich she had purchased.

At five-fifteen p.m., the guard at the door stepped aside as a stream of workers emerged. Unlike Americans, these people proceeded with great discipline, no one jockeying for position. After the first crush, mostly young men and women who looked like clerks and secretaries, a second but smaller clutch of people, all male, emerged. Hopler was among them. Keely noted the time, took a last sip of her chocolate and headed for the street.

Hopler was much younger looking than she expected. His dossier put his age at thirty-seven, but he looked no older than thirty. His wavy blonde hair was perfectly arranged, cut short over the ears and in the back. His clothes were conservative, but expensive. And he looked as though he took great pains to maintain an athlete's physique.

Keely did not think he was attractive, although she wondered if knowing his little side venture affected her assessment. His overcoat was neatly buttoned, and he walked quickly through the crowd, judiciously avoiding contact with anyone. Keely had carefully studied a map of Zurich, where she had marked her hotel, the bank and Hopler's apartment, which was about seven blocks east.

He walked directly home. Hopler's apartment, the Residence Wiedikon, was at the end of the block tucked into a row of similar small apartment buildings. The unmarked entrance had a plain façade. Keely realized the coffee shop across the street would give her a view of the entrance. Again, she circled the block. There was a back entrance, but by the look of the alleyway, it was not often used. Back in front of the apartment, she walked to the door, but saw that it was controlled access. Through the glass, she could see a clean, but puritan lobby and two elevators. The mail slots were inside, but there was a call box on the outside.

Hopler lived in 3B. There was also a call button for the superintendent. Keely pressed the button and immediately a voice responded.

"Wie kann ich Ihnen helfen?"

"Wunderte ich mich, wenn Sie irgendeine leeren Wohnungen haben dürften?" There was a long pause. "You English?"

Apparently, Keely's German was not as good as she thought. "Yes. I'm a graduate student and will be in Zurich for several months. I was passing by and thought by chance…."

"I have two room. You see?"

Keely knew it was unwise to get this close to a mark, but since she'd just begun surveillance, she figured she could chance it. "Yes, I'd love to see them."

She heard the door buzz and she stepped in. The lobby was warm if impersonal and she waited no more than thirty seconds before an old man came from the back. He was hunched, his suspenders gapped in the front where his belly protruded. He eyed her cautiously.

"You come."

He waddled to the elevator and Keely was relieved when he pushed '2.' When the elevator arrived, they stepped in, the man near the controls, Keely to one side. As the door closed, the man mumbled without looking at her. "You study?"

"Yes. Actually, it's more like an internship. At *Aeppli-Ettler-Brunner-Suter Bachtold*. Do you know the firm?" Keely had seen the law firm's name in the guidebook.

"*Nein.*"

That was all he said. When they got off the elevator, they turned right and headed toward the front of the building. Keely noted the numbers. The old man stopped in front of 2A, which was on the left. Apartment 2B was on the right. As he fiddled with the key, Keely glanced out the hall window. She could see the coffee shop easily. Inside, Keely followed him from room to room, making pleasant comments as they went. The bedroom faced the alley. It was quite small, and Keely wondered why a bank official would live in such modest digs. After a few minutes, the old man led her back to the lobby.

"*Zo?*"

"It is very lovely. How much would it be a month?"

The old man scratched his head, knowing he would never be able to give the number in English. "*Neunhundertfünfzig* Euros."

That was a bit over $1,000. Keely thanked him, telling him she would have to think about it. He shrugged his shoulders and walked her back to the front door.

Outside, Keely crossed the street and entered the coffee shop. She spotted an empty table close to the front window, ordering coffee before she sat down. She pulled out her trusty guidebook for cover. Pretending to study pictures of the oldest watches at the Beyer's Watch and Clock Museum, and paintings and tapestries housed in the Swiss National Museum, Keely examined the apartment building across the way, counting up three, marking Hopler's window.

Keely kept Hopler under surveillance four days. She rested in her hotel during business hours then stayed outside his apartment, visiting various stores, but always keeping the front door of the apartment in sight. She would finish up at the coffee shop until it closed around nine each night. She carried several novels and a notepad in a small nap sack in case anyone should ask why she was spending so much time there. No one asked. Occasionally, she would wander around back, but she could not get a view of his bedroom window.

During her surveillance, she noted one man in his late thirties entering the building. His head was shaved, and he wore a leather jacket and jackboots, the uniform of the neo-Nazi movement; Keely considered for a moment if she might be stereotyping an eccentric dresser. She figured he was not a tenant because he usually came and went within an hour. She also noted that he only showed up when Hopler was home.

Hopler only accompanied two people to his apartment in the four days. Both were women-- girls actually. The dossier on Hopler indicated he had no wife or girlfriend. Keely could tell he was uncomfortable walking them through the front door, but his libido seemed to be stronger than his propriety. Both girls had short-cropped hair and wore black leather jackets, various tattoos just visible around their necks. Keely had seen a number of young runaways throughout the city, most making their living as prostitutes. Hopler apparently preferred the very young ones. They would stay for no more than two hours then leave.

On the fourth night, Keely decided to follow one of the girls as she left the apartment. The girl walked casually up the block, turned onto the *Banhofstrasse* and worked her way through the sparse crowd toward the rail station. Keely paralleled her and hurried ahead when she realized the girl was climbing the stairs to the station.

When Keely reached the door, she saw the girl purchasing a ticket at one of the windows, then walk across the cavernous lobby to a row of wooden benches. Keely slowly descended the stairs, stopping to buy an English language newspaper at a kiosk. She took a seat on a bench facing the girl, opened the newspaper and pretended to be engrossed in reading. Keely stole a glance.

The girl could not have been more than sixteen, glassy-eyed, and a row of seven loops dangling from her right ear. She seemed absorbed in thought, swaying slightly as though music played in her head.

Such a waste, Keely thought. This young girl was destined for a life abused, misused and then, when she could no longer attract customers, discarded. Keely stood and passed in front of the girl, wanting to reach down, shake her and tell her what a mess she was making of her life.

Their eyes met briefly, and the bitterness and disdain Keely saw saddened her; she realized the girl was already lost.

Toward the end of the week, Keely was surprised when Jonathan joined her. Since it was early afternoon, Keely hadn't left for the bank yet when there was a knock on her door. When she opened it, Jonathan was leaning against the adjacent wall. "You like my choice, I trust."

He sauntered in and threw an overnight bag on the bed. He picked up the phone and dialed. "*Zimmerservice*? Could you send up a bottle of Scotch, two glasses and a bucket of ice? Oh, and how about a cheese plate?"

He hung up the phone and walked to the armchair facing the window, falling into it.

Keely took the other seat. "To what do I owe this honor?"

Jonathan rubbed his eyes. When he looked at her, he gave the impression of being tired. "Let's wait."

After the Scotch had arrived and he had poured them both a good measure, he sipped then set his glass down. "How's Hopler?"

"He works, he goes home, he shacks up with little girls. A real putz."

Jonathan appeared to not be listening. He drained his Scotch and reached for the bottle.

Keely had barely touched her drink.

"Our contract has been amended," he said casually.

Keely had assumed they would watch Hopler for a while then turn the information over to their client-- although there was nothing to report-- and leave him to deal with the banker.

"Our client has decided that Mr. Hopler has become too much of a... liability. Unfortunately, he does not have enough to go to the authorities."

He withdrew a sheet of paper from his jacket and handed it to Keely.

It was a telex with no address and no name; only one line: *Terminate with extreme prejudice.*

Keely read the sentence twice and looked at Jonathan. "Does this mean what I think it means?"

Jonathan looked honestly vexed. "I've mentioned before that different situations require different responses. This is one of those very rare occasions. I suggested alternatives to our client, but it was no use. Seems Hopler has stepped up activities with the local skinheads and firing him is not an option."

Keely sat in silence for several minutes. She remembered how she had felt in France-- the adrenaline rush firing at the men who tried to kill the French bureaucrat. And she believed she would have killed had her life been in danger. But this was not self-defense. Jonathan seemed to read her mind.

"An old friend of mine, a former Mossad officer, once told me that you sometimes have to step outside the civilized world to protect society. That is the situation now." He took a long drink then looked at her with real concern. "Look, if you wish, I'll fulfill the contract."

"But this is a business contract. We're not working for a government; we're working for a bank."

Jonathan did not seem in the mood for debate. "A contract is a contract, regardless of the source. As I said a long time ago, I will only accept jobs I feel are necessary. Sometimes, that means stepping outside. If I thought this was unwarranted, I would have told the client. In this case, this man is financing death. Is he pulling the trigger? No. But the blood is on his hands just as surely as the person who pulls the trigger."

He walked to his bag and withdrew a stack of photos and handed them to Keely before he returned to his drink. Keely thumbed through the photos she had taken. Several were of Hopler and the man she had seen going into Hopler's apartment.

"The man in black is Amdeus Frindlander. He's a lieutenant in the *Nationalistischen Jugend Schweiz,* a youth party that's a cover for the skinheads. The last two are Frindlander's handiwork."

Keely flipped to the last two pictures. The first was a burned-out house with swastikas painted on the walls. The second was a morgue picture of a young girl not unlike the girl Keely had followed from Hopler's apartment.

"The house belonged to a Syrian family who had come to Zurich six months ago. The skinheads set fire to it and waited for the husband and wife to come out. When they did, the skinheads attacked with lead pipes. Fortunately, both lived. Unfortunately, the wife won't ever walk again. The girl wasn't as fortunate. She was a runaway Frindlander and his buddies picked up off the street. Authorities figured she stayed alive at least a week, if you can call what they did to her living."

"Why didn't they arrest Frindlander?"

"They will."

"But Hopler…."

"…is their banker. Frindlander is bad, but without people like Hopler, he wouldn't exist. Unfortunately, Hopler has been very good about keeping Frindlander and his friends at a distance. There's no direct link. But the money is the key… always the key."

"Okay, so these are bad people. But what gives us the right to execute someone without due process?"

Jonathan turned to her. "Do you think they gave those people due process?"

Keely didn't buy his reasoning. "Couldn't the authorities take this?"

"There is no case against Hopler. Even if they started, he would be long gone before anything would happen. We went through this all before. If you had killed that fellow in France, would it have made a difference if it had been at the behest of the government or not? The man would still be dead. But, as I said, I will take care of this."

For one brief moment, Keely felt relieved. Then she realized she had made the choice to join Jonathan; she had not placed conditions on it. "No. If this is part of the job, then I signed up to do it."

She could hardly believe what she was saying. "Tell me how and when."

The client did not want it to look like an accident. Instead, he wanted it to appear as though local neo-Nazis had killed the banker because they thought the authorities were about to shut down their flow of money. He thought it might make the government crackdown on bankers willing to make deals with the devil; there would also be a story circulated that Hopler had been found working secretly with radical groups to circumvent Swiss banking laws.

Jonathan and Keely were to get pamphlets from *Nationalistischen Jugend Schweiz* and Jonathan had arranged to get a small caliber automatic, the type favored by members of the group. He picked up a knife with a Nazi crest from a stoned-out skinhead anxious for a heroin fix. It was the kind given to the 'storm troopers' in the group.

Jonathan had been told that Hopler would attend a banker's meeting in St. Moritz the following Friday. Because the drive would take over six hours on the winding mountain roads, he assumed Hopler would have to stop. That's when Keely would lure him into an ambush.

Jonathan had offered again to carry out the contract, but Keely insisted this was her responsibility. As she prepared herself in her hotel room, Jonathan looked on. She had slicked back her hair, securing it in a tight braid. She donned black jeans, a black silk blouse that she left unbuttoned to her navel, leather jacket and jack boots. She selected a blood red lipstick and left the jacket opened enough to give anyone interested a good view of her partially exposed breasts.

The only incongruous piece of wardrobe were black kid gloves. When she was done, she turned to Jonathan.

"Well?"

"Bell of a Nazi ball." He stood and adjusted her collar but stared into her eyes. "Are you sure about this?"

Keely didn't answer, but instead went to the dresser and picked up the Ruger .22 Jonathan had gotten for her. It was bigger and heavier than she liked. There was no way she could carry it on her, especially in her skin-tight jeans. She checked the clip and chambered a round, being sure to put on the safety. Jonathan had thought about getting a silencer for it but decided against it. She slipped the weapon into her mini-nap sack.

He stood and walked to her, placing his hands on her shoulders. "Just another assignment. Keep telling yourself that."

Keely didn't respond as she turned and headed for the door.

Jonathan and Keely followed Hopler out of the city along the A3 that traced the western shore of the lake. They had examined the route and decided the best place was somewhere east of Ziegelbrucke. They kept at a discreet distance, making sure another car was between them at all times. After about an hour, Hopler stopped at a rest house and Jonathan pulled in several cars away from where he had parked. He shut off the engine and looked at Keely.

"This looks like as good a chance as any. Maybe you can convince him to drive you someplace."

Jonathan said again. "I really can do this, if you are concerned…."

Keely looked at him briefly, then straight ahead. "I'll tell him my car's broken down. Get him to drive me down the road a bit."

Before he could respond, Keely was out the door.

Once inside, she wandered slowly past the table where Hopler was sitting and ordered coffee. An older couple sat in one corner and a hiker near the door, his pack taking up most of the booth where he sat. She turned around when she got her cup, as though looking for a place to sit. She caught Hopler's eye and smiled. He tentatively returned the smile. She may not be a sixteen-year-old, but Keely figured she looked good.

She drifted over and sat down opposite him, making sure that the other customers in the place could not hear her voice or see her face.

She spoke in halting German. *"Entschuldigen Sie mich, aber ich benötige etwas Hilfe? Sprechen Sie Englisch?"*

The banker looked alarmed but appeared to be tempted by Keely's flashing brown eyes. He responded in impeccable English with the slightest of British accents. "What seems to be the problem?"

She smiled. "Oh, yes! You speak English. I was trying to make it from Salzburg tonight. Unfortunately, my fucking car stopped running. I need someone to take a look at it. The others in here don't look like they know shit about cars. I would really appreciate it."

Hopler looked as though he was weighing the alternatives. "I don't know. I am supposed to…."

Keely leaned forward, knowing he would have a clear view inside her jacket, and pouted while at the same time running her hand up the inside of his leg. "I mean, I could be very appreciative."

Hopler took the bait. He paid quickly and followed her outside. They got into his car and quickly left. He drove rapidly, glancing at her periodically, his rising excitement obvious.

Jonathan's car was parked about two miles away on the narrow gravel shoulder beyond a turn on the mountainous road. The man pulled in behind it and turned off his engine. His hand snaked into her lap before he even looked at her.

"So. Just how do you intend to show your appreciation?"

When he turned, he saw the automatic in Keely's hand. Gradually, his expression changed from excitement to confusion to fear. "What is this?"

Keely motioned with the pistol. "Give me the keys." He complied. "Open the door, but don't get out." After a moment's hesitation, he did as he was told.

"Look, if it is money you want!"

She got out and walked quickly around the front of the car, the weapon trained on his head the whole time. The wind was minimal, but Keely felt cold. It was as though she was watching herself from the outside, unable to control what was happening. When she reached his side of the car, she motioned again.

"No talking. Turn off the lights and get out."

He moved awkwardly, and Keely realized he was shaking. When he was out, she made him put his hands behind his head and walk around to the soft shoulder of the road. The full moon illuminated the mountains and the roadway with an eerie white light. The shoulder was fifteen-feet wide, ending abruptly at a drop-off and a small gorge that in the darkness seemed impenetrable.

She stopped him just at the edge. "Kneel down."

He turned to her, fear contorting his face, shaking uncontrollably. "Wait. I am very rich. I can give you much money."

Keely kept the weapon trained on his head. She was amazed that she was not trembling.

"I said, kneel down."

"Please, don't shoot."

Her only response was to tighten her grip on her weapon. He turned away and slowly got to his knees. She could hear him weeping quietly. She took two steps closer and leveled her weapon.

He whimpered. "Please."

Keely's hands were steady, as she took a two-handed grip of the automatic, using her left to support and steady the butt. With the first spit of the weapon, his body jerked forward. He was dead before he hit the ground. Her lack of emotion stunned Keely as she steadied her grip and, as Jonathan had instructed, fired another two rounds into the back of the banker's head.

Jonathan appeared out of nowhere and gently put his arms around her, taking the automatic from her hand. Realizing she had been holding her breath, Keely released it slowly. She also realized she was extremely cold, her teeth beginning to chatter.

Jonathan started to walk her to their car, but she stopped him, indicating she didn't want help. He put his arm around her to guide her anyway. Dazed, Keely couldn't help but think 'I didn't have the right... what have I done?' Keely was suddenly very frightened-- that she had pulled the trigger without hesitating; that she had killed another human being-- not in self- defense, not in cold blood. She suddenly wondered if she was any better than the young girl she'd followed from the banker's apartment. And when she looked in the mirror, would she see the same lost expression?

Jonathan made sure she was settled in their car before he returned to the banker. She knew what he was doing. The banker would be found with the weapon beside him. A pamphlet from the ultra-right would be found secured to his chest by the blade of the storm trooper's knife.

When Jonathan returned, Keely was pale and mute. He watched her for a moment. "You sure you're all right?"

All she could do was nod. He started the car and headed back toward Zurich. Halfway there, Keely made him pull to the side of the road where she rushed from the car and vomited. When she got back in the car, she looked at him, pain in her eyes. The bile still in the back of her throat, she tried to speak. Jonathan seemed to know the question.

"It is like this at first. But it never becomes easy."

They flew back to London in silence and drove from Gatwick Airport to St. Albans. It wasn't till they had nearly reached the town that Jonathan broke the silence. "I want to stop by Swift House." He pulled in beside the back entrance and turned off the engine. He sat quietly for a minute then turned to her.

"Please come in for a moment?"

She finally moved, opened the car door and got out without speaking.

Once in the house, Jonathan pointed Keely toward his private quarters, while he went upstairs. He was gone for several minutes. When he came back, she was sitting on the sofa, never having removed her coat. Jonathan noticed.

"Let me fix you a drink before I take you home," he said walking out of the room and returning with two filled glasses. She accepted a glass and drank half before she spoke, her eyes fixed on nothing.

"Tell me I did the right thing."

Jonathan finished his drink in one swallow and set the glass down. He watched her for a long moment before answering, sitting beside her. "If you are asking me if that banker deserved to die, I would have to answer yes. If you are asking, have I always been right when I've pulled the trigger...." He shrugged.

Tears welled up in Keely's eyes. Jonathan slid over to her and carefully took her in his arms. They had not touched like this in a long time.

With Jonathan's arms around her, Keely allowed herself to feel vulnerable. She wanted to show she could be as detached about death as he was, but she knew that was impossible. She felt his lips press gently against her hair. She turned her face to his and kissed him. What was meant to be an acknowledgment of his tenderness quickly turned into a need.

Jonathan stood and extended his hand. He led her to his bedroom without a word.

As she pressed her naked body against his, she had forgotten his muscularity. His thighs were rock solid, and as she dug her fingers into his back, she could feel his muscles tighten. She could also feel the ridge of scar tissue that snaked its way from his neck to below his shoulder blade.

There was no tenderness, no gentleness. It was as though Keely was punishing herself-- for allowing the beast to rise up in her and take a human's life-- and punishing Jonathan for unleashing that beast.

It lasted only a few minutes. As they separated, Keely rolled away from him and pulled her knees up in a fetal position. She felt neither relief nor release. She lay still and silent for a moment, then quickly rose, dressed and left.

The next morning, Keely slowly made her way across the small park that separated her apartment from Swift House. She had slept fitfully, her dreams full of blood and darkness. The park was empty except for a mother and a toddler, who giggled each time his mother pushed him higher on the swing. Keely stood and watched for a while, the emptiness inside her almost overwhelming. She had no one. She had nothing. And she had murdered.

As she entered the second-floor office, Jonathan sat buried in his morning paper. He looked up and weakly smiled. Rhonda walked over to her and wrapped her arms around her friend. "Sorry, love. Must've been some bad business, eh? Jonathan told me about it."

Keely pulled back. Why would he tell Rhonda? Wasn't anything private around here?

Keely still couldn't look at Jonathan, staring at newspaper she was certain he wasn't really reading. Had he told Rhonda how the banker had pleaded for his life? How Keely had unflinchingly fired into his head? That the act made her so sick she had to throw up afterwards? Did he tell the rest, of what happened in his bed?

"Jonathan said the man was a bad egg-- needed to be eliminated."

This time, Keely looked straight at Jonathan, but he flipped the pages of the paper and turned it over. "Thanks for your concern, Rhonda. What's done is done, so if you don't mind, I'd rather not talk about it."

Keely walked to her desk and sat down without removing her coat. Rhonda came behind her and patted her shoulder.

"I'll get you a cup'a."

While Rhonda was out of the room, Keely watched Jonathan. He would not return her gaze. Finally, she couldn't stand the silence. "We need to talk."

Jonathan looked up. "I suppose we must. How about a walk in the park."

The mother and child had left, and they had the park to themselves. Keely carried the mug Rhonda had brought her, and Jonathan walked with his hands clasped tightly behind him. Both seemed reluctant to speak, but finally Keely's words cut into the thick silence between them.

"I apologize for last night. I shouldn't have let that happen, again. I guess I just needed something."

"Therapy?" Jonathan had stopped and now looked at her as a teacher might look at a bothersome student.

"Human contact." She turned and walked to the swings, sitting in one and rocking back and forward slowly.

He followed as if in no hurry and stood next to her. "Sometimes, in this business, we make choices. Do we walk away from this kind of job and let the scum continue to corrupt the world? Or do we put a stop to it?"

She put her foot down on the ground and stopped swinging. "I'm curious. What criteria do you use before you say yes to jobs like that?"

He turned and stood in front of her. "If that man had not died, dozens of innocent people may have. I don't ascribe to the theory that within each of us is a good person. I believe some people are evil. And their deaths advance our society."

She looked up at him with disdain. "You actually believe that shit, don't you? You believe I had a right to blow his brains out without giving him any chance to explain. You believe that we can serve as judge, jury and executioner without any moral consequences, as long the price is right."

He began to speak, but she got up from the swing and held up her hand.

81

"And last night, when you were on top of me, did you really think you were providing 'therapy'? Did you think I wanted you inside me because I just needed a little 'boost'? What makes you so damned cold? Last night happened because I wanted to punish myself, you self- righteous bastard."

Jonathan stood silently during her tirade, his expression never changing. Keely sat back down and began to swing. He stepped out of her way and walked over and sat in the swing beside her. He looked through the trees to the overcast sky.

"When I was a child, my mother would walk with me through this park. She would sing to me sweetly and push me high into the air. She died shortly before my twelfth birthday. My father was very responsible, very concerned that I should grow to be a proper English gentleman. But he didn't know how to love. He was the one who encouraged me to enter the service after Cambridge. Even got me a post with an old friend of his. He was livid when I decided to join Special Services; thought it may hurt my 'career'. S.A.S. were considered rogues and mountebanks. He died while I was off in North Africa, hunting down someone or other. I never had the opportunity to say good-bye."

He stood and grabbed the chain of her swing to force her to look at him. "We are in a business that does not allow us to question the morality of our actions. We do not have the luxury of emotions. It doesn't mean we do not consider the consequences; or carry with us the scars of our decisions.

"And as for last night-- there is neither the time nor the emotional space to allow for anything other than professionalism. The first time I killed, I had to find a body against which to throw myself. And the violence of the killing infected that moment, just as your violence in Zurich was matched by your anger last night. Do not confuse the body with the mind. What we did in Zurich was necessary. What we did last night was also necessary... for you."

She jumped up and slapped him. "Fuck you. Moralize all you want. But bottom line, you are a cold-blooded killer. And now you've made me one. And as for last night, don't hand me this bullshit about necessary for me. I was under *you*, remember? That was no 'therapy.'"

Keely turned away. "Look, I don't know what's happening, but it sure as hell isn't what I want. I'm taking the day off."

She walked toward her apartment without looking back. Before she left the park's entrance, she turned around. Jonathan remained where she had left him.

Three days later, Keely returned to Swift House. Rhonda had come around the night before and they had drunk wine late into the evening. Rhonda tried to explain that Jonathan was not the cold-hearted professional he sometimes pretended to be, but Keely remained unconvinced.

"Rhonda, I don't know if I can do this. I thought I could, but I just don't know."

Rhonda leaned forward and put her arm around Keely. "Is it the work or Jonathan you're unsure about?"

"Maybe they've become one in the same. Look, when I first accepted this job, I admit, it sounded intriguing. But now, I'm beginning to wonder if I was just swept up by the fantasy of being some sort of international spy—who knows!"

She stopped and glanced at Rhonda. "You've been a good friend. I'd have gone crazy if you hadn't been here. There's been times I've felt so disconnected from the outside world, but you helped me not feel so alone."

"I'm glad."

"I've been doing a lot of thinking. About leaving." Rhonda's eyes widened. "You mean quit Swift?"

"Why not?"

"Jonathan needs you."

Keely thought Rhonda was wrong. "For what?"

"I know you can't see it, but he's been different since you came. Listen, I shouldn't tell you this, I don't think it my place. I'm sure he won't like it."

"Tell me what?"

She looked hesitantly at Keely a moment, then topped her glass off with the last of the wine without apologizing for not refilling Keely's glass.

"Well, it must have been shortly after he met you. He called for messages from the States and began talking about someone he had met in Colorado, somebody who was not only smart but talented. He asked me to do a background check." Rhonda looked embarrassed. "Then he called back to say he had hired you. You can imagine my surprise. Always the lone wolf-- always glad to be on his own. Since you arrived, there's been a civility about him; nothing I can put my finger on. His world's brutal, Keely. I feel sorry for him sometimes."

Keely had no sympathy whatsoever. "His world is of his own making. At first, I thought I could live there, too, but I can't."

Tears formed in Rhonda's eyes. Keely leaned over and wrapped her arms around Rhonda. "I'll miss you."

Something inside Keely quietly said, 'and Jonathan.' She had been drawn to him like a moth to a candle, mesmerized by his stories about the S.A.S. And underneath it all, there was an attraction that she had tried, unsuccessfully, to keep at bay. But now, she didn't care. A rift had developed between them. He had lost his glamour, and the truth was cruel and hard.

As she walked in the office the next morning, Keely passed her desk and stopped in front of Jonathan's. He looked up from his paper, but there was no smile.

"Jonathan, I can't do this. You said I could quit at any time, that my contract would be voided. Consider this my resignation."

She walked back to her desk and sat down, absently rearranging files. Jonathan didn't move for a while, but finally sorted through the papers on his desk and extracted several stapled together. He stood and walked over to her.

"If that's what you choose. I'm sorry and I do understand. And despite what you might think right now, I will miss you very much."

He turned and began to walk back to his desk, stopping half way and turning back. "I am having a problem motivating some contractors in the Republic of Georgia. I have a business meeting in Washington, so I won't be able to go for another week, but the client wants information immediately. It's a simple reconnaissance job, but our people there need a little 'push.' If there was any other way, I would not ask, but this is time sensitive. Perhaps you could give me two more weeks?"

He didn't wait for an answer, but instead went to his desk, retrieved a folder and walked back to her. He dropped it on her desk.

CHAPTER SIX

Keely sat by the window in the darkened room, staring out at the black sky above St. Albans. She had been sitting there for almost two hours as the gray light of day gradually succumbed to night.

She never had any real plans for her life, or a career, or her future. She had joined the Air Force because it seemed to be the thing to do, but in the end, it was simply a way to postpone actually facing the future. She had joined Swift because the job had seemed exotic and got her out of Cortez and into something that she hoped would be stimulating and rewarding.

Swift had been like the Air Force, only with much better benefits. Jonathan had made all the decisions, and it was obvious he had been guarding her against the nastier aspects of the work. Perhaps he was afraid she couldn't cut it. Maybe she couldn't.

Zurich had been a wake-up call. Jonathan had let her do something she never thought she could do. Why? To prove her worth to Jonathan or because, deep down, she wanted to see if she had it in her. Or she could she be that heartless. Jonathan had warned her this kind of work could affect a person, that it wasn't a game. Of course, it wasn't.

Hopler had been a real person. She shook her head and wrapped her arms around herself.

What had started out exciting and different had become frightening and evil. It was if she had fallen in a deep hole in Zurich, spiraling into hopelessness and fear. She had to find the strength to climb out and run as far away from all this as she could. She swallowed hard and blink back tears thinking it was more than just her job she was walking away from.

The file lay on the coffee table in front her, but she was afraid to touch it, as if it somehow would infect her. She hadn't agreed to take the assignment, but she had not said definitively no. In fact, she had said very little to Jonathan since the park. Killing had left her hollow and disoriented. The sour taste still remained in her mouth, though she had brushed her teeth and rinsed twenty times.

The lights flickering on in the houses across from her apartment caught her attention, and she wondered absently if the families in those houses were sitting down to dinner-- mothers scurrying around kitchens, children under foot, dads coming home from a hard days' work. She had never thought about children, home, family. Because she had assumed the role of mother for her brothers when her mother had died, she did not relish the thoughts of a family of her own. Her father had done the best he could. She still could hear him say, 'let's all do our part.' But her brothers weren't much help around the house. She didn't mind looking after her father; her mother would have wanted her to.

In her darkened room, her thoughts turned to Jonathan. Over the past months, she had felt compelled to be near him, as though his aura somehow illuminated her life. But his business had unleashed something in her she feared could swallow her soul. Taking another's life had brought home how fragile life was. She had stumbled too long through life without much care or thought. That had to stop.

She reached for the lamp beside the couch and turned the knob. Light spilled over the file folder on the coffee table, as she leaned forward, flipping open its cover, and picked up the e- mail from their client at the CIA.

A group of rebels associated with the *al Nusra* front in Syria had overrun a government town. In the bank, they had found a cache of Euros dollars-- worth approximately four million. The group had loaded the loot in two trucks and carried it off. The trucks showed up in Turkey, then in Azerbaijan. They were tracked to the border of the Republic of Georgia. CIA didn't want to alert the Georgian authorities, because they would confiscate the money and they feared it was headed for Islamists in Kyrgyzstan. Tracking it gave the agency a better opportunity to break up a terrorist network.

The idea was to locate the trucks without alerting the rebels they under surveillance and plant a GPS tracking device. Jonathan had been given the contract because if the mission failed, CIA would be cleared of letting the money slip through its hands.

Jonathan had contracted with two locals who as yet had not been able to find the trucks. Jonathan thought they needed a bit of encouragement.

The dossier included a military map of Georgia, a summary of the Kyrgyz terrorists.

There was also a dossier on 'Kestrel.' Apparently, he was to sell weapons to the group when they arrived in Chechnya. Keely remembered that name from her first live fire assignment in France. No one knew his identity, his nationality or his whereabouts. He dealt mostly in small arms-- AK-47s and RPGs-- shoulder-mounted rocket launchers-- stolen or purchased from former arms depots. There seemed to be no political agenda attached to his deals-- he sold to anyone with the cash to buy, often on both sides of a conflict. He was one of many dealers the U.S. had used to get weapons to Kurdish separatists in Turkey, to Abkhazskian rebels in northwest Georgia, and to right-wing revolutionaries in Hungary, Poland, and Romania.

The CIA was worried that if that person made the deal, he could leverage it to start arming the growing Islamic terrorist networks. In other words, they had to get to the truck before he did. And there was the possibility the trucks would lead to his capture.

Keely closed the file and laid it back on the tabletop. She turned to the window again, the night sky pitch black, the low-lying clouds reflecting the lights of the city. She wished Rhonda was there. She had become Keely's constant companion and closest friend. In fact, Rhonda was the first true female friend Keely had had in years. But even Rhonda couldn't help her with this decision, although the decision was apparent. Deep down, she knew what she had to do, and she couldn't let personal connections sway her. Hadn't that also been something Jonathan had taught her? The choices were obvious. She could learn to accept the killing as Jonathan apparently had and stay with Swift, or she could quit and never look back.

That brought her to an even more perplexing realization-- could she really bring herself to walk away from Jonathan. Theirs had become an entangled, emotional relationship Keely had yet to define. Not love. Maybe it had been what Jonathan called it-- a need.

The knock on the door startled her and she jumped slightly before standing. When she opened it, Jonathan stood looking off in another direction. He turned to her and unbuttoned the top button of his overcoat.

"Hello."

Keely didn't answer or move.

Jonathan continued. "I just wanted to make sure you didn't have any questions."

"About the assignment? No."

She bit her tongue to keep from saying what she really wanted to say, what she had been thinking about for the last several hours.

"May I come in anyway? I'd rather not carry on a conversation in the hallway."

She pushed the door wider and walked away. He closed the door and followed her into the living room. He removed his overcoat and fixed them each scotch without asking. He sat across from her, watching. She stared from the drink sitting on the coffee table in front of her to Jonathan, around the room, back to the drink. She shifted in her seat as he set the glass with its near empty contents down beside him on the floor.

"I'm sorry you're angry."

Keely's eyes started stinging. "Neither... just tired."

"Tired of the job or tired of me?"

She stared at him, surprised by his directness. He didn't give her time to respond.

"Was it Zurich or what happened after?"

His detachment loosened her tongue. "Oh, I think we agree we were using each other. It was just-- you know-- a thing. "

"Stop it, Keely. I don't see it that way. We needed each other."

"Don't flatter yourself, Jonathan. I do not like what I've become. What you've made me."

"What do you want me to say? That I turned you into a killer? That the killing was unnecessary? Sorry. Can't. I don't believe either of those. I do believe that banker had to die. And I think we make ourselves what we are and shouldn't lay the guilt on someone else."

She wanted to strike out at him. "We? Lay the guilt? That's the best you can say to me."

Jonathan reached for his glass.

"I don't know what you want to hear. But you must know that we don't live in a world of simple answers."

Jonathan finished his drink, stood and poured himself another.

"I won't deny you are important to me, Keely. But not in the sense you seem to believe. And I won't justify my life to you. I simply can't give you the kind of emotional support you apparently want from me. It's just not in me."

She stared toward the window at the black sky over St. Albans. "Okay. Fine. We're done here. I don't have any questions."

He walked over to her and tried to touch her shoulder, but she pulled away. He sat down next to her and sipped his drink.

"You know, I hate to see you punishing yourself like this. You are at a point we all must come to-- each of us-- to decide what is important to our lives. Unfortunately, sometimes that decision places us in untenable positions. In hindsight, I admit I may have been hasty to make you choose."

She bit her lower lip and looked over at him. Some part of her wanted very much to hold him again. She closed her eyes until she felt his hand on her cheek. She caught his hand and held it at the wrist, opening her eyes to see his face very close to hers. He slowly withdrew his hand and leaned back, held up the drink still in his hand.

After a long silence, she picked up her glass she had left untouched. "I can't believe the killing doesn't bother you."

"I've never said it didn't." He looked directly at her. "I know you think me mercenary, doing whatever our clients ask. You are wrong. People have certain talents. And those talents must be put to use, hopefully for the common good." He looked down into his glass. "My talents just happen to be more distasteful than most."

"You say that so casually. How do you live with yourself? Or look in the mirror?"

"You must remember this world isn't like your little corner of Colorado. My world is full of ruthless people who would kill you without a second thought."

"Knowing that, why did you ask me to work for you?"

He stood up and walked to the window. "The day we met, you flew me to Vegas," he laughed quietly. "Well, actually Overton. I was impressed as hell. I thought about you for days."

"My corner of the world wasn't corrupt enough for you, you mean?"

He turned back and raised his glass to her. "One thing you should know-- you really will be sorely missed."

Keely set her drink down. "I crossed a line I didn't think I ever would. If I continue here, I'm afraid I'll be lost. You said there comes a time when we have to choose. I'm there. I have to make the best decision for me."

He returned to his seat beside her and brushed the hair out of her eyes. "I do understand." He kissed her cheek, put down the empty glass, and walked out of the apartment.

After spending several more days cloistered in her apartment, she returned to the office. Although she had resolved to leave Swift, she felt obligated to take this last assignment. It had not been an easy decision. She had known, too, that if she pressed the issue, Jonathan would find another way to handle the situation in Georgia.

But something inside her couldn't quite let go yet. She wanted to stay connected to Jonathan just a little longer. Inwardly, she knew it was cowardly in a way. She should say no and leave. She knew what it was. She had a last-minute hope that things would change. She knew that wouldn't happen, but she just couldn't bring herself to end it.

She had not thought about where she would go or what she would do. Perhaps to Colorado-- where she would have to face her father's 'I told you so.' She dreaded the thought that he should find out what her job and boss were really about. Maybe she could spend time alone in Europe. She had more than enough money from Swift in her Swiss account. She wouldn't have to stay in one place. She could be free, whatever that meant.

She returned to the office the next day and told Jonathan she would go to Georgia. She listened as he explained the situation she would find. He was all business.

"The trucks should still be in Georgia somewhere near the Chechen border. There are few crossing points. You need to prod the contractors to look more diligently. If you find the trucks, plant the tracker if you are sure you can do it without being noticed. Otherwise, just note the location and we will find another way to monitor. Call on the sat phone either way. However, it would be best if our contractors didn't know you were planting the tracker."

Keely was confused. "Why?"

Jonathan thought for a minute. "It is not that I don't trust them, but I don't know them that well. This is a sensitive part of the job and I'd rather you handle it alone."

"And Kestrel. Why the sudden concern?"

"The CIA thinks Kestrel is brokering a deal. They want to catch in the act. They think he'll use this to establish himself as the go-to guy for Islamic terrorists."

"And all I have to do is get your operatives to find them? Sounds too simple."

Jonathan shuffled several sheets of paper on his desk, resorting folders. "To be honest, I insisted that we not become directly involved in monitoring the trucks.' Once the trucks are located and the track placed, we're done." He reached under his large desk calendar pad and pulled out airline tickets. "You fly through Amsterdam to Tbilisi."

She stood up to accept them.

"On your return, you might want to stop over in Nice. A lovely part of France."

Keely was more concerned about what would happen in Georgia.

"Why haven't your people there found the shipment yet?"

Jonathan pondered the question and leaned back slightly in his chair.

"Niko is a good sort, but not very assertive. He was in the Georgian Army, but decided it was not lucrative enough. He has done worked for the CIA in Chechnya but seems more a follower than a leader."

"And the other one?"

"Ukrainian. She's worked as a contractor for the CIA, British MI-5, and French Duxieme Bureau, whoever has the most money. Her name's Irina. Very competent, very calculating…."

Keely squinted her eyes at Jonathan's hesitation. "But?"

He formulated his words carefully. "I've worked with her before. She can get the job done, but sometimes holds out for more money by feigning failure. I believe a little motivation on your part will get them both back on track."

"What's really the matter with them?" Keely bent over his desk and drummed her fingers on the table, impatient with him. "You might as well tell me, Jonathan. Or rearrange your schedule and go yourself."

Jonathan carefully folded his hands and paused before answering. "The last time we worked together, some tension developed between us."

"Between you and Niko, or you and Irina?"

"You could say that Irina and I had a falling out."

Keely didn't like the way he said that. "Over?"

"Let's just say personalities got in the way."

Keely's pent up frustration got the better of her. "You mean she didn't fall for your 'heat- of-battle' bullshit."

She watched him stiffen slightly, his eyes clouding over.

"You have a uniquely American way of expressing things. But no. Actually, Irina wants to play the game, but she doesn't like the rules. When an operative doesn't follow orders, it can be very costly. In this case, it was only a monetary loss, not someone's life."

Keely leaned in further, grabbing the edge of the desk, her jaw clenched as she spoke. "If she didn't follow your orders, how the fuck am I supposed to believe she'll follow mine?"

Jonathan didn't smile and gathered up the rest of the folders, laying them in a drawer next to him. He avoided looking at her. "We had no choice. The NSA insisted. But you can handle Irina. You should have no problems."

Keely snatched up the material he had for her and started to leave but turned back. "You know I'm serious when I say this is the last assignment?"

"I know." Jonathan never looked up.

Keely stood in the middle of the crowded customs area in the Tbilisi airport, regretting she had agreed to the assignment. The trip from England had taken almost twenty hours and she was exhausted. She had spent her trip trying to convince herself this was her way of showing Jonathan that she was a professional to the end. But now, her bravado wavered.

She fought her way through the mass of humanity to a kiosk where a uniformed man sat and held out her passport. He took the document, studied each page, glanced from her picture to her face and back again, then finally called over a man in plain clothes who repeated the examination. He motioned her to step around, which she did. He stepped close and she could smell the overpowering odor of garlic, onions and unwashed clothing.

"You come here for… business?"

Keely had been through the drill a number of times before. "Yes. Looking to buy folkcrafts."

"Folk….?"

"You know, shawls, hats, trinkets."

The man studied her for a long time. "How long you stay?"

She smiled her best innocent smile. "Less than a week, I suppose. Never know what I might find."

Finally, the man scribbled something in her passport with the stub of a pencil and handed it back to the uniformed man. He stamped it and passed it to Keely, who continued to smile until she was out of their sight.

The sidewalk in front of the terminal was just as crowded as the customs area. Although she had expected a third-world country, she stepped into a lively, modern city. Georgia has suffered incredible hardship under Soviet rule. When the Soviets left, the independent spirit of the Georgians roared into full gear. Now it was a thriving democracy with swarms of investors rushing into the country.

The job Jonathan had outlined was sketchy at best. She had a GPS tracker the size of a donut and a satellite phone, but since the contractors had been unsuccessful, she had no idea what she could do. She also had the address of the Hotel Simpatia in the center of the city where she would be staying and decided to take a taxi there without calling first. In her search for a taxi, she failed to notice the striking woman strolling up to her.

"Keely? I am Irina Pavlychko."

Irina stood in sharp contrast to those around her. In form-fitting leather jacket and skin- tight American jeans, she was several inches taller than Keely, beautiful with deep set blue eyes, a straight, patrician nose, high cheekbones and dark, full lips. Her hair was a white-blonde, cut very short with bangs that dangled in her eyes.

"Jonathan said you would come today. He described you accurately."

Her English had just a hint of an Eastern European accent that made her words sound harsh.

Keely took her hand, feeling Irina's firm grip. "He didn't come close to describing you."

Irina did not catch the irony, even though Keely smiled as she spoke. Suddenly, Irina seemed to get Keely's meaning and returned a thin smile, her beautiful white teeth accentuated by her tanned skin. The smile disappeared as quickly as it had appeared.

"Come, we should get out of the crowd. Niko has our car near the gate."

Niko was much darker than Irina, but he shared the same patrician nose and cheekbones, his face dominated by a bushy mustache. Even through a bulky jacket, Keely could tell he had the body of an athlete. His black wavy shoulder length hair was just unkempt enough to give him a boyish look. His smile came quicker than Irina's and Keely could tell he was used to women fawning over him. Irina made introductions, not bothering to give last names.

They shook hands and he threw Keely's bag into the back seat of a shiny new Peugeot. Keely slid in beside her bag; Irina sat up front with Niko behind the wheel. He negotiated the chaotic road leading out of the airport and entered an even more chaotic highway jammed with a sea of old and rusting cars beside new BMWs and Mercedes.

As Niko concentrated on the road ahead, Irina turned to Keely. "Jonathan should have told you we have found nothing."

Keely could see why Jonathan might not have gotten along with Irina; they gave off the same air of detached control. Irina continued without giving Keely a chance to respond.

"Niko and I have made many inquiries. No one has seen anything."

Keely had learned in her time with Swift that contractors were of varying levels of competence. Some were extremely conscientious, others tended to take the money and do the minimal amount of work necessary to keep their clients satisfied. Jonathan did not seem to have faith in Irina and Niko.

"I'm just here to confirm what you've discovered… or haven't discovered."

Irina gave a thin smile. "I believe your trip may have been… wasted. But then Jonathan has a habit of not trusting people."

"I imagine in our business, 'trust' is a commodity we don't have much of."

Irina looked as though she wanted to say something, but instead turned back to face forward. Her presence justified, Keely leaned back and concentrated on the road ahead.

Niko continued away from the airport at breakneck speed. The other drivers seemed to be oblivious of him and to driving etiquette in general. No one used turn signals; horns seemed to compensate for brakes. Holding on to anything she could, Keely had to turn her attention away from the road for fear of screaming.

The countryside was rugged, and in the distance, she could see mountains rising suddenly beyond the city. Tbilisi hugged both banks of a winding river, ancient bridges crossing at strategic bends. The buildings were a blend of 16th century grandeur and 20th century modernity. But there was a strong sense of place; an impression Keely couldn't articulate but felt instinctively.

After twenty minutes, Niko turned into a side street and pulled up to the curb in front of a two-story building that appeared to be a small hotel. He turned off the engine, jumped out, ran around and held the door open for Keely. "Hotel Simpatia. Best in Tbilisi. I take you to your room."

His voice seemed to suggest that he could stay if Keely was interested in some companionship. Keely gave him her best 'down-boy' look and then turned to Irina.

"I'd like to get started as soon as possible. Jonathan said the trucks have to be found before they cross into Chechnya." She held up a finger and fished the map of Georgia out of her bag. She unfolded it on the hood of the car and pointed to a town. Niko and Irina look skeptically at the map. "Right here. What would you suggest?"

Irina first looked at Niko and then at Keely. "As I said before, it is difficult to find anything in Georgia. The peasants do not talk to strangers. Those trucks would be almost impossible to find."

Irina seemed resolved to end the search now. Keely had studied the maps carefully on her flight. She had paid particular attention to the routes that led through the last town where the shipment was known to have been.

She thought Niko might be more pliable, so she turned her attention to him. "How about these routes. Anything there?"

Niko looked at Irina for an answer. Keely was getting exasperated. She was tired and didn't feel like arguing. All she wanted was a 'yes' or 'no.'

"Well?"

"We have talked to many people. Nobody has seen trucks like that. As for that area, it would be hard to get through to the border."

Keely fought the urge to get back in the car and have them take her back to the airport. But she had made a commitment and she would see it through. "Look, I don't mean to tell you your business. Or what you should be able to find out. All I know is that I have to make a report, or I don't get paid. And without a report, you don't get paid either."

The suggestion he might not get paid had the anticipated effect on Niko. He looked like a small boy who was just told he couldn't go to the circus. He tried to get Irina's attention, but she wouldn't look at him.

Keely smiled. "Tell you what. Why don't we head for the mountains tomorrow? We can check out this Pasanauri. Seems like a good place to make a run through the mountains to Chechnya."

Again, Niko looked to Irina to answer, but she kept silent.

"Okay. Let's just spend a day sniffing around-- I go back home, tell our client we couldn't find anything, and we all get paid."

She caught the glance between Niko and Irina. Niko's eyes pleaded, but the woman seemed unmoved.

"That area is very dangerous. There are bandits in the hills. And the peasants are not friendly."

Keely was not interested in debating the issue. "We're big boys and girls, and can obviously take care of ourselves. We head for the mountains tomorrow, got it."

They may not have understood all her words, but there was no mistaking her tone of voice. Irina shrugged. "As you wish."

Keely's room was small and Spartan, but the quilt on her bed was handmade and inviting. She lay down without taking her clothes off after Niko and Irina had left, pulling the quilt around her. She didn't know how long she slept, but when she awoke, it was dark outside. She went to the window and peered into Tbilisi, the dark of the evening sky made brighter by thousands of lights. She looked at her watch, calculating it was nine local time. She picked up her jacket and went out.

The street where the hotel sat was quiet, but she could hear music and voices in the distance. Many people strolled about the streets. She headed toward the music realizing she had not eaten in a while. When she reached the corner, she searched for a place to eat. Halfway down the block was a storefront, the bright neon Cyrillic lettering above the entrance. She could hear music and headed toward it.

Inside she found a small bar on one side and six mismatched tables crowded with mismatched chairs on the other. Four patrons inside, two young men and two young women, huddled around a table toward the back. American pop was playing in the background. They seemed to all talk at the same time. A fat, old man sat behind the bar, a cigarette dangling from his lips, engrossed in a newspaper.

As she entered, the four at the table looked in her direction briefly and then returned to their discussion. The bartender lowered his paper just enough to peer at her suspiciously.

Keely sat at a table near the door, and the man grudgingly rearranged his girth to waddle over to her. She smiled her best smile. "I'm sorry, do you speak English?"

The bartender just stared down at her. Either he didn't understand or didn't care for foreigners. They stared at each other for a minute until one of the young men disengaged himself from his group and walked quickly over to her. He extended his hand.

"Hello. You are American. I speak English."

Without being invited, he sat next to her. His smile was open and non-threatening. "I am Sando Vukadze."

Keely smiled. "I'm Keely."

Sando turned to the bartender and rattled off something in Georgian. It sounded like a combination of Russian, Turkish and Arabic. The words were spoken in monotone, with little inflection, but the sound of the strange words was not unpleasant.

The bartender waddled away and Sando turned his attention to Keely. "Please. I ordered you Georgian wine and *Acharuli Khachapuri*. That is bread with cheese inside and an egg on top. Very wonderful. Georgian wine very wonderful, too."

There was something about the young man-- earnestness about his eyes, with the wonderment of a little boy. Keely felt very protective all of a sudden. "Your English is very good."

She could see him straighten up proudly. "Thank you. I was an exchange student in America four years ago. You from Atlanta? I lived in Atlanta for year. I live with wonderful family. They love me very much. I go to American high school. Now I go to University."

Impressed by his background, they talked for a long time. The bartender brought the wine and bread, which Keely approached tentatively. After her first sip of the wine, she was sold. It was dark and almost buttery, like a rich Merlot. The bread was hot and when she bit into it, a pungent cheese oozed out. The bread and cheese were flavored with a mixture of herbs Keely could not recognize, but the combination was intoxicating.

Sando talked about America, his university, his family, Tbilisi and Georgia. There was an exuberance about him that was very endearing. He seemed so proud of his country for having chased the Russians out. He told of the centuries of struggle his people had endured. And he told of his plans to graduate the university and enter government. He also talked about his 'family' in Atlanta and how much they meant to him even though it was very hard to keep in touch.

Keely didn't realize that almost two hours had passed, and she had drunk almost an entire bottle of wine until the bartender came over and said something to Sando, who answered him brusquely.

"I am sorry, Keely, but the man must close now."

Keely touched his hand and smiled. "I need to get back to my hotel anyway. But thank you for the company."

She stood and reached into her pocket and extracted folded bills. She had not been able to exchange her Euros at the airport, and she pulled off a five Euro note and showed it to Sando.

"I'm sorry, this is all I have. Will it be enough for the wine and bread?"

96

Sando blushed crimson. "Please. You are my guest. You do not have to pay. I have told the man this."

"Are you sure? I don't want to...."

Sando stood and bowed formally. "No worry. It is done."

His friends had left earlier and Sando walked with Keely along the street until they reached the corner. She stopped. "I can get back from here. It is just up the street."

Sando stood awkwardly, not sure how to say good-bye. He reminded her of her brothers.

Keely leaned toward him and kissed him gently on the cheek. "Thanks for a lovely evening."

Sando blushed again. "No. Thank you. I do not get to speak English very many times.

This is good practice."

"I'm going out of town tomorrow. To the mountains. But I should be back in a day or two. Perhaps we could meet again. Maybe you could show me around Tbilisi."

Sando's beaming smile told her this would be very possible. He searched his pockets, pulling out a pencil stub and a small piece of paper. He carefully wrote something out and handed it to her.

"This is my telephone. Call and ask for Sando."

Keely patted his cheek lightly and walked down the side street. After a few yards she glanced back. Sando was standing at the corner and waved.

"*Nakhvamdis* Gamarjoba."

"Good night, Sando."

CHAPTER SEVEN

Niko and Irina arrived at seven a.m. Keely had slept fitfully, her dreams haunted by Jonathan and the Swiss banker. At one point during the night, she had awakened in a pool of sweat, her heart pounding furiously. Flashes of the Swiss mountains, the London subway, and dark alleyways had collided. Only with great effort was she able to clear her mind and fall back to sleep only to be haunted by her dreams again.

Keely had packed a few things in case they needed to stay in the mountains a few days including a small digital camera the size of a pack of cigarettes. She had dressed in jeans and sweatshirt and tied her hair back. She knew she would not look inconspicuous, but at least she would be comfortable.

Outside, Niko waited by the car and motioned Keely to follow him to the rear end. He opened the trunk to reveal camping equipment and a small arsenal of handguns and rifles. He motioned for Keely to check out his collection.

"You like my guns? We may need in the mountains."

Keely's stomach churned, as the an unnerving adrenaline hit her system. Jonathan had said this was to be a 'safe' assignment, which she had taken to mean there would be no need for weapons. She looked at Irina as if to ask why weapons were necessary. Keely detected a slight smirk on the woman's face.

"We said yesterday that the mountains are full of bandits. We must be prepared."

Keely strongly disliked thinking about the need for weapons, but knew she could not let these two see her apprehension. She turned to Niko. "You are well prepared."

He smiled and indicated she could choose one. "You want, you take."

Keely smiled but shook her head. "Not now, thanks anyway." Without waiting for a response, she dropped her bag on top of the weapons and walked to the front of the car. The two stood beside the open trunk for a second, then Irina said something to Niko, and he closed the trunk. As they came around, Keely spoke directly to Irina.

"If it's all the same to you, I'll ride up front." Without waiting for a response, she climbed in.

The ride into the mountains was uncomfortably quiet. The landscape quickly changed from rolling hills to craggy mountain, and the cityscape quickly gave way to empty fields. The few houses set well back from the two-lane road. Occasionally, Keely caught a glimpse of train tracks that seemed to hug the banks of a small river. They had driven for more than an hour before anyone ventured a comment.

"We will be in Pasanauri in maybe another half hour," Niko said. "Beyond, no other cities."

"Do you know anybody you can talk to there about unusual vehicles passing through recently?"

Niko stole a look at Irina in the rearview mirror, who leaned forward and rested an arm on the back of the seat. "Most mountain people do not like city people. They do not trust us."

Keely sensed that Irina either thought this was a waste of time or she was angry because someone had been sent to check up on her. Keely didn't care either way. "Is there a way to find out if anything passed through, say in the last week or so?"

"Nobody sees anything up here."

"Does that mean you asked?"

Irina answered for them. "We followed all leads. There was nothing. Like we said before."

Keely thought for a moment, ignoring Irina's statement. "Is there an auto mechanic in this place?"

Niko looked at her, confused. "There is nothing wrong with car."

"I know. But mechanics usually notice when strange vehicles come through town. Maybe a mechanic there saw something but didn't think much of it."

Niko shot Irina another look in the mirror. "I know mechanic there. We ask, but I still don't think.... " he didn't finish his thought.

Pasanauri could hardly be called a city. It was just a collection of indistinguishable buildings that followed a river through a mountain pass centered around a dilapidated train station. There were few people on the streets and even fewer cars. A collection of children of various ages played soccer with a worn ball, watched over by three women dressed in black from head to toe. The women seemed to embody the isolation of the place.

Niko pulled in beside the station and the three climbed out. He walked around to where Irina and Keely stood, and motioned toward the far end of the city square.

"The mechanic shop is there. You stay. I will go ask."

Keely watched him walk off, the bravado he had displayed when they had met Keely at the airport replaced with trepidation. Irina remained as stoic as she had been throughout the drive.

Keely felt uneasy with the woman, but felt she had to show that she could be civil. "Do you know this part of Georgia well?"

Irina turned to Keely but didn't answer for a long moment. "I have spent most of my time in Tbilisi or on the Black Sea. These mountains, they are unimportant. The people live as they have for centuries. They care nothing about politics . . . or outsiders."

Keely sensed imperiousness in Irina's attitude that was distasteful. And she wondered whether Irina had the same opinion about Americans as she had about these people.

"Maybe that's a better way to live. At least you don't get caught up in some abstract political game that has no real meaning. They know what counts, staying alive."

Keely didn't know whether she was trying to make a point to Irina or trying to understand her own feelings.

For the first time, Irina looked at Keely with interest. "Odd to say for an American. I thought all Americans loved politics... playing it like some game. You sound like you do not believe in what you do."

"Just calling it like I see it... How about you?"

Irina looked across the square, hesitating before she answered, as though formulating her answer carefully. "I believe in money. I believe in protecting myself. I believe I will do whatever is necessary to achieve those goals."

Keely didn't like the sound of that, but she didn't have time to debate because Niko hurried toward them, his brow furrowed. He began speaking before he reached them.

"He has learned something."

He stopped and looked around as though expecting someone to be listening, though there was no one within earshot.

"The mechanic said three big trucks passed through two days ago. Then they headed north toward the border."

Keely reached inside the car and pulled out the military map. She spread it out on the hood of the car and located Pasanauri.

"Which road did they take?"

Niko stared at the map and Keely could tell he had not spent much time with such detailed maps. After a moment, he traced a line from Pasanauri through the mountains.

"I think this one. It goes along a valley, then climbs to a ridge. It is the only one that goes to the border. The mechanic said there is old Russian border post somewhere there."

Keely followed the line Niko had indicated, but there was no indication of a military installation. That wasn't unusual. The U.S. military had produced the map using old topographic maps and aerial photography. The date on the map was 1980.

"Well, I think it's worth checking out."

Niko looked to Irina for a response. "I think it would be a waste of time," Irina said without expression. "Those trucks are probably gone by now."

Keely could tell Niko was not excited about going deeper into the mountains, but she couldn't quite figure out Irina's motivation. Keely wasn't about to back down. Without speaking, she folded the map so that the road the trucks took was facing up. She climbed into the front seat and settled in.

"Well, we won't know till we check it out. Ready?"

Niko and Irina hesitated for a moment, then grudgingly got into the car.

Any trace of civilization disappeared quickly as they worked their way out of Pasanauri. Keely noted that the power lines ended less than a mile outside the town. The road was paved but had not been serviced for years; huge potholes proved a challenge for Niko's driving skills.

He worked laboriously through a winding valley, often within a yard of the bank of a fast-moving stream, then began to climb. For a moment, Keely forgot why they were there, taken in by the pristine beauty all around.

It took more than an hour to maneuver the road that switched back at least a dozen times before it reached the top. Once on the ridge, they could see the mountains extending in all directions. There was no sign of habitation anywhere.

Keely had Niko pull to the side and she got out and walked several hundred yards in front of the car. She knelt, examined the pavement and then motioned for Niko and Irina to join her. When they arrived at the spot, Keely pointed to the ground.

"See those gouges in the shoulder. They're pretty recent and had to have been made by a very heavy vehicle."

Niko looked as though she had just spoken Greek. Irina was staring off into the distance. Keely was irritated but kept her anger in check. "Looks like we're on the right track. Niko, better drive slowly from now on. We don't want to stumble over any bad guys without warning."

They returned to the car and continued in silence for another hour until Keely grabbed Niko's arm. "Stop!"

Niko slammed on the brakes. Keely pointed ahead. There was a thin plume of smoke rising from around a bend a half-mile ahead. "We'd better check that out on foot. Niko, you stay with the car."

Keely could tell that his male ego had been crushed, but she didn't care. He might look dashing, but she had the feeling he was all looks and no spine. Irina had him open the trunk and picked up an M-16 that had been adapted with shortened barrel and collapsible stock. She chambered a round and set it for semi-automatic. Keely wanted to suggest that such firepower was probably not warranted, but she felt she had to give the woman some latitude. Irina motioned for Keely to take a weapon, but after a moment, Keely closed the trunk.

"You've got the firepower." Without another word, Keely set off toward the smoke.

They followed the road until the bend, then Keely motioned toward the ridge and they began to climb. It took almost a half hour to reach the crest of the hill. Keely was breathing heavily, but not as labored as Irina. They worked their way forward until they could see the roadway below.

The bend was long and narrow, but at the far end it straightened into the upper end of a valley that flared out and ran almost a mile down to a small lake. A gravel path ran about a hundred yards perpendicular to the main road and at the end sat a ramshackle house that looked as though it had been thrown together with discarded building materials.

Keely produced a small pair of binoculars and scanned the area. An assortment of goats, chickens wandered about the yard, and one forlorn cow munched hay from a makeshift trough. There was no sign of heavy trucks. Gunrunners weren't likely to choose such an open location anyway. As she continued to watch, a woman in peasant dress walked out of the house carrying two buckets. Behind her trailed two small children of indeterminable gender. A farming family.

Keely lowered the glasses and thought. After a moment, she motioned to Irina and began the trek back down the hill. When they finally arrived back at the car, Niko was asleep behind the wheel. Keely tapped on the hood and he jolted awake. They gathered around the map Keely had unfolded on the hood.

"Okay. The border is about ten clicks further up the road." Niko and Irina looked confused. "Sorry. Ten kilometers." She traced a short line on the map. "That means the border post must be somewhere there, and that farm is right about here."

Neither responded, so Keely continued. "Those folks up the road have to know something. I don't care how isolated they are. Let's just go in casually. You can say we're from the university doing some sightseeing. Anyway, we need to find out when the last truck went passed them and if they know about that post. Okay?"

Niko and Irina were mute, so Keely took that for mutual agreement and folded the map. She got into the car. The two hesitated, then finally Niko slid in behind the driver's wheel. Irina remained outside the car. Keely was in no mood for insubordination.

"What is it, Irina."

"These farmers will know nothing. It is a waste of time. We should not go further."

"They're on the same damn road those trucks took."

"What can they see? These people will not tell you."

"We're going to the farmhouse. Now get in."

Irina walked up and leaned down resting her elbows on the windowsill as she looked in at Keely. "It is your time we waste. And I get paid the same." With that, she jerked the back door open.

Niko approached the gravel driveway cautiously, and Keely had him pull in far enough to be off the road, but not close enough to panic those in the house.

"Irina, stay in the car. Niko, you come with me. And act natural."

Irina opened her mouth to protest, but Keely shot her a look that indicated discussion was not warranted.

Niko and Keely walked slowly up the path. The woman was feeding the chickens, the children playing at her feet. When the woman finally noticed them approaching, Keely waved casually and called out the only Georgian word she had learned: the word for hello. "Gamarjoba."

The woman looked panicked and glanced toward the house as if deciding whether to run.

Keely whispered to Niko while maintaining eye contact with the woman. "Tell her we're teachers from Tbilisi. That I'm an American. That you are showing me around the mountains."

Niko did as Keely requested. The woman did not move, but Keely could tell that her body relaxed just a bit. They finally reached what passed for a front yard and stopped a few yards from the woman. Keely saw that the two children were peeking out from behind their mother, who was probably in her early twenties, but looked fifty.

Keely thought quickly. It was late afternoon, and she didn't think they would have time to find the camp, reconnoiter, and get out of the mountains before nightfall. She didn't remember seeing any place to stay in Pasanauri but remembered Niko had camping gear in the car. Still smiling, she spoke under her breath to Niko.

"Tell her we didn't realize how late it was getting, and we were wondering if we might be able to camp here overnight."

Niko called out to the woman. She still did not respond, and Keely caught her looking toward the hills that rose from the yard to her right. They stood in silence for a long moment. Suddenly the younger of the children detached herself from her mother and walked toward Keely and Niko. The woman reached out for her, but the little girl had already covered half the distance between them.

Keely knelt and smiled as the girl approached. Through the dirt caked on her face, Keely could tell she was about four and had a cherubic look about her. The girl stopped a few feet away and cocked her head to one side, her eyes intently watching Keely.

She realized the little girl was looking at the rings on her fingers. She removed a silver band she had purchased in Amsterdam and held it out to the child, who stole a glance back at her mother, then walked forward. Keely continued to hold the ring in her outstretched hand and when she could, the little girl grabbed the ring and stepped back. She examined it carefully then looked up at Keely for an explanation. Keely pantomimed putting it on her finger, and when the little girl didn't seem to understand, Keely removed another ring and then replaced it.

The little girl watched carefully, looked at the ring again and carefully fitted it over her pudgy ring finger. It was too large, so she pulled it off and continued to try it on each finger until she settled for putting it on her thumb. When her head came up, she had the most beatific smile on her face that Keely had ever seen.

The sun quickly set in the mountains, and the cold winds began to whip dust around the tiny homestead. Niko had been able to convince the mother that they were in no danger. Irina came up from the car and the woman showed them into the one room building. The smell was overpowering, but Keely kept smiling. The woman offered coffee served in cracked and faded cups.

Through Niko, Keely complimented the woman on her fine home and her beautiful children. Once the four-year-old had broken the ice, her older brother had walked fearlessly up to Keely and stuck out his hand. Keely figured the boy wouldn't want a ring, so reached into her pocket and withdrew a pound coin, placing it gently in the tiny hand. The boy turned to his mother and held up his prize.

They had talked with the woman-- Niko translating, Irina sitting sullenly in the corner-- for almost fifteen minutes when the door opened. A man entered, stopping short when he saw the three of them. He was five inches shorter than Niko, but stockier. His face was olive, dominated by a shaggy handlebar mustache. He didn't look menacing, but Keely did not doubt he could easily defend his family. His wife hurried to him and whispered. The man never took his eyes off the strangers.

Finally, Keely stepped and extended her hand. "Gamarjoba."

The man's gaze moved from her eyes to her hand and back again, but he didn't reach to shake her hand.

"Niko. Tell him we are so sorry that we came here unannounced. It was getting dark and we were afraid to drive through the mountains to Pasanauri at night. We are teachers… from Tbilisi. Tell him I am an American visiting the university. How you were kind enough to bring me into the mountains. I had been told how beautiful they were."

Niko had a hard time translating so rapidly, but Keely didn't want too much silence. As soon as the last word left Niko's mouth, she continued. "If we are a problem, we will leave."

When Niko translated, Keely perceived the slightest softening of the man's jaw muscles. Just then, his daughter walked over to him and held up her thumb. She grunted something. Niko leaned closer to Keely.

"The girl said you gave her a present."

The father examined the ring without touching it, then looked at Keely. Then he spoke, Niko translating. "We do not have many visitors. Too far in the mountains. You are welcome to stay. The road is dangerous at night."

Over the next several hours, Keely learned about the young man and his wife. His name was Vali, his wife's Nana. This land had been in his family for seven generations, each barely eking out an existence in the rocky soil.

Vali had met Nana in Pasanauri. He had gone there to find work, as had she. They had fallen in love, married, and had intended moving to Tbilisi when Vali's father became ill and could no longer tend the farm. Despite their desire to leave the mountains, their sense of responsibility was too great. That had been seven years ago. Vali was twenty-seven, Nana twenty-five.

After a glass or two of homemade wine, and sensing that the couple was less leery about them, Keely got around to quizzing Vali about other travelers in the area. Niko sat across the table translating.

"Where does this road lead?"

Vali had been drinking faster than Keely and seemed to be feeling less threatened. He stole a glance periodically at Irina, and Keely could tell it was more than just curiosity. She didn't bother to return his gaze.

"The border of Russia. Used to be traveled more than now. Many trucks bring goods to Pasanauri, but since the fighting, we see very little."

" No trucks or anything like that at all now?"

"Well, maybe two or three." His lips spread into a knowing smile as he slurped his drink, drops of wine sticking to the mustache. He wiped his mouth with the back of his hand. "But they are not farmers."

Niko leaned forward and asked Vali a question. Keely looked at Niko for interpretation. "I asked him if he knew who they were. Where are they going?" Keely nodded approvingly. Vali looked uncomfortable and Keely feared he might change the subject. There was silence for a few more minutes as Vali looked at Irina again, then leaned closer as though afraid someone might be listening outside the door and spoke to Niko who translated.

"I do not know who they are. But they go to Russian fort. While in the mountains with my sheep, I watch them unload boxes. Big boxes."

Keely smiled and sipped the vile home brew. "Ask him if he would show us?"

Vali smiled back, his teeth a hodgepodge of yellowing fangs headed in many different directions. "I do not think they like company. One time, one of my sheep wandered too close. Before I could bring it back, someone shot it."

Keely heard this and displayed an appropriate level of horror and patted Vali's arm. "I am so sorry."

Obviously, Vali was not used to the attention of a woman such as Keely. Out of the corner of her eye, Keely could tell that neither was Nana, as she tensed and sat with furrowed brow, her arms folded over her ample breasts. Keely leaned back and reached into her pocket, withdrawing currency, but keeping it hidden in the palm of her hand.

"Perhaps tomorrow, you could lead us to this 'fort.' It might be interesting to see. I would be willing to pay."

Any doubts Vali might have had about these 'city people' were erased by the prospect of quick money. He took one more sip, then eyed her carefully.

"In what money?"

Keely opened her hand and showed him the two ten Euro notes. "I am afraid, all I have is this. Is that all right?"

Vali did not have to answer. The wonder in his eyes as he stared at the colorful, crisp notes was enough.

When they finally bedded down for the night, it was decided that Keely and Irina would sleep in the car and Niko in the shed beside the house. Irina said she would take the back seat, giving Keely no option but to slide into the front. Sounds of night creatures filtered through the cracked windows along with a cool breeze. As she began to drift off to a restless sleep, Keely hoped this assignment would be over soon and she could begin planning for her future. As Irina struggled to find a comfortable position in the back seat, Keely whispered, though no one else could hear.

"Can't get to sleep?"

For a moment, she didn't think Irina was going to answer. "This is not my idea of a good bed."

"Staying here just seemed to be the best thing. I think Vali can get us close to that truck park without being seen."

"I do not like it. This family should not be involved."

Keely sat up, her elbows supporting her. It was too dark to see Irina, so she didn't bother looking over the seat. "Why have you questioned every suggestion I've made? What have you got against me?"

There was a moment's hesitation. "You are too eager."

Keely did not like this woman. "Well, you know, if you and Niko had done your jobs in the first place, I wouldn't have had to come."

Irina did not respond, but Keely could hear her take a deep breath. "Or were you hoping Jonathan would come?"

Irina laughed, and Keely could see the outline of her head as she sat up. "You Americans always worried somebody does not like you. And Jonathan… he is just another man who thinks he is more important than he is." She lay back again. "I will tell you again, there is nothing here to find. Personally for me, I will be glad to be back to my own bed."

Keely fell silent. Irina had obviously not been impressed with Jonathan. Keely wondered if the woman was right about Americans-- her. Was she as paranoid as Irina made her out to be? Had she been too eager?

Morning broke gray and drizzly. A tapping on the frost-covered window above her head roused Keely from half-sleep. She rolled it down just enough to see Vali motioning for her to come outside.

He went into the lean-to that doubled as a stable where Niko had spent the night. Keely struggled out of her sleeping position and tried to work out the kinks. She glanced over her shoulder, but saw the back seat was empty.

Niko was sitting on a stool outside the house. She grabbed her bag and as she walked up to him, Keely could tell from his face that his rest had been no more successful than hers.

Keely looked past him. "Where's Irina?"

"She's in the house. Vali suggest we get started."

Keely started to walk toward the house but stopped. There was no way of knowing if there would be any trouble, and though she dreaded the thoughts of touching another weapon, it would be best if they were armed. She turned back to Niko. "How about opening the trunk and getting us some weapons. I'll round up Irina."

"Do you think Vali will be worried if he sees guns? He might not take us."

She nodded. "You may be right. Bring me a handgun. Tell Vali that we will be carrying weapons for protection because we heard there are many wolves in the mountains. Let him take one of the guns and give him one of these as an advance." She handed him one of the Euro notes and headed for the house. Niko didn't look happy about giving away his weapons but did not argue.

The hike was not strenuous, the path well worn by centuries of shepherds driving flocks to feeding grounds higher up the mountain. They walked in silence for almost an hour until Vali stopped and pointed ahead. They were about twenty yards from the crest of the ridge. Keely figured the installation was just on the other side. Vali put his finger to his lips and motioned them forward.

When they reached the crest, all four crouched down and inched forward until they reached a rock outcropping. Below, about hundred yards away, was a makeshift truck park. There were two one-ton trucks and a Russian UAZ-469, similar to an American jeep, parked haphazardly around a small frame building. No one was in sight. Keely removed a pair of binoculars and scanned the area. A dirt road ran through a stand of trees and disappeared around a bend.

She pulled out the military map. According to that, the road continued for another seven miles to Chechnya. Keely marked the exact location of the truck park, wrote down the coordinates on the edge of the map, and folded it. Niko tapped her shoulder and pointed below. Keely saw three men walk from the building to a truck. They wore camouflage uniforms, but none of the uniforms had insignia. They looked Syrian but could have been from anywhere in that general area. Keely took out her camera and snapped a few pictures.

Keely and the others watched for a while longer. The three men seemed in no hurry and finally climbed into the UAZ-469, its engine roaring to life, echoing up the narrow valley. The driver maneuvered the vehicle out of its parking area and headed down the dirt road, kicking up clouds of dust. When it was out of sight, Keely looked around at Irina.

"I'm going down there," she said, handing her the binoculars.

"I don't think that is good idea. Niko or I will go."

"No. Stay here."

Keely did not wait for a response. She scrambled down the embankment and worked her way quietly to the tree line twenty yards from the building. She knelt and stayed crouched until she was sure no one inside had heard her. She circled towards the trucks, making sure to keep trees between her and the building. When she reached the first truck, she went around the far side and peeked in the back. Inside were a dozen large crates with stenciled writing. She took more pictures.

Taking a deep breath, she slipped over the gate of the truck. Once inside, she checked to see if any of the crates were open. They weren't. She tried lifting one but whatever was inside was very heavy. There was a faint smell in the air that seemed familiar, but she couldn't place it. She knelt down and placed her face close to the boxes. The familiar metallic odor had been the same odor she smelled during her weapons training. She examined the crates carefully and noted the stenciled label. It was not in English, but she recognized the letters as being Georgian. It was too dark inside the truck to use the camera, so she found a scrap piece of paper and traced the markings as best she could. She moved to the second truck, making sure to use its body as cover. That one was empty.

She toyed with the idea of looking in the building, but decided it was too risky. She returned to the first truck and keeping her back to the hill, slipped the tracking device out of her bag. Although it was fitted with a magnet, she knew it would bounce off as soon as the truck hit the road. Instead, she climbed back into the truck and placed the tracker against the cab of the truck and turned it on. It made no sound, for which she was extremely glad. She slipped out of the truck and retraced her steps and was soon back on top of the ridge. Irina was waiting for her.

"What did you find?"

"One truck has a dozen crates, the other's empty."

"Maybe just smugglers. Many are in these mountains. Perhaps clothes or food."

"That's not clothes or food. Let's get back."

Irina turned on her heels and walked off. Keely followed, wondering why she was always making excuses. Keely walked below the crest of the hill and pulled out her sat phone. When she dialed the secure number Jonathan had given her, nothing happened. She looked at the display, which read 'satellite temporarily unavailable'. Frustrated, she motioned the others to follow her and headed down the path back to the farmhouse.

Halfway down the trail, they stopped for water. Keely stood next to Irina, sensing her displeasure. Maybe Irina was concerned that word would get out that she and Niko had not been competent enough to find the truck park themselves. Could damage her reputation

Keely didn't really care how Irina felt, but she saw no need in creating problems. Maybe Irina's ego could be saved.

"Look, the sat phone isn't working. Why don't you go back to Pasanauri, call Jonathan with the coordinates?" She extended the map. "Niko and I will stay here to keep an eye out."

Irina seemed to hesitate, then reconsider, and finally smiled genuinely for the first time. "If that is what you want. But I cannot call from Pasanauri. The phones in Georgia do not work very well. I will have to go all the way to Tbilisi."

Keely wanted this assignment to be over but didn't mind spending one more day in the inviting solitude of these mountains.

"Fine. I'll tell Niko. I don't think the farmer and his wife will mind, especially if there is more money involved."

Niko and Keely stood in the dirt path as Irina drove toward the main road. Keely had given her a shopping list of items for the family as a reward for their kindness. It was getting close to evening, and Nana motioned them into the house for a meal of coarse bread and vegetable stew.

After dinner, it was still light out and Keely walked through the plowed fields, occasionally stopping to stare at the magnificent sky. She remembered how she had spent weeks hiking in the Colorado mountains alone. For the first time in many years, she missed her home. She climbed several hundred yards up the hill beside the house and sat on a rock.

Looking down at the worn-out homestead, she wondered who was to be pitied more-- this tiny family tied to land so far from anything, or her, without roots, without a home. A chill went through her and she worked her way back down to the farmyard.

Niko stood outside the house, smoking a cigarette. As she approached, he straightened and smiled, staring toward the night sky.

"Pretty sky. Many stars."

Keely followed his gaze. "Yeah. Really pretty."

She felt his hand gently rest on her shoulder as he moved closer to her. "Very romantic."

Keely sighed. Another time, another place she might have been flattered by the attention of someone as handsome as Niko. But not here; not now. She stepped away.

"Guess Irina is in Tbilisi by now. I assume she'll be back tomorrow morning sometime." She looked again at him. "Well, I think I'll turn in. I'm kinda tired."

Niko looked crest-fallen. He shrugged, resigned he would not have company. He laughed boyishly. "Sure. Me, back with sheep -- you inside."

The sat phone in her pocket vibrated. She had not thought to try the phone in the valley since it hadn't worked on the ridge and had forgotten that it was still in her pocket. She looked at Niko, indicating that she needed to be alone. She walked several paces from the farmhouse before taking out the phone. She flipped it open and saw there was a text message. She entered the number and code. The message came up on the screen-- '?'. She knew it was from Jonathan.

She hit the 'reply' bottom and paused. She couldn't remember the coordinates for the truck park, so she typed 'old Russ outpost @7 clicks from border on road from Pasanauri.' The phone automatically scrambled the message. After a minute, a new message appeared. 'Tracker?' She typed 'placed.' She hit send and closed the connection. She thought about trying to call Irina but figured having her contact Jonathan was a good backup. Jonathan had always insisted on redundancy when it came to messages. She put the phone away and headed back to the farmhouse.

She rose before dawn the next morning. She had slept better than the night before. The family was in an adjacent room-- husband and wife on one bed, the children on another. Niko, indeed, had returned to the sheep pen.

She quietly worked her way out of her sleeping bag. She had kept Irina's M-16 and the automatic Niko had given her beside her during the night, but now thought about leaving them in the house. Afraid the children might find them, she picked up the rifle, slipped the automatic into her waistband and silently opened the front door.

The valley was shrouded in fog so thick that she felt she could reach out and scoop up a handful. She found her way to the trail they had followed the day before to the truck park, and on an impulse began to climb.

Keely knew she couldn't get lost with the trail well marked. In no hurry to be anywhere, she picked her steps carefully. She paused several times to look back, but the fog had quickly enveloped the tiny homestead. She enjoyed the silence and peace. It had been a long time since she had felt such contentment.

Her mind turned to Jonathan. The decision to leave him and his way of life was becoming more and more necessary. Although she knew she would miss it-- him-- she had to move on for her own peace of mind.

A distance humming disturbed her thoughts. She recognized the sound from years before but couldn't believe that was possible. She was getting close to the ridge above the truck park and decided it had to be a generator. In a flash, she changed her mind, admitting it was the sound of a jet, perhaps three miles away and flying high. The noise grew louder, as though it was headed directly toward her.

As she reached the rock outcropping, she heard another sound: a soft whistling that grew louder each second. She did not see the rocket hit, but the explosion threw her back, almost sending her tumbling down the hill, the blinding flash amplified by the fog. A second explosion followed almost immediately, and then a series of erratic secondary explosions as small arms ammunition detonated.

The explosions ended abruptly, followed by an eerie silence punctuated by crackling.

Keely picked herself off the ground and moved forward quickly.

A rocket had apparently hit the truck where the tracker was located, blowing it to shreds.

A second rocket must have hit between two trucks, each lying on its side facing the other. She heard no cries and saw no bodies, but those inside would not have had time to react anyway. She failed to notice the UAZ-469 was missing.

Keely turned away from the destruction and slumped down against the rock. So, that was what Jonathan had meant by handling things. No discussion or negotiation. Jonathan had lied to her-- again. He had made the assignment sound like simple reconnaissance when actually it was a targeting mission. In fact, he had been quite specific.

Once again, Jonathan had put her in the killing zone. And not even the decency to be upfront about it.

It took her almost a half hour to compose herself before she could make the trek back to the farm. There was nothing left now but to wait for Irina's return. She considered going down to the truck park but was not sure if she could handle it. Besides, from what she saw, that place was pretty well destroyed. If Jonathan wanted bomb damage assessment, he'd have to find somebody else to do it.

She was less than a quarter of a mile away from the farm when another sound in the distance broke into her thoughts. It was the motor of a vehicle and its wheels crunching over gravel. Maybe Irina had gotten back sooner than expected. She picked her pace. After another couple hundred yards, she heard automatic weapons fire, short bursts, followed by individual rounds. At first, she thought Niko might be showing off for Vali, but panic swept over her when she remembered she had the M-16. She hurried her steps but avoided running.

Whatever was happening, she couldn't afford to rush headlong into danger.

The fog had cleared around the farmhouse as Keely reached the head of the trail. She saw the UAZ-469 parked just off the road on the dirt path leading to the farmhouse, concealed by overgrown brush. She stood still and listened but saw or heard no one. She worked her way toward the farm. Whoever had left the vehicle had not wanted any one to know they were arriving.

When she was no more than fifty yards away, she could see a body lying face down in front of the barn, a pool of blood around him. Vali. Her heart started to pound with fear. She started to run forward but had just enough time to conceal herself behind a rock outcropping when three men emerged from the house, dragging Niko between them. They were in the same outfits worn by those at the truck park. Each was armed with an automatic rifle.

They dropped Niko to the ground, yelling in Russian. Niko tried to raise himself, but a boot caught him in the face, and he spun backwards. Keely could not understand what they were asking, but Niko did not respond. One of the men raised his rifle and trained it on Niko's head. The man asked a question, but when Niko did not answer, the man fired. Niko slumped in a heap and the man who had shot him fired several rounds into Niko's body. Something snapped inside Keely.

Without being fully conscious of what she was doing, Keely slipped the safety off her M-16 and raised it slowly, taking aim at the chest of the man who had shot Niko. Three quick squeezes of the trigger and the man flew through the air. Before he hit the ground, she had swung the weapon and squeezed again. The other two never had a chance. Keely realized she was still pulling the trigger, but there was no recoil. She had emptied her clip into the men who now lay in the dust in front of the house.

She laid the weapon down and took out the automatic. There was no movement from the three bodies. After what seemed an eternity, she stepped out from behind the rocks and moved forward slowly. The two men lay sprawled across each other, blood spreading across the ground. Keely nudged each body with the toe of her shoe, but there was no reaction. She couldn't bring herself to look at Niko or toward Vali. She had no doubt they were dead.

Keely walked to the house and stood to the side the doorway, her automatic at the ready.

No sound came from inside. Taking a deep breath, Keely moved inside cautiously.

Nana had pulled the morning's porridge from the stove as she fell, splattering it across her apron, her blood mixing with the morning's breakfast. The boy lay in a fetal position in one corner, as though asleep. But there was a pool of blood surrounding his battered head. The little girl was in a sitting position against the other wall, her head slumped forward; her worn dress colored now by a dark stain that expanded from her chest.

Keely went to her and noticed that her tiny fingers were clenched into a fist. Keely gently opened them, and Keely's ring fell to the floor and rolled away.

Keely stumbled backwards out the door. She walked to the-where the killers had fallen and emptied the clip into them. When there was no more ammunition, she threw the pistol as far as she could, fell to the ground. Her moans grew louder as she screamed in agony.

PART TWO

CHAPTER EIGHT

As Keely jogged along the esplanade in Tangier, Morocco, she could see fishermen in rickety skiffs two hundred yards off shore soundlessly pulling in their nets. Keely felt as if she watched it all in a fog-- her senses numb. A month had passed since she had left Georgia, but her mind was unable to escape the brutal images in the Georgian mountains.

After she had cried until there were no more tears in the yard of the farmhouse, Keely realized she was still vulnerable. She didn't know whether more killers were in the area, but she knew she couldn't stay around to find out. She wanted desperately to bury the family, but time was against her. She searched the bodies of the three killers; but as she had figured, no identification or keys. She hoped they had been left in their vehicle. With a final look around the farm, she headed for the road where it had been parked.

Indeed, the keys were in the ignition. She started the engine and pulled onto the road headed for Pasanauri. Her mind drifted to the three men. They could not have been in the truck park when the rockets had hit because they would not have gotten out alive. Which meant they had been somewhere else at the time of the air strike. But how did they know about the farmhouse? And how many others were out here?

She couldn't think about that now; it was more important to get out of the area as quickly as possible. It wasn't until she had driven some distance that she thought of Irina.

The road was the only access to the farm; Keely kept an eye out in case she passed her. The drive to Pasanauri took almost an hour. Anxious to get back to Tbilisi, Keely tried not to think about the two and half hours still ahead. She had not crossed paths with Irina, nor could she figure what had delayed the woman. She chalked it up to Irina's temperament. Maybe she had not come back deliberately to make Keely wait-- out of spite. Irina had already proven she didn't like taking orders and most likely wanted the credit for job well done.

Jonathan hadn't lied about Irina at least. She pulled into the town square, parking adjacent to the railroad station.

Her first inclination was to drive on to Tbilisi, but she didn't want to stay in that vehicle. She couldn't afford to be stopped and questioned by the authorities. Her international driver's license might not help in that situation.

She wasn't sure when or if the murders at the farmhouse would be discovered, but she knew she had to get out of the country as quickly as possible. She decided to leave the vehicle and take the train to Tbilisi. Out of habit, she took the keys and started for the station. Then she stopped, returned and left the keys in the ignition. If Niko had been right about the mountains, it would be stolen within hours-- a good way to dispose of an unwanted albatross.

Inside the station, Keely approached the ticket window and purchased a first-class ticket for the next train for Tbilisi, which would leave Pasanauri at noon. She sat on the wooden bench and tried to compose herself while she waited for the train.

The ride took almost four hours, the train stopping a dozen times along the way. Keely was thankful that the virtually empty first-class cabin allowed her to doze between stops. During her wakeful periods, she tried to figure out what had happened and why the farmhouse had been attacked. Had someone in the camp spotted Vali and followed him? She rocked in her seat, fuming that Jonathan had lied to her about the assignment.

He had promised this was a simple surveillance. But he had also said that once she found the place, he'd take care of the rest. Keely wiped tears from her eyes, her hands trembling as she brushed her cheeks. She hadn't read between the lines. Was it because she wanted to believe he wouldn't put her in harm's way? She fingered a ring similar to the one she'd given the little girl. This time, she didn't stop the tears. Whatever Keely thought about Jonathan had died there in that farmyard.

The train pulled into the central station in Tbilisi at night. Keely still had not eaten; instead, drinking down several bottles of water. She hadn't been able to think about food. She jumped into a taxi and gave the address of her hotel.

When she arrived, she asked the proprietor to call the airlines and see if she could get on the next flight out. She didn't care where. After a half hour of heated yelling on the phone, the proprietor was able to get her on a Turkish Airlines flight to Istanbul that evening.

Back in her room, Keely threw what few things she had into a bag. As she grabbed her hairbrush and lotions, she caught her reflection in the mirror and stopped for a moment staring into the face of a stranger. She hardly recognized herself. She pulled her long hair back and thought of chopping it all off. She would when she had time.

The proprietor had called for a taxi, and she paid the driver extra to get her to Tbilisi International quickly. They arrived with just over an hour to spare. As she waited in the ticket line, Keely stuck her hand in her pocket and realized she still had the sat phone Jonathan had given her. She reached in another pocket and found the number she had for Irina and punched in the digits on the keypad. She was surprised when Irina answered so quickly.

"Yes?"

"Where the fuck are you?"

There was a slight hesitation. "Keely…."

"I said, where are you?"

Irina's voice was cool. "I haven't forgotten you."

"Niko's dead. Those men from the truck park killed him. And Vali and Nana, and--."

Irina interrupted her. "Where are you now?"

"Never mind."

"Will I still get paid?"

Keely's temper flared. "You're a pretty cold bitch, Irina. Did you know that? Amazing-- I tell you your partner's dead and you want to know when you get paid."

Keely clicked the phone off and stood looking down at the numbers on the keypad. She had to hear a friendly voice. She called Sando.

"Hallo?"

Keely knew it was the young man. "Sando, this is Keely. We met a few days ago?"

There was a pause, then Sando responded, "Yes. Yes. My American friend. I wait for your call. We get together again?"

"I'm sorry, Sando, but I'm leaving today. I called to say goodbye and tell you how much I enjoyed our time together. I wish you all the best."

"You will come back to Tbilisi?"

"I-I don't think so."

The long pause told her the young man was disappointed. "Maybe someday I go back to America and we meet. You have a place I can call?"

Keely realized she didn't. She had no clue where she was going or what she would do. She wouldn't return to England. Rhonda could pack up the few things she had at the apartment and send them-- where?

"I don't have a number, but I promise as soon as I do, I will let you know."

"Thank you, Keely. And please, remember me."

After she hung up, she hit the speed dial for Jonathan.

"Keely?" Jonathan said, as if expecting her call.

Hearing his voice, she lost control, despite her promise to herself that she would try to remain calm. "Just simple reconnaissance, you fucking bastard. Do you know what the fuck you have done?"

"Keely, don't get excited."

"Fuck you," she shouted into the receiver. "Your lies cost the lives of innocent people. People who had nothing to do with you or your bullshit."

There was a long pause. "Where are Niko and Irina?"

"Well, Niko has a bullet in his head," she said with all the control she could muster. "Irina, she's in hiding somewhere I guess."

"What happened, Keely?"

"Your little recon mission became a cluster fuck. I was there when the missiles hit."

"You were told to plant the tracker and get out, immediately."

"Yeah, well you should have mentioned missiles."

There was a long pause then Jonathan spoke. "The mission changed. I tried to call, but your phone wasn't picking up. Where are you now?"

"Gone." She closed her phone and realized she had been screaming her end of the conversation. She glanced around at the several people staring at her. She tried to smile but couldn't and moved quickly toward the international waiting area, dropping the phone in a trashcan.

Keely was still numb when she boarded the plane. Again, she was in first class, once more empty, thankfully. Once the plane reached altitude, an attendant brought a meal and a small bottle of wine. She drank the wine quickly and picked at the meal. She wasn't sure where to go or who to trust. All she knew was that her actions had led to the deaths of innocents.

When she arrived in Istanbul, she headed for the British Airways Executive Club. She felt she was being watched but didn't know whether to chalk it up to paranoia of premonition.

Once she signed in, she asked the attendant if there was a place where she could freshen up and was shown to a private room with shower and seating area. Keely stood under the scalding water for a long time. After, she went to the lounge. She ordered a scotch and sat in a trance trying to decide her next move.

Looking around the lounge, she noticed a poster for Tangier. She remembered that Jonathan said it was a great place to decompress. She went to the desk. "How would I get from here to Tangier?"

The attendant smiled and typed in the request. "You could take British Air to London and then get a flight to Tangier."

Keely did not want to pass through England, even if only to stop over. "I know this sounds silly, but is there any way to avoid London?"

The attendant looked confused but turned back to the computer. It took a while, but she turned back to Keely with a smile. "Well, there is a TAP flight tomorrow morning through Lisbon."

"Fine. Can you book me? First class. One way."

The woman nodded and hit some keys. "Certainly. How would you like to pay?"

Keely pulled out the credit card from Swift, thought better of it and took out Visa card from her bank in Zurich. She handed it to the woman. After the ticket was purchased, she looked at the woman. "Is there a hotel in the airport?"

The woman smiled. "There is TAV. You do not have to leave the international terminal."

"Can you book a room for tonight?"

The woman nodded and turned to her computer. "The same card?"

"Yes, please."

When the transaction was complete and the woman gave Keely directions to the hotel, Keely asked, "Do you have a shredder?"

The woman pointed to a room off the main lounge. "I believe there is one in the business center."

Keely went to the room, attended by a woman who could be a twin of the one at the front desk who smiled as Keely entered. "May I help you?"

"I need to shred some documents."

The woman nodded and directed Keely to a desk with a shredder to one side. Seated, Keely went through her backpack, pulling out the Swift credit card, the return ticket from Tbilisi and notes she had taken. Slowly she fed each into the shredder, trying to expunge the past. She knew it would take more, but it was a start.

That had been a month ago, but Keely still felt the pain and anger of that morning outside the farmhouse in the mountains of Georgia. She had spent the month going over and over what had happened. Logically, she knew she should not have involved Vali and his family. And she had not followed directions. That did not assuage the pain or the guilt she felt. Her days were spent thinking 'what if.'

118

What if she had not taken the job? What if she had just continued on the road pass the farmhouse? If she had just planted the tracker and left the farm family? If she hadn't decided to stay and send Irina away?

Irina was another problem. Obviously, the woman was an asshole. Apparently, Irina had not returned to Pasanauri. That was why she didn't pass her on the road. Irina had been playing her own games. Had she come back, things may have turned out differently. Irina may be a bitch, but Keely believed she would hold her own in gunplay. It could have made all the difference for Niko and Vali's family. As far as she knew, Irina never went back to even see the carnage. Her failure to return irritated Keely.

When she first landed in Tangier, her plan had been to stay for just a few days, but the days dragged into a week and Keely stopped looking for places to go. When she had landed, the immigration officer had said she could stay for up to three months without a visa. She had opened an account with 1,000 Euros and got a safe deposit box at the Arab Bank Moroc, transferring 20,000 Euros from her Swiss account. She had been carrying several passports with her, so she put those in the box along with the digital camera she had brought from Georgia.

One of her first acts was to cut her hair. As she watched her long locks fall to the floor, she had thought it meager penance for all the pain she had caused. When she was done, her hair was cropped so short she could have passed as a boy. It was her way of leaving the past behind and starting anew.

Hotel living had been adequate, but she decided she needed something more private.

Through the hotel concierge, she found a simple apartment adjacent to the old city that could be rented by the month. It provided an excellent view of the sea. The apartment had a living room, bedroom and an eat-in kitchen-- about the size of her apartment in St. Albans. It was furnished, but in the month she had been there, she had added little to the décor.

Shortly after she had moved in, she had returned to the apartment after her morning run. She had the strange sense someone had been in it, but she found nothing disturbed. She chalked it up to paranoia.

She avoided all but the most basic contact with other people. She ran each morning, wandered the streets until the heat became oppressive, lay on her bed until sunset, then ventured out again for food. The simple routine seemed to ease her troubled soul, but at night the dreams returned.

When she was stationed in Brussels, she had talked with Army officers who had served in Iraq about post-traumatic stress; how the killing had seeped into their psyches and was almost impossible to move beyond. Keely felt the same, but her trauma included an overwhelming sense of guilt because she had not killed for some cause, but for money. She knew that coming to terms with her pain would take a long time, but the isolation of Tangier had started the healing process.

Part of that process required her to assess what in her makeup had allowed her to pull the trigger. Not so much in Georgia, where there was a sense of self-preservation. It was what she had done in Zurich that continued to haunt her. She had blamed Jonathan for turning her into a killer, but she knew that was an excuse. The real blame lay with her.

She had never thought of herself as a violent person, although she knew that violence did not offend her as it did some people. But what had happened over the last two months was beyond violence. In Zurich, it had been cold-blooded efficiency. In Georgia, it had been rage. Both those mindsets frightened her when she had to face both apparently lay just below the surface. She knew she should seek professional help, but that was out of the question right now. And so, she ran her miles every morning.

Normally, she had the early morning beach to herself. Then a young man appeared.

When she noticed him, she continued to follow the water line about thirty yards west of where he stood and jogged without breaking stride. He stood positioned directly in her path, and she slowed slightly as she was about to pass. She made sure she wouldn't have to run through the water or the loose sand further up the beach to avoid him. He held a camera to his eye focused on the water, and she was not sure he was aware of her. It was not a tourist's camera, but an expensive one with telephoto lens. At his feet was a hefty camera bag.

As she came within a few yards, he turned in her direction. It unnerved her, but she continued past him without acknowledging him. As she continued down the beach, her sixth sense told her he was watching. When she reached the far end, she turned. He was gone.

He was back the next day, and she navigated around him again. He turned and made brief eye contact with her. He looked to be in his mid to late twenties, just a few inches taller than she was. His round face was open, not unattractive, with the complexion of an East European too long in the Mediterranean sun. What she could see of his hair under a ridiculously large straw hat appeared to be light brown, long and disheveled. But he looked out of place-- not a tourist and not an expatriate.

On the third morning, the dawn sky was beginning to brighten as Keely made her way along her jogging route. She had started a bit earlier than usual to avoid meeting the man, but part of her hoped he would be there. As she entered the beach at the west end, she was not disappointed. He was standing on the dryer part of the sand, fidgeting with his camera. He had moved back from the water's edge, Keely wondered if it was so she could pass more easily. She thought the gesture polite and wanted to tell him so, though they had not spoken.

He apparently had anticipated her arrival because he turned in her direction and waved. Bringing the camera to his eye, he pointed it her way. Keely faltered and her face took on a look of concern, but she kept a steady pace as she crossed his path. The moon was a faint parenthesis in the morning sky. She thought how comforting it was to be as invisible as the morning moon.

She tried to concentrate, clear her mind as she ran. But again, she found herself thinking about the man on the beach. By the shabby shirt and pants he wore, she figured he wasn't staying at one of the upscale places, but rather the smaller pensionnes that catered to a younger, less affluent crowd. Keely had learned to be suspicious of everyone, especially those who seemed out of place. But in the fraction of a second Keely saw his face, there was a quiet thoughtfulness, almost painful that made her curious; and that disturbed her.

She had worked hard to avoid all contact except the dutiful interactions with waiters and shopkeepers. But there was something about the man on the beach that made her want to sit and talk with him, to find out what was so interesting to him about the still blue Mediterranean waters. He seemed harmless, but she couldn't shake the thought that he, too, was hiding something.

She made up her mind to stop and talk on the way back. When she reached the far end, she turned. He was walking away from her. Her disappointment amazed her. She fixed her eyes on the sand in front of her and continued her steady jog, trying to put the man out of her mind.

The sound of horns honking in the distance brought her head up, and she realized the man was now only ten yards in front of her, strolling very slowly. She slowed her pace but realized she would soon overtake him. He seemed to sense her presence and turned around. He pulled his hat off and was even more handsome than she had thought. Keely stopped. The man studied her for several seconds without saying a word, and Keely wondered if he had rather she go on by.

Before she could make a decision, he greeted her. "C'est va?"

His accent was definitely not French. "Bonjour."

The man walked the few yards between them, speaking in passable, but strained French. "I hope you did not mind that I took your photograph. I see you every day. You are early riser."

"I like to run before the sun comes up," she said in English.

He did not look surprised that she had switched languages. He turned and faced the water and continued in English, less strained than his French.

"It is quite beautiful out here. So alive, yet so still, isn't it?"

She stared with him to where the blue of the water met the blue of the horizon. In the distance, she could make out the outline of land-- the Spanish coast.

"Yes."

The man turned back towards her. "My name is Stefan Minescu."

"Keely."

His eyes with their unnerving intensity disturbed her as he looked directly at her. His voice interrupted her thoughts.

"Keely . . . that is a different name."

"It's Gaelic." She didn't say that her father had named her that because it meant 'beautiful one.' She had not felt beautiful in a while.

He smiled once again, his brows creasing. "Gaelic? I see. I thought maybe that you were--."

"Moroccan? I'm American."

"Actually, I thought you might be French. Do you live here?"

How could she explain what she was doing in Tangier? "Let's just say that I came here for a vacation and couldn't leave."

He smiled and casually stepped closer to her. "To be honest, I hoped you would stop and talk. But I didn't want to... intrude."

She studied his face. "You haven't. So why are you here?"

He looked toward the water. "I am a freelance photographer. I am supposed to be taking pictures of the city, but I like the sea in the early morning sun." He held up his camera. "I hope I didn't make you upset when I took your picture. You made the beach more-- interesting."

"I didn't realize you had actually taken my picture, but thanks for the compliment."

Silence fell between them, but there was no awkwardness in it. Their eyes met and they held each other's gaze for seconds. He asked quietly, "Have you had your coffee?"

"No. I usually wait until after my run."

"Would you join me? There is a cafe at my hotel."

Keely wanted to say yes, but something inside-- from her training at Swift--made her hesitate. "Thanks, but I'm all sweaty and wouldn't be good company."

He must have sensed Keely's apprehension because he quickly apologized. "I am sorry. That was very impolite of me. We are strangers. It's just that--."

122

Keely wanted to discourage this man. She had no desire for friendship. She had come here for isolation and it had been working. Tourists and locals had tried to start conversations in restaurants and bars, but she had always shut them out. After a while, men seemed to know she did not want to be disturbed and gave her a wide berth.

"Just what?"

"I was going to say how you seem to be so at home in these surroundings."

Perhaps the absence of human contact for so long had not been a good thing; perhaps it was Stefan's intensity, but something motivated her to say yes. And it was just coffee.

"Well, I guess it would be okay, but I can't go like this. How about if I meet you at your hotel in an hour?"

He agreed and told her which hotel. She gave a small smile and jogged off, leaving him standing on the beach.

His hotel was what she had expected-- a small building for budget tourists midway between the beach and the port. It was only ten minutes from her apartment, but something told her to hold back that information. Several tables outside the café shared space with the hotel's small registration counter. Stefan sat at a table offering the best view of the esplanade. When Keely sat down, the waiter set down cups and poured them each coffee without being asked. Keely ordered a croissant, but Stefan waved the waiter away. When he left, Stefan looked across the table at her and smiled.

"Keely, you have found Tangier enjoyable?"

He said her name with added emphasis on the 'ee' that gave it a melodic sound. She had no desire of discussing her reason for being here. Not that she really understood it herself. But she saw no reason to discourage him. "I guess 'enjoyable' is not exactly what I was looking for. More like peaceful."

His smiled broadened. "Was your life before so troubling?"

She leaned forward and pushed the cup back waiting for it to cool down. "I didn't say anything was troubling me. I'm just looking for peace and quiet."

"But so far from home?"

She was concerned by his reference to 'home' since she hadn't mentioned where she lived, but again set her suspicions aside. "I quit my job a few months ago. Got very tired of it. I needed a change." She shrugged her shoulders as if to dismiss the entire subject.

His smile never wavered. "It must not have been very good work."

"It wasn't."

"I see-- Tangier is just a place to unwind?"

Keely's good judgment whispered she should thank this nice young man for coffee, end this conversation and walk away. But something about him kept her there. His eyes, the way he said her name, or maybe it was just the need to interact with somebody, whether she wanted to admit that or not. But she needed immediately to get the conversation off her.

"What are you going to do with the picture you took of me?"

"I shall give it to you, if you like. But if you say I can, I will try to make money with it."

"How would you do that?"

His smiled sheepishly. "I was hired to take photos of people and places to go with a travel article about the real Morocco-- like in Casablanca." As he placed his hand on the table, it came close to touching hers, but didn't. "When I saw you running, I thought it would make a statement about how alone you can be here."

Yes, Keely had been forced to be alone and she certainly didn't want to go any further with that subject. "Your English is very good. You're from--?"

"Romania, although I have not lived there for quite some time. I lived in London for a while. There was much oppression in my country, which is why I left. I studied film in Romania, but now I just sell photos to newspapers and magazines when I can. It gives me opportunity to travel."

"It must pay well."

"I do not need much. I have learned how to live on little money." He broke into a boyish grin. "But I do not turn down a chance to earn money."

They continued to talk for more than an hour. Stefan told her that a French travel magazine was sponsoring this particular trip. He had been in Tangier for a week and had planned to move on to other cities to the South soon. His voice smooth and inviting; she found herself intoxicated by the slightest of accents that made his English sound new and exotic.

Stefan looked at his watch and motioned for the waiter. When Keely reached for her change purse, he waved her off and paid the bill. There was a moment of uncomfortable silence before Stefan offered another possible meeting.

"Perhaps tomorrow, we can have coffee again."

Keely had enjoyed conversing with this man, more than she had expected to. "It's a date," regretting her unfortunate choice of words. She felt, though, meeting him again was another step in her recovery.

They met on the beach for the next several days. Keely would smile as she passed and continue to the end of the beach. Stefan waited patiently until she returned. They tried several of the small cafes along the esplanade, sitting for an hour or more each time. Their talk was usually about Tangier-- its people, its various neighborhoods. Although Stefan had only been in the city a few weeks, he had explored much more of the area outside the city than she had. Keely found the conversation invigorating after a month of silence. Occasionally, Stefan had attempted to ask about her work, her family, and life in America. Keely's answers had been vague, but that did not seem to offend Stefan. Each time they started to leave, Stefan would insist on paying. After the fourth time, Keely felt obligated to return Stefan's generosity.

"Let me repay you for all these coffees with dinner at Ghuria Fowq tonight, near the Medina. Have you been there?"

He looked embarrassed. "I don't go to restaurants at night often. And that seems too much for just buying coffee." He thought for a second. "But, yes, I would very much enjoy it. Shall I come to your apartment?"

Keely smiled and leaned toward him. "Why don't we meet at the entrance to the dock around seven. I think it would be best if we took a taxi. Nights are not always that safe in the Medina."

"I am at your command."

Keely gently patted his arm. "I hope you won't be sorry you said that." She had meant the touch to be playful, but she felt a sensation she had not felt in months.

"See you at seven."

Before he could respond, she stood and began walking away.

The palm trees along the esplanade were cast in ghostly shadows by the infrequent streetlights as Keely made her way down the steep sidewalk from the Medina. A cool night breeze blew in from the Mediterranean even though it was early June. Stefan stood beneath one of the streetlights. As she approached, he gave a shy smile and waved.

"This is first time I've seen you in a dress."

She laughed and had the urge to kiss his cheek but didn't. She extended her hand instead. "I guess it is."

Stefan held her hand a moment then stepped to the curb to hail a taxi. The trip was a short one, made memorable by the recklessness of the driver who seemed oblivious to cars and pedestrians alike. Keely handed him a dinar and wished him a safe journey.

The restaurant was almost invisible; only a small neon sign in Arabic indicated there was a place of business in what appeared to be a block of apartments. Just inside the door was a large room hung with tapestries. The walls were lined with low, pillowed couches barely discernible in the dim light. There was no one in the room, so Keely called out. "*Ahlahlan!*"

An old man in traditional Moroccan dress waddled out of a back room. "*Marabah*."

When he recognized Keely, his face brightened. He switched to English. "My little flower. You are back to visit me."

They kissed on both cheeks and Keely turned to Stefan.

"Stefan, I want you to meet Tayib. He is an old friend. Tayib, this is Stefan. A new friend."

The older man sized up the younger, then shrugged and smiled. "And I thought I was the only man in your life. *Maalish*."

He led them to a corner couch and Keely sat on the overstuffed cushions. The older man departed without asking for their order, but within seconds, he was back with a wine bottle and two glasses.

"A good red wine from Ifrane. You will like it." He poured a glass for each and departed.

Stefan held up the glass to the light. "You must come here often." Keely smiled. "When I find something I like, I tend to stick with it."

She blushed realizing how suggestive that may have sounded. Tayib broke the awkward moment when he returned with a plate of Moroccan appetizers. Stefan poured Keely a glass of wine.

"This place is wonderful," he said. "To think I have been eating my meals in those dingy cafes along the avenue."

"I am glad you approve."

They ate in silence for a few minutes until Keely spoke up. "So how did you get into travel photography?"

Stefan looked confused for a second then seemed to understand what Keely was asking. "I needed a job. Simple as that. I like it because it lets me take the photos I want to take. How about you? Have you traveled much?"

She drew a deep breath and smiled. "Some. Why?"

"Just curious."

She changed the subject. "You said you were born in Romania. Do you miss it?"

"I do not miss the politics. Many good people have died fighting against the government of my country."

"But hasn't Romania changed governments? I thought it became democratic in the early 90s?"

Stefan seemed embarrassed and unnerved. He took a long time to answer. "Maybe, but what is good for leaders is not good for people."

"I don't understand."

"In my country, people say we have democracy so the West will give us money, but the government still does not help the people, so we must fight."

"It seems so senseless for people to waste their lives fighting."

"Perhaps for them it is not a waste." He stared solemnly over his glass at her then set it down. "Sometimes, it is all they have to live for."

"But if they end up dead, what's the use?"

"If you die fighting for a cause."

"I don't believe there is any cause worth dying for." She stopped, knowing that her bitterness had made her sound callous. "I'm sorry. That sounds uncaring. Believe me, it is very much the opposite." She tilted the glass of wine and sipped before changing the subject. "How long do you plan to be in Tangier?"

His brows arched ever so slightly. "As long as it takes to finish what I came to do. And you?"

She leaned back holding his gaze. "I'm not sure yet." She slipped her hand around the stem of her glass and swirled the dark red wine. "That first day I saw you taking pictures, I had the feeling you didn't want company."

He looked puzzled, then smiled. "I thought the same of you."

"Really?"

"Yes. When you didn't return my wave, I decided you didn't want to be bothered." He leaned forward still smiling. "Are you married?"

She laughed. "No." "That's good."

He held up his drink and she picked up hers as they touched glasses. She set hers back down, but Stefan took a long swallow of his. She watched him across the table. She found herself scrutinizing everything and everyone, because things were never what they seemed to be, but she couldn't help hoping this young man was exactly what he said he was.

He smiled innocently at her. "You said you left your job. What kind of work were you doing?"

Keely felt suddenly defensive. "Just a desk job. Very boring-- no chance for advancement."

"Sounds like government work."

He smiled at her, but it didn't help ease her apprehension. The conversation was getting too uncomfortable, but Keely didn't want to spoil the evening because of her own uncertainties. She picked up the glass and took another sip of wine. "I'd rather not talk about my past. Very unimportant stuff believe me. I have a better idea, let's eat."

The room began to fill with diners and after almost an hour, Keely finally had to stop Tayib.

"Please, no more. I'm about to explode."

Tayib looked at the plate in his hands and simply turned back to the kitchen. As he served thick Arabic coffee, three men in traditional garb climbed onto the platform in the center of the room and picked up instruments. With little fanfare, they began playing traditional music, the beat of the drum and the whine of the lute creating a sea of sound.

Keely and Stefan sat for a half hour longer, listening to the music, sipping wine and nibbling dates. Keely stretched and her body brushed against Stefan's. She felt a surge. His hand rested on the table and she gently laid her hand on top of his. When the musicians finally took a break, Keely turned to Stefan. "Perhaps we should leave."

He nodded and began to reach for his wallet, but she stopped him. "Remember, this is my treat."

After paying and bidding goodnight to Tayib, the two walked out into the night air. They found a taxi and Keely directed the driver to take them to the port entrance. Ten minutes later, they were deposited back on the esplanade. Keely was uncertain what to do next. Long ago, she might have invited a man like Stefan to her apartment. But that was long ago. Stefan reached for her hand and wrapped it inside his elbow.

"Would you like to walk some?"

Keely had not felt this comfortable with another human in some time. She smiled and began to stroll with him along the sidewalk. It was not crowded, but there were enough people-- couples, families, groups of young men and women-- not to feel uncomfortable. They walked in silence for a few minutes until Stefan suddenly stopped. He turned to her and hesitated.

"We are near my hotel. Would you... I mean, do you think...."

Everything told Keely no. The last year had made her unwilling to make herself vulnerable. Perhaps it was the night air, perhaps it was this gentle young man beside her, perhaps it was just the need for human contact. Keely leaned forward and kissed his cheek, her lips lingering for several seconds. She pulled back and smiled.

"I would like that."

His room had bare walls, a double bed in one corner, a sink and small refrigerator making pretenses of being a kitchenette. A dilapidated desk faced the French doors that led to a minuscule balcony. On the desk were two cameras and piles of photo packets. Stefan looked embarrassed and attempted to casually straighten the sheets on his bed.

"I am sorry. I did not expect to have company."

Keely walked to where he was standing at the bedside and took his hand. "Don't worry. I'm not looking at the room."

Up-close, she could smell the mixture of wine and coffee on his breath. She wanted so much to kiss him but was reluctant-- reminding herself she was just beginning to regain control of her life, beginning to see beyond day-to-day survival. She did not need entanglements.

Especially with someone she barely knew. But he had stirred something she thought could never be rekindled.

As if reading her thoughts, Stefan leaned forward and pressed his lips to her cheek. His arms moved slowly around her, barely touching her. His lips moved from her cheek to her lips, brushing against them gently. Keely took a deep breath but did not pull back. Gradually the kiss grew more insistent and she could feel the tip of his tongue explore the edges of her mouth. She hesitated only a moment longer before her arms wrapped around him and pulled him to her.

Keely awoke and looked at her watch. It was three a.m. She quietly got out of bed, Stefan breathing rhythmically. She slipped into her clothes and started out of the bedroom when Stefan stirred behind her.

"You are leaving?"

She turned and gave a small smile. "Time to go."

"Is it something I did?"

She sighed. "No, it's something I am."

The esplanade was empty except for a street cleaner who pushed his cart along, occasionally stopping to collect the refuse of the previous evening. Keely walked slowly, the cool breeze carrying the smell of the sea to her.

Sleeping with Stefan had been a mistake. It had taken her a month to loosen the Gordian knot that encircled her psyche. She didn't need more entanglement. Their lovemaking had been comforting. She had never been a sensual being; someone who needed sex to feel complete. But Stefan's excitement had moved her. The analyst in her, however, knew it could not last. Either she would leave, or he would. And she wasn't sure she could take that.

As she neared her apartment building, the evening *Fajr* began. She had come to love the calls to prayer from the many mosques in the old city. The muezzins seemed to echo each other; there was something calming about their voices even though she did not understand what they were chanting. She had looked up the translation of the *Fajr* that called the faithful to prayer. One line caught her eye. 'Come to success! Salat or prayer is better than sleep.' The hopefulness of that line always impressed her.

Back in her apartment, she stripped out of her clothes and lay on her bed's cool white sheets. Darkness gradually shifted to morning light, as she finally drifted off to sleep.

Her morning run started much later than normal, and the sun already blazed in the east. She had not run more than two-hundred yards before her shirt was soaked with sweat. She turned to the beach and started toward the end of the crescent, her head down to watch for debris that might have washed ashore during the night. Halfway along, she lifted her head. Stefan was in his usual place but did not have a camera. He was watching her as she ran toward him. Ten yards away she slowed to a walk. She could see pain in his face. When she reached him, she stopped.

He didn't move. "Why did you leave?"

Keely wondered the same thing. She knew the answer but was not willing to explain to him that her life was in turmoil and he didn't need her complicating his life. "It was lovely, but I think it was a mistake."

"Was I not... pleasing?"

She smiled. "No. You were quite pleasing. But I don't think we need to have our lives more complicated."

Stefan looked down at the sand. "I am sorry."

Keely felt her heart ache. She stepped forward and touched his cheek.

"No, my darling. You have nothing to feel sorry for." Without thinking, she tilted his head up and kissed his lips. "Maybe this is exactly the kind of complication I need."

They began spending every day together-- visiting the market, walking through the back streets of the new city, taking the short taxi ride to outlying villages. Their talk was always in the present tense. Stefan seemed as reluctant as Keely to discuss too much of the past. He told her all about Timisoara, where he had grown up, but said nothing about his family. Keely had been equally as vague about her past, preferring to talk about anything except her personal life.

Stefan had been very inquisitive at first, although not very insistent. He had asked her about her work, where she had been, what she had done. But when she changed the subject, he backed off. After a week, he stopped asking.

She had not been looking for anyone, but she felt like the fractured pieces of her life were finally coming together. After two weeks, she suggested he stay in her apartment. Her apartment was much more comfortable than his shabby hotel room. Stefan was the first visitor she had invited there. She knew there was nothing in the apartment to tie her to her previous life, but still she felt apprehensive.

She was flattered that he seemed obsessed with her. He told her he had never been with someone like her; that his work was suffering because he could not get her out of his mind.

Keely was equally infatuated, but her intuition kept telling her this would not last. Eventually, he would move on or she would; of that she was sure. But in the here and know, she was happy he was with her.

She couldn't understand why Stefan was different. He was no more handsome than some of the other men she had met, but there was an earnestness about him that made Keely want to shelter him. Perhaps she felt that inside, he might be just as troubled as she was. Whatever the reason, she allowed herself to be swept up in their affair.

They fell into a routine. She would run each morning, returning to coffee, juice and croissant he had prepared. They would take long walks through the city in the late afternoon as he took photos, which he seemed to do at random. She was surprised he wasn't more focused on his photography but assumed that was his style. They spent evenings in one of the small cafes along the beach or at one of the crowded clubs that blasted American rock while the Moroccan kids gyrated in their version of dance.

It was Thursday, and the Medina was crowded with shoppers. Stefan had gone to photograph some village farther south for the day, but said he'd be back in time for dinner. When Keely suggested she go along, he discouraged her, saying he would never get any work done with her so near.

Turning into a furniture shop, Keely searched the crowded room for the perfect lamp to go by the bed in the apartment. They had arranged it by the window so that they could see the Mediterranean, and on cloudless days, Spain's craggy coastline.

Keely liked that store. It was larger than most within the walls of the old city and the salesmen were not as aggressive as those in other shops. She never enjoyed haggling over every purchase. She had found two or three shops where the bargaining was minimal and now frequented these almost exclusively. Keely checked her watch. She had a half hour to finish her search before she left to meet Stefan. Back in the corner of the shop, she spied a uniquely shaped lamp that she thought would be ideal.

As the storeowner went to retrieve it, Keely knelt to examine a small table whose legs appeared to be carved from one piece of wood and opened like a tripod to support a carved wooden oval.

The man's voice behind her brought her quickly to her feet. The British accent was unmistakable. Jonathan.

"Don't let him charge you too much for that piece."

He stepped past her and lifted the wooden oval.

"You can tell it was machine made. The edges are too even. He'll probably tell you it is hand-made by Berbers. He'll be lying."

Keely didn't bother to look. She did not take her eyes off him, working hard to gain her composure. "You should know."

"You've been very difficult to find. I didn't know you would come to Tangier."

"I wasn't looking to be found."

"You cut your hair. Not sure I like it that short."

Keely cut him short. "What do you want, Jonathan?"

"I've brought you news from home." He looked around at the few patrons of the store and put his hand on her elbow. "Let's go somewhere and talk."

She pulled away. "I don't want to hear anything you have to say." She amazed herself she could speak rationally to him.

"I assure you, this is something you will want to hear, but this isn't the place."

"My family?" she said, suddenly panicked there might really be an emergency.

"No. This involves you."

"Then just tell me."

He looked around the store again. "All right. Have it your way." He moved even closer to her. "Someone is looking for you." She didn't like him being so close. He bent forward and whispered, "Someone you don't want finding you."

"How did you find me?"

"Friends in high places and all that."

She searched his eyes. "Who?"

"I don't know...yet. Come with me and let's try to figure it out."

"You've got to be joking."

"Oh, I can assure you, this is no joke."

"You followed me here to warn me about somebody, but you don't know who?"

"I felt an obligation."

She backed away from him. When he reached for her, she slapped his hand away and turned toward the open door. She heard him call her name, but she moved quickly through the crowded passageway. She had to get away; she had to escape his grasp... again.

CHAPTER NINE

Keely sat naked in front of a small vanity in her bedroom and stared numbly at her reflection in the mirror.

It had been four days since Jonathan had confronted her in the Old City. She tried desperately to get him out of her mind, but nothing seemed to help. Deep inside, she knew if he wanted to talk to her, he wouldn't give up easily, but she had not been ready to talk with him.

Jonathan's claim that somebody was looking for her had set her on edge. She knew he would not have found her unless he had a very good reason. She had been around him long enough to know that he did not frighten easily. She had also learned the hard way that he was not above 'inventing' the truth. She had hoped to leave his world far behind. Apparently, she had been wrong.

Jonathan had followed her into the market and had grabbed her roughly by the arm.

"Did you hear what I said? Somebody is trying to find you."

"I heard what you said. So what?" She turned to leave, but his grip tightened. She looked back at him. "Look, I quit, remember? Nothing you say or do could drag me back into that hell."

"What happened in Georgia is history. This is now and this threat is real."

She wanted to slap him but couldn't bring herself to strike out. "Those people killed were real. Or don't they count in your world? Oh, that's right. Collateral damage."

Jonathan's look was foul. "Look, I never lied about that assignment or about Swift. It's a bit late to claim you didn't know."

"Really? You weren't upfront with me."

"Think again. I told you from the start that not all our work was clean."

"Yeah. Clean. Odd word coming from you."

"I gave you the chance to walk in Zurich," he said in a voice that barely hid his anger.

"Bullshit. You pushed me into that!"

They had attracted the attention of shoppers and shop owners. Jonathan tried to move Keely away from the crowd, but she wouldn't budge. He gave up trying.

"And as for Georgia, I told you the assignment had change. I told you to get out as soon as you could."

"Nice way to duck the truth."

"I told you from the very start that you could leave at any time. You've made the choice to quit. Fine. But that doesn't negate my responsibility to warn you if you're in danger. After all, if it wasn't for me--."

"Damn straight. If it wasn't for you, I'd be safe, sane and happy. Well, guess what? I've finally started down the road to recovery-- no thanks to you. Just leave me the fuck alone?"

Jonathan still had hold of her arm. She used her thumb to apply pressure between his thumb and index finger, knowing how sensitive that area was. His grip loosened and his hand fell away, but his face showed no hint of discomfort.

"Who's the young man?"

The thought he had been watching angered her to the core. Stefan had shown her more love and devotion in two weeks than Jonathan had in a year. She said nothing.

"Can he be trusted?"

"Leave him out of this. Better yet, leave both of us alone."

"Awfully defensive of the boy. Obviously, he has made quite an impression on you. How long have you two been together? Two, three weeks?"

Keely stepped away from him. Something in his look was cold and primal. She wasn't going to give him the satisfaction of answering. "Fuck you."

Jonathan waved away her defensiveness. "Where is he from? What do you know about him?"

"Stefan is more of a man than you will ever be."

"Stefan... European?"

His presence aggravated Keely. She knew how manipulative Jonathan could be. How he could twist words to make the most innocent statement seem sinister.

"Go play your spy games somewhere else. Why are you really here, Jonathan?"

"To make sure you're safe."

"I absolve you, Jonathan. You are no longer responsible for me."

"Look, this is not something you can just forget. We have to find out who's asking about you and why."

"We? There is no more 'we'. For all you know, it could be the Irish Sweepstakes trying to find me to let me know I won."

"This is no time to be flippant. This is serious."

"What makes it different? How do you know?"

"Let's just call it professional intuition. Somebody has gone to a lot of trouble to find you. And they have done it in a circuitous way. That's reason enough for me. Besides, this is bad for business."

Keely was tired. She didn't want to argue anymore. In a softer voice, she pleaded, "Please, I just want to be left alone. And I want you to go away. Can't you understand that. You represent everything I want to forget."

Jonathan held her eyes for a moment and smiled slightly. "Circumstances have altered what either of us wants."

She felt a tear forming, but she didn't want Jonathan to see her cry. As she turned to go, she heard him whisper, "Just be careful. Don't trust anyone."

She turned back. "Don't worry, you taught me that lesson too well."

She had spent the last month trying to block out the past. But just when she thought she had finally purged herself of her ghosts, they appeared again in her dreams. She also worried about Stefan. What would he think if Jonathan persisted? They had been together for such a short while, she didn't really know how he would react.

Her fingers absently touched the silver pendant that hung from her neck. Stefan had bought it at a Berber market in a small village south of Tangier. The woman who sold it said the intricate swirl of wire-thin silver thread was the hand of Fatima meant to ward off evil spirits.

But Keely knew evil could not be stopped. She surveyed the image in the mirror. The Moroccan sun had turned her tawny complexion darker, accentuating her pale eyes even more. Her face was thin, accentuating her full lips, but when she attempted to smile, the sadness in her eyes did not go away.

She heard movement behind her and saw Stefan's reflection in the mirror. He leaned against the door jam, watching her.

"We'll be late if you don't hurry." He walked over and stood behind her, his hands resting lightly on her bare shoulders, his eyes admiring her body in the mirror. She had been surprised how comfortable Stefan had been with her lack of modesty. It made her feel as though they had known each other for a lifetime.

He smiled. "Every time I look at you, you take my breath away."

She smiled. "Wow, you should write love songs."

His smile broadened. "Is that all you're wearing this evening?"

135

She pushed her breasts out in a seductive pose. "Why not? Don't you think people will enjoy it?"

His slid his hands down and cupped a breast in each hand. "Perhaps this would be less distracting for the waiter. But then, I would have difficulty with my dinner."

He playful kneaded her nipples, and Keely could feel a flush begin to rise in her. "If you want to make it out of this room for dinner tonight, you'll let me finish."

He stepped back and crossed to the bed. As she continued to apply a minimal amount of makeup, she could see he was staring off into space. He had not been himself for the last few days. Keely worried that he might be aware she was troubled.

She turned to face him. "Why such a sour look?"

He smiled but didn't reply. She could tell he wasn't happy. Or maybe it was a reflection of how she felt.

When she turned back, he leaned forward to catch her eye in the mirror. "Is something wrong?"

Her expression didn't change, but the hand holding her lipstick paused. "I'm not sure what you mean."

He stood and walked over to her but did not touch her. "I don't think you have been... happy the last couple of days."

She finished applying the lipstick. "I think you're imagining things." "No, I don't think so."

"Everything's fine. I can't believe how lucky I am to have you." Her words did not sound convincing.

He massaged her shoulders very gently, brushing his fingertips against her skin. "I would hate if you kept secrets from me. Are you sure there is nothing you want to tell me?"

She replaced the lid on the lipstick and tossed it on the vanity, then looked at him in the mirror. "There's nothing, Stefan."

He leaned down and gently pressed his lips against her neck, then straightened. "Please. Forgive me. I am just... I cannot believe how you have taken over my life. I guess I am just worried that this is all just... just a fantasy, a dream. It is very simple. I love you."

"I feel the same way."

She watched him in the mirror walk back to the bed and sit. Keely finished applying her make-up before going to the closet. She had been reluctant to say she loved him-- afraid that Stefan might find it too demanding, too restrictive. She could feel Stefan's eyes on her as she rummaged through the closet. She pulled out a blue dress and turned around to him. "I'm very happy."

Stefan took a deep breath and released it slowly. "Keely. There is one thing. Our pasts, well, we say they do not matter. But some day, we will have to share those pasts. No matter how bad they may be."

She laughed, hoping to cover the trepidation she felt in having hidden so much of herself from him. "I hope we're not going to spoil our dinner with things that really don't matter. Believe me, my past is quite uninteresting."

"I want us to share everything...eventually."

Keely's panic reached deep into the pit of her stomach. How could Stefan possibly love her if he knew the terrible things she had done; how she had killed in cold-blood? No. That secret would remain locked deep inside her. She turned back to the closet and put the dress back and retrieved a different outfit. "Well, true confessions will have to wait. I'm hungry."

She didn't have to turn around to know that Stefan watched her every move. Selecting a simple white cotton shift, she slipped it over her head, making sure to arrange the pendant on the outside. She turned to Stefan for his approval.

"Will this be less distracting for the waiter?"

Stefan's thoughts seemed to be elsewhere. "Is there another man?"

Keely turned away, pretending to adjust the dress. She did not want to answer. For a second, it crossed her mind that perhaps, somehow, he had seen her with Jonathan. But that couldn't have been possible. And, how could she begin to explain Jonathan to Stefan? How could he ever understand the role Jonathan had played in her life?

"Is there?"

Keely did not like his tone of voice. "I don't understand why you're asking me such a question, Stefan. And the answer is, 'no.' I certainly would never have taken you for the jealous type."

She slipped into her sandals, hoping he would drop this line of questioning. Stefan came over to her and turned her to face his.

"It is just that I cannot stand the thought of another man, or anything, coming between us."

She could sense the hurt and suspicion in his voice and could not bear it. She put her arms around his neck and kissed him.

"Please believe me, Stefan. There is no one else."

As his cheek rested against hers, he whispered, "I want to believe that, Keely."

She held on to him for a few seconds longer, feeling like she wanted to cry-- at the thought of hurting Stefan and at the thought of Jonathan invading her life again. Stefan pulled back from her.

"Would you tell me? I don't care if it's someone from your past."

She cupped his face in her hands. "You are the only man in my life."

His sad smile made her heart ache. "You look very beautiful... I cannot think of life without you."

The restaurant was situated just off the lobby of one of the oceanfront hotels. Even though the summer tourist season had not yet begun, it was filled with Europeans who flocked to Tangier for an exotic-- but safe-- vacation. The restaurant had a bandstand against one wall where a combo played 1940s standards. In front of the bandstand was a dance floor, extending to open French doors that looked out onto the Mediterranean. The music and the stars twinkling above the Mediterranean lifted Keely's dour mood.

After ordering drinks, Stefan walked Keely to the dance floor. She seldom danced, particularly to this type of music, and felt slightly awkward, but Stefan held her tightly and led her slowly around the floor.

"This is perfect, Stefan." "Do you like it?"

"Yes."

She rested her head on his shoulder and she could hear Stefan humming softly to the music. As far as she was concerned, this moment could go on forever. Stefan leaned back and smiled at her. "I thought you said you couldn't dance?"

She returned his smile and kissed his cheek. "Maybe it's you."

The music ended, and they reluctantly returned to their table. Their drinks were waiting for them, and Stefan drained his vodka martini. He motioned to the waiter for another and turned his attention to Keely.

"I have done quite a bit of thinking about us, Keely. You are quite different from what I had expected."

She smiled, but not sure how to take the statement. "And, how is that?"

"You are not as unapproachable as you appeared when I first saw you running. It took a while to get the nerve to approach you."

Involuntarily, Jonathan's comments came back to her and she tried to play it off nonchalantly . "You purposely set out to meet me, did you?"

"That's a strange question. I was just curious. This beautiful woman running alone on the beach."

She realized how silly it must have sounded. She could not let Jonathan interfere with her life again. She reached over and covered his hand with hers. She started to speak, but the waiter had returned with another round of drinks. Stefan watched Keely as the glasses were set down in front of them. When the waiter left, Stefan leaned toward her, smiling.

"I must admit, I was a bit afraid of you."

Keely laughed, but didn't quite understand his statement.

"Every morning as I watched you, I would think how you seemed to be distant, almost sad. But now I see there is a strength about you, a softness as well. I cannot explain it to you; I don't quite understand it, but I love it."

"Well, you're the only one of us who sees that."

Stefan laughed, but she could tell he wanted to be serious. "There is also a sense of honor about you. That, I understand. You are like the famous women in Romanian history. Strong. Unafraid. Committed."

"I don't think I'm very brave at all."

She paused, and then looked deep into his eyes. They rarely talked about serious matters. He studied her for a moment and Keely had the feeling he was trying to read her mind. He pushed the drink aside, his mood somber.

"What is important to you?"

She was unsure how to respond. "This is odd dinner conversation. I guess family and friendships."

"But in the world, what about the people who do not live in freedom? You do not understand what it is like to live with tyranny, where no aspect of your life is your own. How far do you think you would go to protect those who you love?"

Dreadful images flashed through her mind. Stefan's intensity was unnerving. She lifted her glass and took a couple of sips. "I don't know anymore. How far would you go?"

He looked past her, focusing on nothing. "Once I would have done anything to win freedom for my people."

She admired his zeal, though it seemed out of character. She recalled her own recent past.

"Yes, but... surely, there's a point where you have to say, 'I won't do that'."

"That would depend on circumstances, yes?"

His comment disconcerted Keely momentarily. Jonathan had once said almost exactly the same thing. She took a sip from her water glass, looking over the rim at Stefan.

He continued but speaking more to himself than to Keely. "But recently, I wonder if my causes are worth the sacrifices."

He drank most of his martini. Then he looked at her and broke into a smile. "I guess that is why I am so happy with you. You have a peacefulness that makes me jealous. I worry that you may be a dream and will go away as quickly as you came."

"I'm not going anywhere. And if there is any peace in my life, you're the reason. I just hope I haven't interfered too much with your work."

There was just a moment's hesitation, and Keely thought she saw a confusion and then distress in Stefan's eyes. "Yes. My work." He looked away. "I no longer care about it."

"Why?"

He did not look at her. "Because of you."

"Me? Have I been that much of a distraction?"

"You have been all I can think of." He seemed to be searching for the right words. "The person who hired me gave me a deadline, but I have decided not to finish."

Keely had tried to avoid interfering with him when he would take photos while they were out on daily jaunts, although he seemed rather casual about his choice of subjects. "I had no idea you wanted to abandon your job."

"Maybe it is not as important as before."

"Don't you have a contract? Why wouldn't you finish it?"

He lifted her hand and turned it over tracing the creases of her palm. "It is my problem; I'll take care of it. Now, all I want is to be with you, to love you."

Keely held his hand in hers. "I would like that very much."

The waiter interrupted them with a message that Stefan had a phone call. Neither of them had many acquaintances in Tangier, nor would anyone know they were here. Flustered, Stefan hesitated for a moment, then excused himself and was barely through the archway into the lobby when Keely felt someone standing behind her. She thought it was the waiter and asked for another drink. She looked up as Jonathan took the seat across from her.

"I'll pass along your order."

She looked past Jonathan toward the lobby where Stefan had gone. "What are you doing here? Stefan will be back in a minute."

"Most likely. Especially when he finds no one on the other end."

"You couldn't be more original?"

"Well, I had considered just walking up and joining you, but your friend seemed so intense that I didn't want to spoil the mood."

She crossed her arms, angry that he was invading her life, again. "Why haven't you left?"

"Rhonda's not done with a bit of research for me."

She knew exactly what he meant. He was investigating Stefan. "Look, how many times do I have to tell you to stay out of my life?"

"Do you think I would come all this way unless I believed there was a serious danger? I don't object to your desire for privacy. I just don't want you to discount my information."

"I don't need you or your information. I'll get what I need from Stefan."

"Will you listen? You cannot afford to trust anyone right now, not even your young, handsome friend."

Neither saw Stefan approach the table until he spoke. "I leave to answer a phone call that did not exist, and now we seem to have company for dinner."

Stefan's smile was ice cold. Jonathan stood, but did not extend his hand. Keely reached for Stefan. "He was just leaving."

Stefan didn't take his eyes off Jonathan. "Oh? Before we are introduced?"

Jonathan held out his hand. "I am an old friend of Keely's family. We go back a long time."

"Really?"

"I was surprised to find her so far from home. I know her father likes to keep up with her. She's bad about calling."

Stefan feigned interest. "You should join us, then."

Stefan sat down, keeping Keely's hand in his. He glanced at her; Keely knew he could feel her trembling. He turned his attention back to Jonathan who remained standing.

"After all, now that you are here, I would not feel right to chase you away."

"Thanks, but it's just a happy coincidence that I happened by. Isn't that true, Keely?" He glanced at her but did not wait for any answer before he looked back at Stefan. "But I would hate to interrupt your dinner. Maybe drinks later?"

Keely refused to look at Jonathan. "Actually, we have plans. Maybe another time?"

Jonathan smiled and bowed ever so slightly toward them, looking at Keely when he straightened. "Be sure to call your father when you get a free minute. He'd be quite pleased to hear that you are safe."

Stefan watched Jonathan walk slowly out of the restaurant before he looked at Keely who had picked up the menu and began to study it.

"That was a surprise. Imagine meeting a family friend so far from home."

She glanced up for a moment. "I guess."

"It must have been some time…."

"Since?"

"You have been home? Doesn't your father know where you are?"

"Of course he does, Stefan. Jonathan knows I have an overprotective father." She laughed nervously and tried to look at him.

"You seemed very unfriendly, though. Do you know him very well?"

"You could say my family was in business with him, but not anymore." Keely knew she couldn't keep her past hidden forever, but for now, she didn't want to talk about any of those things; at least her answer had been part of the truth.

"Your friend is a long way from home, isn't he?"

Keely choose not to answer. He stared at her intently for a long moment, and then seemed to relax. "Well, perhaps we could invite him for lunch. Where is he staying?"

"He never said. To be honest, I'd rather not see him again. He is not that much of a friend." Keely laid the menu on the table. "Do we know what we want to eat, yet?"

Stefan watched her for a long moment. "I don't want to upset you."

"You haven't," she said with relief. "I just want to forget the whole thing."

141

He reached into his pocket and pulled out a velvet box and held it up, then placed it on the table between them. "I almost forgot. Open it."

The lid snapped back to reveal a beautiful silver bracelet. She took it out and held it draped between her fingers but did not put it on.

"You don't like it?"

She looked up at Stefan. "Of course, I like it, but…."

His expression was puzzled. "But what?"

"You can't afford to buy me things like this."

"But I should. When I saw it, I knew I must get it for you. And look how beautiful it is against your skin." He blushed. "Actually, I found it in Asilah. It was a very good price."

She attempted a smile, but Jonathan's appearance had unsettled her. Why would he have traveled from England if there weren't some truth to his story? She tried to get Jonathan out of her head.

"I'm not sure I deserve you."

Stefan had taken the bracelet and fastened it around her wrist. He glanced only briefly at her then double-checked the clasp. "No, you deserve a lot better, but I'm afraid, you will have to settle being with me. Or, at least, I hope that is what you want."

Keely smoothed back a loose strand of his hair. "I wouldn't want to be anywhere else."

He smiled, but she could tell that Stefan had not been able to put Jonathan out of his mind, either.

They had returned home, both strained by the evening. Stefan closed the bedroom door and turned off the lights. Keely, naked once more, sat by the window looking out at the stars above the Mediterranean. Stefan crossed the room and stood behind her, gently resting his hands on her bare shoulders. Keely reached behind her and ran her fingers along his bare arms.

"So many stars."

He leaned past her and looked up into the sky. He kissed her before he straightened up. He turned and walked to the bed. Though he had not mentioned Jonathan's sudden appearance, she got the feeling it was on Stefan's mind. She turned in her chair and looked at Stefan, who sat on the edge of the bed.

"I wish we were the only two in the entire world. No one else."

She stood, walked over to the bed and knelt in front of him.

"Look, I'm very sorry our evening was interrupted. But I can assure you, he has nothing to do with you-- with us. He's just someone from my past. You are my present."

He looked down at her for a long moment, gently stroking her hair. "You and me here. It is all so perfect. I don't want it to end."

"It won't. We won't let it."

"You do not understand how much you have changed my life. How special you are."

"Stefan, you're way too good for me."

"You are wrong. I am not good enough for you. But I cannot help myself." He pulled her up and pressed his lips gently against hers then he leaned her back and looked deep into her eyes. "All I want is to be with you. All I want is for the world to leave us alone."

Keely could feel the tears forming in the corners of her eyes.

"It will, my darling. I promise."

Dreams. At first, her dreams were filled with Stefan-- with kisses and laughter, then they were sailing, dressed in nightclothes. As she watched, seemingly from afar, she found that funny. Then they were on the beach making love, the water washing over them. She felt Stefan deep inside her, his fingers digging into her back. He rose up, and it was no longer Stefan. It was Jonathan. He hadn't invaded her dreams in a long time.

Keely sat up in the bed. It had been two days since they encountered Jonathan in the restaurant. Now images of death had replaced Jonathan in her dreams. Images of a little girl sitting against the wall, her faded print dress stained in dark red by her own blood, a gold ring by her side. How could something so beautiful exist in the same world with murderous animals that could butcher innocent children?

Keely fought back a wave of nausea and turned toward the window of her Tangier apartment. But the peaceful, night-shrouded Mediterranean didn't ease her renewed sense of fear that had surfaced with Jonathan's appearance. If she hadn't talked the young farmer into showing her the truck park, perhaps they would still be alive. She also remembered how coldly she had killed those three men-- regardless of how much they deserved to die. At first, she had convinced herself that shooting them was self-preservation. But she knew deep down that it had been an act of vengeance.

She looked at the empty bed beside her and wished Stefan was there. He had gone off on another of his photo shoots. Stefan's brooding silence made her feel he wanted to say something more about Jonathan's appearance at the restaurant. He blamed his mood on the photo contract and what to do about it, but he promised to be more convivial when he returned.

She got out of bed and felt her way through the dark into the kitchen. She made coffee and sat down at the table near the window; the water bubbling quietly in the antiquated percolator was not as comforting as it usually was. Little seemed comforting since Jonathan's appearance. Though she had tried to forget what she had become-- the way she had assassinated the banker in Switzerland and the men in the mountains of Georgia with no hesitation, no qualms, no remorse-- Jonathan's presence had dredged it all up again.

Keely's thoughts turned to Stefan. She tried to focus on the sensation of Stefan's fingers on her skin, his soft lips, hoping these images would erase the images that still haunted her sleep. Keely felt her wrist for the silver bracelet Stefan had given her; he had been so excited.

Everything would have been perfect had Jonathan not intruded. His arrival disturbed her more than she cared to admit. It was not just his veiled threat that she might be in danger. He represented the life she had hoped to put behind her. She also knew there were unresolved emotions she did not want to explore. She had come to despise what Jonathan stood for, but her sense of attachment to him had not dissipated.

Keely realized the coffee pot had stopped perking, but she didn't move. In a couple of hours, it would be daylight and another two days to wait until Stefan would return. Her thoughts were interrupted by a knock at the front door. Few people visited them and never this early. She wondered if perhaps Stefan had come back early. She went into the living room and to the door.

"Oui?"

After a slight moment of silence, an all too familiar voice called out. "I know you're alone."

She opened the door to see Jonathan leaning against the door jam, his hands hanging loosely at his side. Without being invited, Jonathan walked past her into the apartment, looking around.

"Not exactly up to your standard, is it," he said, his eyes traveling the length of her body. "But the outfit is quite fetching."

Keely shut the door finally and looked down at her outfit. She only wore a t-shirt that barely reached mid-thigh. She slowly turned away from him and walked to the bathroom. She closed the door behind her, harder than she wanted to. She shrugged into her jogging clothes and came back into the living room. Jonathan was standing by the window.

"Nice view. Makes up for the lack of amenities, I assume."

"Whatever you want to say, say it and leave. I don't want you here when Stefan gets back."

"Not afraid he might get jealous, are you?"

"Why the fuck do you keep hanging around?"

Jonathan turned to her. "Let's try to have a civil conversation, shall we? I'm not convinced you are being careful, given that you've been so... preoccupied."

"I don't know how much clearer I have to be, Jonathan. I don't work for you anymore. I'm trying to start a new life."

"With your Stefan. Sweet boy. Kind of soft, though, don't you think? But I admit, it's clear you two are infatuated with each other."

"I'm glad you've finally figured that out. There's no reason for you to stay in Morocco.

Have a nice trip home, okay?"

"I'm afraid I can't leave yet. Not until I know you will take this threat seriously."

"I can take care of myself. You taught me, remember?"

"I also taught you to be more aware of your surroundings, not to take undue risks and to be more vigilant about those with whom you come in contact."

"You mean Stefan?"

"What do you know about him? Has he told you about his connections in Romania? Rhonda has had trouble tracking him down. Seems he's quite the mystery man. By the way, Rhonda sends her love and says she misses you."

She wished she had said good-bye to Rhonda, but knew she had no choice. She had not talked with anyone from her former life since Georgia.

"You had Rhonda check on him? What are you, my father? What have you got against Stefan? Is it because he's able to love me without strings attached?"

She could tell by his face the inference was not lost on Jonathan. "Your relationship with this boy is of no concern to me except if it threatens your safety."

"As usual, you like to play with words. You said someone was looking for me. Who? And why?"

"If I knew the specifics, I would have dealt with it without bothering you."

"I know how you deal with things. That's why I'm through with anything connected with you. Can't you get that through your head? Leave me the fuck alone."

She tried to walk around him, but he stepped in front of her.

"Your gutter language doesn't change the reality of the situation." He grabbed her arm.

She didn't try to pull away. She just stared into his eyes. "You can let go of my arm."

"Listen to me. Somebody is searching for you. I believe they mean to do you harm."

"And who put me in this situation in the first place?"

Jonathan's jaw tightened. "Is that what you want me to admit? That I'm responsible? Okay. Yes, I put you in this position." He let go and stepped back. "But the past does not alter the present. Look, I have no problem that you quit, and when this thing is resolved, you can resume your life with my best wishes. I will be the first to apologize if you think I've gotten in the way of your love life, but I think you'd rather stay alive."

She walked over the window and watched the ocean for a moment. Finally, she faced him. "I don't trust you, Jonathan. But you're not typically hysterical. If there is something I should know, just tell me. Don't play your damn spy games with me."

He walked into the kitchen without answering. She followed and watched him fix himself a cup of coffee. He took another cup, poured coffee for her and carried both cups to the table and sat. She sat opposite him but didn't touch the cup.

"So?"

He took a sip and carefully placed the cup on the table. "One of my friends at the NSA informed me two weeks ago that someone has been attempting to discover your whereabouts for more than a month. At first, he didn't think anything of it. He responded that you were M.I.A. The same person sent another email, this time a bit more insistent." She blinked. "So? Who was it?"

"That's the odd thing." He took another sip of coffee. His insistence on dramatizing everything infuriated her, but she waited in silence until he resumed. "The message was from the CIA, but there was no specific name, just a blind email address. When my friend tried to track down the sender, he was told the address didn't exist."

"Who at the CIA would care about me enough to go to all that trouble? And what's so threatening?"

He ignored her flippant tone. "About the same time, someone was in your apartment at St. Albans. I went there after my conversation with the NSA. The door was locked. When I went inside, it was exactly as you had left it. But I started nosing about. Everything was in perfect order. Too perfect. I took Rhonda by and she agreed with me that something about it was out of order. It was too clean."

For a moment, their eyes met, and Keely could almost believe he really cared about her. But she couldn't allow herself to slip under his control again. "And your suspicion is based on that?"

He turned to refill the glass. "I know when things aren't right. I'm telling you, there is somebody very interested in you. Someone with a very long reach and professional resources."

He went back to the stove and refilled his cup. He walked over to her, then casually pushed a strand of hair out of her eyes. She did not stop him. "Let me ask again. How well do you know Stefan?"

Keely could feel a flush rising in her cheeks. She was embarrassed and angry at the same time, but angrier with herself for letting Jonathan keep getting to her like this.

"If I didn't know better, I'd almost think you were the jealous one."

"Let's just say that I feel I owe you this much. There's no more than that."

"You want me to put my life on hold because some guy in the CIA asked questions about me or because someone was in my apartment? I'm starting to get my life back now. I'm not taking chances. Besides, I have Stefan to protect me."

146

Neither had heard Stefan open the door, and both were startled by his voice. "Protect you from what?"

He stepped into the room and crossed to Keely. He kissed her lightly on the cheek and draped his arm across her shoulders. Keely tried to act natural, though her voice wasn't convincing. "You're back early. How was the trip?"

Stefan looked at Jonathan. "I am very surprised to see you again. Here." Jonathan said nothing.

"It is very apparent to me that she doesn't want your company."

"No offense, Stefan, but my business is with Keely."

Stefan's gaze hardened. "What is important to her is important to me."

"Please accept my apology. I am simply looking out for her well-being."

"Her well-being? I don't understand. Why would that be your problem?"

Stefan didn't give Jonathan time to answer. "Forgive me for saying so, but every time you are with Keely, she looks very unhappy?"

"I'm sorry, I hadn't noticed. Is that true, Keely?"

Keely finally found her voice, "Please, Stefan, let it go."

Stefan stared at Jonathan. "I want this to stop. I do not like how you affect her."

Keely turned to face Stefan. "Our business is finished, Stefan. Jonathan was just leaving."

Jonathan set down his cup. "Certainly. I won't take up any more of your time. Keely, I will be around if you need me."

Jonathan walked out of the kitchen and Stefan followed. When Jonathan reached the front door, he turned and gave a small salute, then left. Stefan stared at the door for a minute then walked to sofa and picked up his overnight case. He glanced over his shoulder.

"How long has he been here?"

She did not like his tone, but knew he deserved an explanation. "Not long."

"This man seems to appear only when I am not around."

"I didn't invite him. But you must believe me, he means nothing to me."

"Yes, you keep saying that. What does he want with you?"

She could not think of an adequate explanation-- one that would not require her to expose her past. He looked at her for a moment then smiled as if all was right with the world.

"Okay. I will stop asking." He reached into his bag and pulled out a carved white porcelain statue of a Diana draped in silk with a crown of garland. "Look, I brought you a trinket."

Keely walked to him, relieved, and tucked her arm around his. "Thank you, Stefan. It's beautiful."

"Strong woman, like you." He smiled, looking around. "It's going to be all right, Keely. I'm going to see to it. We're going to have our life together. And I plan to make you very happy."

147

Stefan left again three days later, early in the morning. He said he was finishing up his work and calling it quits-- whether the contract required more or not. He promised to return in a day.

She rose slowly from bed and threw on her jogging tights and a loose T-shirt. She slipped on her running shoes, tied the strings quickly and left the house. Three days had passed, and he hadn't returned as he had said, nor had she heard one word from him. She didn't want to believe he would leave this way, without even saying goodbye, but reasoned his loose ends for his job had delayed him. She had to bide her time. Stefan would be back; he had said so. Then, she would explain everything and hope he would understand.

Outside, the light mist that shrouded the harbor area seemed to heighten the strange anxiety that sent waves of despair through her. She ran fast, trying to leave the fears behind. Something nagged at her which she couldn't, wouldn't face.

Rain began to fall heavily and drenched her body. She continued to run and finally ran until she was breathless and slumped to the sand. She didn't know how long she stayed doubled over letting the rain pelt the pain away. All she could think was that she couldn't outrun the fear until she had faced it. And his name was Jonathan. Why couldn't he go away and leave her alone?

CHAPTER TEN

She could feel the sand pressing into her skin. She slowly opened her fingers, realizing through the pain that she must have clutched the sand for some time. Like coming out of a trance, she realized she had to know what Jonathan was not telling her. Slowly, she made her way home, the wet clothes weighing her down. Back at the apartment, the front door was unlocked. For a moment, she hoped Stefan had returned. She ran in.

"Stefan? Stefan, are you back?"

Jonathan sat in the far corner of the living room. "No, sorry. Just me."

She stopped just inside the door. "How did you get in here? Never mind-- get out."

"What happened to you?"

She didn't care how she looked. "You happened to me. If you had just left Tangier...."

"Change clothes. I'll get you something to drink."

"I said get out."

"I want to talk."

"Fuck you." She turned away and headed for the bathroom. "When I get out of the shower, be gone!."

She slammed the bathroom door angrily. With a balled fist, she pounded on the door over and over, wishing Jonathan were on the receiving end of her punches. Ripping and tugging at her clothing, she stepped into the shower and twisted the hot water till it ran full blast. Retribution for being so stupid-- for believing any man; for trusting relationships.

When she stepped out of the shower, the only dry clothing in the room was Stefan's cotton bathrobe. She closed her eyes for a moment and imagined it was Stefan-- she would tell him everything and say she was sorry. She yanked the robe from the hook and slipped it around her.

Turning to the mirror, she was shaken by the sight of her swollen, blood-shot eyes-- the woman staring back was no more recognizable to her now than the woman she'd become in Georgia and Zurich where that part of her she now loathed had been unleashed. Keely turned and walked out of the bathroom. Jonathan was still there, pouring coffee into two cups.

"Hope you don't mind. Needed a cup. You look like you could use one too."

"You don't pay attention, do you? I say go; you stay. I say leave me alone; you say let's talk."

He sat on the couch, holding his cup. "It might surprise you to know that I get pretty sick of this myself." He sighed and drank. "I have some new information."

She hesitated for a second, then walked to the chair opposite the couch and sat, making sure to wrap the bathrobe tightly around her. "You're on the next flight back to London?"

"It has to do with Stefan."

Keely could feel the hair on the back of her neck bristle. "Don't you think you've fucked up my relationship enough? Let me guess, you hate to tell me-- he's married."

Jonathan seemed unfazed by her sarcasm. "When things don't add up, it's wise to take another look."

She laughed mirthlessly. "How profound."

Jonathan's somber expression did not change. "Did Stefan tell you where he was going?"

She stood up and crossed her arms. "You say you have information about him, then you ask where he is. I'm surprised. Didn't you have him followed?"

Jonathan smiled. "You know I would." He brought the cup to his lips but spoke before he took a sip. "In fact, I've had your Stefan watched from the first day I saw you here and realized you were not alone."

"You son-of-a-bitch. You have absolutely no respect for me, do you."

"Believe it or not, Keely, I do want you to be happy. You've admitted you know very little about him."

Keely sat back down and picked up her cup, remembering how everything was drama to Jonathan, but now he was making her second-guess everything. She put the cup down. "I only know how we feel about each other."

"I would say that you have let yourself be lulled by your desire for affection."

She looked at him. "Don't give me your psycho-babble. We are in love. But, of course, I wouldn't expect you to understand."

"You call it love, I call it infatuation. Either way, it is such a wonderful narcotic. But it could be dangerous."

150

Keely rose to her feet again, her hands resting on her hips. "Look. Forget whatever misguided loyalty makes you think you have to watch out for me. I'm a big girl. I can take care of myself."

"I know where he is."

Jonathan glanced up at her, then got up, went into the kitchen and poured himself another cup of coffee. Keely remained still, her thoughts racing. He was up to something, she was certain of that. All her questions began with why. Jonathan returned and took his seat again, watching her as he delivered his news.

"He's in Gibraltar. He has an apartment there." Jonathan took a sip of the coffee, staring at her. "I can tell from your expression he never mentioned it."

Keely stared back, stunned. She had suggested going to Gibraltar for a day trip, but he had never seemed interested. It was only twenty miles across the narrow channel, a forty-minute hydrofoil ride. She had seen his British passport once but thought he had come to Tangier from France since he had said he was working for a French magazine.

That Stefan had said nothing about Gibraltar caused the sensation of a thousand needles striking her all over. Why would he take a hotel room in Tangier if he had an apartment just a short distance away? Perhaps he didn't want the hassle of crossing the Mediterranean over and over again. But why did he not say something about it? But then, hadn't she been keeping secrets from him?

Keely finally sat down. "Stefan came to Tangier to take photographs for some sort of travel magazine. It's how he makes his living. I never bothered to ask where he lived." Keely knew her explanation was weak.

He seemed to read her thoughts. "If you two were so close, why would he keep the fact he had an apartment in Gibraltar a secret? Obviously, he is hiding something from you."

Keely got up and walked to the window; wishing she could see Gibraltar. "You always look for some sinister meaning to everything, don't you?"

"Occam's Razor. The simplest explanation is usually the correct explanation."

"What's that supposed to mean?" she said over her shoulder.

"Just that if he's hiding one thing, you can't take for granted he's not hiding more."

"I'll ask him when he comes back."

"You're sure he's coming back?"

She spun around and faced him. "Look, you asshole. He's not like you. He's honest. He's loyal. He makes me laugh. And he doesn't use everybody around him."

Jonathan didn't reply immediately. He twirled the contents of his cup and watched the liquid form a whirlpool. Then he glanced up. "He sounds more like a Saint Bernard. But I am suspicious of people who appear too honest, too loyal."

"Something you could never be accused of."

She went into her bedroom, pulling on jeans and a shirt. She searched through the dresser and pulled out her passport. When she came back out, she grabbed her jacket off the back of the sofa. "Give me the address."

Jonathan stood up and set his glass on the coffee table. "Don't know if that's such a good idea. You probably shouldn't travel alone."

"If you are really that concerned, you can save me the trouble of finding it on my own. One way or the other, I'm going to that apartment. I don't need-- don't want your help."

He walked to her quickly, grabbing her arms before she had time to move away. There was a fire in his eyes she had not seen before.

"You listen to me. Until I know what is going on, you better get used to my being around. You may think you are in control. You may think you can take care of yourself-- you can't." He loosened his grip. "As for dropping in on your boyfriend, I wouldn't think of stopping you."

Algeciras, Spain was a sprawling port city that might have been pleasant had it not been for containers stacked three stories high awaiting trans-shipment. The hydrofoil docked alongside a freighter and Jonathan led the way through customs and to a taxi stand. The ride to the only landside entry point to Gibraltar was as silent as had been the hydrofoil ride across the strait. They passed through British customs and caught a taxi on the other side. She knew that Gibraltar was a British outpost on the Mediterranean, but she hadn't expected it to be so-- British. Keely was struck by a sudden wave of nostalgia.

Keely didn't dwell on sightseeing. She was focused on what she would say to Stefan if he was really there. With Jonathan in tow, she knew she would have to explain her past. But she also wanted Stefan to know that she had left that life behind and how important he was to her, that she was ready to go anywhere he wanted.

They arrived at the address Jonathan had provided the driver, and Keely got out while Jonathan paid. The two-story building was not far from the docks; the imposing rock that defined Gibraltar rising sharply less than a half mile away. The row of clapboard buildings looked weather-beaten; what paint that had been on them now a muddy gray. She could smell salt water, dead fish and diesel fuel. Nearby, cargo ships were moored to docks piled high with crates of all sizes. There were only one or two cars parked along the sidewalk in either direction. No pedestrians.

152

After paying the cabby, Jonathan joined her, and they walked toward the double doors. He glanced casually in both directions as though expecting to see someone. She glanced briefly over her shoulder.

"I hope whoever you have watching is awake." She gathered Jonathan had someone posted somewhere.

He didn't say anything but moved off toward the corner. She watched as an elderly man who looked like a sailor step out of the side street. They talked for a minute then the man handed Jonathan something, which he slipped into his coat. He came back and motioned toward the door. "He hasn't seen anyone go in or out since yesterday morning."

Once inside, Jonathan lingered for a moment, listening for movement. When he was sure no one was moving about, he motioned to the staircase. "Top floor."

She climbed the stairs two at a time and reached the top landing several steps ahead of Jonathan, who seemed to be in no hurry. She was impatient but knew she should wait.

"Which?"

Jonathan pointed to a door two-thirds the way down the hall. He tried to pass her, but she held up a hand. "I'll go first, you wait here."

He shrugged and gestured for her to go ahead.

She reached the apartment door and knocked twice. No answer. She knocked more loudly. Still, no answer. She turned to Jonathan.

"He's obviously not here."

Jonathan moved closer, listening carefully. His eyes searched the hallway in both directions, then scanned the door itself. "Something's not right."

Keely shook her head, disgruntled. "You know, you were awfully sure in Tangier. I bet Stefan never lived here, and you've succeeded in luring me into some wild goose chase."

"You know me better than that. My information is accurate. However, there's only one way to be sure."

He reached inside his jacket pocket and pulled out a small, black leather case, opening it and withdrawing a dentist's pick. He inserted it into the lock gingerly. "Never leave home without it."

The door gave way; Jonathan slipped the pic back into its case. Keely pushed past him and started to push the door open.

Jonathan immediately put his hand on her arm and stopped her. "Wait." Something in his tone suddenly frightened Keely, this time his usual dramatics seemed terribly real. Jonathan's other hand reached inside his coat and withdrew an automatic. Keely realized the sailor had given it to him. He pulled Keely back and stepped in front of her into the doorway.

The room was dark, and it took a few moments for their eyes to adjust. It was deathly calm. A mustiness hung in the still air, as though the windows had not been open in a long while. Another odor she couldn't place, certainly unpleasant.

Jonathan motioned for her to stay by the door. She watched his dark figure move quietly across the room. After a few seconds, Keely heard the sound of drapes scooting across the rod and a crack of light spread wider and wider until the entire living room was illuminated.

Jonathan's face seemed to tense, and Keely glanced in the direction he stared. An archway led into a tiny bedroom. Keely realized what she was looking at and moved quickly, her heart pounding.

Stefan lay face down on the floor beside the bed, his head turned away from her. Keely started to kneel beside him, but Jonathan gently lifted her back up and moved her aside. He squatted and felt for a pulse on Stefan's neck.

"There's nothing you can do for him, Keely."

She leaned over his shoulder. "It can't be...." She fought back a surge of bile in the back of her throat and covered her mouth.

Jonathan quickly examined the body, checking pockets, searching for wounds. In seconds, he stood up and turned to her, putting his arm around her, drawing her completely away. Keely struggled against his tight grasp, wanting to be certain it was Stefan, but the more she struggled, the tighter his grip became.

Jonathan whispered in her ear, gentle and soothing. "Come on, Keely. There's nothing you can do."

Through clenched teeth she somehow managed a word. "How?"

Jonathan led her back into the living room, out of sight of the body, and made her sit. "His neck's broken."

She swallowed hard to keep from vomiting. Jonathan knelt down in front of her. He lifted her face.

"Are you okay?"

She nodded and looked past him, though she couldn't see where Stefan was lying. She slowly forced her eyes away and looked hard at Jonathan. "Did you know this before we came?"

Jonathan dropped his hand to rest on her knee. "Of course not. You must think I'm terribly cruel." Jonathan stood up and went over to the door, locking it. "I don't think he's been dead more than six or eight hours. Whoever did this may still be around."

"Why would anyone want to kill him?"

"I don't believe this was a robbery. He was executed."

"What? Why?"

154

Jonathan stopped and turned. "We need to focus first on other things. Listen, Keely, we must be quick."

As Jonathan began to rummage through the apartment, Keely scanned the small room of threadbare furniture.

Stefan had few personal items in view. No pictures, no artwork. Nothing that suggested a person resided here. She noticed a stack of books on the table and walked over to them. They were a random collection in a language she didn't recognize. As she started back to her chair, she brushed against the stack, which fell to the floor. She bent to recover them and noticed that one had opened revealing a cut-out compartment. In it was a small notebook. She pulled it out and returned to the chair.

She flipped through the pages, but they were written in the same language as the books, but she recognized the handwriting as Stefan's. There appeared to be dates in the margin beginning a week or two before they met. As she flipped through the pages, the notations became shorter, ending beside a date a week ago. Hearing a breaking sound coming from the bathroom, she tucked the notebook in her pocket. Jonathan walked out of the room searching through a manila folder. His expression told her he had found something.

"This was wedged behind a loose board in the cabinet. It would seem Stefan didn't want anyone finding these." He sat on the couch. After a moment, he stopped and stared at what he held in his hand. He looked up at Keely and stood to his feet. "Let's go."

He started for the door, but Keely stood in his way. "What is it?"

He looked at her as though he did not want to cause her any more pain. The folder appeared to hold a number of photos and several pamphlets. Reluctantly, he withdrew a photograph from the folder and handed it to her. It was a picture of her in a park-- a silly smile on her face. Beside her was an equally giggly Rhonda. It was a photo she had kept in a frame beside her bed. In St. Albans.

Walking out of Stefan's apartment-- leaving his body where it lay—took every ounce of strength she had.. Too many questions needed to be answered. She felt cheated and angered. On the street, in the sunlight, Keely still had not been able to catch her breath. Could all his talk of love been lies? Had she given herself to a man-- again-- only to have him betray her?

She could feel Jonathan's hand on her arm. He guided her away from the building quickly, walking for blocks until they found a small pub. Ducking inside, Jonathan placed Keely in a corner booth and walked to the telephone. After a few minutes, he returned with two tumblers of gin.

"Drink this."

Keely threw down the stinging liquid, but it did nothing to take the edge off her anxiety.

After a minute, she looked at Jonathan. He looked truly saddened.

155

"I've alerted a friend in the local police. Everything will be taken care of. Are you alright?"

Keely looked at the empty glass. It reminded her of her life. Finally, she spoke in a voice that was tinged with pure hatred. "I'm going to find out who did this to Stefan. I will find him and then I will kill him."

Jonathan took her back to Tangier. She barely remembered the hydrofoil ride or the customs inspection. Once back in her apartment, Jonathan helped her out of her clothes and into her robe, his gentle hands treating her with tenderness. He led her to a chair, and fixed her a cup of tea, which remained untouched next to her.

Jonathan found a language school in the hills above Tangier, in hopes he could find someone there to translate the notebook and other documents they had found.

Only the silence told her Jonathan had actually left. Keely felt more lost than she had her whole life. Her initial reaction was to seek revenge for Stefan's death, but that had faded into a numbing sense of loss. Sadness seem to enshroud her, and no matter how she tried to shake it, she couldn't stop the pain. She could not think of any kind of future because she couldn't imagine a future without Stefan.

Keely watched as the storm clouds moved in from the Mediterranean; the rain pounding the white sand on the beach and flooding the street in front of her apartment. She had not moved from her chair in more than three hours, numbed by the realization Stefan was gone.

They had only known each other for a short while, but his warmth and his passion had rekindled the fires that had been snuffed out in the mountains of Georgia.

The gray of the stormy day had turned into a starless night. The rain continued, although its fury had subsided. Keely still had not moved from her chair when she heard Jonathan return. She didn't acknowledge him as he let himself in, but she could feel his eyes on her. He didn't speak before he went to the kitchen and returned minutes later with a fresh cup of tea.

He sat on the window ledge and looked into her eyes. "Keely, you must try to drink this."

She looked at him vacantly, as though she barely recognized him. Slowly, almost painfully, she raised the cup to her lips, but her hand shook too much, and the amber liquid splashed into the saucer. After a sip, she rested the cup in her lap and stared back at the night.

"Why would somebody kill him? Is he dead because of me?"

Jonathan took the cup out of her hands, placing it to the side. He reached out and gently turned her face to his. "No, you are not to blame. What happened to Stefan happened because of who he was. You knew so little about him. Don't assume he had no past."

"He had that picture of me from St. Albans. Why would he have it? How?" She attempted a smile, but her chin began to quiver. Tears welled up in her eyes. "I'm not sure I want to know. But I should have known. I should have been…."

"Less trusting? You were emotionally involved, Keely. It made you vulnerable."

He stood and walked to the dresser where he had placed the material he had taken for translation. He carried it back to Keely.

"I found someone at the school who gave me a quick read on these. The language is Romanian. There is a pamphlet from what appears to be some extreme nationalistic group. Has something to do with making sure that Romania rids itself of 'outsiders'… particularly refugees."

Keely looked from the sheaf of papers to Jonathan. "Stefan told me he was from Romania. That he left many years ago."

"The date on the pamphlet is four months ago. Apparently printed in Timisoara… that's in the western part of Romania. Did Stefan ever talk about his political involvement?"

They had avoided speaking of the past, allusions to other places with no details. It hadn't mattered at the time. Neither had talked of the future, either. They had been content to focus only on the present. That dreamy day-to-day existence seemed so far away now, something she couldn't imagine ever finding again.

She looked up at Jonathan. "No."

Jonathan pulled out a small manila envelope stuffed in the middle of the folder. "Take a look at these."

He extended it toward her, but Keely was suddenly afraid to take it, knowing somehow it might confirm her worst fears and alter forever her picture of Stefan.

"Take them."

Jonathan's words forced her hands to grab the folder. She opened the flap and dumped the contents into her lap. Fifteen or so photos fell out. The first one was a shot of her coming out of her apartment that had to have been taken a week before she saw Stefan on the beach the first time. She knew because the hem of the outfit she was wearing got caught on the taxi's door and had ripped. She never wore it after that night. It was also the night she thought someone had been in her apartment while she was out.

She picked up the next one. The shot was taken of her from a distance, as she shopped in the Souq-- she tried to recall when exactly had it been. Was it the day before she had seen Stefan on the beach? She scooped the rest up and put them back in the envelope. She had seen all she cared to. Handing them back to Jonathan, she studied his face. "Have you looked at these?"

"Yes."

"What about the notebook?"

"Seems to be some sort of diary. You are the central character. I've no doubt the pictures match up with the information here. Do you remember when you first saw Stefan?"

Keely thought hard, but Stefan's face-- in life and in death-- clouded her mind. "It was about four weeks ago."

"May 12th to be precise, if Stefan's account is accurate."

Keely looked away. "I don't want to hear this."

"Sooner or later, you will have to face the fact that he met you on purpose."

Keely could feel tears cloud her eyes and escape down her cheek. She wanted to rip the book out of Jonathan's hand and throw it into the night; let the rain wash away the words. But she didn't. She looked down at the pages and Keely could see that someone had written in the margins beside Stefan's small, neat handwriting. Jonathan read quietly:

"May seventh. Apartment in the Medina. Followed to market and back. She has not come out rest of day. May ninth. Followed her to beach. Home until dinnertime. Followed her to Arabic restaurant. While she was there, checked her apartment. Nothing. May tenth. Runs each day at same time. May twelfth. She came close by me. Looks younger than I thought. May thirteenth. Stood on beach in her path pretending to take pictures-- want her to speak first. Will continue to get her familiar seeing me there. Looks sad."

Jonathan looked up, meeting Keely's stare, but neither spoke. He continued reading.

"May fifteen. Talked with her. Tomorrow, I will take the initiative. Is she really that dangerous?'" Jonathan flipped forward several pages. "May twentieth. Had coffee. Won't talk about past, don't want to alert her. I will have to work hard to take her into my confidence." Jonathan stopped reading, keeping his eyes on the words in the book.

Keely glanced up at his silence. "Is that all? He says nothing else?"

Jonathan looked uncomfortable. "There's a couple of entries that involve me and that I seem to be someone from your past. He says I upset you." Jonathan closed the book. "After that, he only has two more entries before it stops."

"Read them."

Jonathan seemed reluctant but opened the notebook again and turned to the last two pages. "May thirty. Things have changed. I am not sure I can continue. Keely is...." Jonathan glanced up and half-heartedly smiled, "-- he has some word here, the translator thinks it is some sort of slang-- probably a term of endearment. May 31st. Told I have no choice. I have delayed too long, but I will not do this. I do not know what I am going to do.' "

Keely's eyes pleaded for an explanation. "What did he mean?"

Jonathan stood and walked again to the dresser, pouring two tall glasses of whiskey. He brought them back and handed one to Keely. "I don't know. Apparently, he was hired to befriend you, but got emotionally involved."

Jonathan put down the notebook and picked up one of the pamphlets. "This suggests he may have been connected to that group in Timisoara. There was also a passbook for a Swiss bank account with a little over 5,000 Euros. The last deposit was two weeks after you... we eliminated that banker. Maybe this has something to do with what happened in Switzerland.

Perhaps the neo-Nazis there are afraid Hopler had talked and somehow got Stefan to find you."

"You're saying Stefan was somehow connected with Hopler?"

Jonathan sipped from his glass. "I don't know. But, apparently, whoever sent Stefan after you was afraid you might have information that could be dangerous. And he or they needed to determine if you had passed that information along."

Keely could feel a flush rising in her cheek. "Stefan was no damn neo-Nazi."

Jonathan started to reach for her but withdrew his hand. Instead, he took a long sip from his drink. "I'm just suggesting that ultra-nationalists sometimes run in similar circles. Perhaps someone from one of those groups approached Stefan. But whoever it was, they seemed to have a pretty tight grip on him."

Keely couldn't respond. Stefan involved with the same group as that Swiss banker? The thought that Stefan had betrayed her should have been crushing, but Keely believed that he loved her. And he had died because of it. That alone was enough for her to want to find his killer. She owed that much to him, even if he had deceived her.

She watched the rain splatter against the window for a long while without saying a word.

If only the rain could wash away memories. But Keely knew she was trapped. In a voice she hardly recognized, she whispered, "If I hadn't seen him myself, I wouldn't believe he's really dead."

Jonathan had no reply. She cocked her head to glance briefly at him then slowly looked back at the darkness. He wandered toward the bedroom, telling her he wanted to search the apartment.

"Maybe he left something here. A mail receipt if he had sent photographs to someone. He had to have been taking pictures for some reason."

Keely could hear him rummaging in the other room. He came back to the living room and searched the desk, then the closet in a far corner. He found a strip of negatives. He held it up to the lamplight.

Keely stood up and looked over his shoulder. She recognized herself running toward the camera on the beach. Her eyes met Jonathan's, but neither spoke. For a moment, she wondered if she had actually seen a flash of anguish in his eyes.

Jonathan spoke softly. "If it means anything to you, I really am sorry."

She spoke matter-of-factly. "No, you're not. You're only sorry he died before you could interrogate him."

He gently touched her shoulder. "I am not the cold bastard you think I am. I understand a lot more than you think."

"Really? Tell me."

He turned away. "It's not important. Emotions can muddy a situation. They have no place in our line of work."

Keely grew angry. "Your line of work, not mine." She returned to the couch. "The real scary part is I understand you-- that any emotion can jeopardize the mission. But that seems to have completely stripped you of all emotions. That's what I had to run away from. And now, here you are."

"I'm sorry you feel that way. I thought we made a good team."

Keely didn't answer. Jonathan walked into the kitchen and returned with a glass of juice.

He handed it to Keely along with a pill.

She stared at it then at Jonathan. "What's that?"

"Something to help you sleep."

"I don't…."

Jonathan knelt down in front of her. "Yes, you do. Now take this."

Keely reluctantly reached out and took the pill and the juice. When she had swallowed it, Jonathan stood and held out his hand. "This works pretty quickly. Let me help you."

Keely tried to stand, but realized she was already woozy. Jonathan helped her up and walked her toward the bedroom. She could hardly put one foot in front of the other. Finally, Jonathan picked her up like a rag doll and carried her to the bed. He laid her down gently and pulled a throw over her. She was asleep before he left the room.

When she awoke, she thought she had only been out for a few minutes, but the clock on the nightstand read 5:45 am. She had not dreamt, had not moved. She struggled to sit up and when she finally was able to, got out of bed and went to the bathroom. A long, hot shower revived her, and she slipped into her jeans and a t-shirt and went into the living room.

Jonathan had spent the night on the couch but was sitting up talking in a hushed voice on his cell phone. When she entered, he motioned her toward the kitchen. He had already prepared coffee and she poured both of them a cup. She returned to the living room just as he hung up and handed him his full cup. She noticed he had been taking notes, but his look showed he had not found out what he had hoped to.

"That was my friend in Gibraltar. He found some information about Stefan, but it doesn't make much sense."

Stefan had passed through Gibraltar customs using a British passport for the first time two weeks before he had met Keely. The passport number was real, but it was a new issue, so there was no way to trace his movements before Gibraltar except that he had arrived from London. A company in Switzerland with no address or telephone number owned the building where he was staying. Apparently, the company was a front for somebody, but Swiss officials couldn't or wouldn't say who. The building was probably a safe house of some sort.

Keely sipped her coffee quietly as Jonathan spoke, but she still didn't understand. "I don't get it. What was going on? Is there any connection with Hopler?"

"Nothing directly links Hopler with Stefan except Switzerland, and that might just be a coincidence."

Jonathan stood, walked into the kitchen returning with the coffee pot and poured them both more.

"Here's my take. Stefan was told to find and follow you. I have no clue why he was chosen. Apparently, he was to find out where you were staying and search for something in the apartment. When he didn't find it, he was ordered to befriend you. Again, why and to what end, we don't know. Then he had a change of heart. He must have told whoever was controlling him that he was through and that's when he was murdered."

Keely rested her head in her hands. "What could they want?"

"We don't know. I've gone over the last few months you were at Swift. The only possible assignments that could have caused this were Zurich or maybe Georgia. But a direct connection between either of these and Stefan eludes me."

161

They were silent for a few minutes then Jonathan's expression changed. "I think my only course is to start in Romania, since that's where Stefan was from. I might be able to find out who was pulling his strings, which might answer who's looking for you. You should go back to England. Rhonda will arrange for a safe house."

Keely looked at him as though he was a stranger. "Why are you doing this?"

Jonathan put his coffee cup down on the table and spoke without looking at Keely. "For one, to prove to you that I'm not the cruel bastard you think I am, and second-- obviously, Stefan failed to complete his assignment. He paid dearly for it. Which means whoever sent him may try again." He looked at her then. "You're still very much a target. We can't sit around here and wait. You will not be totally safe until I find out what this is all about."

"Then I'll go with you."

He leaned back in his seat. When he finally spoke, his voice was stern and low. "It is too risky. Besides, you have told me a number of times, that you can no longer stomach all this."

She let his words sink and turned to watch the rain. It was softer now, the wind having died down, but the storm clouds still hung over the seaside city. Lights of ships passing far out to sea blinked in the distance. The rain muted even the traffic noise that usually drifted through the morning air.

Keely finally turned to face Jonathan. "You've always said that the best defense was an aggressive offense. My feelings for Stefan aside, it is my life in danger, and I'm not sitting around waiting for someone else to show up. I know why I have to do this. Why do you?"

Jonathan refused to meet her eyes but looked past her to watch the rain. "Tangier can be beautiful, especially in the rain." He paused for a long moment. "Why? Because I have to know you are safe, perhaps for my own peace of mind."

She glanced over at him. "Why can't you admit it?"

"Admit what?"

"That there's something more."

He smiled briefly. "I admit you have come to mean a great deal to me. More than I had realized until this. I also see that my decision to bring you into this business was clouded by, let's just say, considerations other than professional. That's why I think it best that you return to England and allow me to do the investigating."

"It's my life, it's my call. I'm going with you."

Jonathan looked at her in consternation. "I'm sorry, but I don't think that wise. Obviously, someone is very interested in getting close to you. I wouldn't feel right letting you get in harm's way again."

"Little late for that, don't you think? Besides, how can you protect me if I'm in England and you're who knows where?" With that, she stood up. As she walked slowly to the dresser, she realized she had been sitting so long her joints ached. She poured a bit of the whiskey into her coffee cup and drank it in one swallow. She poured more and turned around to Jonathan, walking slowly toward him.

"I appreciate what you are trying to do. I really do. But I can't be left out. This is my fight, my loss. Whoever caused this must answer to me."

She put down her cup and leaned forward reaching for his hand to take in hers.

"Surely you can understand that. Surely you understand this is the way it has to be. Please, don't shut me out of this."

Jonathan looked into her eyes for a moment then smiled wanly. "I'll have Rhonda make the arrangements."

CHAPTER ELEVEN

It took two days for Rhonda to arrange for a flight to Romania that met Jonathan's concerns for security. Keely did not want to give up the apartment, although it now held very painful memories. She paid the landlord for the next month and said she would be away for a while. Jonathan asked her to get her other passports just in case.

When she went to her safe deposit box, she left the passport she used to enter Morocco and the Euros, but as an afterthought picked up the small digital camera and dropped it into her purse.

The trip to Romania was long and convoluted, as Jonathan had required. They had to catch a flight from Tangier to Madrid on Air Maroc. They changed to Austrian Airlines bound for Vienna, and then on to Timisoara. Jonathan wanted to make sure if they were followed, he would be able to spot them in transit. In all, the trip took eighteen hours during which the two spoke little. Keely's mind was on Stefan. She still had trouble believing he had deceived her, and worse, plotted against her. Jonathan had also found some letters among Stefan's papers. The translator had said they contained typical family news and that the handwriting was female. The contents gave no clue who the author might be, and Keely didn't want to know. Keely rested little during the flights, and when she managed to sleep, her dreams were invaded by visions of blood. She would wake to find Jonathan staring at her with concern.

In the darkened cabin, Keely grappled with the events of the past month. She still could not accept that Stefan had betrayed her. But she knew he had fallen in love with her, an act that had cost his life. She wondered if her feelings for him were as strong, would she have sacrificed her life for his?

She had told Jonathan she was in love with Stefan, but in her heart, she wasn't sure. Her feelings might have been more the need for something good and comforting. Keely wasn't even sure what love-- true love-- felt like.

They had never talked of the future, which indicated to Keely she had not committed to Stefan the way he seemed committed to her. If she was honest, the relationship always felt somehow impermanent, and that may have been one of the reasons she'd fallen into it so easily.

She was also plagued by her reaction to Jonathan. She hated what he had made her, but she could not help feeling there was still an emotional connection she could not dismiss. She knew that someday, she would have to confront all this, but she could not think about it now.

They arrived in Timisoara shortly after ten p.m. Romania's second largest city sat less than 100 miles from the Hungarian border. The airport was almost deserted, but the customs official poured over their passports so meticulously, Keely wondered if something was out of line. Unlike some agents, Jonathan refused to use forged passports. Instead he had used his connections to obtain Keely passports from Canada, Ireland, England and Australia to accompany her American one. All the names were slightly different, but all had the initials K.G. Finally, the officer returned their documents and waved them through.

The taxi ride into the city took another half hour. Ornate gas lamps illuminated turn-of-the-century buildings along well cared-for streets. Few people walked the streets-- couples headed to or from a number of small clubs, workers trudged to late night shifts.

Rhonda had made reservations for them at a hotel just two blocks from Victory Plaza, the hub of the city. The hotel was small by American standards, but with a grandiose facade. Keely took passing notice that a second entrance led to a casino. Jonathan checked in as Keely slumped against a marble pillar in the hotel's lobby. He led her to an antiquated elevator, which rose slowly to the fourth floor. Only after the bellman had deposited their two small pieces of luggage in the room, collected his tip and closed the door quietly behind him, did Keely realize that Jonathan's luggage had been left as well. She turned to him wearily to ask, but he apparently anticipated her questions.

"I didn't think you wanted to be alone. I did, however, ask for twin beds."

The room was actually a suite. Keely could see two beds through the bedroom door. Jonathan followed her gaze.

"I could sleep out here if you prefer."

She didn't say anything but picked up her overnight case and went into the bedroom. When she came out, she had stripped off her travel clothes and had pulled on an oversized T- shirt.

"Is there a mini-bar?"

Jonathan, now seated on the couch, had anticipated her and had two drinks poured. He was already sipping his as Keely slumped onto the couch beside him. She stared at the glass, then took it and drank it down in two gulps. She held the empty glass in both hands.

"This is all so unreal."

Jonathan put down his glass, stood and reached out a hand to her. "Don't think. We will take this one step at a time. And the first step is to get some rest."

He led her into the bedroom and helped her under the covers, pulling the downy comforter up to her chin. She shivered despite the fact she was not really all that cold. He went to the other bed and started to take the pillow and blanket, but she stopped him.

"Look, you need rest as much as me. And that couch won't cut it. Stay in here." Jonathan looked at her for a moment then lay down on his bed still fully clothed.

When Keely finally struggled from sleep in the morning, she realized she had not moved a muscle all night. Morning light seeped in the windows and the faintest sounds of morning traffic sounded in the distance. She also smelled the distinct aroma of coffee. She stiffly sat up, pulling the blankets around her. Jonathan's bed looked as though he had hardly slept in it. Through the bedroom door, she could see a silver trolley with coffee service and a pile of croissants. She heard water running in the bathroom, which stopped and a moment later Jonathan appeared, wearing a new outfit that looked as if had just been pressed.

"Good morning. I had hoped you would sleep a bit longer."

Keely smiled weakly. "What time is it?"

Jonathan glanced at his wristwatch. "Little past six a.m. Juice?"

Keely nodded. Jonathan went into the sitting room and returned with the trolley, poured a glass of juice and carried it to Keely, sitting at the foot of her bed. She took the glass and drained it. The tinny orange juice was room temperature, but Keely did not realize how parched she was. Jonathan took the empty glass and returned to the trolley.

"How about a little breakfast?"

Without waiting for a response, he fixed a cup of coffee-- touch of cream and one spoonful of sugar as she liked it-- and selected a croissant. He carried the plate and cup to her and placed them on the nightstand, falling back against the pillows of his bed.

She sipped the coffee, savoring the European blend that was much smoother than the Arabic coffee she had grown accustomed to in Morocco. She tore off an end of the croissant, astonished by its buttery warmth. She finished the coffee and rested her head against the pillow.

166

"What if the people who live at the address on Stefan's letters turn out to be his family? I am not sure I could face them. Do they know, I wonder?"

He looked away. "We'll see."

Keely felt queasy but knew they had to follow the leads wherever they led.

In the morning light, Timisoara looked like a movie set. The streets were lined with beautifully excessive rococo design. If it had not been for the occasional Cinzano umbrella at the sidewalk cafes, Keely would have sworn she was in pre-World War I Europe. The streets bustled with pedestrian traffic, but no one seemed to be in a particular hurry. Fashion ranged from peasant frump to haute couture to American casual. The people were handsome, albeit weathered by years of hardship and rugged winters.

They caught a taxi outside the hotel and as they made their way east, Keely could just make out mountains in the distance, although the city itself was rather flat. She tried to imagine Stefan in this setting and wondered how long it had actually been since he had been there.

In less than ten minutes, they had moved from the bustle of the center city to sleepy urban streets lined with three-story flats. The cleanliness to the place reminded Keely of Germany. The taxi finally pulled over, the driver pointing to the address on the envelope Jonathan had handed him when they had gotten in. He nodded at a building across the street.

Jonathan peeled off several bills and handed them to the man.

"*Aşteaptă-mă.*"

The man looked reluctant to wait, so Jonathan peeled off more Romanian lei and handed them over. The man nodded.

As they approached the door, Keely suddenly panicked. She didn't know whether she could face who might be behind that door. Jonathan must have sensed her dread, took her arm and gently led her up the front stoop.

Inside, he located the apartment number and led Keely through the interior door to a first floor flat.

Jonathan rapped gently on the door and they could hear movement inside. In less than a minute, a small woman in a worn housedress opened the door. Her hair was silver, and her face creased by an intricate array of wrinkles. But Keely could see Stefan's eyes in hers.

"*Buna Dimineat?*" Her 'good morning' was tinged with a considerable amount of trepidation.

Jonathan responded gently. "*Buna Dimineat. Vorbit, Englezes te?*"

Keely assumed he asked if the woman spoke English. The woman eyed them warily, then called back into the apartment.

A girl of fourteen or fifteen came to the door. She was beautiful; a female version of Stefan, dressed in baggy jeans and a Mickey Mouse T-shirt. "*Da?*"

Jonathan spoke for them. "Do you speak English?"

The young girl looked from one to the other. "Yes."

"We are friends of Stefan."

The girl looked at them for a long moment, then turned and said something to her mother. The mother stiffened slightly, but motioned Jonathan and Keely to enter. For the moment, Keely felt relieved.

The apartment was small and crammed with overstuffed, threadbare furniture. The older woman motioned for them to take a seat and she sat at the edge of an armchair, the girl casually seated on one of its arms. The mother gestured as she addressed the girl.

The girl turned to them. "She asks how you know my brother."

Jonathan glanced at Keely, his eyes asking if she wanted to answer. "I met him in Tangier. About a month ago."

The girl translated and the mother responded. "We did not know where Stefan was. He only writes now and then. My mother would like to know how you come to be his friends." The girl's English was heavily accented, but precise.

Keely kept her focus on the mother. "Please tell her that I loved your brother; we meant a great deal to each other. He was a very gentle and kind man."

The girl did not look at her mother as she translated. The mother nodded gently as she listened, looking from Keely to the girl. The mother spoke.

"She says you speak in past tense. Where is he now?"

Keely hesitated, and Jonathan shifted uncomfortably then answered. "I am sorry, but we have sad news."

The girl did not translate, so Jonathan continued. "He was killed several days ago… in Gibraltar."

The girl absorbed the information, then turned and slowly spoke to her mother. Her eyes saddened, but Keely could tell this was a woman used to suffering in silence. The older woman whispered something, and the girl turned back to Jonathan.

"She says that she knew this; her heart had told her something bad had happened to him."

Tears welled up in the older woman's pale eyes. She stared at Keely for a long moment, then spoke. The young girl had tears in her eyes as well, translating.

"My mother says that Stefan was a good son. She thanks you for bringing her this news."

Keely stood and walked over to where Stefan's mother sat. She knelt down and took the older woman's hands in hers. "I am so sorry. We were very happy."

As soon as the girl finished translating, the mother smiled at Keely and placed her palm against Keely's cheek, speaking close to her. Her words, though Keely didn't know what she was saying, were soothing and for a moment, Keely felt exonerated. When her mother finished speaking, the girl translated.

"She says you are very sweet. Your eyes are kind, and she can see why Stefan would have loved you. She is sorry for you as well." There was a pause as the mother said something further and the girl interpreted, though, tentatively. "She asks how he was killed."

Keely could feel her spine stiffen, not wanting to tell this woman how her son died, or why. "Someone broke into his apartment and killed him. We don't know who, but I will find who did this."

When the girl finished translating, the old woman lifted Keely's hand to her face and pressed it against her lips. She sat in silence for several minutes before she rose, said something and walked out of the room.

The girl looked at Keely. "She is going for tea."

"What did your mother say just now?"

The girl looked as though she didn't want to translate, but finally did. "She said that there is much revenge in your voice. To be careful that it does not consume you. Hatred was what sent Stefan away. And she wouldn't doubt it had killed him, as well."

She paused, looked to make sure her mother was out of earshot, then continued.

"Stefan was trouble. He had to run away before the government arrested him. He made my mother very sad. At first, we were proud because he was part of peace movement, but then he and his friends became angrier with everybody. They get in fights, they break windows of refugees, they march in streets. No good. My father die of sad heart because of Stefan. I am now left with no father and a broken-hearted mother. Stefan think he is doing right thing, but he only leaves unhappiness behind him. He hang around bad people and they only get him in much trouble."

The girl stopped because her mother returned with an ornate tea service on a tray. She busied herself with preparing tea for her guests and finally sat back in her chair, sipping tea from a cup that shook noticeably as she raised it to her lips.

Jonathan set his cup down and looked at the girl. "We want to find out who murdered your brother. We found this in his apartment."

He took out the leaflet and handed it to the girl. The mother glanced at it but turned away.

Keely saw the look of recognition. The girl handed it back to Jonathan without reading. "That is from group Stefan member of. Bad people."

"There is no address. Do you know where we could find them? It would be very helpful to us."

169

The mother patted her daughter's hand, asking what they were saying. The girl told her, and she responded. The girl nodded slightly and stood, walking to a small desk in one corner. She wrote something on a piece of paper and returned, handing it to Jonathan. It was a name and an address.

"My mother says to give you name of Stefan's friend. He may help."

Keely and Jonathan stood and walked to the door. The girl and mother followed. As they were about to leave, Keely turned. "Was Stefan… involved with anyone?"

The girl looked confused.

"Was he married or…?"

The girl shook her head. "He had no one here."

The mother asked what had been said. When the girl translated, the mother rested her hand gently on Keely's arm. "*Cum va numit, I?*"

Keely looked at the girl. "What is your name?"

Keely rested her hand over the mother's. "Keely."

When they exited the apartment building the sun was blazing, although there was a chill in the air. As they walked down the front stoop, Keely leaned against Jonathan for support.

They reached the street and pulled at his coat sleeve like a little girl. "I need coffee. Bad."

The cafe was crowded even though it was past nine. Keely found a table while Jonathan ordered coffee at the counter. A young woman in her early twenties brought the two steaming cups a few minutes later, smiling brightly. When she left, Keely sipped the rich coffee. Jonathan stirred his for a moment, then spoke gently.

"I'm sure that couldn't have been easy."

Keely put down her cup and stared out the window. "I didn't expect them to look so much like Stefan. I guess I didn't know what to expect. There was no love lost between Stefan and his sister, was there?"

"Apparently not." Jonathan busied himself with his coffee, took a sip then finally met her eyes. "Have you thought about what you will do, after?"

Keely looked confused. "After what?"

"After this is settled, what will you do?"

Keely smiled weakly and leaned back. "Like you said, I'm taking it one day at a time."

His expression seemed to soften. "Perhaps you might think of returning to England. Rest awhile, before you make any decision."

Returning to a life that had caused her such anguish was unthinkable. "What would be the point?"

"A safe harbor. I know you wouldn't come back to Swift, even though you've been… important to me."

"Important?" She just shook her head and sighed. "I don't know. Maybe I'll head back to Colorado. When we were talking to Stefan's mom, I suddenly wanted to see my father. I feel sort of like Dorothy-- there's no place like home. I wish I had a pair of red shoes."

Jonathan smiled warmly at her. "Movies aside, I'm afraid 'home' will never be the same. You are a different person than you were when I first met you in Colorado. And no matter how much you try to bury your past, it has a tendency to resurrect itself at the most inopportune times. But the choice, as always, is yours."

Keely wished he would be less circumspect. But he had come to Tangier and was here to protect her. That spoke more to her than words.

The address Stefan's sister had written down for them was in a seedier part of the city. Shabby storefronts and deserted warehouses replaced neat row houses. Grimy windows were plastered with posters. Keely couldn't read them, but the erratic printing was enough to let her know these were not signs of peace.

Turning her head to look out Jonathan's side of the taxi, she caught him looking at her.

"Doesn't appear to be a very happy place."

Jonathan sighed as he briefly glanced past her out the glass. "I imagine this is the type of place that breeds revolution."

"Revolution? Don't you think Stefan was just caught up in some misguided attempt to protect what he thought was his country?"

"Don't kid yourself, Keely. He knew what he was doing."

"I think I knew him better than you."

"Did you?" When she turned away, he reached out and patted her hand. "I'm not looking for an argument. It's that we have to keep our emotions out of this. I told you this would be hard. But if we want to catch a killer, we have to think like a killer."

"That's what's wrong with your business, Jonathan."

He withdrew his hand. "Perhaps, you're right," and looked to the front as the taxi slowed.

The driver stopped across from a storefront whose glass windows were plastered with posters. Jonathan asked the driver to stay. The man hesitated, feigning he didn't understand what was being asked of him. Jonathan peeled off enough lei to increase the man's comprehension.

His mumbling was a thick accented English. "No like place. I wait, maybe, ten minutes."

Jonathan patted him condescendingly on the shoulder. "Good man."

171

Jonathan led the way across the street. The building was no different from those on either side. Jonathan gently tried the front door and found it unlocked. The interior was a jumble of paper and boxes illuminated by a 25-watt bulb. Smoke filled the air and made it much more difficult to see the dim interior. A sickly buzzer had gone off in the back as they had entered, and in a minute a pale young man in his mid-thirties ambled into the front room. He was dressed in jeans and a sweater that looked worn and dirty. He had a three-day's growth of beard. His hands were smudged with blue ink as though he had been working on a mimeograph machine. He sized up Jonathan and Keely and spoke in clear English.

"Can I help?"

Jonathan smiled graciously and stepped to the man. Keely remained by the door. "Good morning. I'm glad you speak English. My Romanian is atrocious."

Keely noted that Jonathan was laying his British accent on generously. "I've come to see Stefan Minescu."

Keely watched the young man's face carefully. At the mention of Stefan's name, his jaw tightened, and his eyes darted toward the back of the shop. His reaction lasted only a second, but it was clear he knew Stefan.

"Sorry, that name does not mean anything to me."

When Jonathan took another step closer, Keely knew he, too, had seen the same reaction. He placed his hand casually on the shorter man's shoulder. "Now, my fine young man, you don't want to be lyin' to me, do you?"

With a swiftness that stunned Keely, Jonathan brought his free hand around and slapped the young man just at his jaw line. The blow was not meant to injure but to gain the man's attention. Fear flooded into the young man's eyes as his cheek reddened where Jonathan's hand had landed. He looked like a trapped rabbit and would have fled had Jonathan not held tightly to his shoulder. In a voice that belied his actions, Jonathan continued.

"Perhaps you didn't hear the name. I said Stefan Minescu."

The young man was trapped, and Keely could see any idea of resistance drain from his face.

"Yes, yes, sir. Perhaps I do know Stefan. But I have not seen him in a very long time."

Jonathan released the man's shoulder, patting it gently as though to smooth out the man's sweater. Jonathan glanced around the room and motioned toward a table and some chairs at the back.

"Why don't we sit down and chat."

Over the next ten minutes, the young man-- an earnest, but sensible revolutionary named Marco-- divulged everything he knew about Stefan Minescu.

They had met as college students during protests against the corruption rampant in Timisoara. Stefan and Marco had gravitated to the mass demonstrations more to meet girls than for the politics. When the local officials promised to address the demands of the students, they all celebrated.

But over the next several years, the promises had not been kept. Adding to the situation was the flood of refugees from Syria. Some Romanians blamed these foreigners for sapping the resources of a destitute country and wanted them deported. They also feared that the government may be coerced by Western governments to accept the refugees.

Stefan, who had dropped out of college, had grown up listening to his father rant about foreigners. Stefan had taken a series of low-paying jobs, but each time, he was fired because a refugee would do the work for less. Eventually, he joined the ultra-nationalists. Because of his youth and mild manner, he was often the spokesman for the group. Members found him a job, but he spent most of his time organizing.

Tensions grew with other protect groups, especially when Stefan's group called Romania Motherland began harassing refugees in Timisoara. It started with pranks; throwing paint on windows, throwing rotten eggs into stores. Soon, it escalated to violence. When the ultra- nationalists were defeated in city government elections, a fire broke out in an apartment house filled with Syrians. Seventeen were killed; scores of others were injured. No one could prove whether it was an accident or arson, but Romania Motherland was blamed. Stefan had been seen in the vicinity of the building the night of the fire.

Keely sat in silence through the young man's story, unable to connect the man she loved with the revolutionary Marco described. When he finished, Keely leaned toward him. "Was Stefan responsible?"

Marco shrugged. "I do not know. I was out of the city when the fire happened. When I returned, Stefan was gone. The police looked for him. They questioned everyone, including me."

Keely leaned closer. "What did you tell them?"

Jonathan put a hand on Keely's arm and spoke softly to the young man. "When was the last time you saw Stefan?"

He began to drum his fingers on the table as though playing a tune on an imaginary piano. He watched his fingers intently. Keely knew he was debating how much to give away. She wondered if the Romanian police had managed to pull information from him as easily as they had. Jonathan reached into his pocket and extracted a roll of bills. They were all 100 new lei notes, each worth about twenty pounds. He peeled off lei notes and arranged them on the table. When he reached five notes, he paused.

"We would be very appreciative of any information you might be able to provide. We are not looking to harm Stefan in any way. Have you heard from him recently?"

Jonathan's soothing voice and the money had the desired effect on Marco. It was a powerful incentive. Marco was hooked.

"About a month after he left, he called. He said he had a job with somebody. He sounded frightened, but said he had no choice. He said emails might come for him. I was to pass them on to his gmail account. He didn't say where he was."

"What sort of messages?"

Marco was very uncomfortable, but he couldn't take his eyes off the stack of notes.

"They made no sense. Just times, dates maybe a place. He had me send them on to other email addresses. He also showed me how to change the information."

He stood, went into the back and returned with a tattered book. He handed it to Jonathan. It was a flight schedule for *Tarom,* a Romanian air transport company. He took the book and flipped through the pages. "I was to locate the place, find the page number here, then use it in the email. I reversed the time and used letters for the date. I thought it was silly, but I did it for Stefan."

He looked up. "The last email to Stefan was about a person. That was, maybe one month ago. That is the truth."

His hand began to slowly move toward the stack of money, but Jonathan casually rested his hand on top of the bills. "You wouldn't happen to have that email around, would you?"

Marco looked crushed. "Stefan told me to delete all emails for him and from him."

Jonathan removed his hand and nodded slightly. Marco gathered up the money. He sat for a long moment as though trying to correlate the information Marco had given them with what they already knew. Jonathan smiled graciously and counted out five more bills.

"Where is your computer?"

Marco motioned toward the back, and Jonathan followed as Marco led the way. They were gone just a few minutes then returned, resuming their places at the table. Jonathan turned to Keely. "I tried to retrieve the deleted files, but they're gone. Stefan's address was through Yahoo's U.S. site. Interesting, isn't it. It would be hard to pinpoint where exactly he emailed from." He turned back to Marco. "Does anyone else know about these emails?"

Marco looked sheepish, as though there was something, he was reluctant to admit.

Jonathan noticed it, too. He raised his eyebrows, as he held his hand over the extra money.

Finally, the young man spoke. "Sometimes, his sister picked up messages for Stefan. She sent them on in her letters. She picked up the last email to him."

Jonathan peeled off more money and held it out. "Here is five-hundred more, but this is very important. Did you tell the police about Stefan's sister?"

Marco raised his eyebrows. "No. Never. Stefan would have... he would have been very angry with me."

Jonathan handed the money to the man. "Thank you for all your help. We greatly appreciate it."

Marco took the money and stared at it as though in a trance. Finally, he looked at them. "Do you know where Stefan is?"

Keely couldn't answer, just nodded.

"Is he safe?"

Keely stood and walked out the door. Jonathan answered. "Stefan was killed three days ago."

Neither talked on the taxi ride back to the hotel. Once inside the lobby, Jonathan led the way to the coffee shop and ordered each a coffee. After the waiter had left, he leaned in.

"Seems Stefan's little sister was not as forthcoming as she could have been."

"Do you think what that guy said about Stefan was true?"

The waiter returned and placed the cups on the table. Jonathan sipped his before he answered.

"Keely, blood hatred runs deep here. Like it's imprinted genetically. I know I've been harsh about Stefan, but you seem to have found a side of him that was good. After all, it seems he might have paid with his life for his refusal to carry out his... last assignment. You need to focus on that and forget what else he might have been."

Jonathan's compassion touched Keely. She also knew that she had to keep her emotions in check. She didn't know if her anger was driven more by revenge for Stefan's death or to protect herself.

"I want to talk with Stefan's sister. Alone."

Jonathan leaned back and opened his mouth as if to protest but said nothing. Then he nodded his head.

"All right. But I will be across the street."

The young girl looked surprised when she opened the door. Then she looked frightened.

Keely smiled. "Hello."

"My mother has gone to light a candle for Stefan."

"Actually, I wanted to talk to you. May I come in?"

The girl hesitated then opened the door enough for her to enter. "What else can I say to you?"

175

Keely smiled at the young girl. "What is your name? I told you mine before, but you never told us yours."

"Neda."

"You speak good English. Like your brother."

"Stefan was an exchange student when he was in high school. He went to England for a year. He was very smart. When he returned, he taught me. Stefan promised to take me there someday."

"You must have been close to him."

Neda lifted her chin and nodded. She remained silent but moved to sit down. Keely followed.

"You looked up to Stefan, didn't you?"

"I love him very much." She covered her face with her hands. "I am so very angry at him for leaving us."

Keely stood up and went to her, putting her arm around the girl's shoulders. The girl cried for a few moments, then looked up, brushing the hair from her face. Up close, she favored Stefan even more. A strange feeling passed through Keely-- a chance to say good- bye to Stefan. "Are you okay?"

Neda nodded.

"When did you talk to him last?"

Neda wiped her tears away on her sleeve. "He would call to see how mother was. He sounded very unhappy, but said he was trying to help us. One a month, he would send us money. At first, my mother didn't want it, but we have no other way."

Keely was quiet for a moment, her arm still holding the girl. "Neda, Stefan's friend said you sometimes picked up messages for Stefan."

Neda looked as though she was about to protest, then said quietly. "He asked me to get them and put them in a letter. He told me how to change the words. I was to destroy the message after."

"I know you picked up the last one he received. It is very important that I see it."

"Will it help you to find who killed my brother?"

"It might."

She sat still for another moment before she left the room. She returned with a brown pouch and opened the flap. "Everything I keep in here. Stefan would not come here. He would send word where he was, and I write to him. This is book I used." She pulled out a tattered copy of 'The Prince' in English and handed it to Keely.

She flipped through the pages. In the same precise handwriting, she had seen in the notebook from Gibraltar, there were notations in the margins. She looked at the girl.

"I was to find words in message in the book then send page, line and word number in letter. If I couldn't find the word, I would use numbers to replace letters, always with a clue he would give me. I thought it was good game. I guess it was not a game."

Keely wanted to hug the girl but continued through the book. Toward the back she found a single sheet of paper folded neatly. Slowly, she unfolded it. It was a copy of an email. There was nothing in the subject line. The text contained three lines in English.

Tangier. Rue de Portugal. American Female. Brown hair, brown eyes. Follow.
Determine what she has. Remove when you have finished.

The first line listed Keely's apartment and street address located in Morocco.

CHAPTER TWELVE

Keely sat quietly in the coffee shop watching Jonathan's eyes scan the lines of the email Neda had given her. After he had finished, Jonathan stared off into space for a moment, then re- read the words.

There was no ambiguity to the message. Stefan had been ordered to follow her, find out what she had-- which remained unclear-- and then he was to eliminate her.

That last bit was disturbing. Never once had she been afraid of Stefan, but the idea that his mission was to end her life was too much for her to accept. If Jonathan hadn't come along, she might not have been able to defend herself. But she knew Stefan had decided he could not carry out that order. A decision that cost him his life.

Keely looked across at Jonathan and the paper in his hand. "I can't believe Stefan would really have tried to kill me."

Jonathan glanced up at Keely briefly and half-smiled. "Glad you didn't have to find out."

Keely moved her cup around but didn't pick it up. "I came to Tangier because it seemed the best place to disappear. How did they find me?"

Jonathan laid the note down and rubbed his eyes with the heels of his hands. "We would like to think we can disappear, but there are always ways to find us. I found you because you used your passport entering Morocco. Others could have done the same."

"But how can they access passport control in Morocco?"

"In our current age, passport information is often shared with other countries, especially intelligence agencies." He studied her, thinking for a moment. "There is one other explanation. Some of my clients have this information when I believe it's necessary for security."

"Somebody had the name and number on my passport, traced me to Tangier and sent Stefan?"

"Well, he had been taking pictures of you at least a week before you met. He may have had your picture. More likely, he had your description, and you would be relatively easy to pick out of a crowd here. So, he took your photo and got confirmation from whomever hired him."

Keely caught her breath. Jonathan stared at her. "What is it?"

"About a week before I met Stefan, I had the strangest feeling someone had been in my apartment. I thought it was just paranoia, but--."

"It could have been him looking for something, something he was ordered to find you supposedly have."

Again, they sat quietly, both absorbed in thought. Finally, she spoke, more to herself than to Jonathan. "How did he get involved?"

Jonathan was sitting next to her at the table. He reached out gently to place a hand on her arm. It felt reassuring. "I've wondered that myself. Given what little I know of him, and what you've told me, he doesn't fit the profile. Maybe that's why he was sent. As to motivation, it could have been money, political, or--."

"Or what?"

"He could have been coerced. The fact he didn't go through with it suggests his heart wasn't in it. Falling in love with you was the reason he couldn't do it."

Keely turned to him. "That's the first time you've admitted he loved me."

"I doubted his sincerity. Apparently I was wrong." He stopped for a moment and studied her. "You told Stefan's mother you loved him, not that you were in love."

Keely had wanted desperately to believe she loved Stefan without reservation. But the truth was she wasn't *in* love with him. If she had been, she would have shared all her secrets with him.

But Jonathan's question started her thinking about her feelings for him. She knew there was something more than friendship between them. It wasn't because they had been intimate. It had more to do with sensing that below the surface, Jonathan had come to see her as more than a colleague. And she truly believed it scared him as much as it scared her.

As she looked at Jonathan, she realized it was not that she couldn't love; she couldn't trust. She had to keep telling herself that Jonathan Swift could never offer her the unrestricted love Stefan had.

Jonathan waited patiently until he realized she wasn't going to answer. He changed the subject. "I can't help but feel he came to Tangier under a certain amount of distress. The big question, however, is not why he came, but who sent him."

He reached for the email, examining it again. Suddenly, a look of disquiet clouded his face and he held the paper up to the light.

"What is it?"

Jonathan lowered the paper, took a pencil and small notepad out of his pocket and jotted something down, then studied it for a long moment. "Very interesting."

"What?"

He looked up as though surprised by Keely's presence. "Sorry. The address of the email-- I didn't notice at first because the ink is smudged."

Keely didn't want technicalities; she wanted answers. "What?"

Jonathan stood and walked outside, leaving her sitting there. She could see him pull out his cell phone. In a few seconds, he began talking with whomever answered. The conversation lasted less than a minute and he returned to Keely.

"What was that about?"

"Rhonda. I asked her to check on this email address."

Keely looked confused, so Jonathan continued. "It seems I've seen this kind of address before." He slid the email across the table to Keely. "Look at the name."

She picked it up and examined the address. Where she expected to see a name there was a series of ten numbers. The suffix was '@axxuster.org.'

"Am I supposed to know this?"

He leaned forward and took the email from her, pointing to the number and suffix. "It's a blind address. Meant to be untraceable and if you respond, you get your message bounced back."

"But who does it belong to?"

"Perhaps our little computer genius can tell us."

Keely sat in silence as Jonathan drank his coffee. She was tired, physically and mentally. "Are we chasing shadows?"

Jonathan looked at her. "It's one step at a time. We won't get the answers any other way."

"We could be running around for nothing. Maybe whoever sent Stefan was tying up loose ends. Maybe it is over. You told me long ago that these people didn't do things out of revenge."

Jonathan motioned to the waiter for a refill. He didn't answer until the man had come and gone. "Have you lost your need to find Stefan's killer?"

She leaned back in the seat, exhausted, and shook her head. "I don't know. I'm tired.

Knowing you've been sleeping with someone who was sent to kill you is overwhelming."

Jonathan reached for his cup of coffee. "Whoever is behind this assumes you have something that could cause serious repercussions if passed along. Apparently, Stefan did not find it. We have to assume you are still a target."

"And I still have whatever it is! So why kill Stefan?"

"He failed."

He put down the cup, never taking a drink from it. "I've been thinking about your last assignments, Switzerland and Georgia."

Jonathan gently laid his hand on top of hers. It was a protective gesture, as though he truly felt responsible for her safety. "Is there anything you remember that could lead to this?"

Keely had gone over Switzerland and Georgia a hundred times in her mind trying to figure out if she had seen something worth being killed for. As far as she was concerned, there had been nothing. "You were in Switzerland. What do you think?"

Jonathan pondered the question. "Did something happen before I arrived? You said you kept Hopler on a very loose leash."

"I did."

"What about Georgia?"

"We could have been spotted at that camp. Or maybe Niko told those guys something to save himself, but it didn't work."

"That doesn't sound worth such an elaborate scheme to get to you." His cell phone buzzed, and he answered quickly and listened intently. Shortly, he thanked Rhonda and ended the connection.

He sat for a minute staring at the phone then he looked at Keely. "I thought it looked familiar. It's one of the backdoor accounts for CIA headquarters."

"You mean that email originated at the CIA?"

"Or from someone intimately familiar with CIA computers."

"Why would they be looking for me?"

Jonathan toyed absently with the spoon in front of him. Finally, he said decisively, "The only way to find out is to ask."

"Ask who?"

"CIA, naturally. I think we have to follow this lead."

She sighed. "This is getting totally out of hand. Should we really go running around on just a whim?"

Jonathan held up two fingers. "There are two approaches. Reactive and proactive. With reactive, we wait for them to come to us, but then we are sitting ducks. With proactive, they might not see us coming. We also don't know if they have given up. I do hate to be blunt, but killing Stefan suggests they are still on the hunt.

Jonathan called for the check, paid and led Keely onto the street. More people were about as they walked toward the center of the city. They walked past the storefronts exhibiting the latest fashions, but few customers inside purchasing goods. The chilly air, even though it was late May, caused Keely to tighten her thin jacket around her. They reached their hotel and started for the elevator, but Keely stopped Jonathan and pointed toward the restaurant. Neither had eaten since early morning and although she wasn't hungry, she knew that had to keep up their strength.

Jonathan was particularly quiet during lunch and picked at his salad. Keely swallowed another bite of her grilled mushrooms with potatoes and polenta sprinkled with a thick garlic sauce, watching him off and on. She picked up a napkin, switching her fork to her other hand.

"What's bothering you?"

Jonathan put down his fork and sipped his glass of wine. "It's the CIA connection. That creates a new wrinkle. I don't think the agency's looking for you, I think someone inside may be helping, which suggests this may have been authorized."

"I don't get it."

"Until we know for sure, I have to assume that whoever is trying to find you might be doing it under orders. If that's true, we have to approach this so as not to set off any alarms."

Keely leaned back in the chair, tossing her napkin to the side. "Are you saying the CIA set me up? Why? We've done so much work for them."

"The answer to your first question is just one possible explanation, although I think it's highly unlikely. Especially since 'they', unidentified right now, would have hired Stefan and that's very unlikely given their resources already in place. As for your second question, the Agency is a big bureaucracy, where one section often has no idea what another section is doing. And it is not unheard of for them to turn on anybody if the mission requires it. Just because we've worked for them in the past doesn't make us safe. We're cannon fodder as much as those three men who killed Niko, and certainly would have killed you and Irina."

He toyed with his salad a bit more. "I had thought we might be able to do this long distance, but if this has an official sanction, we can't risk being exposed. We'll have to do this another way."

Keely cradled her face in her hands. This wasn't supposed to happen. Stefan was dead, she was on the run and Jonathan had put his career on the line. She looked up, and picked up her fork, but wasn't hungry any more. She watched as he continued to eat, wondering why he was so protective.

"You don't have to do this, you know."

He looked mystified. "But I do. Not only did I get you into this mess, but if someone is after you, they are after Swift. This is business. I have to see this through to the end."

"Meaning?"

"Meaning we go to Washington. That's where the trail leads."

Keely dropped her head into her hands. When she looked up, Jonathan could see the fatigue etched in her face. She shook her head slowly.

"Jonathan, this is too much. We could be following leads forever. When is it time to stop?"

He gave a small smile. "When it's over." He reached across and stroked her cheek. "Look, I warned you in Tangier that this wasn't going to be easy. You were in the business long enough to know things don't just fall into place like they do in detective stories. We find a lead, we follow. Sometimes we get lucky, but not always."

She touched his hand, not to push it away but for reassurance. "Will we win?"

Jonathan's smile grew bigger. "Don't we always?"

CHAPTER THIRTEEN

Colorado looked different to Keely. As the commercial flight circled the Denver airport, Keely had a hard time remembering when she had left. It seemed a million years ago.

The jet touched down and pulled into the terminal. Keely followed the crowd through the jet way toward baggage claim. As she stepped onto the escalator leading to the ground floor, she saw her father. When she reached him, he grabbed and hugged her. She didn't want him to let go.

During the flight from Timisoara to Paris, Jonathan suggested Keely spend a few days in Colorado. At first, Keely was unsure. She had come to accept Jonathan's role as her protector, but he confided that it would take several days to locate the person who originated the email.

There was no sense for her to stay in D.C.; besides the fact she may be safer in a familiar environment. They had separated in Paris. In the international terminal, Jonathan pulled Keely aside.

"This is a good move, but don't get too relaxed. It seems your pursuers have a long reach."

She hugged him, and as she held him, she whispered. "Thank you."

Now she was with her father and she felt really safe for the first time in two weeks. She released him and examined his face, shocked at how much older he appeared. His hair was grayer, and he looked tired. Suddenly, she realized how much she had missed him. She hugged him again. The tears came easily.

Her father pulled her close and patted her on the back as if she was a little girl again. Keely stepped back, collecting herself, and wiped the tears off her face with the tips of her fingers, then laughed shyly.

"Look at me, a babbling cry baby."

"I was really happy when you called. Haven't heard from you in a while. Last time you called you were somewhere in Morocco?"

"Yea, sorry I've been so bad about calling. Just trying to get my act together." He reached out and touched her hair. "What the hell did you do to your hair?" "Trying a new look."

"Well, looks okay, I guess. One good thing, it will grow back." She hugged him again. "I'm really glad to be here, Dad."

He placed his hand under her chin and tilted her face to him. For a moment, his intense look frightened Keely. Instead, he put his arm around her shoulder and led her toward the baggage carousel.

They took a taxi to Centennial municipal airport and her father checked in with the attendant. She stood staring at the runway until he joined her.

"You want to fly us home?"

"No, you better."

When they landed in Cortez, her dad led the way to the office. It still smelled of oil and dust. Keely ran her fingers along the metal counter as her father topped off two cups of coffee and handed one to her. She took a sip, anticipating the coffee to be strong, because that was the way Jim Greer drank it for as long as Keely could remember. He came around and followed her to the small waiting area and sat down heavily in one of the over-stuffed chairs.

"You look tired."

Keely looked at him, a slow smile came across her face. "Some R&R and I'll be fine."

He gulped his coffee, and then balanced the cup on his knee. "I dreamed the other night you came home."

"You mean before I called?"

He nodded his head and sipped the coffee. "How's what's his name?"

Keely wasn't surprised that he had conveniently forgotten Jonathan's name. Though he had not been happy when she had taken the job with Swift, he had finally resigned himself to it and had told her so in one of his letters.

"Jonathan. He's fine. He's the one who suggested I come here."

Jim Greer leaned back and frowned. "Is he coming later?"

"No. He's in Washington. Business." She left it at that and hoped he would not ask more.

She had not mentioned she had quit. Her father stared so hard at her that she forced a smile. Keely wondered if he could read her mind, the way she thought he could when she was a little girl.

"What is it, Dad?"

"Oh, nothing. 'Cept I was thinking you look so much like your mother. She'd be so proud of you."

Keely took another sip of the coffee to keep from losing her composure. "That's debatable."

185

He watched her a moment, then leaned forward. "Let's you and me go over to Brandell's."

"It's four in the afternoon. "

He was already on his feet. "I know what time it is. I think I can make up my own hours here. I am the boss. Besides, I'm letting McCallen take on more flights. He's due back at five, so he can lock up."

He stood up and walked to his desk, locking the file cabinet and turning off the coffee pot. He signaled her to follow and they walked outside. One of her father's Cessna was coming in for a landing.

"That's one of my new guys, Jeremy Hawkins. Let me speak to him a minute."

Keely waited by the truck while her father walked toward the taxiing plane. The comparison to her mother had unnerved her. Keely looked down at her hands. She wondered how proud her mother would be if she knew her daughter was a killer.

Brandell's hadn't changed in all the years they had been going there. As they settled into a booth near the front, a fifty-ish dishpan blonde waitress named Betty ambled over. She placed napkins and silverware in front of each of them as she spoke.

"Hey there, Jim. Back so soon?"

Her father seemed genuinely flustered but glanced up and cleared his throat. "You remember my daughter, Keely?"

"Sure. How you doing, hon? It's been a long time. Jim said you live in England now?"

Keely just nodded her head.

"He talks about you kids all the time. Your dad's a good man. What can I get you?"

Jim busied himself with the menu he knew by heart. "How 'bout bringing us two pieces of blueberry pie."

"Sure thing. Good seein' you again, Keely. I'll bring you some coffee in just a sec." She winked at Jim as she walked away.

Keely smiled. "I think I was in high school when she started here. You two seemed to have gotten awfully friendly."

He looked across at her. "Hey, I like the food here. Besides, since Collin joined the service, not much need to cook just for me."

"What happened to that girl he was dating? Think he'll get married?"

"I think she scared him. Too intense."

"Intense? Is that your word or Collin's?"

"Mine. Collin doesn't need to get married yet. He did the right thing to join up. He's got a real good job. They'll probably keep him at Mather his whole tour. Another Air Force type like his big sister."

"Well, at least he's away from all that craziness in the Middle East."

Betty brought two cups to the table and poured the coffee from a battered pot. "I know your dad's glad to have you home. How long you here for?"

"I actually haven't decided yet. It depends."

Suddenly Keely didn't want to talk about why she was there or how long she'd stay. She knew the woman was only making conversation, but Keely shifted in her seat uncomfortably and changed the subject. "Could you bring me some ice cream with my slice?"

"Sure thing." Betty winked again at Jim. "I guess our movie's off, huh? That's okay. You enjoy visiting with your daughter. Call me later."

Jim Greer cleared his throat as she walked away and looked timidly at Keely whose face broke into a grin.

"Date?"

He flapped his hand as if to brush away her comment. "Nothing like that. We just see a movie together now and then, share a dinner or two."

"I think that's wonderful. You should go out; see people. You're entitled."

"Thanks for the permission."

Keely turned serious. "I don't think Mom would want you sitting home alone."

"I'm not alone," he said defensively. "I just enjoy Betty's company. She makes me laugh. She wants to be an actress."

Keely nearly choked on the coffee she had just swallowed. "Actress?"

"Don't laugh. She's been in two plays at the library. She's part of a group that puts on plays they write themselves."

"I'm not being critical, Dad. I just-- how old is she?"

"Now, I haven't asked her that. That wouldn't be proper."

"You're right. Sorry. Age doesn't matter."

"And what's wrong with her wanting to be an actress?"

"Nothing. Don't be so defensive. I say more power to her."

Betty returned with the plates and put them down. "Anything else you need, just holler."

Keely picked up her fork and took a bite of the pie. "Not bad. I see they still know how to make a crust." She looked up at her dad who smiled.

He chewed on his food a minute then put down his fork and picked up his coffee. "Now, that's better."

"Yeah, this place always had great coffee."

"No, I meant you."

Keely stopped chewing. "Me?"

"You seem more like yourself now. A minute ago, you told Betty 'it depends' when she asked you how long you'd be here. What does it depend on?"

"I said I hadn't decided how long."

"Same difference."

"I was making conversation."

"Okay. Then let me ask you. How long you staying?"

"Ready for me to leave already?"

Jim took a deep breath and picked up a fork. "Far as I'm concerned, you never have to leave."

Keely pushed the pie around on her plate for a moment. Jim shoveled in another forkful. After a minute, he stopped and looked at her. "Remember I said I dreamed about you? You were very sad and crying. What really brought you home, Keely girl?"

Memories of her childhood brought on her tears. She reached for the napkin and dabbed her eyes. "Just wanted to be home."

Her father reached across the table and held her hand, concerned. "Want to leave?"

Keely nodded, and Jim stood up reaching for his wallet. He walked over to the counter.

Keely went outside. Jim followed minutes later with two 'to-go' boxes. By the time they had driven the three miles back to the house, Keely had regained her composure and wished she hadn't lost it like that. She knew it would open up a subject she couldn't face.

Keely followed behind her dad as he unlocked the door. He excused himself and took the boxed food to the kitchen. Keely looked around the room. It was as if she had never left.

Newspapers lay scattered near the couch where her father would sit and read. He was determined to read every article. The only problem was they piled up until they would topple over. A blanket was thrown casually over the back of the sofa where he often fell asleep with the television going. A basket full of laundry occupied the chair closest to the hallway door.

Her father returned with two glasses in hand. "Here. The latest batch."

She tasted the homemade blackberry wine and winced. "I think you've outdone yourself."

Jim sat in the recliner next to the chair. "I remember the time you and Collin-- and maybe Seth-- drank the better part of a gallon of my best."

Keely laughed and sat across from him on the couch. "Seth put us up to that. He said it was grape juice. That's also the time he swore to us we were adopted. Keely laughed again. "I remember how sick we were the next day. I remember you sitting on my bed and telling me if you ever caught me pulling that again, you'd tie me to a propeller and fly to Denver."

The smiles and laughter faded. Her father put his glass on the table. "You ready to tell me what's wrong?"

Keely looked over at her dad, knowing it would be pointless to avoid explaining her visit any longer. She twisted the base of the glass around in her palm, collecting her thoughts before she spoke.

"I met somebody. He was so…." Tears rolled down her cheeks, but Keely didn't wipe them away, "I thought he loved me. His name was Stefan." The tears choked her suddenly and she turned up the glass for a swallow to wash them away.

"Sounds pretty serious. What about Jonathan?"

"Jonathan was my boss, Dad," hoping her denial didn't sound shallow, "I'm not involved with him."

"Okay. This Stefan, you're talking about him like it's over now. You two broke up?"

Keely stood up and walked around the small room, but then sat back down. When she spoke, the voice sounded like it belonged to someone else. "Somebody killed him because of me."

Her father's face registered uncertainty. "Killed him?"

"He was protecting me."

"From what? From who?"

"I don't know, Dad." Keely stood up again; crossed her arms and walked to the window. "I quit Swift. Actually, I ran away from it." She glanced over at her father and could see a look that said he approved.

"That's good news, Keely. How come you didn't let me know?"

"Don't take this wrong, Dad, but I needed to be alone. I didn't recognize myself anymore. Things had gotten very complicated in my life. I went to Morocco. I just wanted to be somewhere no one would find me for a while. I guess I thought if I could stay there long enough, I could get everything back in some kind of order. Then, I met Stefan. We became inseparable. He became a lifeline for me and brought me back to my senses. I started to feel human again."

Keely wiped the tears off her cheeks and looked at her father. He was waiting for her to continue. She looked back out the window.

"Then Jonathan showed up. He said I was in some sort of danger, but he didn't know what. When he found out I had met someone, he wouldn't leave. I pleaded with him to go back to London and leave me alone, but he was suspicious of Stefan."

Keely turned and sat down in a chair near the window and clasped her hands in her lap and leaned forward. She swallowed hard and continued.

"Jonathan told me he thought Stefan may not be who he said he was. We went to an apartment he had in Gibraltar that I didn't know about and that's when we found him-- dead."

The phone rang and Keely jumped, her heart racing from the sudden noise. Her dad quickly got up and answered the phone, then hung up almost immediately.

"Damn salesman." He turned back to her but didn't sit down. "What made Jonathan suspicious?"

"Instinct, I guess. And he has ears everywhere. We found out Stefan was actually ordered to find me."

Her father sat down. "By who?"

She shook her head. "Someone who thinks I have something important."

"This why Jonathan's in Washington?"

She nodded, and not able to get comfortable, stood up, but remained at the window. "Once he decided to go to Washington, he suggested I come see you. He'll call when he finds what he's looking for."

Her father scooted forward on his seat and spoke after a moment. "I'm glad you're home safe, Keely. I think you should consider not going back. Let Swift handle this. It's more his racket, anyway."

She smiled weakly. "It's not that simple, Dad. I have to find who killed Stefan."

"Why?"

"Whoever hired Stefan is very likely still after me. And I owe it to him."

"You don't owe anything to somebody who put you in harm's way. I don't like it." He stood up. "I didn't like it when you told me the things you were up to. Going around spyin' on people-- it's not right."

Suddenly she was weary and didn't have the energy to defend herself or Swift. Besides, her dad was right.

"I need to lay down a while, Dad. Do you mind?"

He lost his scowl. "You don't have to ask. Your room's in the same place it's always been. Get some rest. When you wake up, we'll talk some more if you want."

Keely walked over to her dad and hugged him. "I'm sorry, Dad. I didn't come home to lay all this on you."

"I'd been disappointed if you'd left me out. I'm just glad you're all right. I still want you to consider staying."

She kissed him again and turned to go down the hall to her old room. She stopped and turned before she went in. "Dad? You won't leave, will you?"

"Honey, I'll be right here when you wake up."

Keely had not realized how tired she was but found it impossible to sleep soundly. She would awaken from a dream to the sound of clattering dishes in the distance. It would take her a second to remember where she was, that she was safe, and she would close her eyes again.

She was roused by the television and her father's quiet laughter. The smell of sage and thyme drifted in the air and somehow she knew her father had a meal in the oven. It was comforting, and she drifted back to sleep.

When Keely finally awoke, she had no idea how long she had slept. Thoughts of Jonathan in Washington suddenly popped into her head, and she wondered briefly if he would be able to uncover any useful information. It seemed like they were going around in circles. But she knew that following the smallest lead might pay great dividends. It was useless to berate herself for what had happened. The past could never be change. Only the future could.

Jonathan had said very little to her during their flight from Romania. At times, he had smiled at her sympathetically. She wondered if he knew how it felt to lose someone like Stefan, but Jonathan's compassion had been puzzling; as if he let his guard down and genuinely cared. Jonathan remained as much a mystery to her as he had the day he came to Cortez.

She threw her pillow across the room and sat up. If she had never gone to work for Jonathan, she'd never have found Stefan. But she wouldn't have cost him his life. She swung her feet off the bed. She thought about calling Jonathan and telling him to go on without her, but she knew she couldn't stop until she found Stefan's killer.

Her father sat on the sofa, his feet propped up, reading the newspaper. He folded it in half, tossing it when he saw Keely come down the hall. "Well, did you get any sleep?"

Nodding, she dragged herself toward the sofa and sat down beside him. He put his arm around her and drew her near. She rested her head on his chest.

"I'm glad. I made us some supper."

It was dark outside. "What time is it?"

"Ten."

"Why didn't you go ahead and eat?"

"I couldn't eat without my Keely girl. What kind of father would I be? Besides, it isn't often I get to fuss over you, is it?"

She lifted her head from his chest and looked at him, then kissed his cheek. "I love you, Dad. Just in case you forgot."

He smiled at her and looked embarrassed. "Come on, you got to keep your strength up. Let me make you a plate."

They both got up and went into the kitchen. Her father picked up a pair of potholders and reached in the oven for the hot covered dish.

"I made stew, the way you like it."

He removed the lid and aroma from the meat, potatoes, carrots, and onions permeated the air. Her mouth watered and she realized she was actually hungry for the first time in days.

He bent over and pulled another pan from the top rack. "And I made biscuits."

"Well, you have been busy, haven't you?"

191

He set the food on the table and sat down across from her. "Maybe I'm trying to make you want to stay."

Keely said nothing. Instead she got up and poured each of them a cup of coffee. She returned to the table and put his down near him. Then she slid into the seat and picked up her fork. After a couple of bites, she laid the fork down, looking at the plate.

"I need to tell you all of it, Dad."

"What's that, honey?"

"What made me leave Swift."

He stopped chewing and looked across the table. He laid his fork down, swallowing the bite of food in his mouth. "Okay."

Keely chose not to tell him about the banker in Switzerland. She wasn't sure she could tell her father how that man had died.

"Two people in the Republic of Georgia were supposed to find something. I went to help things along. We headed into the mountains and stumbled onto this family-- husband, wife, and two kids. The man had seen some trucks parked at a place not far from their farm. He led us to the place. They were what we were looking for. I sent one of my people back to report. I stayed behind to keep an eye on things."

She cast a glance at her untouched food. "Early the next morning, I decided to take another look. While I watched, the area was rocketed. That was not supposed to happen. When I got back to the farm…."

Keely stopped and brought her head up to look at her father. His expression showed he understood. He finished for her. "The family had been murdered."

Tears escaped easily but she didn't bother to brush it away. "Three armed men were in the yard and they shot my friend like an animal."

For a moment they sat in silence, their eyes never leaving each other. More tears spilled down her cheeks. "Without thinking, I shot them. It wasn't self-defense; it was anger."

Her father's face paled, but he said nothing.

"That's when I decided I'd had enough. I drove to Tbilisi and called Jonathan to tell him I quit. Then I went to Tangier."

Keely stood and walked over to the counter, looking out the window over the sink. "You said mom would be proud of me. I doubt it. Nothing can change what I've become."

Her father pushed back his chair and came over to her. He wrapped his bear-like arms around her and held her tight. "Sounds to me like you had no other choice. If they'd seen you, they'd have killed you, too."

"You don't understand. I could have escaped. They wouldn't have found me. Instead, I gunned them down. Which makes me no better than they were."

"I don't know about that. I'm not saying it was right, but--."

Keely pulled away and walked back to her chair. She shook her head and turned toward him. "The only thing I could think of when I found Stefan dead was that I was going to kill the person who did that to him."

He watched her carefully. "Lots of people want to take revenge when they lose someone. Hell, I wanted to kill the doctors after your mother died."

"Dad, the difference is, I have it in me to actually kill someone."

Her father walked the few steps and stood behind his daughter, resting his hands gently on her shoulders. "It's not your fault. You're not like that." His tone became authoritative. "I don't want you to go back.""

She leaned against him. "I know. But I must. And I am like that."

"No. This is Swift's doing. You're kind and compassionate, Keely. You're not killer."

"No one made me pull the trigger. I really thought I could never kill someone. I was wrong." Then she began to sob.

She didn't know how long they had stayed there, her father's tender voice saying everything would be all right. Soon, her tears ended, and she allowed him to lead her back to her room where he tucked her into bed. Keely felt like a small child again. It was part of the reason she knew she had to come back to Cortez. She needed to remember who she had been and where she had come from.

Her father turned off the light. "Things always look different in the morning. You'll see."

She could see her father's outline in the doorway, then he softly closed her door.

Morning light trickled through the rippling curtains, blown by a gentle mountain breeze. She watched them quiver in the chill morning air, much like the leaves on the aspen trees that covered the mountains. She sat up in bed, brushing her hair back with her fingers. It had been a good night's sleep-- there had been no dreams. She picked up the alarm clock on the nightstand.

It was a little past nine. She had not slept that long in years. Her overnight bag was on the dresser, and she fished out a change of clothes and went into the bathroom across the hall.

The hot water seemed to wash away some of the anguish of the previous night. She toweled dry and put on fresh clothes. Her hair still wet, she wrapped it in the towel and came out.

"Dad?"

"In here."

He was at the kitchen table writing out bills. "Taking care of some business. Get some coffee. I haven't made any breakfast yet; trying to get this done first."

"Go ahead. I'll make something."

"Coffee's fine for me. Heat up those biscuits from last night."

"I'm not really hungry." She sat down and watched him.

He put the lid on his pen and closed the bankbook. "I've been thinking about what you said last night. I'm scared for you, Keely."

She attempted a laugh. "So am I."

"You said there's still somebody after you, but you don't have any idea why?"

Keely was embarrassed. She didn't want to explain about the banker in Zurich. "No. Jonathan seems to think it might have something to do with a past assignment." "I still think you should stay here where you're safe."

"But I'm not safe, Dad, until I know who's after me. I'm a sitting duck. If they could find me in Morocco, they can find me here. That puts you in danger. I can't do that."

"That's the least of my worries. I don't like what's happened to you. You've changed, Keely. That scares me more. Even if you don't come back here, don't go back to that life. Get as far away as you can from people like Jonathan."

"I'm not sure if I know how, Dad."

"Yes, you do. You just walk away."

"This is not the kind of thing you walk away from. You always taught me to stand up to my fears."

"Honey, that wasn't the kind of fear I was talking about. I didn't teach you to put yourself in harm's way."

"Dad, you have to understand. If I don't find these people, I'll never find peace no matter where I go."

"You willing to risk losing yourself?"

Keely was never going to convince her dad. She reached across the table and placed her hand over his. He sat a moment longer looking intently at her, then reached under his bankbook and pulled out a slip of paper, handing it to her, almost reluctantly.

"You left your cell out here and it rang while you were sleeping. I answered but didn't want to wake you and I told him so."

She didn't understand until she saw the name her father had scribbled. 'Jonathan.'

Keely was glad the first-class section of the United flight from Denver to Washington was virtually empty. She knew she couldn't handle idle chatter for the four-hour flight. She stared out the window as the plane lifted off, the snow-capped mountains a dramatic backdrop for the sprawling city.

Keely's father had insisted on flying her to Denver. She had packed quickly, and they arrived at her father's airstrip just as the mechanic was topping off the fuel tank. As they approached the plane, her father pointed toward the pilot's side.

"You fly."

It had been over a year since Keely had sat in the pilot's seat and the take-off was less than spectacular. But as they rose to cruising altitude, the feel of the stick helped Keely relax.

Her father had not said much, but finally he turned to her. "I don't like this, Keely. I think you're wrong to go back. I see what all this has done to you and I can't imagine how walking back into it will help."

In a way, Keely had to agree with her father. But she also knew that the ghosts of the past would continue to haunt her until she found closure. And finding Stefan's killer was part of that process.

"Dad, I love you for being concerned, but this is just something I have to do. If it's any comfort to you, I am through with Swift. Please don't worry."

He didn't look convinced, but he dropped the subject.

They landed at Centennial Municipal Field, and her father offered to ride to the airport with her, but she suggested he return to Cortez.

"I'll be okay. Don't worry."

"Don't ever tell a father not to worry. It's what we do for a living. I may not have shown it-- to you or your brothers-- but I still constantly worry that you all are safe and happy."

She threw her arms around him and buried her face in his neck. "You're wrong, Dad. You always have been there for us, and I've never doubted you loved me. Thank you for that. And for being here now."

With that, she kissed him goodbye and headed for the taxi that would take her to the Denver airport.

It was dark and drizzly as she deplaned at Washington's National Airport. She was surprised Jonathan was waiting for her. When she reached him, he gently bent forward and kissed her on the cheek, taking her overnight bag. There was an expression in his eyes that Keely read as relief.

"You look worried. Thought I wasn't coming back?"

"To be honest, I wasn't sure." He took her by the elbow. "Sorry to cut your visit short, but I believe I have found something."

They made their way out of the airport and to the Metro station. Jonathan hated driving in Washington, although he had a rental car at the hotel. He said the drivers were too eager to play bumper cars. He always stayed at the Omni Shoreham, which had a Metro stop one block away. They made their way in silence, Keely glad that Jonathan was not in a talkative mood.

195

In the cavernous lobby of the Shoreham, Keely walked toward the registration desk, but Jonathan took her arm and led her toward the elevators.

"Thought it would be more judicious if you did not register."

He led her to the end of the hall on the fifth floor, opening the door only after checking a tiny slip of paper he had secured just below the lock. It was his way of insuring no one had entered the room while he was gone.

Inside, Keely realized he had taken a junior suite with bedroom and sitting room. He carried her bag into the bedroom, returned and headed for a service cart with a bottle of scotch, ice, and a variety of snacks.

"We're going to splurge a bit. I'll tack this on to some future CIA bill. You will have the bedroom; I'll take the couch. It's actually quite comfortable."

Keely went into the bedroom, dropping her jacket on one of the twin beds. She kicked off her shoes and stretched her neck working out some of the tension. When she returned to the sitting room, Jonathan had prepared each of them a drink. She accepted hers and downed half of it, then slumped on the couch.

"Who is it?"

Jonathan finished his drink and made himself another. Then he walked to the chair facing the couch and sat down casually, as though at a cocktail party.

"He is in Operations Management. They are the folks who pay our bills, by the way. Handles contractors. Anyway, the email address was a cut-out assigned to his department. What happens is that the address is only used once or twice then discarded. Makes it almost impossible to determine who used it, but I was able to persuade a friend to trace the account."

"What's his name?"

"Arnold Schwiller. I've made discrete inquiries. He seems clean on the surface. However, our Mr. Schwiller apparently has a Swiss bank account, which happens to be in his mother's maiden name. By the way, his mother's dead. Has a balance in the low six figures, which means, based on his salary, he is either very frugal or he has some other sources of income. We will find out when we pay him a visit tomorrow."

Keely finished her drink as Jonathan related his information. She stood and walked over to the bar setting her glass down on the counter.

"Is there any way to tie this guy to one of the assignments?"

"I checked with Rhonda. Schwiller has handled a number of our contracts, which certainly gives him access to our information."

Keely returned to the couch. Though it was late afternoon, the day was catching up to her and all she wanted to do was curl up in bed and forget the world. "How do we get to him?"

"Schwiller likes to lunch alone. We'll join him for a little chat."

196

Keely watched Jonathan for a long moment. Her opinion of Jonathan had undergone a change since he'd shown up in Tangier. She was seeing a side of him she never thought he would have allowed. Keely had been moved when he admitted his worry that she wouldn't return. She could almost believe he actually regretted her leaving, but he still hid behind his baffling British reserve. She stood and walked over to his seat, bending down and kissing his cheek.

"Thank you. For caring." She headed toward the bedroom and turned at the door. "Look, I want to tell you something. I'm sorry I was such a bitch when you came to warn me. And, I know it's not your fault about what happened to Stefan."

She started into the room, not wanting to hear any reply from him, but stopped suddenly and turned back. "You don't have to sleep on the sofa. Take the other bed."

Langley, Virginia, is carved out of rolling farmland like the dozens of bedroom communities surrounding the ever-expanding DC area. It is the model of suburbia replete with crowded roads and strip shopping centers jammed tightly between redundant sub-divisions.

Jonathan and Keely had been inside Schwiller's favorite restaurant for almost a half hour when Schwiller came through the door. Jonathan had gotten a description of him from one of his contacts in the agency. He was a mousy little man in his early fifties in a cheap, gray suit. His thick glasses looked smudged, and as he made his way toward the counter, he looked as though he could be frightened by his own shadow.

After he picked up his sandwich, he found a seat at a free booth, sitting with his back to Keely and Jonathan. They wandered over to where he was sitting. Keely pushed her way in beside Schwiller as Jonathan slid in across from him, smiling disarmingly.

"Hope you don't mind us joining you, Arnold. My, that corned beef looks good."

Schwiller looked at the two of them, and then turned to Jonathan. "Do I know you?"

Jonathan continued to smile and leaned forward, his voice soothing. "Not personally. But your organization often uses our services. However, today, we need information from you."

Schwiller eased back against his seat. "You're contractors?"

Jonathan gave a quick and easy nod and placed his hands palm down on the table. "I'll be brief. Seems my friend here was a topic of an email you sent a while back. We were curious why you sent it."

Schwiller's expression remained blank as he glanced again at Keely and back to Jonathan. "I send emails out all the time--you think I remember all of them?"

197

"You sent one to an address in Romania about six or seven weeks ago. It directed the recipient to locate someone at a specific address in Tangier, to follow that person and to remove her, if necessary."

The man's brow furrowed as he looked between the two of them. "I still can't help you."

Jonathan raised his hand for silence. "Interestingly, a friend of mine has access to bank accounts in Bern. Fascinating the kind of information you can get from friends."

Jonathan pulled out a piece of paper from his jacket pocket and read. "Do the numbers 7-3-1-2-0-9-8 mean anything? Seems it's the account of a Mrs. Ida Otterbein. Isn't that your mother? My condolences on her death."

Schwiller stiffened, but his expression did not change. Jonathan continued.

"If you'll just give me the name of the individual who requested the email, I'm sure I could forget that account exists. Then you can return to your lunch." He took a potato chip off the man's plate.

Schwiller was not as easily rattled as he appeared. He looked at Keely; his eyes said he was calculating his options. He took his time answering. "I still don't know what you're talking about."

"Just take a look at the email. Maybe it will jog your memory." Jonathan reached into an inside pocket and pulled out the paper. He carefully unfolded it and laid it flat on the table where Schwiller could see.

Schwiller shifted and leaned forward, unwilling to touch the paper in front of him. "Look, I just do my job. I'm sorry, as trite as that sounds, but it is just business."

Keely could see Jonathan's jaw tighten; he said nothing.

Schwiller glanced at the page, then at Jonathan. "It's not my job to look out for you."

Keely felt mortified to be put in the same category as the people who killed Stefan, but inside she had to admit there was a certain logic to what the man said. To him, they were nothing more than guns for hire.

Jonathan suddenly picked up a fork and sunk it into Schwiller's hand hard enough to get the man's attention, but not break the skin. Schwiller winced. "You have made me unhappy, Arnold. Now either you tell me who told you to send that email or I'm obliged to pass along this bank account information to your boss. After all, business is business. I'm sure your superiors would be curious how you amassed several hundred thousand dollars on your salary." Jonathan dug the fork in deeper. "But then you may not be in shape to care what happens to you."

Schwiller's expression turned a bit more panicky with the pain. "Okay. Okay."

Jonathan withdrew the fork. "I'm listening."

Schwiller massaged his hand and looked across the table at Jonathan. "But no one can know where you got this information. I could be in deep shit."

Jonathan smiled. "You already are."

Schwiller paled. "I got a message from one of our contractors. I've done some stuff for him in the past. He asked me to search for info on a job in Georgia at the end of May. We didn't have anything, but I checked with State, Defense and NSA and found your report. I thought it was just some disagreement between contractors. You guys are always after each other. I try to keep you people happy."

"And?"

"And I sent him the report. Couple days later, he sent that, and I relayed to that address."

"Who's the contractor?"

Schwiller hesitated and Jonathan twirled the fork.

"Guy calls himself Kestrel."

CHAPTER FOURTEEN

Keely sipped her scotch slowly, savoring the warmth that spread through her body. She had been sitting in the living room of the Omni Shoreham suite for more than an hour. The fading light through the French doors coloring the sky shades of blue and pink. She walked to the doors, opened them and walked on to the balcony. She could hear the traffic on Connecticut Avenue, but it was muffled by the expanse of Rock Creek Park that wrapped itself around the hotel. Below she could see cars pulling up to the entrance, but in the distance, the forest lay in ever deepening shadow. The air was surprisingly dry and cool for Washington in May, and Keely wished she could walk into the woods below and never come out. But she also knew that wouldn't help.

Jonathan had spent the better part of that hour in the bedroom on the phone to Rhonda in England. The meeting with Arnold Schwiller had been disconcerting for both of them. After he had told them that Kestrel-- the illusive gun dealer whose shipment had been destroyed in Georgia and who probably ordered the attack on the farmhouse-- had requested the information about Keely, things began to fall into place.

Schwiller said the CIA had used Kestrel to move arms into areas where American client groups were fighting, especially in Syria. Kestrel fell out of favor after he was caught selling arms to Serbian paramilitary forces in Kosovo. But he had not been 'sanctioned'-- a euphemism in the Agency that meant he had been marked for elimination. Schwiller saw no harm in passing along information about Keely.

Jonathan asked Schwiller if Kestrel had asked about Keely specifically, but Schwiller insisted that Kestrel had only asked for the agent involved in a covert air strike in Georgia.

Schwiller tracked down a copy of the incident report Jonathan had filed. The CIA had been copied on it. The NSA liked to rub its sister agency's nose in trouble. Keely had been listed as the field agent in charge. He had found Keely had entered Morocco and used the country's *Deuxième Bureau* to get her street address. He swore he didn't know who received it or what it meant.

Although Stefan's friend had told them he was mixed up in something shady, Keely found it hard to believe that Stefan was connected to Kestrel. Was it possible Stefan had also been part of the weapons deal in Georgia?

Jonathan returned to the sitting room, prepared himself a drink and joined Keely on the balcony.

"Lovely evening." He sipped his drink then looked at Keely. "Tell me about Georgia."

Trying to hold her emotions at bay, Keely recounted what she had done from the time she arrived in Georgia until she returned to Tbilisi and called Jonathan.

"I was angry. You said the job was simple reconnaissance, but when they rocketed the trucks, I thought you had lied to me." For a moment, Keely wondered if she read disappointment in his expression.

He stared into the dusk. "Originally, the contract had only been to locate the trucks. But our friends at the NSA got nervous and decided it was too risky to let the shipment go through.

Apparently, there was an inter-agency squabble going on. NSA never told the CIA about its intentions until after the air strike." He slowly raised the glass to his lips. "Believe me. Had I known that was going to happen, I would not have sent you."

Keely knew that intelligence agencies competed, even when they were from the same country. But their silly games often cost innocent lives. She turned to Jonathan and studied him. Despite all that had happened, she believed that he had not deliberately sent her into harm's way.

"I believe you."

Jonathan looked up from his drink and turned to her, a slight smile on his lips. "Thank you." He returned to the sitting room.

Keely followed, leaving the doors opened. "Kestrel had Schwiller locate the report to see who else might have been there. The question is, how did he know it was the Americans?"

Jonathan smiled. "We're the only ones with the ability to strike like that. He must have been around when the trucks were hit and surmised that somebody had to direct the attack."

"Irina was supposed to call you when she got to Tbilisi. What did you tell her?"

Jonathan walked over to the bar and started to refill his glass. He turned back with a look of surprise.

"I didn't hear from her until a couple of days after you called."

201

"What do you mean? When I thought my sat phone wasn't working, I sent her with the coordinates."

He sat down, staring at his drink. "No, it was after the raid."

"You mean that bitch left us up there?"

"Seems you ruffled her feathers quite a bit. She didn't have many flattering things to say about you-- called you an amateur." Jonathan glanced at Keely. "She hung up on me before I could get any significant details. She only wanted to know if she would get--."

"Paid." Keely finished his sentence. "Arrogant bitch."

Jonathan laughed quietly and then sipped his drink. "Irina is only concerned about Irina."

Images of the farmhouse in the murderous aftermath flashed in Keely's mind as she had recounted her story to Jonathan. She had tried to eradicate those memories, but they could not be purged. She shuddered.

"The children affected me most. There was no reason to kill them. I put them in harm's way. My suggestion we camp there. My suggestion to involve Vali."

Jonathan sat back down next to her. "You can't blame yourself for what evil people do."

He settled back against the sofa. "You said when the gunmen came out of the house, they were questioning Niko. Kestrel must have assumed Niko wasn't alone. Asking if there was anyone other than the family with him."

Keely nodded. "Maybe Niko told them he was it, to protect me, so they killed him. Maybe later somebody else went back to the farmhouse, saw their guys dead and realized there was someone else. Me."

"Or Irina." He stood up and walked across the room. "However, the email message specified you, and something you have-- an item, perhaps? Did you pick up anything at the camp? Anything at all?"

Keely didn't answer. She got up, went to her purse took out her wallet. She searched the compartments until she found a scrap of paper and carried it back to Jonathan. He opened it and looked at the scrawled marks she had copied at the truck park.

"What is this?"

"I got that off one of the crates in the truck."

"This was on the crate?"

"Yes. Thought a label might be useful. Is it Russian?"

"Georgian." He took out his cell phone. "Looks like we will have to go back to where all this began-- Georgia."

Keely took a step away from him. "No. I can't go back there."

Jonathan walked to her and escorted her to the window. "Come, look at the sunset."

Keely looked at him in wonder. "Are you kidding? Sunsets? I don't want to ever see that place again. We know Kestrel is looking for me. Why can't we get to him?"

Jonathan turned to look at the setting sun. "Believe me, it's not that easy. A number of folks have been chasing him for years without success. That's why I think we can pick up his trail in Georgia."

"How about the CIA?"

Jonathan finally looked at her. "Remember, the agency hired him in the past. And although they have cut him out, doesn't mean they won't go back in the future. No, they won't care. This is something we have to do ourselves."

He stood and walked toward the bedroom, "I'll have Rhonda make the arrangements."

"I haven't said I'll go."

Jonathan hesitated, his hand stroking his jaw. He didn't face her. "Of course, you will. You can't give up until you know who killed Stefan. Isn't that true?"

Keely stiffened. When she didn't answer, he continued into the bedroom.

"I'll also see if she can track down Irina. She should be warned that Kestrel may be looking for her; her name's in that report as well."

Keely walked back to the French doors as Jonathan made his call. Night had settled over the area and Keely could see the lights of houses in the distance. She felt lost and confused, and she wished that the trail would not lead back to the farmhouse. Jonathan knew her all too well, that she had made the commitment to herself to see this to its end, and if the trail led there, then so be it.

Jonathan joined her back by the window. "We fly out tomorrow through Amsterdam."

She bowed her head, tears fell down her cheeks.."

Jonathan faced her, turning her as he took her hands.. "I know this is painful. I know you would rather this all go away. But we started this for your protection and to avenge Stefan, and possibly the other deaths in Georgia. Too late to stop."

She looked at him. "I know."

They sat in darkness as the jumbo jet made its way from Washington to Amsterdam, the first leg of their trip to Tbilisi. Despite the comfortable first-class seats on British Airways, Keely turned every which way fitfully. Jonathan had chosen to either ignore it or hadn't noticed her fidgetiness-- at least, he had made no comment. As the rest of the passengers settled in to watch the in-flight movie or catch some sleep, Keely looked over at Jonathan, his eyes closed. The last few days had been tense for both of them, and Keely knew the tension would not diminish until they had answers.

Without really thinking, she rested her hand lightly on his. He opened his eyes and looked at her questioningly but did not withdraw his hand. She studied his face for a moment.

Keely didn't know how to approach what she wanted to say, but the past and the future both required it. "When you first arrived in Tangier, were you jealous when you found out about Stefan?"

He raised his eyebrows and smiled. "Always the romantic."

"Not an answer."

"I can assure you I was not jealous."

"Then, how would you explain your reaction to Stefan?"

"Suspicion." He gave his patented quirky smile. "I came to Tangier because I believed you might be in danger. Stefan seemed out of place."

"I think it was more."

"I felt you had become too involved too quickly with someone you hardly knew."

"It amazes me that you can't just say that you have feelings for me. Nobody puts his life on the line for a... business associate."

He reached with his free hand to brush back a curl that had fallen across her eyes. "Don't misread what I say, but affection is a luxury I cannot afford. Right now, neither can you."

He withdrew his hand gently and closed his eyes again. Keely nudged him in the arm. "Have you ever been in love?"

"No," he said with eyes still closed.

"I don't believe you."

Jonathan's jaw tightened, then relaxed. He opened his eyes and looked at the small screen as though turning his attention to flight details. Finally, after what seemed to Keely a very long time, he turned to her.

"Under other circumstances, I would stand by my answer. But these are unusual circumstances, and I believe you deserve a more complete explanation. Her name was Geetha. She was Indian, working in the South African Department of Defense. Low-level clerk. However, she also did some freelance work for British Intelligence. I was in South Africa on business and a friend introduced us. She was quite beautiful and quite taken with helping a 'spy.' We saw each other on and off for several months. I found myself accepting more assignments that would take me to Johannesburg. I even suggested she come work for me in England."

Keely looked at him carefully, but he did not react to the irony.

"After a while, I noticed that we were being followed. At first, I thought it might be Security Forces keeping tabs on a foreigner. But whoever was following us was too expert to be regular police.

"One evening, we returned to her home and after I left her, I watched the house for more than an hour. There was nobody. The next morning, she was found in her garage. She had been beaten severely, raped repeatedly and her throat slashed.

"The police claimed it was done by some right-wing Afrikaners, to teach a 'non-white' girl not to associate with a white. I didn't believe it. My guess is that some agency wanted to ensure that Geetha did not pass along information to me. Her death was a warning to me that I was not wanted in South Africa. They must have assumed that the death of a 'colored' would not be investigated too thoroughly."

Keely felt embarrassed for having wanted him to reveal what must have been a devastating experience. "Did you love her?"

Jonathan looked out the window at the black sky. "Love is such an obtuse word. It is too easily used as a weapon or an excuse." He looked back at her.

Keely waited for him to continue.

"It's true that I wasn't as forthcoming about this work as I should have been. I knew after Zurich that you were not meant to be in this business."

Keely stared straight ahead. Jonathan was right. The glamour of the job had disappeared on that cold road outside Zurich, and she knew that was the end for her. But he was wrong to assume so much responsibility for her. She had decided to go to Georgia, and although on one level she blamed Jonathan for the killings at that farmhouse, she had been horrified when she realized how easy is was for her to kill again.

Jonathan brought Keely back from her thoughts. "Were you in love with Stefan?"

She had been wrestling with that very question since his death. She had told Stefan she loved him, but it was not that simple. She started this journey to avenge her lost love and protect herself. But Keely had come to realize there was more to it than that. She had worried that her feelings for Stefan had been based on the fact he seemed to love her with such passion. And that realization made her feel guilty because he apparently gave his life for that love.

Mixed with those feelings were her feelings for Jonathan. She had despised him for showing up in Tangier, for re-entering her life just when she thought she was coming out from under a dark cloud. But being around him had rekindled the emotions she had tried-- sometimes unsuccessfully-- to keep at bay. She looked at him, wondering if he, too, had tried to figure out their tangled relationship.

"I thought I loved him, or at least the person he pretended to be. Now, I think I was just amazed that someone could love me."

"Don't be so hard on yourself. You may think you are 'damaged goods.' You'll get past that. As for Stefan, he must have cared for you." Jonathan leaned forward. "You have to forget about revenging Stefan."

She looked at him for a long moment. "Then why should I be chasing a phantom around the world?"

"Self preservation."

He looked at her for a long moment, smiled gently, laid his head back and closed his eyes.

The Tbilisi airport was just as crowded and chaotic as Keely remembered. There seemed to be more men and women in business clothes milling about, perhaps Europeans and Americans rushing to get a foothold in the country as it worked its way into a world power. The line through Customs took about twenty minutes. Once they gained the main terminal, Jonathan searched the crowd.

"If Rhonda was able to contact Irina, she should be here."

They both scanned the faces surrounding the exit, but neither located the tall blonde. Finally, Jonathan motioned for Keely to follow and they worked their way to a corner that was less trafficked.

"Wait here, I'll call Rhonda and find out what's going on."

He stepped away and took out his cell phone. He tried several times to dial but came back frustrated. "I must remember to charge this damn thing."

He handed the cell to Keely and worked his way across the lobby floor to a telephone kiosk. Keely watched as he negotiated with the young woman behind the desk who looked confused, then concerned. Finally, she turned away and began dialing. It took almost ten minutes for Jonathan to complete his call and return to where Keely was standing. He looked troubled.

"Rhonda couldn't find her. Called her apartment, one or two other places. She hasn't been seen for more than a month." He paused, as though deciphering his own words. "She must have sensed some heat. Anyway, looks like we'll have to do this on our own, Captain."

Without waiting for a reply from Keely, he turned and again worked his way across the lobby, this time to a Euro Car desk. Keely watched as the young woman behind that counter made several phone calls and finally turned back to Jonathan with a weak smile. He signed several documents and returned to Keely. He showed her a rusted key ring with two worn keys attached.

"Our transportation ought to be quite interesting."

It took nearly a half hour to locate the rental, a Mercedes-Benz that had seen better days. The interior reeked of Turkish cigarette smoke and stale sweat. Keely rolled down the window despite the brisk, chilly wind that swept through the airport parking lot. They worked their way carefully out of the airport and onto the main road to the city. Jonathan seemed to know the streets and he headed toward the upper section of the city, away from where Keely had stayed last time.

This section of the city was much fancier than the area where she had been before. Shops along the wide, tree-lined boulevard looked well stocked and busy. Several sidewalk cafes were crowded with patrons despite temperatures in the low fifties. It was getting toward dusk, and lights began to appear in stores and street lights blinked on.

Jonathan entered a traffic circle anchored by a military statue of a woman in medieval uniform holding a banner in one hand and a fallen comrade in another. Almost immediately, Jonathan veered out of the circle and up a sweeping driveway that led to the entrance of an ornate hotel.

The doorman reached them before the car stopped, opening Keely's door and offering a salute at the same time.

"Gamarjoba."

Keely smiled and accepted his proffered hand. Jonathan came around the back and spoke, in halting Russian, to the man, who appeared to be in his seventies. Jonathan took Keely's arm and led her through the doorway, leaving the doorman to gather the luggage.

After Jonathan registered, they rode a creaking elevator to the fourth floor, emerging in a dimly lit hallway with threadbare Persian rugs running in both directions. A bellman motioned them toward the end of the corridor and opened the last door for them. The room was small but ornate, a French window offering a view of shadowed church spires in the waning evening light.

Once the bellman departed, Keely sat on the edge of one of the two beds and looked at Jonathan.

"This one room thing is beginning to be a habit."

Jonathan smiled for the first time since they had deplaned. "Why, Miss Greer, do I detect a sense of propriety in your voice?" His smile lessened. "You should know by now that I don't want you out of my sight until this is settled. Clear?"

After a light supper in the almost deserted restaurant, they had a nightcap in the lounge where two tired hookers waited patiently for tricks to escort them upstairs. Keely didn't realize how tired she was until they reached the room and she collapsed on the bed.

When Keely awoke the next morning, the rays of the sun were just beginning to streak across the sky above Tbilisi. She rolled over and noted without alarm that Jonathan was out of bed, the covers barely mussed. She wondered how long he had rested. He seemed to be able to function on little or no sleep and moved about the room so quietly that Keely hardly knew he was there. Now he sat at a small table beside the French doors intently studying the sky and the skyline. He sipped coffee, a tray set with coffee service and a plate of bread and fruit on the table beside him.

Keely sat up in bed, pulling the cover around her chin for warmth. "Morning. Up early as usual? Man, I didn't even hear them bring that in."

Jonathan looked in her direction and raised his cup. "Actually, went downstairs and retrieved it myself. Didn't want to disturb you. Cup?"

Keely nodded and Jonathan poured the steaming coffee in a cup and carried it to her. She took it, sipping the black brew, its deep aroma and taste attacking her taste buds with a vengeance. When she had finished half of it, she set the cup on the nightstand.

"Have you made a plan?"

Jonathan didn't bother turning from the window. "Thought we'd head into the mountains as soon as you are ready. You said it was about a four-hour drive?"

Keely didn't answer. Panic swept over her. She knew that the area was probably safe, but she didn't know if she was up to facing her demons so soon.

Jonathan looked over at her, aware of her fears. "You'll be okay. Will it take you long to get ready?"

Keely hesitated and then shook her head.

The drive into the mountains was just as startling as it had been the first time. The sudden shift from 21st century urban to 18th century rural still unsettling. Jonathan had stopped at a non- descript building on the way out of Tbilisi, emerging after a few minutes with a box tied loosely with twine. He had placed it between them and, after they had left the city behind, had Keely open it. Inside were two automatics and several clips. He had her check the clips; load both weapons and chamber rounds in each. She complied, but the feel of a weapon in her hand again felt as though she was holding a poisonous snake.

They rode in silence for a long time, both caught up in their thoughts. Finally, Jonathan spoke. "We'll go to the farmhouse first. We'll see if Irina was able to sanitize the place before she disappeared. One way of knowing she made it out. Then we'll check out where the trucks were."

They passed through Pasanauri, the same rag-tag collection of kids playing soccer in the main square, the same clutch of black-clad women keeping a watchful eye. As they approached the stretch of road where the farmhouse sat, Keely could feel her stomach knot and the muscles of her neck tighten.

As they came to the curve in the road before the farmhouse, Keely touched Jonathan's arm lightly and motioned ahead. "It's just around that bend."

He slowed to a crawl and worked slowly around the sweeping curve. They had not seen another vehicle since Pasanauri, but Jonathan was intent on approaching the area with due caution.

Around the bend, the dirt path to the farmhouse came into sight, but there were no signs of life anywhere. As they pulled off the road, Keely noted that the chickens and goats were gone, and no smoke rose from the chimney. Jonathan stopped the car and watched, apparently looking for movement. There was none.

After several minutes, he shut off the engine, picked up one of the automatics and got out of the car. "Stay here." Without waiting for a response, he headed up the path toward the house. Keely hesitated a minute, her hand hovering above the weapon. Finally, she left it on the seat and opened her door.

Cold gusts swept up the valley and dampness hung in the air. Keely was glad for the biting wind because it steeled her nerve as she followed Jonathan. When he was about ten yards from the house, he stopped and scanned the surrounding hills for activity. Keely reached where he stood and pointed toward the path that wound toward the summit.

"That's the path that leads to the top. From there, you can see down into the truck park." Jonathan nodded and turned his attention on the farmhouse. "You wait here."

He started forward; Keely stopped him with her hand. "We'll do it together."

They moved forward, Jonathan holding his weapon loosely at his side. He had not said anything when Keely joined him without a weapon. The door was ajar, and Jonathan pushed it slowly open with his foot.

Sudden movement from inside startled them and he brought his weapon up. A pigeon flew past and out the open door. They both relaxed and Jonathan smiled weakly. He opened the door completely, sunlight racing across the rough-hewn wooden floor. The sweet smell of decay permeated the air, a fine veil of dust floating all around as the outside air disturbed the interior.

Irina or someone had been there. The room was empty. No furniture, no blood stains, nothing. Keely looked around the room, her mind recalling the last time she had been here. She turned and walked back into the yard, gulping air to keep from vomiting. Jonathan joined her after a moment and gently massaged her neck.

"Looks like Irina cleaned up well. Not a trace."

He patted her gently on the shoulder and then began circling the house. After a minute, Keely followed. About twenty yards behind the house, at the edge of a furrowed field, was a six- foot square section of newly turned soil. Jonathan knelt beside it, picking up a clot of earth and rubbing it between his fingers.

"Must have buried them here. Probably figured no one would think to investigate too thoroughly."

Keely walked to the edge of the turned earth and dropped to her knees. She rested her hand lightly on the ground. She found herself praying silently-- words she had not said for years. She stayed there for a long while. Jonathan stood and returned to the front of the house, but Keely could not bring herself to desert the family again. Tears fell from her eyes, quickly absorbed by the soil. If she sought absolution, the silent graves did not provide it. As she mourned, Keely realized that death had come to many by her hand. She could not imagine a just God would-- could-- forgive her.

When her tears stopped, Keely stood and turned away. She walked slowly to the front where Jonathan stood intently staring at the hills.

"Lovely place, this. Quiet. Serene." Keely couldn't answer.

Jonathan reached an arm around her waist and began directing her back to the car. "Let's check out the truck park. I imagine the bad guys have moved out, so no need to hike over the hills."

They reached the car and Jonathan rested a hand on Keely's shoulder. "You sure you're all right? You want to stay here while I go check?"

Keely shook her head and opened her door.

It took only five minutes to work around the hill separating the farmhouse from the truck park. The driveway was almost hidden from the road by underbrush, but they could see tire marks on the soft shoulder that indicated where the trucks had left the main road. Jonathan pulled off the road and shut off the engine.

"Let's do this on foot. Just in case."

They got out and began working their way along the rutted dirt track that led into the forest. This time, Jonathan insisted Keely bring a weapon. The steep hill rose to their right and effectively kept the area in shadow even though it was early afternoon. It was cold beneath the trees and they could hear birds rustling through the branches above their heads. But there were no other sounds.

210

After several minutes, Jonathan raised his hand and then pointed ahead. Keely could just make out a shape through the trees. It looked like the burned-out shell of a small building.

Jonathan waited, and when he heard nothing, motioned them forward. They halted again at the edge of the clearing, both dropping to one knee and holding their weapons loosely at the ready.

From this vantage point, they could see all that was left of the building was a charred frame of timber hanging from blackened brick walls. Two trucks lay on their sides, their bellies facing each other. Fragments of twisted metal had been splattered in a circle around a shallow crater. After a moment, Jonathan nudged Keely's arm.

"Thermite. No huge crater, but deadly effective."

He rose and started forward, his weapon making a steady sweep from one side to the other. Keely rose as well, keeping her weapon at her side, but watchful of the area surrounding the building.

They spent the better part of an hour combing through the wreckage. There was little left.

At one point, Jonathan called to her, and she wandered over, only to be confronted with two bodies burned beyond recognition. Apparently the two had started out the back of the building but had been engulfed by the fire. There was a third body inside the cab of one of the trucks.

Keely noticed that the trucks apparently had been empty when hit. Inside the building were shipping crates, several with twisted rifles sticking out haphazardly. Jonathan meticulously examined every inch of the building, paying particular attention to the crates. He called her over.

"I don't see any boxes with the writing you showed me."

"I don't either." Keely looked around the area where they stood, and then quickly back to Jonathan, a gleam in her eye.

He leaned toward her. "That look means you remembered something?" "I have pictures."

"What?"

"The camera you gave me. I took pictures. Didn't think of it till just now."

Jonathan smiled, "Very good. Where is the camera now?"

"Back at the room, in my suitcase."

He motioned Keely outside. They walked several yards away and sat on the ground. "Those weapons-- what were they?"

Keely shrugged. "Junk. Old AK-47s, a few used RPGs, some handguns."

Jonathan's frown deepened. "I didn't tell you everything about this assignment. Or, to be more factual, I didn't find out until after you left for Georgia."

"What?"

He spoke as though to himself. "They apparently knew they were being observed."

"Kestrel?"

"I was told that small arms were being shipped to rebels in Chechnya. When the air strike was ordered, I asked my contact why. He said that along with those arms there were a dozen guidance systems for SA-19s. Apparently, the Chechens had gotten their hands on some surface to air missiles that didn't have the guidance gizmos. They're about the size of a small suitcase. The reason for the bombing raid was to keep those systems from arriving, not these weapons."

Keely's expression hardened. Just when she was starting to trust him again! She had let herself be duped again.

Keely stared at Jonathan for a few moments, bordering on tears and resentment at the same time. "What you're saying is that Vali and his family would have been killed even if we hadn't come?"

Jonathan met her look, though regretfully. "Chances are very likely. You said Vali had already been warned to stay away, when they killed his sheep."

Keely spun on her heels, looking toward the mountains, unable to fathom a world where people could die simply because their livestock wandered into forbidden territory. She could hear the crunch of dirt as Jonathan came closer to her.

"Could have been a surprise to them when they came across Niko."

Keely turned around. "Somehow, that just doesn't make me feel better." She turned around again, staring at the two destroyed trucks. As she fixated on the now burned out shells of transportation, something clicked in her mind's eye, trying to recall some detail. She looked back at Jonathan. "There were three trucks."

Jonathan looked at the two trucks. "You're sure?"

"Got the pictures to prove it."

Jonathan ran his fingers across his lower lip in thought. "Perhaps the systems left on that third truck."

She sat staring at the destruction around her as Jonathan went back into the building and returned with a piece of crate. He showed her the faint stencil marking, but Keely couldn't make out the writing.

"What's that?"

"A shipping stamp of some sort. Two actually. One is in Georgian script. The other --." He looked up. "I believe the other is in Russian."

Keely was totally confused. "I don't understand."

Jonathan laid the piece between them carefully. "These are the kind of stamps usually used to mark crates aboard ship. I am guessing that some of the weapons must have entered Georgia through a seaport. That might have been the third truck."

He stood suddenly and reached down for Keely, but she ignored his hand.

"Look, I know you despise secrecy, but I didn't get the information about the guidance systems until after your call from the airport."

Keely was angry. "How can I believe you?"

"I'm here."

She knew Jonathan was right. "What do you suggest?"

He bent down and picked up the held up the crate fragment. "Head for the coast. See if we can track down the ship that carried these crates. Let's find out what that writing you found means."

CHAPTER FIFTEEN

The wiper blades had seen better days. Jonathan attempted unsuccessfully to clear the windshield of the rain that had begun to fall. Keely lay in the back seat, the rocking of the car causing her to doze off.

They had been on the go for almost thirty-six hours and she could hardly keep awake. Jonathan leaned forward to get a better view through the streaked windshield. The radio blared American rock music, broken periodically by a squeaky female disk jockey speaking Georgian. Beside Jonathan, as though he had no care in the world, sat Sando.

On the journey back from the destroyed truck park to Tbilisi, Keely had been quiet. She hadn't been able to shake the images whirling through her mind. At one point, she had thought she was going to be sick and asked Jonathan to pull over, but the nausea had passed.

Jonathan had been quiet as well, watching her off and on, his concern obvious. Keely was appreciative, but it was hard to reconcile the Jonathan before Morocco and the Jonathan sitting beside her now.

She stared out the window at the empty mountains. Jonathan cleared his throat, but didn't say anything as he looked over at her again. When he finally asked his question, Keely felt warmed by the worry she heard in his voice. It acted like an elixir soothing her frayed nerves.

"Are you alright?"

She didn't bother to turn.

"I can't get that family out of my mind. If I… we hadn't entered their lives, they very likely would have grown old quietly in these mountains. Their kids would have grown up, gotten married and someday might've taken over the farm. Where's the justice in all this?"

Jonathan let her words hang in the air for a few minutes before responding. "The truth is terrible things happen to good people. And bad people don't seem to be affected at all. They go on living to cause havoc another day. It is one of the reasons I got into this business. In a way, I thought I could reverse that. But sometimes, my best intentions…." He didn't finish.

She looked at him then. "So why stay in it?"

Jonathan smiled slightly and bent his head a bit to look into the side-view mirror. He hesitated so long that Keely started to ask her question again, but he spoke first.

"You see things in black and white. Strangely, I find that admirable. But I have to look at things many different ways, and I have to take into consideration all alternatives. That's part of the job."

"You could walk away. Just like I did."

"You make it sound very simple. I just wonder… is it?"

He had not looked at her while he spoke, but Keely had watched him, listening for some meaning. She sat quietly for a moment, waiting to see if he would add more. Shortly, she turned away from him, staring out the window at the barren mountains.

They had arrived at their hotel late in the evening, but Jonathan insisted they look at the pictures on Keely's digital camera. She retrieved it from their room and brought it to Jonathan in the small bar off the hotel lobby.

The batteries had died, but Jonathan was able to talk the concierge into finding two AAA batteries. He turned on the LCD and began flipping through the pictures, Keely looking over his shoulder. There was a series of wide-angle shots from the hills, then several when Keely had entered the camp. It showed three trucks just as Keely had indicated.

Jonathan skipped through the rest of the pictures but stopped when he reached one of the farm family with Niko and Irina in the background. He held the camera up for Keely.

"The family?"

"Vali and Nana… their kids." She returned to the seat opposite him, knowing the next picture was a close-up of the little girl.

Jonathan continued to look, reviewing each picture more carefully. After a few long minutes, he turned off the camera and slipped it in his pocket.

"Well, seems just as you said. Three trucks. I think if we find where that third one went, we'll find who is after you."

Jonathan went to the bar and returned with a bottle of wine and two glasses. He poured for both of them and began studying over a map of Georgia, focusing on the country's Black Sea coastline.

"Those markings were in Georgian and Russian. It wouldn't make sense to move them into Georgia and then back into Chechnya by land. I believe they came by sea, probably from the Ukraine."

"Why the Ukraine?"

"Kestrel has ties to former Russian military types, so the Ukraine would be the most logical transit point for material being smuggled out. With the Russians in Crimea, it may be too hot to ship from there. The safer bet would be someplace like Odessa. Turkey has too many controls in place and Bulgaria is too unstable. Has to be the Ukraine."

"So how do we find out?"

"We'll have to get some help. You mentioned some kid you met when you were here."

"Nice kid, good English."

Jonathan tapped his fingers on the table. "Irina's disappeared, Niko's dead. We need help, but I am not sure if I want to enlist some other professional here. Obviously, we need to be discreet, so as not to draw attention to ourselves. That means we need an outsider."

"Are you suggesting we use Sando?"

Jonathan smiled, "Yes."

Keely stared into the ornate lobby, its original paintings of famous Georgian kings and queens badly in needed of restoration. She looked at Jonathan. "I don't want this boy hurt. In any way."

"All he has to do is accompany us to the coast as an interpreter. When we find where that shipment came from, we'll return him to Tbilisi none the worse for wear. I will pay him handsomely, and I'm sure he could use the money."

Keely was reluctant to get Sando involved, but knew Jonathan was right. They could spend weeks searching the Black Sea coast without someone to lead the way. Keely dug the faded piece of paper containing Sando's phone number out of her wallet. She walked over to the concierge's desk. The sleepy bellman spoke passable English and Keely asked him to ring the number. She waited as he dialed the number and handed her the phone. A woman answered on the fourth ring. She said something in Georgian. Keely didn't know what the woman said, so she spoke in English.

"Is Sando there?"

The line was silent for a long moment, but Keely could hear movement and a muffled conversation. Finally, a young man's voice came on the line speaking English.

"This is Sando. How can help you?"

His English was more heavily accented than she had remembered.

"Hi, this is Keely Greer. We met about two months ago. In Tbilisi. At a small cafe." She waited.

216

"Hello. Hello. Yes, I remember. Keely. How are you? You call from America?"

"No. Actually, I'm at the Cron Palace Hotel. I thought, perhaps, we could get together for a drink. Do you know where the hotel is?"

"Yes. I would love this. When?"

She knew it was late and didn't know how long it would take him to get to the hotel. "How about now?"

He hesitated only a moment. "Oh, yes. Now. I will be at hotel in maybe fifteen minutes?" "Fine. I'll meet you in the lobby."

After she hung up, she looked over at Jonathan who sat at the table sipping his drink as though he had not a care in the world. She walked over to him, and he smiled up at her.

"Did he remember you?"

"Of course. He's on his way."

"Perhaps you should meet him alone. Be careful how you approach the subject. I don't want to frighten him off. See if he knows the most likely port for a shipment coming in from someplace like the Ukraine. If he is amenable to helping us, tell him it will require driving to the coast. It will only take a day or two and then we'll return here."

"Are you sure we need him?"

Jonathan stood up. "Don't worry. Nothing is going to happen to him."

"You've said that before."

Sando entered the lobby ten minutes later. Jonathan had retired to their room. The young man had obviously dressed up for the occasion; his clothes clean and pressed. He beamed as he saw her walk across the lobby and stood up straight as she approached. When she reached him, she took his outstretched hand and kissed him on his left cheek as she had seen others in the hotel do.

"Sando, you look great. How have you been? I've thought a lot about you since we met."

Keely could see a blush creep up his neck and cheeks. She took his arm and led him toward the small bar at the back of the lobby. It was deserted except for the same two hookers sitting silently at one of the small cocktail tables. Keely directed Sando to a table at the other end of the room and allowed him to hold her chair for her. When they were seated, Sando turned and said something to the drowsy bartender who grudgingly pulled himself off his stool and reached below the counter.

"I order a bottle of Georgian wine. You remember?"

Keely couldn't help but smile at his earnest innocence. After the wine arrived and they toasted, Sando told Keely he had completed his term at the university with the highest marks in his class. He wanted to go on to graduate school but didn't think his family could afford the expense. He and some friends had talked about starting an English language primary school.

"We must teach our children English. Many investors are coming to my country. We must be ready."

She was amazed by his optimism about his own career and about his country. When he had exhausted all of his news, she decided it was time to discuss her current situation.

"Actually, Sando, that's why I'm back in Tbilisi. An associate and I are interested in exploring shipping possibilities here and thought you might be able to help."

She hated misleading this sweet boy, but the less he knew the better off he was. She realized Jonathan had used the same tactic on her.

"We need someone who can act as guide and interpreter, but someone who is also very smart and knows how to keep a secret." She could see his ego expand. "Would you be interested?"

He tried to act sophisticated, but she could tell he was like a small child just told he could run amok in a toy store. He sipped his wine, but his smile never left his face. "I would be very happy to help. What do I do?"

"The first thing we need to know is where cargo ships on the Black Sea are most likely to come into Georgia."

"Well, Sukhumi is very big, but it is in Abkhazia, and that is now Russian. Next biggest is Poti, about 300 kilometers from here. There are some others, but really Poti is biggest."

Keely nodded. "We would like to take a look at the port. Would you be willing to go with us tomorrow? We will probably only be gone two days. We already have a car."

Sando didn't have to think about it. "Oh, yes. Easy drive. Very beautiful."

"Then it's settled. We will meet here in the morning and go." Keely lifted her glass for a toast to their success, but set it down. "Sando, how much does graduate school cost?"

He looked puzzled. "School is free. Of course, we all have to work. Food, books."

"What will you study?"

"International Business. Georgia needs people who can help build."

"Here is the deal, you help us, and we will pay you," Keely wanted this young man to have a future, "three thousand Euros. That should help."

Keely could tell by his stunned look that 3,000 Euros was more money than he ever imagined having in his life. He stared at her for a long while and then nodded in response. Before he could speak, Keely lifted her glass into the air toward him.

"Then it is agreed. Tomorrow. Say around eight?"

Sandro lifted his glass and they had one last drink. Keely set her glass down, stood up and kissed his cheek.

"We'll be waiting."

She left him sitting, still unable to fathom the windfall he had just been offered.

The next morning, Keely and Jonathan came down early. Sando was already there. After Jonathan had informed the desk clerk they would be away for a few days, they walked over to where Sando stood and Keely introduced Jonathan.

"This is Mr. Jonathan Swift. He is my business associate and he will be driving our rental car."

Sando stuck out his hand. Keely detected just the slightest bit of jealousy in Sando's eyes, but it quickly passed. "Like writer?"

Jonathan smiled his most appealing smile. "Why, yes. Like the writer. Have you read any of his works?"

Sando was back to his eager self. "Yes. He was great social critic. Wrote about the oppression of common people, like some of our great poets."

"Actually, he was my great, great, great uncle."

Sando's jaw dropped slightly and he stared at Jonathan with new admiration. Jonathan had won him over just as he did most people. He motioned them to a seating area where he produced a sheet of paper on which he had traced the Georgian characters from the piece of crate they had found at the truck park.

It was a fair representation of the characters. Jonathan explained that a friend had given it to him to track down a shipment that seemed to have disappeared. It was a lame story, but Sando accepted it. He deciphered the Georgian words, which was the name of a ship and its destination --Poti. The Russian words repeated what was written in Georgian.

Jonathan was pleased. "So, Poti it is. And you will show us how to get there?"

Sando nodded and they headed for the car.

The rain had begun shortly after they left the city. The road followed a river basin through the foothills to the west of Tbilisi, the area as desolate as the mountains to the north. The road continued through the mountains for almost sixty miles before it sloped down to a broad plain leading toward the Black Sea. The land was lush; the expansive fields dotted intermittently with small farms. They had lapsed into silence after Jonathan had quizzed Sando about his schooling, his hobbies and soccer. It was a comfortable silence, none of them seeming to need conversation.

The drive took just over five hours with a stop along the way for a drink and khachapuri, the cheese-stuffed bread Keely had tried on her first visit. As they crested a small hill in mid- afternoon, Sando pointed toward the distance.

"Poti just there. Maybe ten kilometers."

Poti turned out to be a rather large city, blending modern and old buildings on either said of a river Sando called it Rion. There were newer buildings, mostly high-rise apartments further up the valley, but the ornate steeple of a church anchored the center of town.

Sando directed them through the maze of streets toward an expansive system of warehouses and docks. He had been to the city several times with friends. They would drive from Tbilisi hoping to buy clothing and other goods, as they were unloaded from the Black Sea ships, which they would take back to Tbilisi and sell. He explained that anything could be purchased for the right price.

Jonathan had suggested they find a hotel first; they located a guesthouse about a mile from the dock entrance. A typical Soviet-style place in need of repairs, but the tiny bar on the main floor made up for its outer appearance, which let out onto a secluded patio. He had told Sando that the first order of business was to determine when the ship had arrived and what company handled offloading.

Sando did not bother to question the rather flimsy story. In Georgia, all business was handled in a circuitous fashion. Once they had checked in-- each with a single room-- Jonathan laid out his strategy as they sat on the tiny patio.

"Keely, I want you to stay here. Too many people will only confuse the situation. Sando, you and I will go down to the dock master's office and see if we can track down the shipping company. I don't expect this to take long."

Before Keely could protest, Jonathan stood and headed for the front door. Sando hesitated a moment, shrugged and smiled weakly, following him. Keely had no recourse but to wait.

She didn't have to wait long.

In less than an hour, Jonathan and Sando were back. Jonathan seemed almost jovial and Sando was beaming. "Some young man you got here."

Keely had moved to the front porch where chairs afforded a view of a rather forlorn shopping area. She had carried a beer with her but had taken only a few sips.

"Things went okay?"

Jonathan and Sando slid into the chairs around the small table. The owner wandered on the porch and Sando spoke to him. He looked at the group, shrugged and went inside. In a few minutes, he returned with a bottle of wine and three glasses. After the wine was poured and the owner had returned inside, Jonathan leaned forward.

"If this boy doesn't become president of this country, he'll be its greatest con man. Or perhaps, they're one in the same."

He sipped from his glass before he continued.

"We found the dock master rather easily. He was, however, a bit reluctant to discuss shipping companies based on a piece of paper. Old Sando here took over. I didn't know what he was saying, but by the time he was finished, the dock master was sweating up a storm and rummaging through his paperwork faster than a rabbit in a carrot patch. We got the name of the shipping company and the ship and were gone before the man knew what hit him."

Sando was blushing during Jonathan's retelling of the events. He smiled and shrugged. "Just tell the man sort of the truth."

Jonathan slapped him on the back and raised his glass in salute. "What did you say to him?"

Sando smiled more broadly. "I tell him you are important man from England here on official business. That the minister of interior-- he takes care of port-- is personal friend who wants you helped without any interference. I also asked him his name and how long he is dock master. That is when he gives you information."

Jonathan roared with genuine laughter. "Boy, you are a born con man."

Sando didn't seem to know that term, but he knew the implication and blushed even more fiercely. "In Georgia, you must understand the system."

They continued to sit on the porch as the late afternoon turned to dusk. By the time Jonathan made a move to leave, the table was filled with two empty wine bottles and Sando was more than a little intoxicated. He had entertained them with a detailed-- and lengthy-- history of Georgia, recounting the glorious and inglorious with equal passion.

What was most poignant was his description of the brief war between Georgia and Russia in 2008. The Russians had entered two areas with large Russian populations on the pretext of protecting them, much as they had done in the Crimea. When the dust settled, thousands had died, tens of thousands had been displaced and the disputed areas, South Ossetia and Abkhazia, were designated autonomous regions. Georgians long had enmity toward Russia. This was just another reason why Sando hated the Russians.

221

Jonathan stood and motioned for the waiter, pulling bills from his pocket to pay for the wine. He seemed a bit tipsy himself, and he suggested that they all rest for a while and then go out for a late dinner. Sando looked as though he would fall asleep the moment he hit the bed, and rose unsteadily, saluting Jonathan lazily and heading for the front door.

As soon as he entered the lobby, Jonathan glazed look and wobbly stance promptly disappeared. He sat back down and leaned toward Keely. "You up for a little nighttime reconnaissance?"

Keely had seen him pull his phony drunk act before and was amazed that he could have drunk so much with so little effect. "Sure. Where to?"

As they walked through the early evening throng of people on the town's main thoroughfare, he outlined his plan. The dock master had given Sando the shipping firm's address, and on the way back Sando had pointed out the building, which sat outside the dock area.

Jonathan assumed the company kept bankers' hours and would have closed for the evening by now. He also felt that the local constabulary was probably not the most efficient, so a little nighttime door rattling would not arouse suspicion.

They headed away from the center of town, the strong odor of salt water, dead fish and diesel fuel building as they moved closer to the docks. Fewer people moved about on the streets at this end of town, but Jonathan linked his arm in Keely's to give the impression of a couple out for an evening stroll. The stiff breeze and chill in the air heightened Keely's adrenaline evident by the beads of sweat at her temples.

They reached the building and passed by, the front door inset several feet from the street. Jonathan glancing casually up at the second floor. They reached the corner and paused. Jonathan put his arm around her shoulders and drew her close to him, his lips just inches away from her ear.

"As we walk back, pretend to stumble just before we reach the door. Then lean on me and we will move into the entry way."

He leaned back and smiled at her. "Don't think anyone's about but shan't take a chance."

They retraced their steps and Keely stumbled on cue, grabbing Jonathan's arm to break her fall. She cursed and tried to put weight on her foot but lifted it up quickly. Jonathan half carried her to the entry way, the shadows obscuring what to any observers was a gallant gentleman helping his lady friend. Once in the shadows, they separated, Keely standing close to the front, making sure no one was watching. Jonathan worked on the door, and within seconds, it swung open.

Once inside, Jonathan used a small penlight to locate the office of the shipping company, comparing the Cyrillic lettering on a small piece of paper the dock master had given Sando with the names on a dinghy directory. He motioned toward the stairs and they climbed silently to the second floor and moved to a door, which Jonathan opened with equal speed.

Inside the single room were four desks forming a square in the middle, ancient roller chairs facing inward behind each. Against one wall was a collection of mismatched file cabinets, and Jonathan headed immediately to them and began to examine the tabs set in the front of each.

"Good! They're numbered."

Keely stayed by the door as Jonathan quickly located the right drawer and withdrew a file folder. "Got it."

They retraced their steps to the front door, making sure to lock the office first. Once outside, Jonathan re-locked the building and they stepped into the half-light of the street, Keely limping noticeably, Jonathan supporting her around her middle. Total lapse time was five minutes.

They proceeded slowly until they were several blocks away, Jonathan constantly peeking behind them in case they were followed. When he was sure they were in the clear, he leaned down and kissed Keely on the forehead.

"Think you're all better now, love."

They didn't stop until they were back in the hotel and in Jonathan's room. They had only been gone a half-hour.

"Think we should rouse Sando for dinner?"

Jonathan smiled. "From his look before we left, I think he'll sleep the whole night." Jonathan had purchased a bottle of scotch at a small store close to the hotel and now poured them both a double. Keely sipped hers as Jonathan finished his in two swallows. Keely toasted him.

"Just like old times, Jonathan."

She instantly regretted the comment, not wanting to give any false hopes that she was ready to get back into his twisted world. Her comment didn't go unnoticed by Jonathan, who looked at her in fascination. But it quickly faded as he stood up.

"You mentioned food. Shall we grab a bit at the café next door?"

Jonathan kept the conversation over their late dinner casual. He told her Rhonda had found a 'special friend' and was spending a lot of time in London. He also mentioned that he was leaning toward taking a hiatus from work for a while. He gave a vague explanation that he was tired of traipsing around like some playboy of the western world.

It was so casual that Keely almost missed it. She wondered why he was telling her now; why he didn't say that driving back to Tbilisi. It was the first time since Tangier Keely felt really comfortable around him though, and she didn't want to spoil it by questioning him further. She just let him talk. She could tell he was working hard to put her at ease... with him and with the situation. As they returned to the hotel, Jonathan led Keely to the staircase, but stopped before they began to climb.

"I can't help but believe your life would have been much better had you turned me down when I offered you a job."

Keely could see the sincerity in his eyes. She reached her hand behind his neck and kissed him gently on the lips. She held her lips to his for a moment then leaned back.

"When you offered, I was just treading water. It didn't turn out as I expected, and my heart is broken over the pain and suffering I have seen... and caused, but I've learned a lot about myself, Jonathan, and you're responsible for that."

She leaned forward and kissed him again, with more passion. Then she stepped back and started up the stairs, turning after a few steps. "You have become a very important part of my life. And of all things that I want to forget about, you are not one."

For just a moment, she wanted to ask him to come up with her. She felt the need for intimacy, but she quickly she changed her mind. She didn't want to start something she knew she couldn't finish.

The next morning, Keely came down to the lobby to find Jonathan and Sando immersed in conversation. When she approached, Sando stood and smiled weakly as Jonathan waved cheerfully. She reached them and patted Sando on the cheek gently.

"How are you feeling this morning? I hope you didn't get sick."

Sando looked down at his scuffed shoes. "No. Just sleep all night."

They sat and Jonathan filled Keely in on what they had found the night before at the shipping office.

"The ship's name is the N.M.B Varna. Ukrainian registry. Works the Black Sea coast from Istanbul to Odessa to Poti. It off-loaded three items there, a shipment of grain from Bulgaria, approximately four tons worth, and twenty pallets of condensed milk from Turkey."

"The third?"

"Twenty crates of farming equipment. The first two were clearly identified by the originating company. The last only by a transit number. It appears that one was a short haul." He paused expectantly.

"Jonathan, stop playing games."

"Keely, you never appreciated the dramatic pause. The equipment arrived in Poti from Odessa. I have the name of the company that owns the ship. As soon as we get Sando home, we're heading for the Ukraine."

It would have taken only three hours to fly from Tbilisi, Georgia, to Odessa, Ukraine, on a direct flight. Unfortunately, the airline had no direct flights between the cities. Jonathan and Keely found themselves on yet another circuitous route that took them through Vienna.

They left Tbilisi long before sunrise, the airport practically deserted except for a few hardy souls, mostly European businessmen, headed west to Amsterdam. Sando had driven them to the airport, his pocket stuffed with Euros.

On their return from Poti, Jonathan had ceremoniously presented Sando with an envelope containing eight 500 Euro notes. He had told Keely the bonus was well deserved, and when Sando opened the envelope at the small restaurant around the corner from the hotel, his eyes began to tear up. The money was more than enough to start his adult life in style.

He began to protest, but Jonathan would have none of it. He explained that the money was actually an investment. Jonathan expected him to be very important in Georgia someday, and it would be good to have a friend in high places. Keely knew that meant having Sando in place for any future needs Jonathan might have there, but she didn't protest.

As Sando left them at the front portal to the terminal, he shook Jonathan's hand seriously and wished him good luck. He then turned to Keely and extended a hand, but she folded her arms around him and held him for a long moment. After kissing his cheek, she smiled at him.

"You be good. I can't tell you how much you have helped us."

She could see he was tearing up again, so she left him, walking through the doors, glancing back only once to see him still standing out front.

Not many passengers had boarded the four-hour flight to Vienna. Keely managed to take two seats in first class. Images pounding through her mind from the last two weeks kept her from sleeping. Two weeks ago, she thought she had finally conquered her self-loathing. She thought she had begun to regain normalcy, and that she had found someone with whom she could share a life. That dream had been destroyed in a rundown Gibraltar apartment. Now she found herself racing around the world trying to find Stefan's killer. The chase had preoccupied most of her mind, but in the stillness of the flight, she had time to reflect. She didn't know if she wanted to.

At first, she had been sure this frantic hunt had been to find a killer. But she had to admit that the pursuit was driving her now, and, maybe, the sense of security she felt being around Jonathan. He was different. He still had the self-assuredness that made him almost irresistible. Few questioned him because he seemed to know exactly what he was doing.

She had been in love with Stefan, or at least a maybe just the idea of what being in love should be. She wasn't sure they ever really had any future together. Eventually Stefan would have had to confess to her that someone had hired him. That someone wasn't going to let Stefan walk away. She believed she knew him well enough to say he would have kept that from her. Instead, he would have spent their relationship looking over his shoulder.

Being around Jonathan these past weeks had resurrected feelings that went beyond complicated. Now she found herself in an airplane across the aisle from the man who was perhaps second only to her father in shaping her past and perhaps her future. She had thought once or twice about suggesting they stop their search; allowing Keely to return to Cortez, and hope Kestrel would forget her. She knew too well that people like that had long memories; she also remembered Jonathan had told her that people in this business rarely seek revenge. If it didn't impact the bottom line, it wasn't worth the effort. In her case, it seemed whatever information she supposedly had, Kestrel would not give up till he had found her.

Keely also knew that once Jonathan had made up his mind, he would not turn back until he was sure she was safe. Part of her wanted Jonathan to continue this search a while longer. Not just to find a killer, but so she could feel the sense of security she felt when close to him.

Jonathan had arranged for a connecting flight to Odessa, but the only one available was late in the evening, the same day they arrived in Vienna. Their plane touched down shortly after seven a.m.

After deplaning, Jonathan led Keely through customs and into the small terminal.

Morning travelers were hurrying to flights as overnight passengers with bleary eyes wandered aimlessly through the halls. Jonathan had decided both of them needed a decent rest and had arranged for rooms at the Imperial Palais Schwarzenberg in the city's historic district. He was unusually quiet during the taxi ride to hotel and followed Keely through the grand lobby to the front desk. An earnest young woman checked them in-- each with a single room. On the elevator to the third floor, Keely studied her key card.

"Single rooms, huh? What, I snore or something?"

Jonathan smiled without looking at her. "Thought you might like a bit of privacy, at least here."

"Kinda late for that, isn't it?"

226

Their rooms were adjacent. Jonathan left a call for four so they could grab a real meal before returning to the airport. It took Keely almost an hour to drift off to sleep; images nagging at her mind. The past would not stop haunting her. She thought about Stefan, the family at the farmhouse, the banker in Zurich, the frightened bureaucrat in Paris. Intertwined with these images was Jonathan. She had held their relationship at bay for a long time. Only when her mind was weary, and her defenses down did she recall memories of their more intimate moments. They had never talked about their sexual encounters. In fact, Jonathan acted as though there had never been anything intimate between them. Keely was not as good at sublimating her past.

Keely slept fitfully and awoke at the first ring of the telephone. It was Jonathan. Keely noted he was calling an hour early. "Thought we had till four?"

"Sorry. Guess I didn't pay attention to the time. I'll let you go back to sleep."

"Too late now. Give me about a half hour and I'll be ready."

Keely took a long, hot shower, letting the water stream down her body; the tension of the past two weeks had turned her neck and shoulder muscles into Gordian knots. The water helped some and she tried to focus only on how the water caressed her skin. Afterward, she dressed and threw the few pieces of clothing she had into her bag. Sooner or later, she needed to do laundry; it would have to wait for a later time. Keely brushed her still-damp hair, finally comfortable with its length. She had peered at her reflection in the bathroom mirror and didn't like the circles under her eyes and lines creasing the corners of her mouth. She was too weary to bother with makeup.

Jonathan was in the lobby and smiled when he saw her. "Ah, freshly scrubbed. Makes you look like a schoolgirl."

She laughed. "In which case, would that make you the perverted school teacher?"

He held out his arm. "Well, Lolita, would you like some dinner?"

Keely had only been into Vienna proper once. It had been late fall, the trees bare of leaves, snow heavy in the air. In late spring, Vienna was bursting with color and new life. The doorman hailed a taxi, and Jonathan gave the man the name of a restaurant. It was just a few minutes from the hotel, but Keely was glad Jonathan hadn't suggested walking.

It was upscale without being pretentious. Patrons wore casual-- though expensive-- clothes. Despite the main room was virtually empty, Jonathan asked the maitre d' if they could sit on the patio. The man led them through tables to the back of the building where a flagstone patio held a dozen tables. The air was brisk, but not too cold.

They were seated at a table adjacent to arching trees. After ordering a bottle of wine, Jonathan settled in to examine the menu. Keely realized she was famished. When she looked up from her menu, Jonathan was looking at her.

"What is it?"

He adjusted himself in his chair, sipped his wine judiciously and placed the glass precisely in front of him. "Talked to Rhonda while you slept."

Keely motioned him to continue.

"Seems we've been offered a very interesting contract."

Keely was becoming impatient. "Dammit, Jonathan. Can't you just get to the point? Just tell me."

He raised his glass and toasted her before drinking. Then he set it down again. "My always-impatient Keely. Always quashing the theatricality of life. Anyway, it was from the British. Seems an individual has finally worn thin on their nerves. They want him."

"And?"

"It is Kestrel."

Keely slumped in her chair and stared up at the early evening sky. Then she looked back at Jonathan with mistrust. "Are you sure you just found out? Or has this whole thing just been your way of suckering me into helping you?"

Jonathan looked genuinely hurt. "No, my dear. This started out just as I have always told you, an effort to insure your well-being. This just happened."

They sat in silence for a while, breaking it only to order. Keely's hunger had disappeared. She ordered now only to eat to keep up her strength. The bottle of wine was almost empty when she leaned forward and spoke.

"I am sorry if I sounded bitchy. It's just that all this has unnerved me. And you must admit, it does seem odd that the person we're looking for just happens to be on somebody's hit list. Tell me why the Brits want him."

Jonathan seemed relieved. "The missile guidance systems. Apparently, he never got them to Chechnya. However, he did put them up for sale."

"Wouldn't they be hard to peddle?"

"Maybe. In reality, building a missile is child's play next to developing a sophisticated guidance system. Look at it this way, without the guidance system, a missile could, at best, hit within a three-hundred mile radius of a target. Not very strategic. With the system, it could drop a missile within a three-hundred meter radius. That makes the system very dangerous and very pricey. London believes the asking price is $5 million."

'A significant sale,' Keely mumbled, understanding the potential danger of such a system falling into the wrong hands was apparently more than the British were willing to allow.

"Why don't they send their own people after him? Why us?"

Jonathan looked embarrassed. "For one thing, they don't want their friends across the pond to find out. Afraid it would be bad business to kill a CIA contractor. For another, the British are worried the missiles would be used against its forces in Kenya where it has a significant presence. Finally, word's gotten out that we are looking for him."

"What happened to discretion, and keeping things quiet?"

Jonathan shrugged as if he'd never said that, "Well, naturally, when we made the connection in the States, I had Rhonda get in touch with MI6 to see if they had any information about his whereabouts. When they realized we were already out here looking, they figured why not just have us do the job. Plus, there are the Americans."

"Meaning?"

"Apparently the Americans are not as concerned as the Brits and have tried to convince MI6 to leave Kestrel alone. The British reluctantly agreed. Of course, if a third party got into the act."

Jonathan didn't need to continue. It was what Swift Enterprises did. Keely was skeptical but realized arguing with Jonathan would be futile. Besides, there was something about making this an assignment that seemed to make it less personal. Even though she had to keep reminding herself that she had quit that business-- she was there because it had become personal. Yes, she wanted to help Jonathan find the person who killed Stefan, but not at the risk of being drawn back into assignments laced with more killing.

When the food arrived, Keely found herself diving into it with more gusto than she expected. When the meal was done and coffee served, Keely sat back and looked at Jonathan.

"I still don't know why we are following a trail that seems shaky at best. Can't we just find out where Kestrel is hiding and go there?"

Jonathan sipped his coffee then smiled. "Have you ever been on a fox hunt?"

"What's that have to do with it?"

"Well, you could ask the hounds why they don't just find the fox's lair and wait. They don't because the fox has many lairs and if he senses the hounds at one, he merely skips to another. We are following the scent, no matter how faint. Eventually, we will stumble across something that will lead us to his hiding place."

"You relish this whole thing, don't you? I mean, the chase, the intrigue."

He put down his cup and dabbed the corners of his mouth with his napkin. "Less than you would imagine. I told you a long time ago that I do not do this for sport. I believe in what I am doing. Not so much in a 'rah-rah-rally-around-the-flag' way. It is just that after my years in the S.A.S., I realized there were some very nasty people about; people who have no compunction about destroying lives for monetary gain or political or religious zealotry. I realized I had a certain talent for ridding society of these nasties. Don't get me wrong. It isn't something I want to talk about or think back on, but the rewards, and not just the tangible rewards, can outweigh the guilt."

He reached across and rested a hand on hers. "I know you have had a horrendous experience. And in many ways, I blame myself. But deep down, I am happy you joined me. You have given me, and please do not misinterpret this, great pleasure. Your smile, your sense of wonder, even your quirky sense of humor and gutter language have been a great joy. I was sorry to see you go, but I did understand. I wish it could be different. I wish I could say, 'stay and we'll do some other kind of work,' but as long as there are folks like Kestrel around, and as long as I am able to provide my special services, I will have to continue."

Keely held his hand lightly. "I don't blame you anymore; for any of this. I knew, or should have guessed, what I was getting into. But you've given me a chance to see what I am capable of doing. Most of it surprised me, some of it frighteningly so. But I think I have a clearer picture now of who I am. And I have you to thank for that."

CHAPTER FIFTEEN

The entrance to the Hotel Londonskaya sits two hundred yards from the Potemkin Staircase, the 193 steps that lead up from the port of Odessa. Keely and Jonathan had arrived at the hotel around nine p.m. There had been a long queue at the airport as they passed through customs. The agent behind the glass spent a long time scrutinizing their passports, checking each page carefully. Eventually, he returned them and motioned Jonathan and Keely to move on.

It was a short ride from the airport to the center of the Black Sea port. Jonathan had been quiet throughout the trip, and Keely had been lost in her own thoughts. He had not said what would happen in Odessa, and Keely didn't bother asking, knowing that Jonathan often waited until the last minute to formulate a plan.

At dinner in Vienna, he had talked about finding the company that had shipped the crates they had found. He wanted to find out the origin of that shipment, hoping it could lead them to Kestrel. He assumed Kestrel would have covered his tracks carefully, but something in the raid in Georgia had apparently unnerved the gun dealer, and that may have made him careless. It couldn't be the weapons themselves. Jonathan wondered if somehow this illusive dealer's identity might have been compromised because of the raid. It was the only reason Jonathan could imagine causing such an intense effort to find Keely.

Keely wondered if their chase would ever end. If Kestrel was as secretive as he seemed to be, she couldn't imagine Jonathan would be able to run him to ground. Of course, that was Swift Enterprises' specialty; doing things other intelligence agencies could not. She was only slightly relieved she was now the hunter rather than the hunted. And the hunt had kept her from thinking... about Stefan, about her future.

231

The Hotel Londonskaya, turn of the century but in remarkably good shape, sat on a boulevard lined with Western-style boutiques and coffee shops. They registered, once again in the same room. They rode the creaking elevator to the third floor and entered a spacious suite with French doors that led to a small balcony. As Jonathan directed the bellman to put their luggage in the bedroom, Keely strolled over and opened the doors, stepping out into the brisk evening air. She could smell the salt from the sea. Jonathan joined her.

Keely turned to him. "Have you noticed that every hotel we've stayed in has French doors and a balcony?"

Jonathan looked genuinely embarrassed. "I have Rhonda find hotels with this amenity. I find it somehow comforting to be able to step outside without actually going outside. Did you notice the staircase over there? Very famous stairs, those."

Keely looked in the direction he pointed. Between the trees she saw a wide staircase at the foot of a huge statue leading down from the promenade.

"Did you ever see *Battleship Potemkin*? Where the Cossacks are firing on protesters? A baby carriage starts rolling down the stairs?"

Keely nodded. "I think I saw a clip or something."

"Well that's where it was filmed. Very famous."

"What happens to the baby?"

Jonathan looked at her briefly. "You never find out. The baby just keeps rolling down the stairs."

Keely shuddered to think how much that carriage ride seemed a metaphor for her life and wondered if her ride would ever end.

After watching the still street for a minute, they returned inside, and Jonathan called down for a bottle of Scotch and ice. Keely busied herself in the bedroom, emptying her few belongings. She had bought some clothes in the duty-free shop in Vienna, throwing out others. Not quite as economical as finding a laundry, but much simpler.

She could hear the bellman at the door and returned to the sitting room as Jonathan poured them both a stiff drink. He crossed to the couch and slumped down next to Keely, handing her a glass.

"Hope you are enjoying your tour of the Black Sea."

He drained his drink but didn't rise to get another. Keely sipped hers, the amber medicinal-tasting liquid sending a shiver through her.

"I suppose you plan to go to the shipping company tomorrow."

Jonathan had his head back and his eyes closed. "That is my intention."

He stood, walked over and fixed himself another drink, but stayed by the table. "Perhaps we'll learn what the relationship was between Stefan and Kestrel. But whatever it was, obviously Stefan wasn't important to Kestrel's operation."

Keely brushed away images of Stefan dead in his apartment and finished her drink quickly. She stood up, strolling out to the balcony and leaned over the balustrade. She gazed at the people walking along the boulevard. Jonathan joined her. Keely finally turned toward him.

"I don't understand how I could be that important. If Kestrel had discovered I found the truck park, why wouldn't he just move the weapons? Why kill the family? Why chase me? And what's happened to Irina?"

"I feel confident Irina has gone underground."

"And this running around we're doing, this can't go on forever."

Jonathan patted her gently on the shoulder. "I've followed leads a lot shakier than this. Besides, this is no longer just something personal. We've got a job; we're on the clock. And as long as the leads keep popping up, we'll keep pursuing." He caught her expression of dismay. "Unless you're ready to throw in the towel."

She leaned forward and kissed him gently on the cheek. Something inside her wished the kiss could last longer, but she knew that was wrong and leaned back.

"How did I end up back on the clock?" she asked sadly. "I thought I had escaped all this. Obviously, I haven't."

She turned back to the railing and looked down below. "We started this together and we'll finish it together." She glanced toward him, her eyes darkened. "Besides, for me this is still personal."

Jonathan hesitated, looking as though he was debating whether to return her kiss. Instead, he went inside. Moments later, Keely could hear him speaking on the phone, but couldn't make out the conversation.

Despite the late hour, Jonathan suggested they take a walk through the center of the city, although he made sure to steer them toward the district where the shipping office was located. He had talked with the concierge, showing him the bill of laden from Poti with the shipping company's name. The man had gone into the back and returned a few minutes later with the company indicated on a street map.

They made it within two blocks of the office. Jonathan led her in another direction.

After walking for more than a half hour, casually but purposefully, Jonathan pulled Keely to a stop and pointed at a small cafe with light and music streaming from its open door. Above the door was a neon sign that blinked 'New York Cafe.'

"We have an appointment inside. A friend."

He didn't explain further but took Keely's arm and led her toward the cafe. Inside, the long, narrow room was crowded, and a sound system blared American rock. Jonathan stood just inside the door scanning the crowd until he located someone.

They worked their way to a table where an African-American woman with cropped black hair sat sipping on a straw in her drink. She was about Keely's age and very attractive.

When she saw Jonathan, she casually waved but looked excited. She pointed at the empty chairs. When they reached the table, Jonathan leaned down and kissed the woman gently on both cheeks.

Jonathan spoke in a voice loud enough to be heard at the adjacent tables. "What a pleasant surprise. I didn't know you were still in Odessa."

He slipped into the seat beside the woman and Keely sat opposite. Jonathan pointed at Keely.

"Let me introduce Keely Greer. Keely, this is Peery Vanavich. Peery is a lecturer in English at the Polytechnic University here. You've been here a while, haven't you?"

Peery smiled graciously. "Five years now. Of course, I've been back and forth a bit. Went back to my school for two years before they let me come back again."

Jonathan leaned toward Keely but spoke loud enough for any inquisitive listener. "Peery was, I assume still is, a professor at McGill University in Montreal. Specializes in Russian literature, culture, language."

Keely finally comprehended. This was no coincidence. Jonathan continued small talk for a quarter hour, asking about her family, what she had been doing, relating his travels. Keely watched the performance, but she sensed there was a history there that wasn't coming out in the conversation. Finally, he looked at his watch and glanced around the cafe.

"Say, Keely and I are famished. Would you care to join us for a bite?"

The woman thought for a moment, then smiled broadly. "I'd love to. And I know just the place."

They left the cafe and began strolling along the wide boulevard, Jonathan standing between the two women, his hands holding each one's elbow. They stopped periodically to look in shop windows, but Keely knew Jonathan was trying to determine if they were being followed. After they had walked several blocks without talking, Jonathan spoke softly without looking at either woman.

"Peery has agreed to serve as an interpreter." Jonathan didn't need to say more. He had established an extensive network of contacts throughout Europe-- some who provided innocent services such as interpreting, others who were more clandestine. But by the way Peery acted, Keely felt they might have been more than just colleagues. Keely was more intrigued by that than jealousy.

No one spoke again until they were inside the small restaurant Peery had suggested. It was on a side street, away from the boulevard, and looked expensive. More importantly, it was only one-third full. Jonathan asked for a table toward the middle that afforded them a view of the front door.

They settled in and Peery ordered wine and late-night dinner for all of them in Russian. Although Keely didn't speak the language, she could tell Peery spoke like a native. With her jet-black hair and blue eyes, she could have passed for a Ukrainian. Just for a moment, she was reminded of Irina.

After the waiter poured the wine, Jonathan held up his glass in a toast. "To friends." They set down their glasses and Jonathan leaned forward, his voice no longer audible beyond their table.

"Have you had a chance to ask about the company?"

Peery raised her glass and smiled. "Looks pretty legit. Asked around and the company's been there for about fifteen years. Of course, in Odessa, that doesn't mean a whole lot."

"Do you think it's safe for you?"

Peery thought it over for a few seconds. "I guess it's as safe as any place in town.

Depends on you."

Jonathan smiled. "You know I wouldn't do anything to jeopardize your position here. It will be very innocuous. If anybody asks, you were referred to me by the British consulate as an interpreter."

"Then I guess we go tomorrow."

After dinner, during which the three made small talk about England, Canada and Colorado, they parted company, Peery hailing a cab, Jonathan and Keely walking. After a few blocks, Keely's curiosity couldn't be contained.

"Who is she, really?"

Jonathan skipped a step then continued walking. "Peery does some freelance work for the Canadian Foreign Service-- nothing dangerous, just keeps her eyes and ears open."

"And?"

"And we have known each other for a number of years."

Jonathan would say no more.

The next morning, Peery was already in the hotel lobby when Jonathan and Keely came down. She was dressed in a colorful short skirt and peasant blouse and looked for the entire world like a woman about to go on a picnic. She greeted both of them with a jaunty wave and walked to meet them.

"Are we ready? The office is an easy walk."

Jonathan and Peery lingered in the lobby for a moment while Keely started toward the office. Jonathan wanted to make sure they weren't being followed. It was a routine they had employed before. Keely would stroll for a block or two looking at shop windows. She would stop at one, ostensibly to examine the merchandise inside. Not so coincidentally, she always stopped at a window with a dark background. Jonathan-- and now with Peery in tow-- would stroll along the opposite side of the street in the same direction, passing Keely's position. Through the reflection in the window, Keely could observe anyone who might be following.

Jonathan was adept at stopping abruptly, back-tracking a few yards to look in a window or at a sign. This would force anyone following to change direction suddenly, a sure give-away to Keely. After Jonathan had passed, and only when Keely was sure there was no one following, she would proceed. In the next block, Jonathan would stop, and Keely would pass, Jonathan now checking to see if she was being followed.

The whole process was well choreographed, but from an observer's perspective they would appear to be tourists strolling the city.

After their *pas de trois* had continued for several blocks, both Jonathan and Keely were satisfied that no one was following. They continued quickly to the shipping company's office, staying on opposite sides of the street. Keely would serve as lookout while Jonathan and Peery went inside. Keely was to look for-- she didn't know what. Jonathan had spent months teaching her how to identify someone who was in the wrong place at the wrong time.

It had to do with how people carried themselves. Those who were up to no good usually tried too hard to look casual, nonchalant. It was a dead give-away. She positioned herself opposite the building in an alcove, but half a block away. She took out a guidebook she had purchased, and spent the time slowly turning the pages.

Jonathan and Peery were in the building less than twenty minutes. Peery exited first, smiling as though she had just had a pleasant conversation with a friend. Jonathan followed and they kissed on the sidewalk before Peery headed off in the opposite direction. Jonathan watched after her for a minute, and then crossed to where Keely stood.

"Some kind of girl, that."

Keely smiled as she pulled a lock of hair out of her eyes. "Do I detect something more than just professional interest? She's very attractive."

Jonathan smiled back. "Better to charm people, which she certainly did to the clerk inside. Let's get some coffee."

Over rich, dark coffee at a cafe several blocks away, Jonathan recounted his visit to the shipping office. Peery had played her role perfectly. The young clerk in the shipping office couldn't keep his eyes off her.

She had introduced herself and offered her card that indicated she was an 'authorized' translator. She had explained that several crates from Jonathan's company apparently got mixed in with those from a shipment on the N.M.B Varna after it arrived in Poti, Georgia. He hoped to find the owner of the shipment to recover his missing crates. Peery gave the arrival date and the shipping number Jonathan had taken from the office in Poti.

The clerk stiffened when he heard the name of the ship and Poti. He said he could not give out any information about shipments. While they stood there at an impasse, a manager came from the back and asked what the problem might be. Peery explained again. The manager roughly pulled the clerk aside, and although Jonathan and Peery could not hear the conversation, it was obvious the manager was not happy. Embarrassed, the clerk scrambled through his files until he located the shipping order. It was from an import-export firm called Tokanska-Bresk in Odessa. Satisfied, the manager returned to his office.

Peery asked the young man how to contact that firm, but the clerk, still smarting from the upbraiding he had received from his boss, indicated that he only dealt with them over the phone. She tried to get the address, but the clerk seemed very reluctant to say more, so she smiled graciously and left with Jonathan in tow.

After he had recounted the visit to the shipping office, Jonathan sat for a long while staring at his coffee. Finally, he looked at Keely.

"I get a sneaking suspicion that the young man was not completely forthcoming. There must be a listing somewhere for that company."

They returned to the hotel by taxi and Jonathan went straight to the concierge. After a brief exchange, the concierge disappeared into the back. It seemed to take a long time before he returned. When he did, he seemed reluctant to hand Jonathan a piece of paper, but he did.

Jonathan thanked him profusely and walked to where Keely was sitting.

"Seems our Tokanska-Bresk is in a seedier part of town. The concierge was quite surprised I would be inquiring after such a place and cautioned me against going there. I assured him I would be careful."

They sat in the light of the fading sun as it streamed through the open French doors of their hotel room. The afternoon had been spent scouting the area around the import-export office. They had seen very few visitors enter the building. By mid-afternoon, Jonathan had signaled it was time to leave and they had worked their way back to the hotel in silence.

Jonathan had stood at the doors of the balcony for a long while in thought before finally explaining his plan to Keely. It was simple, but very uncharacteristic. He had always preached to Keely the most preferable move was to employ a circuitous approach. Now he proposed a frontal attack.

"I'll simply go in and intimate that I have some unusual equipment that needs shipping. Hopefully, that will draw somebody out."

She didn't like the idea at all. "Seems kind of risky, putting yourself in the open like that."

Jonathan's voice held an obvious determination. "As you pointed it out before, this little dance we are doing around Kestrel is not producing results. Perhaps it is time we became more proactive. Baiting a trap might help. I do not believe our illusive Kestrel is here, but we may be able to get closer to where he might be hiding."

Over the next hour, Jonathan outlined his plan. He would go to the office in the morning, pose as someone interested in moving some 'fragile' equipment from Bulgaria to Turkey, and wait for something to happen. Keely countered that something could go wrong. If it were actually a legitimate business, the people would probably want to know what he wanted to ship. They might even call the authorities. If it was a front operation for Kestrel, they might panic. And that could be even more dangerous. Jonathan did not seem concerned.

He intended to drop the name of an individual who, if it was a legitimate business, would not raise suspicions. On the other hand, if it was a front, there was a good chance that name would mean something, and they would be interested, especially if he made the offer unavoidably attractive, no matter how vague the cargo. The point was, if they took the bait, he would insist on seeing the person in charge-- and that person most likely knew how to get to Kestrel.

Keely was not convinced but knew Jonathan had already made up his mind. She was to watch from outside, note anyone who came in and out and be prepared in case of trouble. They had scoped out a rear entrance, though from a distance, it looked like it hadn't been used in years, dust having collected in a thick layer of the rickety steps leading down from the doorway. Whoever was going to enter or leave the building would do so through the front. Jonathan also felt going to the building early in the morning when street traffic was at its height would provide a bit more security.

That night, Keely slept fitfully. When she finally dosed off, her dreams were invaded by dark and foreboding figures and she would wake with a start. When she looked at Jonathan in the bed next to hers, he slept quietly, seemingly without a trace of concern.

In the morning, they breakfasted in the small cafe next to the hotel and moved out in the same pattern they had used the day before; Keely leaving first, walking two blocks, stopping to window-shop, watching Jonathan as he passed on the opposite side of the street.

The import-export firm was just ten blocks west of the shipping office they had visited the day before, but the area quickly deteriorated from business-like to seedy the closer they came to the harbor. There was a small shop across the street from the import-export firm that Keely had already selected as her vantage point. It had a grimy picture window where Keely could watch the street undetected.

Keely had asked if Jonathan would take Peery along to interpret, but he thought that might put her in too much danger. Besides, Peery lived in Odessa, and she was better off if people could not connect her with him.

They reached the block where the firm was situated. The street was crowded with people, mostly workmen headed for the docks and older women out for the day's shopping. Keely took up her position in the small store. It appeared to be a cross between a family grocery and a pharmacy, with a few kitchen utensils and tools hanging haphazardly from nails driven into the wall behind the counter.

As she entered, Keely smiled at the shopkeeper who lounged behind the counter, putting down the newspaper he had been reading. She smiled even more broadly and walked toward him. She had asked the concierge at the hotel how to say 'I am waiting for someone. Is it all right to stay here?' in Ukrainian and had rehearsed the phrase a number of times on her walk over. Now she approached the man and spoke the words she had practiced. To add enticement, she extended a fifty Hryvnia note, about twenty dollars.

The man hesitated, looking between Keely and the note. Finally, he smiled a toothless smile and reached for the note. He turned back to his paper and Keely wandered to the front of the store. She took up her position just as Jonathan walked into sight. He walked casually, a man for whom it seemed perfectly normal to be on this street at this time. He climbed the stairs and went inside.

The minutes dragged. Although there were a number of people on the street, none entered the building. Her mind wandered and she suddenly thought about marathon runners. She had always been a short distance runner and marveled at the tenacity of those who could run twenty-six miles. She had read how running took on a Zen-like quality, where the runner's mind and body seemed to exist on separate plains. That's how she felt now. She was going through the motions as Jonathan instructed her, but she had no idea where the finish line was or how she would reach it.

She was brought out of her reverie as a mother entered the store pulling along a small child. The little girl was irritable and whining. The mother spoke in a firm tone to quiet her, though Keely couldn't understand what she said. She watched them as they went to the counter and the shopkeeper held up a stick of candy. The mother took it, bowing thanks, and handed it to the little girl. Keely couldn't help but think of the little girl to whom she had given her silver ring. She looked away and back to the street, almost missing Jonathan as he came out.

He seemed totally in control and headed back toward the center of town without bothering to look in Keely's direction. She waited a few more minutes to see if anyone followed, but no one left the building across the street. Satisfied, she turned and waved to the shopkeeper, who just shrugged and continued reading.

They strolled-- separately-- until they reached the cafe where they had eaten breakfast. By the time Keely entered, Jonathan was already seated in the back and the waiter was walking away from the table, leaving a tray of food. Jonathan waved jauntily and Keely made her way to him.

Once seated, she looked at him expectantly. "Must have gone well."

Jonathan smiled innocently. "I've ordered us coffee and rolls," Jonathan said as he meticulously spread jam on his roll. "Seems they've taken the bait. At least it appears they have. When I mentioned that I was not at liberty to divulge the contents of the shipment and dropped a few names, the clerk seemed to stiffen. He said that his manager would have to handle my request and disappeared into the back. A few moments later, an officious-looking weasel appeared. He chased the clerk away brusquely. I intimated that he could earn himself a bonus if he helped. He looked nervous and indicated that the office might not be the best place to discuss matters. He asked if I could meet him this evening. In Shevchenko Park."

"And of course, you said yes."

Jonathan took a bite of the roll and washed it down with coffee. He smiled at her patronizingly. "Of course."

Keely started to protest, but Jonathan held up a hand.

"He wanted to meet inside the park, but I was able to convince him that would not be acceptable. We compromised. I'm to meet him at the corner of Marazlievaya and Nakhimova just outside the park. Much more public. You, my dear, will be in the park behind us."

Keely knew that to protest was pointless. If Jonathan felt the arrangements were acceptable, she would not be able to convince him otherwise. But there was something else he wasn't telling her.

"What else?"

Jonathan hesitated, but finally said, "I got the distinct feeling that the man had been expecting me."

"A trap?"

Jonathan sipped his coffee and stared into the middle distance for a minute. "Perhaps. But traps can always be turned on the trapper. Vision is the art of seeing things invisible."

Keely laughed. "Your thought for the day?"

"Not mine-- the first Mr. Swift. Just a thought that we may draw out our invisible friend."

After their coffee, they took a taxi to the meeting place and began to reconnoiter. The streets were busy, with shops and cafes facing into the park along Marazlievaya. The tree line began about thirty yards inside the park, obscuring a gentle rise into the interior of the park. They strolled up the rise, evaluating the cover available--both for Keely and for anyone else who might wish to observe. A rock outcropping afforded an unobstructed view of the corner. Someone standing there could watch who came and went without being seen. It was the only logical place for a person interested in observing the street corner to hide. The break in the trees provided an unobstructed view but far enough inside the tree line to be invisible at night.

Jonathan spent minutes walking the tree line to ensure that his analysis was correct, moving ever deeper into the woods until he was satisfied that he had a clear picture of the location. He motioned to Keely to follow him and moved at an angle to the rock outcropping. Thirty yards away, he stopped and pointed to a slight depression.

"Here's your position. From here, you can just make out the corner, but have a lovely view of the rocks over there." He pointed in a sweeping motion from the street to the rocks.

They returned to the rocks and worked their way deeper into the forest along an unused path that wandered for several hundred yards, exiting onto a paved walkway that meandered off in either direction. He smiled.

"If someone else is observing our little meeting, chances are they would come up this walkway, sneak along that little path and camp out on those rocks."

"That's an awful big assumption, don't you think?"

Jonathan wasn't paying much attention to her. "I don't assume, I plan."

With that he sauntered off along the pavement as though out for his morning constitutional. Keely didn't have the confidence he had, but knew Jonathan had a sense about these things. She had seen him make similar calculations before-- invariably accurate. He seemed to sense her concern and turned, waving for her to follow. When she reached him, he smiled.

"Don't worry, I will position myself so that the gentleman from the shipping company is between me and the trees. He'll make an adequate shield. Besides, I will have you up here. Why should I worry?"

241

The meeting was scheduled for nine p.m. and Jonathan decided she should be in position by seven. It would mean a long wait, but he wanted to be sure she did not cross paths with anyone. They wandered through the shops around the hotel, and Keely purchased a black sweatshirt, black jeans and hiking boots. She also bought a small blanket and a novel. If someone should happen to stumble across her, she would be just another tourist seeking solitude to read. Jonathan had offered to get a weapon, but she refused without explanation.

They had lunch and returned to the room, Jonathan suggesting she get some rest before the evening. She couldn't sleep, but the cool sheets help calm her nerves. By six, she was up and dressed. They had decided to leave the hotel separately.

Before she left, she turned to Jonathan. "Take no chances. I need your ass. You got me?"

He smiled condescendingly. "Of course, my dear. And I love you, too." He leaned forward and kissed her on the forehead. "Now go and enjoy your book."

Keely entered the park several blocks south of the meeting site. She walked casually along the paved walkway, passing only a few elderly men hobbling along on canes and a few mothers herding children before them. When she reached the point where she was to leave the path, she glanced around and moved into the trees quickly. It was fortunate they had walked the area so thoroughly earlier in the day. The deep shadows of the early evening had already closed in, and she could tell that by the meeting time, the area would be in total darkness.

She approached the outcropping, pausing to make sure of no others following. She then left the path and worked her way through the trees until she found the depression. She tried to gauge the quickest route between her location and the rocks but realized that cutting back to the path would be the easiest. When she felt she had that route in her mind, she returned to the depression and laid out the blanket. She positioned herself so she could see both the street corner and the rocks. The trees were sparser around the outcropping so it would be less difficult seeing movement there than if someone looked in her direction. She glanced at her watch: Seven.

Time seemed to drag. She daydreamed about Colorado and her father. She wondered where life would take her when this hunt ended. She wondered if they would ever find Kestrel? If they did, what then? Being with Jonathan these past weeks had softened the pain of Stefan's death, but had not dissuaded her decision to leave this life behind. The problem was deciding what to do next. She knew, though, no matter where she went, her past would haunt her.

It was close to eight-thirty when she became aware of movement in the distance. She focused her attention on the rocks. It was dark now, but there was a full moon and the absence of trees around the rocks made visibility acceptable. She peered into the darkness until she saw a figure move along the rocks. She could not make out much, but by the movements, the person was alone and did not want to be detected.

She wished they had picked a location closer so that she could have a better view, but there was no place between that would have afforded as much cover. She glanced at the corner; Jonathan was not there.

Despite what Jonathan had suggested, she realized she needed to be closer. She left the blanket and book and moved quickly but quietly through the trees. Her years in Colorado had taught her how to move through forests, and she was comfortable in the fact she would not be detected by whoever was on the rocks.

She gained the walkway and stood for a moment to make sure no one else was on the path. The park seemed deserted. She moved east quickly, passing the opening that led to the rocks. She stopped twenty yards beyond, ostensibly to tie her shoes. She heard no movement.

Assuming the person on the rocks was alone, she returned to the opening and began working her way along the path. She moved slowly, hoping that the person's attention would be on the street and not behind him. After she had gone fifty yards, she stopped and knelt down. The rocks were another fifty yards, and she checked her watch to determine how much time she had left before the meeting. Fifteen minutes.

She started forward again, stopping every ten yards, closing her eyes and listening carefully. She knew her ears would be better in the dark than her eyes. She heard nothing. For a fleeting moment, she wished she had taken Jonathan up on his offer of a weapon.

Finally, she was within twenty yards and stopped. She could make out the rocks ahead but was not sure where the person was. There was no sound. There was no movement. She waited. After what seemed hours, she heard the distinct sound of metal against metal. She knew that sound. It was the bolt action of a sniper's rifle.

Without waiting, she moved forward. The figure was crouched in a shooting position, one leg tucked under him, the other resting on a jacket that served as a rest for the rifle. He must have heard her, because he fired quickly, the report muffled, apparently because the rifle had a noise suppression attachment. She lunged forward. He began to rise, but his position impeded him. She was on him as the rifle swung in her direction, but he didn't have a chance.

Her first kick with the heel of her boot caught him in the jaw, snapping his head around.

She stepped through the kick, grabbing the barrel of the rifle and yanking up. As his arms followed, she buried her knee into his rib cage, hearing a sudden rush of air that prohibited any attempt to cry out. Her fist came up and smashed him across the bridge of the nose. Blood spurted. His body sagged, his hands released the rifle and he slumped to the ground dazed.

Keely was breathing hard and knew she should attack, but she turned quickly toward the street instead. A body lay on the ground and someone was moving quickly in her direction, the movement indicating that the person was in distress. She chambered a round in the rifle and swung it toward the advancing person. She recognized Jonathan.

She began to lower the rifle when a hand grabbed her from behind. The shooter had revived enough to make it to his feet and lunged for the rifle. Keely spun, stepped back and fired point blank into the shooter's chest. Again, the report was muffled, but he flew back a few feet, crashing into a tree, a dark stain spreading from the hole in his chest.

When Keely turned back to the street, Jonathan was no more than thirty yards away. Behind him, she could see people stopping by the body on the ground and looking around. When Jonathan reached her, she saw a stain of blood extending from just under his left arm to his waist. She didn't know if it was his or the person's on the street. He took in the scene, took several deep breaths and walked over to where Keely stood. He gently took the rifle from her and touched her cheek.

"You all right?"

She nodded. "You?"

He glanced at his chest. "'Fraid I caught one. Not bad, though." He motioned toward the street. "Seems it passed through my friend there before hitting me."

Keely looked at the shooter lying at the foot of the tree. "I guess when I spooked him, it threw off his aim. What happened down there?"

"We were talking amiably when the firing began. My friend from the shipping company did seem a bit distressed when he first arrived. Like he was afraid of something." Jonathan glanced at the shooter's body. "Doesn't look like he gave you much trouble. Though, I would like to have chatted with him."

Jonathan walked over to the man, turning him over with his foot. It was hard to make out his face in the deep shadows. Jonathan motioned Keely over.

"Familiar?"

Keely glanced at the dead face. "No."

"Me either."

Jonathan searched the body and found a wallet. He stepped away from the body and rummaged through the wallet, stopping suddenly and withdrawing a business card.

Keely stepped closer to him. "You recognize something?"

Jonathan held up the card. Keely didn't understand. "What is it?" "Peery's business card. The one she gave the shipping clerk yesterday."

CHAPTER SIXTEEN

Jonathan sat impatiently as Keely tended to his wound. In the half-light, she could not tell how much damage the bullet had been done, but from the amount of blood covering Jonathan's shirt, it was more than a flesh wound. She reached under her sweater and unfastened her bra, slipping it off through one sleeve. She held the padded cups against the wound and wrapped the straps around his chest and tied them tightly over the cups. It was makeshift and very tight, but it was secure.

Jonathan wanted to find Peery immediately, but Keely counseled that a man wandering the streets in a bloody shirt would attract too much attention. And, they needed to tend to his wound properly. He gave in and agreed to return to the hotel briefly.

Keely went to where the shooter had been laying and picked up his dark jacket. She helped Jonathan slip into it and began to lead him toward the path. In the distance, they heard the whine of a police car, but he stopped and told her to wait while he went back to the shooter. He took the rifle, placed the barrel against the man's chest and fitted the man's thumb against the trigger, then he returned to Keely.

"When they find him, the first thought will be that he shot the other fellow then killed himself. Since he won't have identification, it will take a while for them to figure out who he is."

They worked their way slowly along the path to the walkway and proceeded west to the park entrance. As they gained the street, they could hear a police siren close by. Keely had Jonathan's good arm around her shoulder and helped him to the curb.

She flagged a taxi and helped Jonathan inside. She gave the driver the address of the hotel. Jonathan rested his head on her shoulder. A drunken husband helped home by a dutiful wife.

Once inside their hotel room, Keely led Jonathan to the bathroom and made him sit on the edge of the tub. He was pale but made no indication he was in pain. She went into the living room and poured him a tall scotch.

As Jonathan drank, Keely noticed the slightest tremble in his hand. She stripped off his shirt, carefully laying it on top of the shooter's jacket. They would be discarded later. She retrieved the first aid kit Jonathan had in his bag. It contained more than the typical bandages and iodine. This kit was designed to handle serious injury.

Keely gingerly removed her blood-soaked bra from the wound. In the harsh bathroom light, she could tell the bullet had dug a gash in Jonathan's side two inches long by an inch deep. Blood oozed from the wound, but the bullet had passed through.

Keely gently washed the area with peroxide before she applied a coating of antibiotic cream. She covered the wound with a gauze pad and secured it tightly with more gauze. She took a bottle of penicillin from the kit and put two tablets into Jonathan's hand, which he took without complaint.

"We need to head off any infection."

When she had finished, he inspected her work and smiled wanly.

"Thanks."

"I don't think it'll need stitches, although we should probably have a doctor look at it."

Jonathan shook his head.

"Figured you would say that."

She cleaned up the area as Jonathan went into the living and sat on the couch. She could hear him pick up the telephone and dial, but he didn't say anything. She made sure no blood had spilled onto the tub or floor, then wrapped up the discarded clothes. She walked into the living room. Jonathan was struggling into his jacket. Keely walked over to him and helped him with it.

"Don't you think you should rest? You lost a lot of blood."

Jonathan expression told her resting was not an option.

"Peery doesn't answer."

She went into the bedroom and returned, putting on her jacket. She carried his small leather case that contained his lock tools and a small flashlight. She handed them to him.

"Let's go find her then."

Jonathan looked as though he was going to suggest Keely stay at the hotel but thought better of it.

"We'll start at her apartment. I doubt she'd be at school this late."

Peery lived south of the center of the city close to the Polytechnic Institute where she taught. The street of neat, but utilitarian apartments was virtually empty. The taxi let them out and Jonathan asked the driver to wait, which he agreed to do after Jonathan handed him several Hryvnia notes.

Jonathan led the way to a two-story building. Inside the poorly-lit hallway, Keely could just make out a row of five mailboxes without names. Jonathan apparently knew his way and started to climb the stairs to the second floor. That hall was totally dark, the bare bulb hanging from the ceiling extinguished. Jonathan touched the bulb, turning it in its socket until the light flickered on. He walked to the door at the front of the building, listening carefully before he rapped softly on the doorframe. There was no answer. He tried again, this time a bit louder. Still, no sound from inside.

Jonathan tried the door and it opened. The main room was dark, and Keely could just make out the florescent glow of a kitchen clock in the distance. Jonathan moved through the room slowly. He studied the area then moved deeper into the apartment.

A door toward the rear was ajar and Jonathan stood beside it and moved it open with his foot. It was Peery's bedroom and by the looks of things, there had been a struggle. The bedclothes were in disarray and a small table had been knocked over. Jonathan stepped around to the other side of the bed and let out an angry moan. Peery lay face down, her head at an unnatural angle. Jonathan knelt down and placed two fingers just below her ear. He then gently examined her, attempting to lift her body onto the bed. His wound wouldn't let him, and Keely knelt beside him and helped. They stood in silence looking down at the still figure that seemed to be in deep sleep. Jonathan pulled the sheet over her face and walked out of the room without a sound. Once they reached the street, Jonathan stopped and stared into the starlit night. Keely walked to him and touched his arm.

"Jonathan?"

"She was killed quickly. Doesn't look like whoever did it was after information."

Keely stood beside him for a moment then moved him toward the taxi. Once they were underway, she touched his arm again.

Jonathan looked vacantly out the window as he spoke. "We met while I was still in the S.A.S. She was a graduate student in London. I was taking a course in Russian at the same university. She offered to tutor me and-- well, one thing led to another. I even contemplated leaving the service for her. Take a normal job. She never asked about my work, but one night several of the boys were over, drinking a bit too much, and recounted some of our adventures. Later that night, she asked me about the service for the first time.

"Theoretically, she understood the reason for people like me, she just didn't know if she could spend the rest of her life in such an atmosphere." He looked at Keely for the first time. "You understand."

He took a deep breath. "There was no earth-shattering break-up. We just drifted apart. She returned to Canada. As fate would have it, she was recruited by Canadian intelligence. When I was wounded and left the service, I went to Ontario to see, if perhaps, we could start fresh. But what might have been no longer existed. We discovered we were better as friends."

They rode in silence back toward the hotel. Finally, Jonathan seemed to awaken from his reverie and leaned forward. When they arrived, they got out, but Jonathan turned toward the promenade. Keely followed.

They walked several blocks before Jonathan stopped and sat on a bench, obviously in pain. Keely sat beside him.

"What are you thinking?"

Jonathan stared out at the blackness of the harbor. In the distance, lights from ships left shimmering trails on the water. He looked at Keely.

"We have to continue."

Without another word, he stood, walked to the street and hailed a taxi. When they entered, he leaned forward and spoke to the driver. "Take us to Tushnarova, north of the steps."

Jonathan sat back in silence and said nothing more until they were within several blocks of the import office and he ordered the taxi driver to stop. They got out and this time, Jonathan did not ask the driver to wait. When the taxi was out of sight, they headed toward the import office building. When they were in the same block, Jonathan pulled Keely into the shadow of a doorway. He waited several long minutes, trying to determine if they may have been followed. But the street was still. Finally, he stepped to the sidewalk and started walking briskly toward the building where the import office was located. Keely hurried to keep up with him. Jonathan paused to see if anyone was around. Satisfied, he motioned to Keely. "We have to see what's inside that place."

He quickly picked the outside door lock, and when they entered, he made sure it was locked behind them. He moved to the entrance of the import company.

"Obviously, the guy I talked to today was not supposed to meet me at the park. I believe that bullet was meant for him, as well. The shooter was most likely ordered to take both of us out. Whoever killed Peery must have gotten her address from the clerk at the shipping office we talked with yesterday."

"I don't get it."

"I never mentioned Peery today. The only person who knew she was involved was the first clerk."

"You think that guy gave Peery's name to the shooter in the park?"

"Peery has been dead less than an hour. The shooter was in the park well before that. There must be somebody else."

Without waiting for a response, Jonathan opened the office door. Inside the small, crowded office, several desks and a row of mismatched cabinets sat along one wall. Moonlight from a side window illuminated the desks, but Jonathan didn't bother them. Toward the back was a smaller office, containing only a single desk and no filing cabinets. Behind another door was a storage room. Jonathan stood in the middle of the room, his eyes surveying every square inch of the place. He stopped and seemed to concentrate on the sidewall. He walked over, pacing off the distance from the window to the back wall. Without saying a word, he motioned her to follow.

Outside, he walked around to the side of the building and paced off the distance from the window to the back corner of the building. There he stopped. Keely walked to him.

"What is it?"

"The dimensions don't match. Inside the distance from the window to the back wall is approximately fifteen feet. I get twenty-five to thirty feet out here. Where's the extra ten feet?"

Without waiting for a response, he turned the corner. Keely followed. The darkened alley afforded them little visibility. They moved cautiously toward the back door. Jonathan withdrew the penlight and began to examine the door. What looked like an unused backdoor to the casual observer was not. The doorframe was metal painted to look like wood, and the door jamb at the foot of the door was a shiny steel plate. The door did not have a lock. Jonathan traced the frame, finally pointing to almost invisible wires attached to the frame with screws.

"Alarm."

They returned to the offices. Jonathan rested against a desk and Keely could see perspiration on his forehead. His wound must have been giving him problems, but he didn't complain.

"That door out there hasn't been opened in a while. I bet there's a way in from here."

He studied the room a moment, and walked to the back wall, running his fingers at shoulder height along the wall to the storage room. Finding nothing, he opened the door to the tiny room and stepped inside. Keely followed. He shut the door and turned on the overhead light. It was ten feet by five feet with built-in shelving along the wall adjoining the small office. The back wall was lined with filing cabinets, boxes piled on top almost to the ceiling.

Jonathan tested each cabinet, rocking it gently from side to side and then tugging on the first drawer handle. When he tested the third one, instead of the drawer pulling out, the entire cabinet rolled forward, the boxes perched on top apparently anchored in place. Along with the cabinet, a portion of the wall seemed to be attached as well. When Jonathan had pulled it completely out, they could see an entrance into a small room behind. Jonathan motioned for her to stay put and he moved through the opening slowly. He disappeared, but after only a moment, a light went on and he called to her to come in.

The room was in stark contrast to the front office. There was no clutter, just a single desk with four modern file cabinets behind. On a table to one side was an expensive copier and fax machine. A computer terminal dominated one side of the desk.

They looked at each other and Jonathan pointed at the computer. "See what you can do with that. I'll check the cabinets."

Keely sat down in front of the computer and turned it on. The screen came to life and the computer went through the booting procedure, finally presenting Keely with a desktop that asked for the password. Rhonda had spent more than a year showing Keely how to manipulate computers and Keely tried all the tricks she had been taught, but she could not find a way around the security program. Behind her, Jonathan rifled through the cabinets. She heard him say 'good' but without any satisfaction.

"Jonathan, I can't get around this system. You have any luck?"

"Kestrel may be a real bastard, but he's an anal bastard. The files are in chronological order."

He withdrew several folders, placing them unopened on the desk. He moved to a lower drawer and called over his shoulder. "When were you in Georgia?"

"Early May."

Jonathan withdrew another folder and placed it on the pile. He closed the drawer, walked around and sat on the edge of the desk. Keely shut down the computer.

"What did you find?"

Jonathan was flipping through sheets of paper in the top file, a look of fierce concentration on his face. "Very thorough records," he said more to himself than to her. He stopped at the last piece in the folder and looked confused.

"What is it?"

"Seems to be the military map of the area where those trucks were situated."

He flipped the map to her. She glanced at it, looking more closely, the blood drained from her face.

251

"Jonathan," she barely whispered. She couldn't speak more but pointed at some scribbling on the side of the map. Jonathan walked around and looked over her shoulder.

"Coordinates."

Keely turned her face up to him. "I know. I wrote them."

For the next few minutes, Keely described how she had written the coordinates on the map, gave it to Irina who left for Tbilisi.

"I assumed she called them in to you when she got there."

Jonathan looked at her intently. "She never called them in."

"What? But the air strike…?"

"Was based on the coordinates you texted me."

"Does this mean Kestrel may have found Irina? Maybe that's why Rhonda couldn't get in touch with her."

They sat in silence for a moment then Jonathan stood and started through the cabinets. "We will have to worry about that later. Let's deal with what we have here right now."

She and Jonathan had spent the better part of two hours combing through the files in the secret room at the back of the import office. They found detailed records of all types of transactions. Kestrel had been smuggling weapons, equipment and medical supplies. Anything that could be sold, Kestrel sold it. Although most buyers were not identified, it was not difficult to ascertain which groups bought what material because of the destinations. Kestrel seemed to have a pipeline from the former Soviet satellite states to terrorist organizations in Eastern Europe, the Middle East and North Africa. He was non-sectarian in his dealings, selling to governments as well as insurgents in the same country. It was smart business to fan the flames of conflict, increasing his sales potential. Keely wondered why he would keep such detailed information.

"Probably as insurance, assuming that if someone came down on him hard, he could barter information for his freedom."

Jonathan had quietly examined the files, jotting down notes periodically, but returning the files to their original locations. He had Keely turn on the copier and made several copies of what appeared to be invoices. He also copied the map Keely had used to pinpoint the truck park in Georgia. Keely also rummaged through the desk, finding nothing more than a collection of office supplies. She moved on to a file cabinet set off from the others, picking the lock on the bottom draw. Inside she found several handguns, mainly Russian military issue. Jonathan examined the collection.

"Samples."

"Pretty eclectic if you ask me. Some of this shit is twenty years old."

Jonathan reached into the drawer and removed an automatic that had been fitted with a silencer. He checked the clip and finding it full, stuck it into his waistband.

"Souvenir."

Jonathan made a copy of the most recent file after examining it. When he finished, he closed the drawer, told Keely to turn off the copier and surveyed the room. Assured that everything was as they had found it, he led the way out of the room, sliding the fake cabinet back in place. When they were finally outside, Jonathan checked his watch and shook his head.

"'Fraid we'll have to walk. Don't think there'll be many cabs in this area at this time of night."

As they walked along in silence, Keely could see Jonathan was testing the mobility of his side. She could only assume that the wound was causing him pain, but he would never admit it. They had walked several blocks, getting closer to where most of the tourist hotels were located. There were more lights and a few more people on the streets. They could have continued walking, but Keely flagged down a passing taxi and open the back door.

"Get in."

Jonathan started to protest, but relented and slipped in, Keely right behind him. She gave the driver the name of their hotel. As they pulled away from the curb, she glanced at Jonathan.

His eyes were closed and by the tightness of his jaw, she knew his shoulder was causing him considerable distress. The ride took less than ten minutes. Keely paid the driver while Jonathan headed for the door. They proceeded to their room and once inside, Keely headed directly for the dresser and the bottle of scotch. She poured a tall glass and went to the couch where Jonathan had slumped. He reached for the glass gratefully and drained half of it. Keely knelt in front of him and pulled gently on the lapels of his coat, made him sit up and helped him take it off. She saw a trace of blood on his shirt. The wound must have leaked through the dressing.

"I need to change that."

Without waiting for a reply, she went into the bathroom, returning with a damp cloth and the first aid kit. He was reading one of the copies they had made from the office.

"This file indicates that those guidance systems have been diverted to someone named Ibrahim. No address, but a fax from him. Rhonda should be able to tell us where it came from."

He started to get up, but Keely pushed him gently back. She had sunk to the floor beside him, holding the first aid kit. "Let's get that shirt off."

He didn't protest. She worked carefully, but quickly, removing the dressing; pouring a bit of peroxide on the gauze pad covering the wound to help loosen it. When she finally removed the pad, the wound was swollen and angry, but there was no indication of infection. She wiped the area gently, applied more antibiotic cream, and re-wrapped the wound. When she was done, she looked into Jonathan's eyes. There was a mixture of weariness, pain and appreciation.

"I believe you missed your calling, Florence. You'd have made a wonderful nurse."

"Not me," she laughed, "but growing up with brothers I saw my share of cuts. Of course, none by gunshot." She began to button his shirt. He caught her arm with his good hand and pulled her close. He kissed her forehead, then tilted her head up and gently kissed her lips. It was more friendly than passionate but it still sent a current through Keely she knew she could not allow. She pulled herself away and stood up, gathering the kit and the soiled bandages.

"You need rest."

He smiled up at her feebly and winked. "Nice way to say, 'easy chum.'"

She shook her head, took the material to the bathroom and returned. She took his empty glass, went over to the dresser, and poured them both a drink. After she handed it to him, she plopped into the facing armchair and drank half of hers.

"Why do you think Irina didn't call you?"

"Several possibilities. Irina does not like to be ordered around. She may have been angry with you and decided to wait until you got back to Tbilisi and make you call."

"And the map? If Kestrel had it... doesn't sound too good for Irina. I don't much care for her, but I don't want to think she's dead, too."

"I'd like to think she simply left it in her room in Tbilisi. Someone broke in and stole it."

Keely preferred that idea as well. "You said all along that Kestrel might be looking for me to tie up all loose ends. Which means Irina is just as much a target as I am. Do you think we should try to find her?"

Jonathan sipped his drink, apparently in deep thought. "I'll have Rhonda try again to track her down through other sources we have. Should we get off track and head in another direction? I don't think so, when we seem to be at Kestrel's doorstep. I think that's how we can best help Irina... and you."

Keely was put off by the callous way Jonathan seemed to dismiss Irina's fate, but she knew that he could not waste time worrying about what he could not resolve.

"That manager might have helped, but he's... unavailable. We don't have a clue where Kestrel actually is, or whether he even comes to Odessa. That office may just be one of many." He stared out the window, then back to Keely. "There was the clerk in the shipping who passed on Peery's card. I can't figure what his role in all this is, but he's not an innocent."

He shifted and Keely could see the pain register on his face. She stood up, put her glass on the table, and held out her hand to him. "We can work this out in the morning. You really do need to rest if just for a few hours. Maybe we can come up with a plan."

Jonathan did not argue and allowed Keely to lead him into the bedroom. She helped him onto his bed and he gingerly lay back against the pillows. She adjusted them to make sure his side was supported and drew the blanket over him. He smiled up at her as his eyelids closed.

"Thank you."

Keely lay on her bed in the darkness. She was bone-tired, but her mind would not let her sleep. She kept flashing on the map and worrying about how Kestrel might have gotten it. She was petrified to think that another death had been caused by her misadventure in Georgia, although Irina had known the risks. And somehow, she had to stop blaming herself for what happened there-- she had only been doing her job. She glanced over to Jonathan. Swift had been at fault. She also thought of Stefan for the first time in days, realizing that his face was quickly fading from her memory.

The first rays of the morning sun spread across the still waters of the Odessa harbor, promising respite from the chill of the night. But Keely was unimpressed. With bleary eyes and a throbbing head, she continued to stare at a copy of the military map bearing her scribbling. As the sun crept over the horizon, Keely stirred and looked over to where Jonathan slept. He had not moved. She wondered if Peery's death had hit him as hard as Stefan's death had hit her. She knew he would never tell her. That was too private, too intimate. His eyes opened and he looked toward Keely.

"Morning."

Not at all rested, she stood, stretched and walked toward the sitting room. "You stay there. I'll order breakfast."

Over coffee and rolls, Jonathan outlined a plan. After dressing quickly, Jonathan stayed in the room while Keely made her way to the concierge, asking if a rental car was available. The concierge telephoned an agency and within twenty minutes, the car was at the hotel. When it arrived, she phoned Jonathan to come down.

Outside, Keely drove while Jonathan directed her. Before going to the shipping office, Jonathan led her through traffic to a side street. He told her to wait while he got out and went into an office without any signs. He came out with a package and got back in the car. Keely then drove them to the district where the shipping office was located. When they got within a block, Jonathan told her to find a parking spot. Keely noticed Jonathan's slow movement as he got out of the car on the passenger side. "You okay?"

"Yes. The package is for you."

She looked inside. There was a small automatic. She looked at Jonathan. "An enticement for the clerk to join us."

He directed her to park across from a bakery diagonally across the street from the office.

They entered the bakery and took a table near the window. The baker leaned over the long counter and looked at them a moment, then spoke in broken English.

"You want?" waving his hand over his baked goods on display.

Jonathan smiled. "We haven't decided." He looked back to her and then out the window in time to see a young man a block and a half away. "There. In the brown coat and pants. Has the newspaper under his arm."

"I see him."

"Invite him to talk. I'll pick you up in the car."

They moved quickly.

The man was unlocking the door when Keely walked up behind him. She smiled politely when he turned around to see her. His disgruntled expression indicated he wasn't yet ready for business.

He spoke to her in Russian. When she smiled and shook her head, he switched to crisp, practiced English. "We are not open."

"Good. You speak English."

His expression turned from irritation to fear as she stepped closer to him and let him see her other hand holding the automatic inside her jacket.

"What is this about? I have no money."

Keely continued to smile. "That's okay. I just want to talk with you."

His eyes scanned the sea of pedestrians trying to find help.

Keely took his arm gently. "Just smile like we are old friends and come with me."

He seemed unsure what to do. Keely sensed he might try to overpower her.

"If you try to run or shout, I will kill you," she said passively although she questioned if she really meant the words.

"You think you shoot me here and no one would notice?"

"What difference will it make if you are dead?"

The color drained from his face.

256

"Walk to your left, please."

Keely looped her arm firmly through his and pulled him tightly to her, letting him feel the barrel of the gun in his ribs.

"Do you mind telling me what...?"

"I do mind. Just keep smiling."

Keely saw that Jonathan had pulled the car to the curb. She approached quickly and opened the front door, telling the man to get in. He started to turn around to her, but she jabbed the barrel of the gun very hard against his rib cage. He straightened in surprise, and got in. Keely slipped in behind the young man and Jonathan moved rapidly from the curb as Keely pulled her door closed. The young man was staring at Jonathan.

"You were in the office. Two days ago. What is this about?"

Neither Keely nor Jonathan answered, but Keely pressed the barrel against the man's neck to remind him that he was to sit quietly. Jonathan drove them through the business district, past a residential area, then well into open country. Jonathan had shown her on a map where they would take the man for questioning. He had told her he wanted privacy, complete privacy. The trip took more than a half hour during which no one spoke.

Jonathan found the road he wanted and turned. It was the entrance to a park and as Jonathan slowed, Keely read the sign marked Danube Wetlands in English. He followed the gravel drive through manicured lawns dotted periodically with statues. As they left the entrance behind, the surroundings became more natural until they reached a clearing closed in on three sides by large oaks. He pulled the car well off the drive. He got out and walked around to the front passenger door, which he opened.

"If you would...."

The man climbed out with Keely right behind him. "What do you people want with me?"

Jonathan smiled and motioned toward the trees. "What is your name?"

The young man looked frightened. "Andriy."

"Fine, Andriy. Let's walk, shall we?"

He motioned to Keely and she handed him the automatic, which he held non-threateningly at his side. They strolled toward the trees, Keely unobtrusively behind them. After several yards, Jonathan stopped and motioned for the man to sit on the grass. The clerk did as directed and Jonathan sat beside him.

"We just want to ask you some questions." The smile faded. "I want you to tell me about the owner of the company where you sent me."

"Tell you what?"

"Let's start with his name."

His eyes darted between the two of them settling on Jonathan. "I do not know. I have never met him."

Jonathan's hand brought the automatic up to the man's temple. "You've never met the man?"

The clerk shuddered and looked on the verge of tears. "I only dealt with Kimro Budell."

"The manager at the import office?"

The man nodded his head.

Jonathan lowered the weapon. "How do you know him?"

"He often does business with my company."

"Did you know he was killed last night? By someone trying to kill me?"

The man's mouth tried to form words. He finally found his voice. "No."

"Who did you give my friend's business card to, Andriy?"

At first, the clerk was confused, glancing at Keely. Then he understood. "I gave it to Kimro. I told him someone may be coming to him."

"And obviously, my inquiries disturbed someone. My friend was also killed last night."

Jonathan let that sink in before he continued. "You say you've never seen the man who owns the import company. How do you conduct business?"

"I was told the man who owned the company lived far away and Kimro would personally handle all his orders."

"What about that room in the back? The one behind the fake filing cabinet."

The man shook his head, as if he didn't understand. "Room? What room?"

Jonathan placed his hand on his shoulder as if they were old buddies. "You are telling me the truth?"

"Yes."

"The way you said that, I don't believe it."

"I swear."

Jonathan released the hold on the man. He stared at him a moment, thinking. "Did Kimro tell you about any visitors out of the ordinary?"

"Visitors?"

Jonathan's response was so quick, it startled even Keely as Jonathan swung the barrel of the automatic across the man's jaw. The clerk's head snapped sharply to the side as blooded trickled from his lips.

"Visitors." Jonathan's tone was sharp and demanded a response.

"Not really." He seemed to be searching for some bit of information to keep the Englishman from striking him again. "There was one who came often."

"Who?"

"I do not know."

Jonathan raised the weapon but did not hit him. "A name."

The man's eyes pleaded for mercy. "I do not know. That is the truth."
"What did he look like?"

"It was a woman," he answered quickly to avoid being hit.

Jonathan glanced toward Keely. "A woman?"

The man answered again quickly. "A tall, blonde woman. Ukrainian. She came every three weeks to see Kimro. He seemed frightened of her."

There was no hint of surprise on Jonathan's face, but Keely's mouth opened in shock, inhaling sharply. Jonathan continued matter-of-factly.

"When was the last time she was there?"

"Two weeks ago, I think."

The man had begun to weep. Jonathan touched him gently on the shoulder. "Don't think. Be exact."

"Yes, it was two weeks ago. An order going to Tunis." A look came across his face as if he wanted to say more. Jonathan grabbed a lock of hair and tilted his head back.

"Is there something else?"

"I overheard her tell Kimro that someone named Kestrel would meet the shipment." Keely felt weak. Jonathan stood up. "Is that it? Is that all you can tell me?"

The man wiped blood off his mouth. "Yes. I know nothing else."

Keely walked a step or two toward the car, expecting Jonathan to bring the clerk back to the car for the return trip to the city. She heard the spit of the automatic and whirled around to see the young man pitch forward on the ground. She looked at Jonathan, then at the automatic. She ran back to Jonathan who was bending over the man positioning the automatic into the dead man's hand. Jonathan stood up.

"That should work."

She raised her voice. "For what?"

"Needs to look like suicide."

"Does this fucking shit ever stop?"

He stood up and came close to her, the frustration apparent in his eyes. "Look, this isn't some dime-store spy novel where the good guys have the luxury of acting honorably. That boy was a threat to us. He was instrumental in Peery's death. There was no way to know whether he would tell Kestrel we were on his trail. That is why he had to die. This is a war, Keely, and he is another casualty. Like Stefan. Like Peery."

With that, he walked away, leaving Keely alone, shaking in her own fear she was never going to be free.

CHAPTER SEVENTEEN

The sky above Tunis was black in the early morning hours, with only a few streetlights to puncture the darkness. It reminded her of Tangier with its French architecture and the warm salty air of the Southern Mediterranean.

Keely stood on the tiny balcony of the Hotel Belvedere in a quiet section of the city, staring through the night. In the distance, a faintly amplified voice called the faithful to prayer. She listened closely to the sound. The first time she had heard it in Tangier, the sound so captivated her that she had found herself praying, something she hadn't done in years. Now, on the balcony in Tunis, the call to prayer forced her to reflect on the pain and suffering of the past few weeks. She had lost count of the people dead because of her. Perhaps, she was afraid to count.

Into her memory crept the oil painting that had hung in the third-grade classroom at Our Lady of Mercy School. Christ, kneeling at a rock, His hands folded as He prayed. A stream of light captured Him in the darkness. She recalled every detail vividly. That painting had always made her feel safe and secure. She wondered why she had remembered now but was glad for the sudden comfort that came with the memory. She looked into the room where Jonathan slept quietly on the bed next to hers. She wondered if he ever prayed.

After Jonathan had executed the clerk in Odessa, they had driven back to the hotel in silence. Keely wanted a better explanation why Jonathan had to kill the young man, but she knew he would not provide one. She couldn't help but wonder if it had been out of revenge for Peery's death, although Jonathan would never have admitted that. Looking down at the man's body, Keely thought about the three men in Georgia and wondered if she used the same rationalization to justify killing them.

When they had returned to the hotel, Jonathan had gone into the bedroom, and she could hear him talking on the phone. When he returned, Keely was already on her second Scotch. He made a drink for himself and sat across from her.

"I talked with a friend at MI-6 to check out the information we found on that fax—somebody named Ibrahim and the reference to something called a Vector+2076-A. He said he'd get back to us."

Keely was not interested. "You feel no guilt at all?"

Jonathan at first looked puzzled, then disturbed. "Without getting into it, again. He was instrumental in Peery's death. That was enough for me." His look was hard. "You know the rules as well as I do."

Keely set her drink down so hard that some of it sloshed over the side of the glass. "Rules, my ass. You killed some poor slob just because he worked in the wrong office. Don't you feel the least bit uncomfortable about that?"

He leaned forward and stared at her. "I'll ask again, you ready to throw in the towel?"

She bit her lower lip and leaned back. "Haven't I proved I'm in this for the long haul? But to kill innocent people-- that makes no sense to me."

He stood and walked to the French doors. The street below bustled with midday activity. "I think we may be getting close, and I need to know if I can count on you, when and if we catch up to Kestrel."

Keely thought for a long moment. She knew what he was asking. Jonathan would give Kestrel much less quarter than he gave that clerk. If they found Kestrel, Kestrel would die.

Jonathan's question was simple. Could Keely pull the trigger if she had to?

She wasn't as sure now as she had been the day they found Stefan's body. The answer then was an automatic 'yes,' but this chase had drained her. It had become an end instead of the means. She knew that she and Jonathan would never see eye to eye on certain things, but now she didn't know what she wanted. After Stefan was killed, Jonathan had been comforting. But all the pain that had driven her to Tangier had resurfaced in Georgia and Odessa. She longed for the solitude and detachment that the Moroccan city had provided.

261

Jonathan waited for an answer. Keely lifted her feet to the edge of the cushioned seat, and wrapped her arms around her knees, resting her chin on her folded hands. After a minute or two of silence, Jonathan headed for the bedroom.

"We need to pack up. If Kestrel plans to meet a shipment in Tunis, we need to beat him there. I told my friend where to find us." He stopped and looked back at her. "The choice is yours, but just so you know, I will continue until it's over regardless what you do."

He didn't wait for an answer.

Keely hesitated, not wanting to move, but knowing she had to see this through to the end, whatever the end might be.

They had arrived in Tunis, the seaside capital of Tunisia, close to midnight. It was a short ride from the airport to the hotel. The Belvedere sat in a commercial block, and at this time of night, few people were on the streets. Despite being dead tired, Keely was impressed by its expansive white marble lobby. Rhonda had phoned ahead, and the night manager showed them to one of the penthouse suites. The suite had a small sitting room, a spacious modern bath and a large bedroom with a balcony. It was too late for food, but Jonathan talked the manager into getting them a bottle of wine.

Once they had thrown down their bags, Keely made Jonathan take off his shirt. The wound looked as though it was healing despite all the movement he had done. She washed the area with soapy water, applied a new coating of antibacterial ointment and redressed it. When she was done, she examined her work. Without comment, she returned the material to the first aid kit and went out on the balcony, sucking in the warm moist air. Her head was pounding, and she wanted to fall into bed, but she knew from experience that sleep would be hard to come by. She glanced behind her at Jonathan on the phone then leaned on the balcony railing. Jonathan did not speak much and hung up only a few minutes into the call. She looked back to see him staring at the phone. The manager had brought the wine earlier and now Jonathan poured both of them a glass and joined her.

"Very odd." He sipped his drink. "Our contract has just been withdrawn."

"Really?" Keely asked genuinely surprised. "Why?"

"Don't really know. He didn't give a reason. Just said that we were no longer to locate Kestrel. Did say he would pay for expenses up to this point. Awfully kind of him, don't you think?"

Keely wanted Jonathan to be serious. "What changed their minds?"

"Said he had word from the Americans to back off. I have a sneaking suspicion it has something to do with this Ibrahim fellow and the cargo on that ship."

"Is it because the Americans want it to go through?"

"Our friend didn't have answers to the questions I posed in Odessa. I just asked again but got a curt 'never mind.' I can only assume that someone in Washington either panicked-- which I think is highly unlikely-- or was worried we might inadvertently spoil a separate covert operation. Just like the government. You Americans sure are a confusing lot."

Keely ignored the slight. "But we're still going to look for Kestrel, aren't we? Isn't that what all this is about? Why we're running all over the place?"

Jonathan stared out over the quiet city as though he hadn't heard her questions. Finally, he turned to her. "That is why this started. Someone wanted you eliminated, and we still don't know why or if there's still a contract out on you." A smile formed on his face. "Since we started this adventure without a contract, guess we can finish without one. Does that answer your questions?"

"Yes. What do you propose we do now?"

He cast a glance toward lights in the distance. "I can't help but wonder why the Americans are no longer interested in Kestrel."

Jonathan said nothing more, returned inside, and went into the bedroom, flopping back on the bed. Keely followed, wanting to hash out some sort of itinerary and discovered Jonathan had fallen quickly to sleep. She walked quietly into the room and stared down at him a moment, watching his peaceful slumber. For a moment, she could detach him from the world he deliberately chose to be a part of. She reached down and pulled the covers over him, tucking him in. She almost reached to stroke his cheek but stopped and backed away from him.

Keely watched the night wane, wishing she too could fall asleep. She knew that wasn't possible. Part of her wanted to wake Jonathan and tell him it was over. She would go back to Tangier and grieve the loss of Stefan. Maybe she would head back to Colorado and get on with her life. But another part of her knew that she would never be free of this life without finding Kestrel.

Keely finally fell asleep close to five a.m., waking in a sweat three hours later. Jonathan was gone, but he had scribbled a note saying he would return in a bit and would have breakfast. Keely wandered into the bathroom, filling the tub with scalding hot water. She gingerly lowered herself into the steam, hoping the heat would relieve some of her tension. She leaned back and closed her eyes. She must have fallen asleep in that position when she heard the door to the suite open and Jonathan call out.

"You awake?"

Keely didn't move. "In here."

Jonathan nudged the door partially open with his foot, his hands holding a large tray. He did not seem to notice her nakedness.

"Brought you breakfast. Coffee, juice and a special treat. Did you have 'brique' in Tangier? It's an egg concoction-- in pastry. Quite nice. Got you one."

263

Keely opened her eyes and reached for one of the fluffy terry cloth robes hanging near the tub. "Be out in a second."

When she walked into the sitting room, Jonathan had set up tray on a small table and was filling their cups with thick coffee. He held a cup up to her.

"Sit here. The whole object of this brique is to eat it without spilling any of the contents."

She watched as he bit into the triangular pastry, noting that along with a runny egg, there were chopped vegetables and a sauce. She picked up one and absently bit into it, the egg running down over her fingers. She noticed a flight bag they hadn't brought with them in one of the chairs.

"What's in that?"

Jonathan finished his pastry and meticulously wiped his hands.

"Insurance."

He reached over and opened the bag, extracting two small automatics and several extra clips.

"Prices are quite good here even though your government will pick up the tab. I have a man." He had a man in almost every city. Keely avoided looking at the weapons.

He finished his coffee and poured another cup. He sat back and sipped. "By the way, before I went out this morning, I placed a call to a friend at the CIA. You remember Roger Vengling? Think he visited St. Alban's once when you were there. Short fellow with a pot belly."

Keely was in no mood for a protracted exchange. "What about him?"

"Seems 'Ibrahim' is the *nom de guerre* of the head of Algerian intelligence. Uses it when dealing with other intelligence agencies. His real name is Mamoud Al Fasali. Roger said he's quite the manipulator. Took Roger a bit longer on those numbers, though."

He leaned forward and tore a croissant in half, buttering part and biting into it. Keely wanted to scream.

"Quit with the games. What is it?"

Jonathan's demeanor suddenly turned serious. "Those numbers are the Russia designation for weapons-grade Phosgene gas. Vector was the code name of a research center in Siberia. The number is the box number for Stepnogrosk in Kazakhstan. Apparently, Kestrel has made a deal with Algerian intelligence for nerve gas. He must have gotten it from some base in the Ukraine-- bought it, most likely-- and cut a deal with Mamoud. From what Roger says, that could be a big score for Kestrel."

"Was that part of the shipment in Georgia? I thought you said that original shipment was some guidance system. Now you're saying there was nerve gas?"

"Apparently. Our friends at NSA were leery about telling me the truth the first time around. There are actually two elements to the gas, and they are shipped in separate canisters. They only become toxic when mixed. I assume the NSA thought the air strike would dissipate the gas in the mountains with little damage."

Keely thought about the family at the farm. Had the gas canisters been ruptured by the air strike, their lives might have been in danger anyway. "The canisters survived?"

"Since we didn't find anything remotely resembling gas canisters, I think Kestrel was tipped off and got them out of there before the strike."

Jonathan rose and went into the bedroom. He returned in a moment with the digital camera. Turning it on, he reviewed the pictures Keely had taken. When he was through, he set the camera down. "Nothing. But then, I don't expect the canisters would have been in the open."

"And so now the NSA doesn't want to stop the shipment?"

"Roger believes they may actually be sponsoring this little transaction. He thinks Mamoud will use it on his home-grown fundamentalist radicals. Everybody has them. Kinda makes sense in a perverse way. Mamoud gets rid of some real nasties for his government, the NSA gets Mamoud in its back pocket from some future pay back, like maybe help with Al- Qaeda."

"What a fucking piece of shit."

"I think our friends in Washington would prefer to call it 'covert international diplomacy'."

"What's that mean for us?"

"Not a thing. The NSA can play all the little games it wants. Our problem is locating Kestrel. And when we do...."

Jonathan didn't have to finish. Keely knew that he didn't care if he displeased the NSA or CIA. They always came back. Outwardly, Jonathan seemed as brash and nonchalant as he always had been, but Keely sensed the strain of the chase was wearing on him. Perhaps it was the fact this chase had become personal for him as well.

They had both thrown themselves into the hunt because they believed they were looking for someone out to kill Keely. But every day, Keely felt there was deeper meaning to all this than either cared to admit. Jonathan had never truly explained why it was so important for him to protect her. Keely had blamed Jonathan for Stefan's death. She had wanted to believe that if he had not shown up, Stefan might have eventually told her of his situation, but in all honesty, she wasn't sure. Perhaps he was looking for a way for them to escape. Unfortunately, Stefan had made a choice-- a choice that cost his life.

The last weeks-- never more than three days in any one city or country-- began to wear thin on both of them. She knew Jonathan was used to stressful conditions, but none with as many twists and turns. His wound and the death of Peery added to the stress.

Jonathan broke into her reverie. "Thought I'd stroll over to the docks, perhaps find out when that ship is due to arrive."

Keely stirred and stood. "Want me to go with you?"

"No. You look like you need to get your mind off things for a bit."

"I think that is a good idea. If you're sure you don't need me...."

Jonathan stood and reached for the flight bag. He took one of the automatics and an extra clip. "By the way, if you feel up to it, the Souq here is quite interesting. About a ten-minute taxi ride."

After dressing, Keely sat alone in the hotel room, trying to decide what she felt like doing. Too restless to go back to bed, she rode down to the lobby and asked the concierge for a taxi. She was glad everyone spoke French here; it was comforting to be able to deal with people in their own language, even if her French needed refreshing.

Jonathan was right about the Souq. Unlike the market in Tangier, this one was covered and flowed down from one of the hills above the city, anchored by a broad square with churches and mosques at each corner. She followed the crowd of early shoppers into the winding alleyways of the area. The narrow pedestrian walk lined with small shops sold everything imaginable.

Keely wandered the alleys looking at nothing in particular, comforted by the crush of people. She would stop occasionally to admire some lace or a leather purse, the storeowners hovering just a few feet away ready to pounce. She knew better than to pick something up; a sign she was interested in buying.

These merchants waited for a sign to distinguish who was really interested and who was just sightseeing. Some called out half-heartedly, more to strike up a friendly conversation than to make a sale. She would just smile at them and say "*la, shukran.*" No thanks.

She had walked for almost a half hour, purposely allowing herself to get lost in the winding maze. She wasn't afraid. Someone was always willing to point the way out. She was looking at carved picture frames, finding herself wishing she had some of the photos Stefan had taken, when something in the corner of her eye caught her attention.

She looked up just in time to see a tall woman around a corner at the end of the block.

Something uncomfortably familiar about the figure impressed Keely, despite the fact she disappeared in a fraction of a second. Keely moved forward, making the corner quickly. The woman walked about twenty yards ahead of her, but her height made her easy to keep up with, being several inches above those around her. She moved with determination. Keely saw the alley led to the outside.

266

Keely quickened her pace and was within ten yards when the woman stopped suddenly, apparently to examine something in one of the stalls. As she turned to look, Keely caught her breath. It was Irina.

The white-hot noonday sun bathed the square beside the Kasbah Mosque in unbearable light. Keely stood just inside the entranceway to the cavernous souq staring at the pavement in front of her, panicked that her eyes were not adjusting to the light fast enough. After what seemed like an eternity, her eyes had adapted well enough for her to scan the square.

When she saw Irina in the Souq, Keely's first instinct was to confront her. But she hung back, not sure what Irina was doing in Tunis and if it might be connected to the shipment Kestrel had sent. After all, they had discovered Irina had more than shown she would work for anyone. Keely followed Irina through the winding alleyways, keeping far enough back to avoid detection. Irina spent a half hour more wandering the stalls, stopping periodically, but buying nothing. Finally, she reached a portal and Keely moved forward quickly.

Irina was almost to the line of taxis waiting for passengers. Keely assumed Irina had not seen her because the Ukrainian woman walked with a casual gait, never glancing back. Once her eyes adjusted, Keely angled toward the curb keeping Irina slightly ahead of her. Irina headed for the front of the line while Keely headed toward the back. They reached the curb at the same time. Keely knew she was violating protocol by approaching a taxi at the back of the line, but she pulled out a wad of Dinar, and peeled off several holding them up as she slid into the back seat. The driver looked uncomfortable, but his eyes on the Dinar told Keely he was not stupid.

"See that taxi at the head of the line?" Keely spoke slowly, and her tone was serious. "It's my sister, and I must find out where she is going. Can you do it without being seen, if I give you an extra fifty Dinar."

The driver nodded and pulled quickly into the flowing traffic. He obviously knew his business, because he was able to keep three cars between the two taxis at all times. They moved away from the old city and toward the section of Tunis where many of the tourist hotels were situated. They drove for about ten minutes before Irina's taxi turned onto a side street and came to a stop. Keely's driver pulled to the curb waiting for orders.

Irina got out and headed down the street away from Keely. She paid the driver, including the extra fifty and got out. Irina had reached an intersection and had turned to the right. When Keely got to the corner, she stopped and peered around. Irina was a half block ahead. It was an upscale neighborhood with haute couture shops and jewelers lining both sides of the street. Most of the men and women were Tunisian, but their clothes were French and Italian. Keely moved carefully, glancing occasionally in shop windows, but never long enough to lose sight of Irina.

The tall blonde was not hard to follow because she was at least a head taller than most of the women on the street.

After two blocks, Irina pushed through the front doors of a posh hotel, the Oriental Palace. Keely hurried ahead but stopped at the door. The lobby was small, but well appointed, and Irina was at the desk talking with a clerk. The young man handed her a key and she walked toward a bank of elevators in the rear of the lobby. Keely sized up the situation, figuring the clerk might be hesitant to reveal what room she was in, but Keely needed to find out. She pulled out her Dinar, peeled off ten of the bills, and entered. She walked to the front desk, holding the money at her side. When the clerk saw her, he smiled cautiously. She returned the smile and stopped, leaning on the marble counter.

"Excuse me. But I think one of your guests lost this." She spoke in French and held the money out to the young man. He did not reach for it but looked dutifully concerned.

"Do you know who it was, Mademoiselle?" He answered in impeccable English.

"No. I think it was a tall woman with blonde hair. We were in the same shop down the street. It must have fallen out of her purse as she was paying for something. The shop girl thought the woman was staying here."

The young man seemed to accept the story. He smiled and extended his hand. "That would be Mademoiselle Sorenski. I would be happy to take it up to her room."

"Good." Keely hesitated. "By the way, this lady is an American, with long hair."

"I am sorry. Mademoiselle Sorenski has short hair and is, I believe, from Russia."

Keely looked dejected. "Oh. The shop girl was sure she was American, and I'm sure she had long hair."

"Would you like to leave a message, Mademoiselle? She can contact you."

"Sure. Do you have paper?"

The young man handed her hotel stationary and a pen. She took the paper, walked toward a writing desk on the far side of the lobby. She scribbled a few lines on the page, placed the note in an envelope and returned to the clerk. "Here you go. I put my number there in case she wanted to call me." She watched as the young man place the envelope in the message slot for Room 28.

Back on the street, Keely walked quickly to the corner, turning down the side street.

Halfway down, an alleyway ran behind the hotel. Keely moved deliberately down the alley, passing a loading dock where a security guard was asleep in a chair leaning against the door frame. Further along was a single door inset in the wall. Keely looked back at the guard and then tried the handle. It was locked and looked as though it had not been used in a while.

She exited on the adjacent street, noting there was no other entrance to the hotel. She walked around to the front of the hotel, surveying the area. Across the avenue and several doors down was a small café with several umbrella-shaded tables outside. Keely crossed to the café and walked inside. She asked the proprietor if she could use the phone. She dialed Jonathan's cell.

He answered on the fourth ring. "Yes?"

"You won't believe who I just saw."

"How many guesses do I get?"

"One. Irina."

He spoke after a long pause, the humor gone from his voice. "Where are you now?"

"Across from her hotel. The Oriental Palace on Avenue Jean Jaures. I'm in the café directly across from the hotel entrance."

"I'll be there in about fifteen minutes."

He arrived in ten. Keely had ordered coffee and sat in an inconspicuous spot where she could watch the front of the hotel without being seen. Jonathan got out of the taxi and walked over casually.

"Nice place." He motioned to the waiter for service. "Pretty swanky area. You know, the port is only about a half mile from here."

They sat quietly for a while. Jonathan finally leaned forward and spoke softly. "This certainly complicates things. The most obvious question is, why is Irina here? And does her presence have anything to do with that shipment coming in from Odessa?"

"I keep thinking about the map, the one I gave Irina is Georgia. Given what that clerk you killed said and the fact Irina is here and in good health, I think we can rule out that Kestrel took it from her by force. Maybe he offered her money for it. More money to help with this shipment."

Jonathan sipped his coffee, ignored the comment about the clerk and pondered Keely's conclusion. "Or maybe she knew more than she even told Niko. How did she behave when you were in Georgia?"

"She didn't seem too interested in finding the weapons, that's for sure. But not enough to make me suspicious. When I first got there, she tried to steer me away from the mountains. But when I insisted, we go, she relented. I just thought she was a bitch."

"An interesting assessment, and probably accurate. She's never seemed the type to let things like loyalty stand in her way. Somehow, I don't think a little thing like a few innocent bystanders getting killed would upset her, either. After all, she's a freelancer just like you and me. Maybe she took the map to Kestrel when she left you at the farmhouse. Maybe she saw the map as marketable somehow."

To be placed in the same category with Irina vexed Keely, but she ignored it. "There is also the fact that she never contacted you."

"If she was playing both sides, it certainly explains why she didn't. Had nothing to do with you ordering her around. You just provided her an excellent out."

"That's very comforting." Keely leaned forward. "All these maybes' add up to it's not pure coincidence she's here at the same time that shipment from Kestrel is due. I think she is involved in this, and that's what happened in Georgia."

The anger deepened in her belly, making her hands tremble and her face feel flush. Keely had been focused on Kestrel, but the thought that Irina, someone who was supposed to be on her side, might have betrayed her, putting her life in jeopardy and maybe causing the murders of the family and Niko, made her anger all the more palpable.

Jonathan sat quietly until he seemed to come to a decision. "I checked with the harbormaster and the ship is scheduled to arrive this evening at ten. I think we should keep an eye on Irina in case she is involved. I'll camp out down there; you stay here. Fair?"

Jonathan finished his coffee and stood, not waiting for an answer. "Don't be heroic. And don't lose sight of her." Then he stepped to the curb and hailed a taxi.

Day turned into evening and the sidewalks filled with couples in search of dinner or drinks. Keely had strolled among the stores on the street, but never lost sight of the hotel's entrance. She had eaten a light dinner back at the café and now sat nursing a glass of wine. Although she had done this kind of surveillance a lot when she had worked for Swift, she had never gotten used to the inactivity.

She was just about to grab a cab, race to the pier and suggest she and Jonathan swap places when a man on the other side of the street caught her eye. He was coming out of the Oriental Palace in a hurry, bumping into people as he made his way down the street. At first, Keely pegged him for just another rude tourist, but when he turned to look for a taxi, she knew she had seen his face before. It was the man Jonathan and she had confronted in Langley-- Schwiller.

Keely quickly evaluated her predicament and decided to follow the man. She dropped a few bills on the table and crossed with several other people to the same side of the street as Schwiller. She signaled for a taxi and one pulled to the curb. She slipped in and leaned forward.

"See that man waving for a taxi? Do you think you could follow where he goes? I'll pay you extra to not get too close." The driver nodded.

Schwiller got a taxi a moment later, and as his pulled out into traffic, so did Keely's. They traveled south, then east on the main boulevard. It was a short ride, ending at the entrance to the port. Keely sat in her taxi until Schwiller had gotten out of his, paid and began walking toward the quay. Keely got out and followed at a distance, wondering where Jonathan might be lurking.

The wharf area was U-shaped, with a dozen berths. Out of the four docked ships, Keely could see two of them were being unloaded. Schwiller seemed to be heading for the ship docked at the end of the southern arm of the horseshoe and moving with determination. The area was lighted, but there were large areas of shadow away from the water's edge and Keely kept to the shadows. After about twenty-five yards, Schwiller slowed down, as though unsure where to go. A figure moved out of the shadows and came up behind him. Keely could see Schwiller turn quickly and then step back, but the figure grabbed him and pulled him into the shadows. Keely moved forward, wishing she had carried a weapon as Jonathan had suggested.

She stopped at the corner of an alley formed by stacked crates that ran from the middle of the pier to the corrugated wall of a warehouse. She hazarded a glance around the corner and was trying to decide her next move when she heard a familiar voice.

"Well, imagine meeting you here." It was Jonathan, his voice almost pleasant.

Jonathan had backed the man all the way to the wall, their faces no more than a few inches apart. Jonathan had a tight grip on Schwiller's arm. Keely stepped into the shadows and called out in a stage whisper.

"Jonathan. It's Keely."

Jonathan didn't move. "A regular party."

Keely moved forward and stood a foot or two behind Jonathan. "I followed him here from Irina's hotel."

At the mention of the woman's name, Schwiller tensed more. In the half-light, Keely could see the panic on his face, his hands held weakly in front of him in an ineffectual attempt to keep Jonathan away. Jonathan brought his other hand up to rest lightly on Schwiller's shoulder.

"Isn't that fascinating. You know the captivating Ms. Pavlychko. How?"

Schwiller chanced a glance toward Keely. There was dismay in his eyes, as if he had stepped into more than he had bargained for. Schwiller looked back at Jonathan. "I don't know…."

He didn't have a chance to finish because Jonathan dug his thumb deep into the soft flesh just above Schwiller's collarbone. The man would have cried out, but Jonathan covered his mouth with his free hand, moving his lips close to the man's ear.

"I'm going to ask once more. Answer incorrectly and this," he applied more pressure with his thumb, "will seem pleasant to what will happen to you next. Were you at the hotel to meet Irina?"

Jonathan removed his hand from the man's mouth and eased up on his shoulder. Tears of pain and fear were in Schwiller's eyes as he slowly nodded.

Jonathan smiled warmly. "There. That wasn't so hard, was it? Now, why were you meeting her?"

"I was ordered to meet her." "Who ordered you?"

Schwiller's momentary silence had Keely wondering if he would tell them the truth. He finally answered. "Kestrel."

Jonathan stepped back from Schwiller and looked over at Keely before he began questioning the man again. "Since when did you start taking orders from him?"

Schwiller, adjusting his tie, cleared his throat. "I didn't have much choice. At first, I refused to come, but Kestrel threatened to expose me if I didn't."

"That bank account coming back to haunt you, after all? What was your meeting with Irina about?"

"She wanted me to meet with the captain of the freighter and give him this envelope." Schwiller reached in his pocket.

Jonathan motioned him to be careful as he handed over a wrinkled white envelope, which Jonathan opened. Inside was a thousand Tunisian dinar, about $1,500.

"What was this for?"

"I was to say that it was a bonus."

Jonathan handed the envelope back to Schwiller, stepped a few paces back from the little man and spoke softly to Keely.

"A CIA man all the way from Washington to deliver a tip. Bit odd, don't you think? Why would Kestrel want Schwiller here?"

Keely shrugged, looking at Schwiller. "Insurance? Maybe he told Kestrel somebody was out to get him, and Kestrel figured Schwiller could run interference."

Jonathan turned back to the man, who looked slightly less frightened. "How do you contact Kestrel?"

"Only by email. Blind accounts that change regularly. I get an email directing me to pick up messages at a certain site. I never go to the same address twice."

"Did you know about a contract from the NSA to find Kestrel?" Schwiller looked stunned. "I-- I heard something about it."

272

"You wouldn't happen to know who rescinded that?"

"Look, all I know is that Kestrel was selling some stuff to some intelligence types in Algeria. I pointed out to my boss that letting Kestrel go ahead with the deal would put the Algerian in our pocket. He was the one who called the NSA."

Jonathan smiled amiably. "How astute of you. Aside from costing us our normal fee, you've caused us some significant anguish. What do you get out of this?"

Schwiller's eyes darted about for a place to hide. Keely could tell from his expression that he was weighing other options. "I told Kestrel that delivering his shipment would not be stopped by the Americans. He told me that if I wanted my cut, I'd have to come here because he wouldn't have the money until the material was delivered."

Jonathan patted the little man on the shoulder. "Very mercantile of you. When is the delivery and where?"

"I was to make the arrangements with the captain to off-load the shipment tomorrow morning. A truck will be here to pick it up.. Irina said I was to make a big deal about showing the captain my identification. Guess Kestrel thought that would make the captain more docile and not ask unnecessary questions. Irina said the transfer would take place at someplace called Tbessa, just inside the Algerian border. I was to get my cut sometime late tomorrow night."

"Well then, by all means, carry on. Of course, we'll just tag along--if you don't mind."

They kept to the shadows, Jonathan and Keely on either side of Schwiller. Keely kept her hand gently on the man's elbow. Anyone watching would think they were three friends. As they approached the ship, the late evening call to prayer could just be heard over the sounds of the shipyard. As they entered the lighted portion of the quay, Keely noticed a car parked at the far end. When they were half way across, Keely sensed movement to Jonathan's right. The car was creeping forward with its lights off. Jonathan noticed as well and pivoted in that direction, his hand reaching for the automatic tucked in his belt. By the time he had dropped to one knee, the car had swerved to a stop and a man jumped from the passenger side.

The man yelled something in French, but the boats hitting the sides of their berths drowned out his words.

Suddenly, the man raised something in his hands, the chatter of a silenced automatic weapon discernible above dock noises. Bits of concrete erupted in a line working toward the three of them. Jonathan swung the weapon in a small arc as though he was on a target range. He squeezed off three rounds in rapid succession.

Prompted by the gunfire, Keely started to push Schwiller to the ground, but something burned into her thigh and spun her around. She dropped as Jonathan continued to return fire, slowly and deliberately. He hit the windshield of the car and then the gunman, who stumbled backwards with his finger still squeezing the trigger, the barrel jerking in an erratic dance.

When the firing began, Schwiller had stopped, looking around in confusion as though uncertain what to do. The first round struck him in the stomach and pushed him backwards. As he stumbled, a second round ripped through his chest below his knotted tie. A final round caught him in the side of the head as he spun, exiting through the opposite temple carrying with it a shower of blood and gray matter. Keely pulled herself toward him, but knew that he was dead.

CHAPTER EIGHTEEN

Although Jonathan had hit the gunman, he must have still been alive because the driver had dragged him into the front seat and sped away. Jonathan had kept his weapon trained on the car but didn't fire. When the car was out of sight, he stood and approached Keely checking Schwiller's pulse.

"Dead."

"Are you hit?"

Keely sat down beside Schwiller's body, examining her own wound. The wound was more messy than serious. The bullet had ripped through her slacks and dug a gash into her upper thigh, but she had had more serious injuries playing soccer.

"Nothing a little antiseptic and a bandage won't fix. What was that all about?"

Jonathan looked up at the ship, but apparently the gunfire had not attracted any attention. He searched the body, extracting the man's wallet and the envelope.

"Apparently, Kestrel was worried about leaks. I assume those folks would have picked Schwiller up after he had delivered his message and then deposited him somewhere where he wouldn't be found for a very long time."

"They obviously changed their minds."

He straightened and held a hand out to Keely. "Probably weren't expecting a crowd and panicked. But they may come back for the money. We should be going." Jonathan walked her back to the shadows. "Wait."

He walked back to the body and dragged it quickly to the edge of the quay. He pushed it over. There was no sound of a splash. Keely thought what a sad end that was to a person's life, but no sadder than the other deaths she had witnessed-- and caused.

Jonathan held her tightly as they made their way as quickly as Keely's wound would allow. They walked between two warehouses, finding themselves in a quiet, but shabby, portside neighborhood. Keely's halting steps didn't draw the looks of the small amount of people on the streets. They walked toward a main road several blocks ahead. When they got within a half block, Jonathan suggested Keely wait and he would find a taxi. There was no need attracting attention with Keely's bloodied attire.

The ride to the hotel was short and the hotel's lobby empty. Jonathan led Keely directly to the elevators and returned to the quizzical clerk at the front desk to get the key. Jonathan whispered something to the young man who nodded knowingly. When Jonathan got back to Keely, he wrapped his arm around her waist and practically carried her into the elevator.

"What did you tell the clerk?"

"I told him you had been drinking a bit too much and had fallen off the curb. Didn't want him too suspicious. "

"No, can't have that. Better he thinks I'm a lush."

Jonathan smiled, "Well, your injury hasn't hurt your sense of humor."

Keely didn't respond. Fleeting as it was, the thought that some semblance of normalcy was comforting.

Once in their room, Keely hobbled to the bathroom while Jonathan retrieved the first aid kit she had used on him in Odessa. She gingerly peeled of her slacks. The blood had already coagulated around the gash, only a few inches long. She ran the water as hot as she could, soaked a face cloth, and carefully wiped the area. Jonathan came in and studied the wound. He found the small bottle of peroxide and poured it over the gash, pink foam springing alive. He dabbed away the foam and applied antiseptic. Finally, he bandaged the wound with gauze, wrapping it tightly around her thigh. When he was done, he admired the work.

"Almost as good as your handiwork." Jonathan gathered up the first aid kit. "Test that to see if it'll hold. I've got a call to make."

He went into the bedroom and Keely stood slowly, applying more and more weight to the leg. It was not very painful, and Keely knew from her soccer days she healed quickly. She took a few halting steps around the bathroom, placing more weight on the leg. She could walk without a noticeable limp, although she assumed tomorrow it would be stiff. From the next room, she could hear Jonathan's muffled voice. She checked the bandaging, which remained secure.

She wrapped a bathrobe around her and joined Jonathan in the bedroom.

He was replacing the receiver as she entered, a look of optimism on his face. She went to her overnight bag and dug out a pair of light jogging pants, which she slipped into carefully.

Without commenting, she went into the living room to get a drink.

276

The wound was not nearly as disturbing as watching Schwiller get gunned down. She had no personal feelings about the man, but it was another death to chalk up to Kestrel. She was tired of the chase, tired of death, tired of this anguish that seemed to govern her life. From the deep recesses of her soul came the cry to end it all right there. Jonathan strolled in, making his way to the bar for a drink and then took the seat across from Keely. He watched her as he drank and finally set his glass on the table, leaning toward her.

"Want to quit, don't you."

Keely hated the fact that Jonathan seemed to live inside her head. "Yes." He retrieved his drink and finished it in silence.

"I just can't take this shit anymore. It's not this," she patted her thigh, "it's the whole idea. I mean, do we really expect to find this Kestrel? And is blowing him away the only way to find resolution?"

She could feel tears of frustration forming, but she fought them back. "This fucker had Stefan killed. He's after my ass, or at least that's what we think. But I'm tired of the whole thing. Can we move on and hope this clown decides I'm not worth all this?"

Jonathan sat passively while Keely ranted. When she finished, she raised her glass to her lips and noticed that her hand was trembling.

"Have you ever seen someone killed by poison gas?" He said it so matter-of-factly that at first Keely didn't understand the question.

He stood and carried both their glasses to the bar, refilling them as he spoke.

"When I was still in the S.A.S., several members of my unit were sent into Northern Iraq to help organize Kurdish resistance to Saddam. Simple assignment and one we had done many times before. Things were going fine until we lost contact with the team. We waited three days before we sent in a recovery unit, which I led. When we got to within a mile of the village where the original team was based, we could smell death in the air. The stench was so strong that our Kurdish guides refused to go closer, but we pushed on.

"The village had a population of around one hundred Kurds and our four team members. We began finding bodies several hundred yards beyond the cluster of wattle houses. Not just men, women and children, but animals as well. They all lay in contorted twists and turns, blood that had gushed from mouths and bowels. It had dried in pools around them. They had been dead for several days and the sun had already caused massive decomposition. But there was no doubt that the people had suffered terribly before they died.

"We located our team in one of the huts. The leader, a sergeant who I knew personally, had apparently shot the other team members and then himself. He was probably afraid of being taken alive, or maybe he wanted to spare his men the agony of a slow and painful death.

"Before he died-- his name was Jonah McAllister-- he scribbled a note, wrapped it in foil and put it under his tongue. It's a way we could let others know what happened to us. I found the note. It just said. 'bio.' Later, through some sources inside Iraq, we found out Saddam had used Phosgene on the village. Not because he knew our people were there, but to see how effective it was and as an example to the Kurds."

He finally turned back to Keely and his look was more pained than she had ever seen. He walked back to the chair and slumped into it handing her the drink.

"I promised myself then that I would stop that from happening to anyone else. There is no way I am going to let that bastard deliver that shipment."

She picked up his hand and held it between hers. "A rather noble endeavor."

"Perhaps, and removing Kestrel removes the threat to you, so you can pull out if you like. But I intend to see this thing through."

Keely leaned back and didn't speak for several minutes, then looked at him with a new resolution. "Okay. We're still a team. All the way to the finish. What's your plan?"

"Well, do you feel up to flying an airplane?"

Keely looked at him dumbfounded. "What?"

"That was Maloof on the phone."

Maloof Boubouwal was Jonathan's contact in Tunis. He was a member of the Tunisian Secret Service but was not above making a few dollars on the side working with agents from other countries. His superiors turned a blind eye to it-- since most had similar arrangements-- as long as it did not negatively impact their country.

"Maloof says the only route to Tbessa runs through the mountainous region west of here. Only one road. It passes through a small town called Maktar. He says there is a landing strip there… and his brother Khalif."

Keely hated how Jonathan rambled on, but this time gave him leeway.

"He has arranged for us to fly to the field where Khalif will meet us with a truck."

"Okay. We get to this Maktar, assuming I don't crash the plane. Then what?"

Jonathan smiled. "I trust your flying skills as much now as I did back in Colorado. Anyway, Khalif will also have some material for us to stop that truck." "Material?"

"AK-47s and land mines."

Over the next hour, the two debated how to stop Kestrel's shipment before it crossed into Algeria. They had no guarantee that Kestrel would even be with the truck, but Jonathan argued that if not, hijacking it would surely bring Kestrel into the open. Not to mention the awkward position he would be in with his Algerian friends.

Keely was not completely sold on his plan. Stopping the shipment was important, but they had set out to find Kestrel. What if this operation just sent him further underground? Keely sat for a long while trying to piece things together. "What about Irina?"

"I've been pondering that myself. She had to have set up Schwiller. What's in it for her?"

"Why don't we just pay Irina a visit and ask her directly?"

It was close to two in the morning when the taxi deposited them across from the Oriental Palace. At Jonathan's insistence, Keely had changed into a pair of jeans and a thin T-shirt. He had suggested she not wear anything under the shirt and pull it tightly around her. Keely complied without question.

Outside the hotel, Jonathan had Keely peek in the lobby to make sure the clerk was not the same man she had talked to earlier. It wasn't, and the new clerk looked half asleep. Jonathan outlined his plan.

"Go in and ask for the key to Schwiller's room. Look like you've been drinking. If the clerk gets nosy, lean in and explain that you are a special guest of Schwiller's and he sent you on ahead to meet him here."

"First a drunk and now a hooker. Remember I told you I wasn't into playing Mata Hari?"

"We play to our strengths, my dear. Once in the room, call me on my cell. I'll come up.

From there, we will check on our mysterious Irina."

Keely followed Jonathan's instructions. The clerk was more interested in trying to see through her shirt than in her explanation. He smiled licentiously as he handed her the key and followed her with his eyes as she sauntered to the elevator.

Once in the room she dialed Jonathan's number. "Number seventeen, third floor." Jonathan arrived in five minutes; Keely had already begun to search Schwiller's room.

There was little to find. He had packed lightly and there were few personal effects. Jonathan re- examined everything in the room. Finally, he went to the bedside table and looked at the notepad next to the phone. He took a pencil and lightly scraped it across the top page.

"Saw this in a Humphrey Bogart movie once. Actually works, you know."

Looking over his shoulder, Keely could see a faint mark appear. It was the number 28.

"That's Irina's room," Keely said.

279

They took the stairs to the next floor, Keely walking slowly. The wound was not painful, but she didn't want to aggravate it. They entered the hallway and worked their way down, passed the elevator to the far corner. Jonathan motioned Keely to stand to one side and drew his automatic. His knocked softly and said in French, "Mademoiselle Sorenski, I have a message."

There was no sound from inside. He knocked again, a bit more forcefully. Nothing. He handed the automatic to Keely and examined the entire doorframe. He pointed to something just below the lowest hinge, and Keely saw that the small piece of paper pinned into place by the closed door.

"Very old trick."

Jonathan measured the distance from the floor to the paper with his hand and put the piece in his pocket. He pulled out his lock-picking kit and quickly opened the door. He took the automatic back and held his finger to his lips. He slowly moved the door open.

It was a suite and the hall door led into a sitting room. A lamp on one of the end tables just barely illuminated the room. Jonathan motioned Keely to stay put as he worked his way to the bedroom. That room was dark, and Jonathan moved through cautiously. There was no sound for a minute and then he re- emerged.

"Looks like the occupant is out for the evening."

Jonathan directed Keely to check out every nook and cranny. While she did, he searched the luggage in the bedroom. There were three pieces, matched and expensive. Jonathan ran his hand around the inside lip of the case, feeling for unnatural shapes. Finding nothing, he closed it and turned it over, examining the seams carefully. Finally, his fingers stopped at a point on the edge and he smiled at Keely.

"Very professional."

He worked the leather with his fingers and it finally gave way. There was a compartment the size and width of a file folder, and Jonathan moved his hand inside extracting a small manila envelope. He carried it into the living room and gently opened it. There were several sheets of paper inside, including the shipping form Jonathan and Keely had copied in Odessa. There were also three passports: one Russian, one British, and one American. Each had Irina's picture with variations of her name. Jonathan unfolded the final piece of paper that seemed to be a fax transmittal form. Jonathan read it and looked up at Keely with disbelief. He handed her the paper and she read it.

It was dated the day before and was brief: "Ibriham. Shipment on way. Should be in Tunis on 17th. Have ordered S to join me here. He will be taken care of before we reach Algeria. I will deliver personally to Tbessa on 18th."

It was signed "Kestrel."

At four a.m., the pier next to the S.S. Vilushka was deserted. Jonathan and Keely sat in the front seat of the beat-up Peugeot that Maloof had lent them along with a young driver-- Amin-- who was snoring softly in the back seat. Jonathan had been withdrawn since leaving Irina's room, commenting only that they should stake out the ship until the transfer was made. His plan was to follow the shipment until he was sure that it was actually headed for Tbessa and then return to the small airfield outside Tunis where Maloof had arranged for their use of a single-engine plane. Maloof had calculated that a truck traveling at top speed could make it to the Algerian border in a little less than six hours. By air, even in a slow plane, the same trip would take forty minutes.

Jonathan and Keely would have ample time to get to the Maktar airstrip, pick up the waiting truck and find a secluded location to stop the shipment.

Maloof had said he could have men at Maktar to assist, but Jonathan felt it was better to keep the number of participants to a minimum. Jonathan had explained all this to Keely on the way to the pier. Neither broached the subject of the fax they had found in Irina's room.

Peering into the still night, Keely tried to figure out why Irina might have that fax. Perhaps she had made a deal with Kestrel to compensate for her involvement with the incident in the Georgian mountains. But that didn't make a whole lot of sense. Finally, had the S stood for Stefan, or Schwiller?

Jonathan finally spoke up. "I have a very uncomfortable feeling." Keely turned to face him. "About?"

"Irina."

They sat for a moment then Jonathan turned to meet her gaze. "You said she was at first reluctant to help in Georgia, but finally acquiesced."

"Yeah. I just thought she was afraid I'd show her up and she'd look bad."

"Was she ever out of your sight?"

"No. From the time we left Tbilisi until she returned to call you, we were all together."

Jonathan looked like he was making some calculations in his mind. "When did she leave the farm?"

"It was right after we saw the trucks. We hiked back down the hill, I marked the map, and she took off."

"Can you give me a specific time?"

"I'd say about two in the afternoon. She said she wouldn't be able to get to Tbilisi and back before dark. That's why Niko and I stayed. Why?"

"You texted me the coordinates around nine. I remember because I had to interrupt the dinner of the NATO commander in England involved in the operation. The travel time back to Tbilisi-- how long?"

"I'd say four hours."

"Then, if Irina drove straight through and got a secure phone, which shouldn't have been difficult, she should have reached me at least by six. She never did. Where was she?"

Keely couldn't answer, but she began to get a nagging feeling that Irina was involved with Kestrel before the farmhouse. "Do you think…?"

Jonathan rubbed his face with both hands slowly, as though trying to keep awake. "That's she has been working for Kestrel all along. I can't come up with any other conclusion. And that may be why you became a target. Perhaps she told Kestrel that if you put things together, we may come after her, and she might have led us to him."

Keely thought that was stretching logic, but she couldn't come up with any other explanation.

"She's obviously involved in this— and Schwiller's murder. You think she'll come down here?"

Jonathan smiled kindly and patted her hand. "Why don't you stop trying to figure it all out for a moment and get some rest. You need to be fresh."

Keely settled down as best she could. Her leg had begun to ache, but she refused to take any painkillers. She didn't want to fly hopped up. Despite the adrenaline coursing through her, she dozed. She dreamt of her father's house. She entered, calling his name. From the back room, Stefan walked into the living room, which seemed perfectly natural. They talked about nothing in particular. Then Keely reached out to touch him. A look of absolute terror swept over his face.

She woke with a start. The sky reflected the first traces of morning. She could hear Amin still snoring in the back. When she looked at Jonathan, it was as if he had not moved a muscle.

"How long have I been asleep?"

"Not long enough-- maybe an hour. You haven't missed anything."

Just then, Keely heard the dull roar of a truck engine. Looking back down the pier, she saw a covered two-ton truck rumbling slowly toward them. Jonathan had parked the car between two warehouses. It afforded a reasonable view of the ship without putting them in the open. The truck passed and pulled alongside the S.S. Vilushka. Two men got out, glanced around and climbed the rickety gangway, disappearing into the ship.

Fifteen minutes later, the men reappeared with a uniformed officer who seemed to be calling out orders to the crew. It took another half hour to transfer a pallet stacked with olive-drab metal containers from the ship's hold to the truck. There were a dozen containers, each about four-foot-long and two feet in diameter. By the way the men loaded them into the truck, the containers appeared not to be heavy.

Halfway through the loading, a sedan pulled alongside the truck from the opposite direction. It parked between the truck and the ship, so Keely and Jonathan could not see the occupants. The two men loading stopped and walked to the car. After several minutes, the loading continued. By the time the two men climbed back into the cab, morning had broken, and Amin had awakened in the back seat.

"We go now?"

Jonathan ignored the question but turned to Keely. "Did you notice how many people were in the car?"

"Couldn't see from this angle. Think one of them might be Kestrel?"

Jonathan didn't answer for a long moment. "He said in the fax he would be accompanying the shipment. Maybe he'll follow in the car, maybe he'll ride along. Either way, we should stay with the shipment."

When the truck pulled away from the ship, Keely saw the car parked close to the gangway. It was empty. She turned to Jonathan.

"Well, whoever was in the car is now in the truck. I get a feeling it'll be a lousy ride."

Jonathan started the engine. "We'll follow to make sure they are headed in the right direction, then we'll circle back and get the plane." He turned to Amin. "You tell me if they take the road to Tbessa, then to the airfield." The young man nodded.

The journey through the early morning traffic of Tunis was tortuous, which was in Jonathan's favor. The truck had to creep along, allowing Jonathan to follow at a safe distance. By the time the traffic thinned, they were well past the built-up sections of the city and into a more ragged area of ramshackle houses and farms. The truck was picking up speed and there were fewer cars to provide cover.

"Well?"

The young man hesitated then smiled. "Yes. This is road. Now we go to airport?"

Jonathan pulled to the side as the truck grew smaller and smaller. "Get us to the airfield as quickly as possible."

It was a twenty-minute ride to the airstrip, which in actuality was a cracked asphalt runway bordered by two corrugated steel hangars. An old Cessna 185 sat beside one hangar, a bored guard lounging nearby. They pulled in beside the plane and Amin got out, walking quickly to the guard and talking animatedly. He turned and motioned Keely and Jonathan to join them. When they did, Amin formally introduced the man.

"This is my brother Akmud. He is in the army."

The brother saluted and smiled. Jonathan returned the salute and pointed to the plane. "That ours?"

The young man nodded. Keely eyed the airplane suspiciously. She had flown similar planes, but this one looked as though its better days were long past. As Jonathan talked with the two Tunisians, Keely make a quick inspection of the plane. It looked worn out but would probably make it if they didn't have to do any intricate maneuvers. Jonathan walked over to her.

"Well?"

"All things considered, I'd rather not trust it. But if we have no other choice...." Without waiting for a response, Keely opened the pilot side and climbed in. The interior had been modified and the area behind the front seats was an open cargo area. Jonathan returned to the men and talked a minute longer, then joined Keely.

"They said there is an aeronautical map in here that shows the airstrip we're headed for." He searched a second and found it on the floor. He studied it and then handed it to Keely.

She had studied hundreds of air charts, and this one was decidedly less complicated than those used in the States. The airfield at Maktar was circled in red. Keely looked at Jonathan and shrugged. "Ready?" He nodded and she waved to the two men standing beside the car.

The engine turned over on the first try. Keely was pleasantly surprised it sounded as though it had been well serviced. She taxied slowly down the runway, turning at the end.

"Well, here goes nothing."

She throttled forward and the plane picked up speed rapidly. Three-fourths of the way down the runway, she eased back on the stick and the plane rose effortlessly. Banking to her right she headed west, gaining altitude slowly. In a matter of minutes, the ground below them turned into desert-scape broken rarely by a road or structure. Jonathan studied the map, suggesting over the roar of the engine that they parallel the highway to Tbessa to be sure the truck was still headed in that direction. Keely leveled off at 2,000 feet. They located the highway and identified the truck moving along at a steady pace. It was not hard to pick out because it was the only vehicle on the road. They watched for a minute or two then Keely increased speed, quickly losing the truck behind them.

Jonathan reached behind his seat and pulled out a bag. "These are for you." Inside were two British desert camouflage uniforms.

"Slip in the back and put them on."

Keely did as she was instructed, Jonathan taking over the controls. She slipped out of her shirt and jeans. The loose military pants and top were lightweight and fit perfectly, which she expected. She laced the camo boots and fitted her hair under a cap with a cloth extension that covered her neck. There was also a pair of sunglasses.

284

When she was finished, she tapped Jonathan on the shoulder and slid into the pilot's seat.

Jonathan looked her over. "Regular desert warrior."

He went into the cargo bay and changed into a matching outfit. When he was back in the front, he glanced down at the terrain passing below. "Now we are ready."

They flew one for several minutes until she glanced over at him. "We still don't know what Kestrel looks like-- how can we be sure he's in there?"

Jonathan didn't respond immediately to Keely's question. He seemed to be working out the possibilities in his mind. He answered, not looking at her.

"All the evidence seems to suggest he is. There's no other vehicle, and I doubt he would have allowed such an important shipment to be handled by lackeys. The faxes-- what that clerk said. I think we should work on that assumption."

"And if he isn't?"

Jonathan looked at her. "We still take the shipment. And we just keep looking. Although I have a feeling that stopping a sale this big will bring him out of the woodwork if he's not there. We might want to leave a little message for him if he's not in the truck, just so he'll know where to find us. It's time he came to us rather than us running after him. Let's take it one step at a time, though. First things first and all that."

The sun was at their back and the vista in front of them was astonishingly similar to western Colorado-- rolling sun baked hills devoid of most vegetation except for a truculent scrub pine. There were no signs of habitation, although Keely guessed Bedouin drove their herds of sheep through this area.

Jonathan's question disrupted her thoughts. "Very possibly this could be over soon. Have you decided what happens after?"

Keely had avoided thinking about that for the last several weeks. She was certain that returning to Swift was out of the question, although being with Jonathan had made her wonder if she wanted to stay with him after all. That thought had been fleeting, but she knew it was one she had to assess more carefully. However, now was not the time.

"My first thought is to go back to Colorado. You know, start over. Probably go to work for my dad." She dipped her right wing and straightened. "Forgot how much I like flying. Besides, I still have a tidy sum in Switzerland."

Jonathan watched the desert below. "Sounds very comfortable."

Keely could feel embarrassment rising in her. "Well, maybe it's not your cup of tea, but it'll suit me fine."

285

He looked at her. "Didn't mean to imply… In fact, I've been mulling over options as well. Perhaps my hiatus will stretch into something more permanent. This business is getting just a bit too wearisome for me. Perhaps it's my age. Anyway, I may just close down Swift; become that gentleman farmer. Of course, I'd set Rhonda up nicely, a little sex shop somewhere."

Keely shook her head, laughing at his notion and keeping her thoughts to herself. He might do that for Rhonda, but she couldn't imagine him leaving behind his world or closing down Swift Enterprises.

They followed the highway as it meandered through the rolling hills, finally arriving at Maktar, a disorganized cluster of buildings wedged into a valley, the highway running through its center. Jonathan pointed to the area west of the town where a small airstrip had been carved out of the land. They circled once and then Keely set the plane down. She taxied to the only building at the airstrip. Sitting to one side was a flatbed truck. As they drew near a man got slowly out of the front. He wore Bedouin headgear and appeared to be quite elderly. Keely shut down the engine as Jonathan got out and walked to the man, kissing him in Arab fashion on both cheeks. By the time Keely got to them, they were both smiling. Jonathan turned to her.

"This is Issam, Maloof's uncle. A very important man in Maktar."

Issam smiled a toothless grin and bowed slightly as he enthusiastically shook Keely's hand. He led them to the back of the truck. There was a large tarp and several coils of rope. There was also a crate, which Issam opened proudly. Inside were a pair of AK-47s, one fitted with a scope, and a pair of automatics. The crate also contained several Claymore mines that had been haphazardly thrown in, along with several magazines of ammunition.

Keely looked at Jonathan quizzically. "Claymores?"

"Old S.A.S. trick. You set one in the middle of the road propped up at a 45-degree angle. When a vehicle gets close enough, you detonate. Blows out the tires and gums up the engine but doesn't affect the rest of the truck."

Jonathan shook Issam's hand and smiled broadly, addressing the old man in French. "Thank you very much. We should not be more than a few hours. We shall meet you here at, perhaps, five this afternoon."

The man nodded and smiled.

They headed east along the highway, which was little more than a two-lane hardtop. The landscape was less appealing on the ground than it had appeared from the air. The road snaked through rolling hills devoid of vegetation. They made sure no other trucks were headed west on the road, and both felt confident they could pick out Kestrel's truck if there were. After a few miles, Jonathan slowed, peering at the sloping hills on either side of the road. He finally pulled over and retraced their route. He stopped past a particularly sharp curve and pulled onto the soft shoulder. He got out and walked around for a few minutes, then returned and drove another three-hundred yards to a dirt road that wound its way behind one of the ridges that bordered the road. He pulled in far enough not to be seen from the road and turned off the engine.

"This is the place."

They got out and collected the equipment, Jonathan taking the AK-47 with the scope and handing Keely several magazines of ammunition.

"That should be enough. Before we set up, I want to make sure you understand. This is 'no quarter given'."

Keely understood. There would be no prisoners.

They set up on opposite sides of the road. Jonathan situated Keely a hundred yards further east than his own position. He set up the Claymore and set a second one opposite Keely's position.

When she asked about it, he explained.

"If my calculations are correct, the tires will blow about here." He drew a line with his foot. "It will take about sixty feet for the truck to stop. That means it will pass over the second Claymore, which will then be facing the rear of the truck. Just in case you need it. I will take out the driver and anyone coming around the left side of the truck. You have the passenger side of the truck and anyone coming out the back. Just be sure not to fire into the cargo area. Wait until they are out."

After Jonathan had placed the mines, he touched Keely softly on the cheek. "You ready?"

She nodded, but inside she was not sure she could go through with this. They got to their positions and the waiting began. Keely couldn't help but dread the inevitable firefight about to take place. And even though it might end the fear of being hunted, she knew that the killing would throw her back into the same depression she had felt before Stefan. And as she thought of him, she tried to remember his face, saddened by the realization his image was no longer easy to capture. Tears began to fall-- for Stefan, for her. For all the things that could have been, even with Jonathan.

CHAPTER NINETEEN

An hour and fifteen minutes passed while Keely and Jonathan waited on opposite sides of the road. But Keely's mind was not on the impending battle. Jonathan's comments about giving up Swift kept coming back to her. She wondered if he really meant what he had said or was he trying to ease any guilt she might have about not returning to the company. With each passing minute, she agonized over something else Jonathan had said. Once they stopped the truck, they would take no prisoners. She imagined the ensuing battle and wondered if she still had the stomach to fire on another human being again, even if it was Kestrel.

Jonathan stood up abruptly, snapping her back from her reverie. She checked her weapon to make sure the safety was off and set for fully automatic. When she looked up, he was crossing the road and hurried to where she crouched. He wiped the sweat off his forehead and looked down the road.

"That truck should have passed here forty-five minutes ago."

Keely agreed. "What do you want to do?"

He clicked on the safety of his AK-47. "Let's double back and see if we can find what's happened to them." He smiled at her. "Wouldn't you rather be moving, anyway? The heat is oppressive. Who knows, they might have broken down. Good thing you're a mechanic."

"I don't work on trucks. Just planes, remember?"

He smiled again and reached down for her. As she stood, she could feel her thigh muscles tense. The wound had not bothered her until now but sitting in one position for so long had aggravated it. She held his arm as they worked their way to where the truck was parked. Once on the tarmac, she released him, but he reached out and held her under the elbow.

288

"The thigh?"

Keely nodded, thankful that he had offered. They walked slowly for a hundred yards until the pain eased then she picked up speed and Jonathan let go. She followed him to the truck and got in, resting her weapon on her lap. Jonathan backed into the roadway and headed the truck east.

"I was thinking about what you said before-- about when Irina finally contacted you. Did you tell her about the air strike?"

"I couldn't have. I didn't know until you were in the country. There was no way she could have found out. Maybe she just warned Kestrel that someone was spying on the site."

"But why didn't Kestrel just evacuate the truck park? I couldn't have done anything about it. And why sacrifice some of his people and those weapons to cover the missing truck?"

"Cutting his losses. Maybe when he discovered the park had been hit, he thought whoever hit it would do BDA. From the air, it would look pretty much destroyed. Of course, how he found out in advance and moved the trucks before the strike is beyond me."

Keely could not comprehend such a callous disregard for human life, even after her experiences of the past year. "Why kill the family?"

"Irina must have told Kestrel you and Niko were at the farm. The family was just collateral damage. I believe they were after you. They just took out anybody around."

"But how did he know I wasn't dead?"

"Irina must have come back, found the bodies and panicked. She would have assumed you were the one who killed the men and couldn't be sure if you had seen the truck park after the strike. If you had, you might have realized one of the trucks was missing. And of course, she knew you had taken pictures. That would open a whole can of worms."

Keely knew that, in a perverted way, it made sense. She looked at Jonathan. "She told Kestrel I could be a threat. And that was when he brought in Stefan, first to find the camera and then to find out if I had discovered the ruse and passed the information on." She frowned. "But why would he go to all that trouble? After all, he was hired back by the CIA."

Jonathan shrugged. "Some people just don't like loose ends. It is odd he would be so single-minded about finding you. As for Irina, she was just looking for a way to profit from both sides. It's a strange business. One minute you're looking for the enemy, the next you're working for them."

"Don't you think Irina would assume that if something happened to me, you'd step in?"

Jonathan didn't say anything for a moment, then shot a look her way. "Well, actually, I told Irina that you were quitting after Georgia, and would probably leave directly after the weapons were found."

"Since you had no reason to go looking for me, my death would be chalked up to terrorists killing an American."

They didn't speak for a while, the road weaving its way eastward. The topography didn't change much and nothing that indicated human habitation. She looked over at him, but he continued to watch the road ahead. Her respect for him had grown these recent weeks. She found him even more humane, and by extension, more vulnerable than he had been in the year they worked together.

"Thanks."

"For what?"

"This. Coming to my rescue, even if it did cost the life of someone I cared a great deal for."

"Like I said, I felt obliged given the circumstance." He paused. "It should be over soon. Are you okay with what we still have to do?"

She had not taken her eyes off him, and he glanced at her for a second. She smiled, "I think so."

Jonathan slowed down. "Up there, looks like a turn-off." He tapped the brakes as they came to a dirt road on the right.

It was the first passable trail they had seen since leaving their ambush site. He stopped and pondered. Without speaking, he got out and wondered over to the path, bending down to inspect it. He studied it for some time before returning to the truck and climbing in.

"Looks like some vehicle of some kind has driven in there recently." He backed the truck up to a bend in the road. Once around the bend, he pulled onto the shoulder.

"You wait here. I'll take a look." He pointed to the curve. "You'll have to post yourself there. If the truck gets this far, shoot out the tires. Once it's stopped, take out whoever's in the front." He glanced at her. "Don't hesitate."

He walked away quickly, and she took up her position. As he hurried out of sight, she could feel her hand tremble. At the earlier ambush site, she had been comforted by the fact he was only a few yards away. Now, she was alone.

The minutes dragged by without a sound then she heard a soft whistle. Jonathan rounded the bend walking as though on holiday.

"Didn't want you taking a pot-shot at me. There's a shack about two-hundred yards down that path with a truck parked in front. I believe it's the one from the dock. Looks like I was right about mechanical problems. The hood's raised. Let's check it out."

Without waiting for an answer, he turned and marched down the road. Keely scurried to follow. The area was concealed from the road by a rise nine feet high that ran down from the rugged hills to the west. Once at the entrance to the path, Jonathan pointed to his right.

"You circle that way, I'll come around the other." She started to move when his hand stopped her. "No chances. If it looks too exposed, just hunker down."

Keely slowly worked her way, stopping every few minutes to listen. She had moved fifty yards from the path when she decided to see where she was. She slowly moved to the top of the rise and looked over. The shack was off to her right and she realized staying at the base of the rise would only take her further away. The wattle shack looked abandoned, a portion of the mat roof having collapsed. A large opening in the front apparently served as a door along with two smaller openings. The side was solid. She couldn't see Jonathan but assumed by the direction of the rise he was a good twenty yards closer to the shack. She had to leave the safety of the rise to get closer.

Cautiously and stopping every few feet, Keely traversed the fifty yards in minutes. When she had gained the relative safety of the side of the shack, she stopped to collect herself. She could hear voices from the front, but they seemed to come from inside the shack, angry voices.

Keely moved to the corner of the shack and glanced around. She had a good angle should anyone come out the front door. As she held her position, she saw Jonathan appear and make his way to the truck, but she lost sight of him when he stepped past the cab. Suddenly, Keely heard scuffling. She stepped away from the wall. Jonathan had taken a man working on the truck by surprise. The man had pulled a knife, but Jonathan grabbed the man's arm, pushing against the elbow. The man went down on one knee and Jonathan brought his knee full force into the man's throat.

Keely had brought her weapon up but didn't fire for fear of hitting Jonathan. She heard something behind and started to turn, but the barrel of a rifle dug into her back. The man ordered her to drop her weapon. She stretched her hand out to the side, slowing letting her fingers dangle the weapon by the handle.

The front door flew open. A man rushed out, but not in time to save the one fighting with Jonathan. The man fell to his side, writhing in pain. The other man stayed out of Jonathan's reach. Jonathan looked as though he was ready to spring but stopped when he realized an Uzi was aimed at him.

Keely started at the sound of the woman's voice but was not surprised to see Irina come through the front door, a small automatic held loosely at her side. She turned toward Keely, and her eyes looked as cold as they had when they first met in Tbilisi.

"Well, the determined American." Without looking back, she motioned to the others. "Bring him over here."

291

"Irina. We've been worried about you." Keely hoped her tone sounded genuine.

Irina's brows rose slightly. "Really? How flattering. Why?"

"We thought you might be in danger. After what happened in Georgia."

Irina's facial expression did not change. "Yes. And you are alive as well."

Keely fought hard to maintain her composure, all the while her heart pounded. So far, Irina had not raised her weapon. Keely tried to keep her voice concerned. "Sorry I ran out on you."

"Unfortunate. And unfortunate we cannot continue this friendly chat. But once more, you have stumbled into things none of your concern."

She looked in Jonathan's direction. "And you, Jonathan? I thought you had more sense than this." She laughed at a private joke. "Too bad we won't have time to reminisce."

She looked at the two men on either side of Jonathan and the man behind Keely. "Take them out back and get rid of them. Then get that radiator fixed." She began to walk away.

Keely raised her voice as the men started to shove her. "I don't think you want to do that, Irina."

She stopped but didn't turn around. "Why is that?"

"I don't think my employer would like that. We were hired to make sure the contents on that truck get to Algeria. Kind of an insurance policy. You kill us, you run the risk of making him angry."

She turned and studied Keely for a moment. Irina seemed curious; her hard stare apparently trying to decide Keely's game. After a moment, she motioned the men to wait. "Go on."

Relieved she had bought a few more minutes-- or seconds-- Keely glanced at the man guarding Jonathan. Her eyes met Jonathan's, hoping that he realized they had only one chance. She needed to know how close the man was behind her. She causally moved one foot back as she spoke.

"There's not much more than that--Swift was hired to see the package through. Apparently, someone did not trust you. Unfortunately, we didn't get all the details before our contact was gunned down at the pier." Keely slid her foot back again.

Irina paused; the perplexed look on her face didn't match her tone of disbelief. "Your contact?"

"CIA guy... Schwiller. Arnold Schwiller." Another gradual step back.

Irina's eyes flashed, but there was no other change in her expression. Her tone remained even. "And he hired you?"

"No. He was just a go-between. Kestrel hired us."

Irina's stoic expression turned to disbelief as she turned toward Jonathan, waiting for him to say something. Keely moved her foot back again and bumped into the man's foot. The man holding the rifle seemed not to notice. Keely wanted to use Irina's apparent confusion to her advantage, but she didn't want to give the woman too much time to think.

"It's crazy, isn't it? This business. Never know who will hire you."

Irina's demonic smiled told Keely she had struck a nerve. "I am positive Kestrel did not send you."

"Let's ask him, then. He's supposed to meet the shipment at some point. Right?"

Jonathan had been silent throughout the conversation. His guard had moved closer and now held tightly to his arm. Jonathan allowed him to assume control. He knew he needed to help Keely keep up the banter until the moment to act presented itself. "You're not trying to double- cross him, are you?"

Irina whirled around at Jonathan. "You idiot. Kestrel did not hire you." She laughed, throwing back her head. "He doesn't even exist. I invented him."

Keely took advantage of Irina's sudden outburst. She glanced at Jonathan briefly, and then taking a deep breath, pivoted to her right. The balled fist of her right hand swung in an arch with her pivoting body, catching the man full force at his right temple.

Taken by surprise, the man squeezed off a single shot before Keely grabbed the weapon with both hands and pulled it toward her, breaking the man's grip. At the same time, she coiled her right leg and snapped her foot into the side of the man's knee. He crumpled to the ground with a cry of agony. She now had a weapon and turned to face Irina.

When the weapon fired, Jonathan slumped, the man holding him turning slightly to catch his fall. Jonathan stepped back, forcing the man to follow, then quickly using his freed hand to chop across the windpipe of the man. He grabbed for his throat, releasing Jonathan, who turned and thrust the heel of his hand into the man's nose, breaking it with a loud snap.

At the sound of the gunfire, Irina flattened herself against the building. By the time she moved away and tried to bring her weapon up, both Keely and Jonathan had weapons trained on her. Irina hesitated for only a second then dropped her weapon and raised her hands slowly over her head. The entire confrontation had taken less than fifteen seconds.

Keely's hand tightened around the AK-47's grip, her finger tapping the trigger. What Irina had said began to sink in. Dozens of images flashed through her mind: Niko, Vali, Nana, the children, the two people in Odessa, Peery and Stefan.

Jonathan herded the two men to where their comrade lay writhing in pain.

293

Without taking her eyes off Irina, Keely spoke matter-of-factly to Jonathan. "Let them go."

"What?"

"The killing stops here. Let them go. We'll turn Irina over to the authorities."

A clouded look passed Irina's face as she glanced at Jonathan, jerking her head toward the men. "You trust them to just leave?"

Jonathan smiled. "I'm sure we could work out something." He looked toward the men and spoke in French. "The lady's doing you a big favor. You will come with us." The men hesitated then nodded. Jonathan shortened the distance between himself and the two women.

Keely stared hard at Irina. "You're Kestrel?"

Irina met her gaze. "I do not expect you to understand, but surely you can see the logic. What better way to cover my own identity than to create Kestrel? It worked better than I planned. Everyone thought they were dealing with a man."

Jonathan nodded his head. "And by continuing to work as a freelancer, you stayed abreast of perspective business. Very clever, Irina."

Keely stepped forward abruptly. "Vali and Nana-- what did they ever to do you?"

"I could not take the chance the farmer might have seen me at the camp, especially since he had been snooping around. It was simply business, nothing else. There can be no loose ends."

"And Niko," Jonathan asked.

Irina shrugged her shoulders and spoke to Jonathan. "Niko had his talents, but he was a very bad operative. You know that as well as I. He would have gotten himself killed sooner or later."

Jonathan looked at Keely before he turned back to Irina. "Keely was a 'loose end' as well."

"When she became insistent about going into the mountains, I thought I would let her see the place and take her back to Tbilisi. And then I would have chance to move to another location. But then she starts taking her pictures, what choice was there but to kill all of them? When I returned and she wasn't there, I could not take the chance the photos would show one of the trucks wasn't there when the strike occurred." Irina looked at Keely. "As for that Romanian, if I had known he had lied to me, his death would have been much slower and more painful."

"What are you talking about?" Keely felt her cheeks flush with anger. "Stefan convinced me you were dead."

The implication was overwhelming. Stefan had said he was going to find a way to make them safe. Keely's voice sounded constricted. "If you thought that, then why kill him?"

Her eyes showed no expression. "He was expendable. Stefan was not cut out for this work. Like you. Soft. You proved that when you let those three go. Me? I would have killed them. You don't understand the realities of this world. You think everyone has the right to live. You are wrong. Only those willing to kill will survive."

Keely still had her weapon trained on Irina. Something snapped. Keely's eyes burned.

"You know what, Irina? I understand you perfectly."

She pulled the trigger-- once, twice, three times.

EPILOGUE

Keely sat alone on the deck of the Costa Victoria as it plied the Mediterranean. Before dawn, the sun was sending streaks of gold across the dark blue waters. After hours of trying to force her eyes to close, she gave up and found an empty chair. She had been sitting long enough to meet the sunrise. Her arms were wrapped tightly across her body-- in part to keep out the night's chill, in part to hold in her emotions.

Jonathan had insisted they take a cruise ship, and had talked their way onto this ship, docked for the day in Tunis and headed for the Playa De Mallorca in Spain. He had said they both needed to 'decompress,' and the sleek Italian liner was certainly suited for that. But Keely could not decompress. Her mind still had trouble grasping all that had transpired over the past months, and the fact it was now really over.

After the sounds of the AK-47 had stopped reverberating through the empty, barren hills of western Tunisia, Jonathan had walked to where Irina's body lay crumpled against the stucco wall of the shack. He checked her neck for a pulse, but the close pattern of three bullet holes in her chest was indication enough that she was dead.

Keely lowered the weapon and turned to the man whose knee she had smashed, kneeling and inspecting it. "Is it painful?"

The man searched her eyes, his face reflecting his fear that she may turn the weapon on him.

"Can you stand on it?" Keely's voice was so sincere that the man nodded slightly. She helped him to his feet and steadied him as he tried to take a step. It was halting, but apparently, the knee was not dislocated.

Jonathan had motioned to the man he had injured and whispered something. The man dragged Irina's body behind the house. Jonathan walked over to where Keely stood. "I told him to bury her."

Without waiting for a response, Jonathan turned and entered the building. Keely continued to assist the man. Her soothing touch seemed to reassure him, and he smiled weakly at her as he took uncertain steps until he could walk on his own. Jonathan came out, searching through a small leather bag. He walked to Keely.

"Irina's. Several passports, odds and ends, and this." He held up a roll of Dinar secured with a rubber band. "Looks to be about 20,000 Dinar. Hefty sum. Probably pay-off for these fellows with some bribe money thrown in."

The man who had carried off Irina's body returned, and Jonathan motioned the two men to come over. He held the Uzi he had retrieved casually at his side. Keely stood by him as Jonathan explained in French that the situation had obviously changed. They had a choice. They could join Irina in the back of the house, or they could come to work for him. He held up the roll of Dinar. The men glanced only briefly at one another before agreeing to the new arrangement.

It took fifteen minutes to transfer the canisters from the stalled truck to Jonathan's. Keely sat silently on a rock outcropping, staring at nothing. When the job was finished, Jonathan walked over and offered his hand.

"Time to go."

They rode to Maktar in silence, the two Tunisians complacently tucked in the back of the truck, each with 5,000 Dinar safely in their pockets. Once at the airstrip, they transferred the canisters to the Cessna, Maloof's Uncle Issam looking on passively. When the loading was completed, Jonathan walked over to Issam, kissed him on both cheeks and asked him to call Maloof. He was to say that he was bringing a special cargo to Tunis and that their friend Barnaby should be there. Barnaby Fredricks was a military attaché at the British embassy and a member of Britain's Secret Service. He gave the older man the rest of the money as payment for the truck. Jonathan cordially said goodbye to Irina's men, apologizing for not being able to take them to Tunis.

Jonathan helped Keely into the pilot's seat. He looked as if he was about to speak, changed his mind, and shut her door, coming around to the passenger's side. Keely's natural instincts took over as they lifted off and began to fly. After a while, Keely seemed to awaken from a trance.

"It was always Irina. Even in that alley in France, that was Irina."

297

Jonathan rested a hand on her shoulder but didn't look at her. "I feel so silly not having figured it out before now. But it makes perfect sense. A freelancer who works with several Western governments has access to all kinds of insider information. Makes trading guns all that much easier. She must have seen the Chechen deal as stepping up in the world and didn't want anything confusing the situation. Like you."

Keely's jaw tightened. "But all the killing. The farmers. Stefan. And Peery. Just for asking questions. I just don't get it."

Jonathan's hand tensed a moment at the mention of Peery. "And that's the reason you need to get out of this business. You see, in my world, killing is just part of business, something that must be done to advance the financial interests of your operation. Irina was right when she told you her decisions were just business. And, Irina-- or should we say Kestrel-- was just another businesswoman.

"Her product may have been repulsive and deadly and her tactics unfathomable in polite society, but within her industry, she was just another player. Therein lies the logic of it all. If you can't see that-- as perverted as that logic might be-- then you can't understand the spy business."

Keely finally looked at Jonathan, tears beginning to well up in her eyes. "And that is a world you enjoy?"

"Enjoy is perhaps the wrong word. It is the thing I'm good at. When I first got into the S.A.S., I thought I was doing something noble for Queen and country. Now, I see that all this is just another form of business."

Silence fell between them. Then Keely glanced over at him. "What are you going to do next?"

Jonathan didn't answer for a long time. "When I said I wanted to get out of this business, part of me believed it, but like I said, it is what I do best. I suppose I'll return to England and Swift. And you?"

"You still want me to come back, don't you, after all this?" He didn't answer and Keely stole a glance at him. "You could say it. You don't have to be afraid of feelings. Regardless of how they might make you seem vulnerable."

He looked toward her but focused his eyes on her side of the windshield. "I would like for you to come back to Swift... for me."

She didn't answer and neither spoke the rest of the flight.

Maloof and a sandy-haired, overweight man were waiting for them when they landed. Keely taxied to a spot next to a covered truck, and two serious-looking men were at the cargo door of the airplane before the engine stopped. Jonathan was out and shaking hands with Maloof while Keely sat in the cockpit.

298

She tried to comprehend it was finally over as the pressures of the last month slowly dissipated. But a great sense of loss made her feel hollow inside; she knew she would be leaving Jonathan, again. By the time she stepped down from the plane, the containers had been transferred to the truck and it was pulling away. Maloof and the man Jonathan introduced as Barnaby shook her hand and thanked her for a job well done. She didn't answer.

They had stayed in Tunis a day longer while Jonathan arranged for passage on the cruise ship. They would be on board for only two days, even though Jonathan had paid full price for the cabin. She had boarded the ship unsteadily and hardly noticed the modern, hardwood décor of their cabin. Jonathan had arranged for dinner to be served in their cabin, which also contained a well-stocked bar. Keely sat sipping a scotch as the ship made its way out of port. Jonathan absently flipped through the ship's directory.

"Appears there is a flamenco show this evening."

Keely didn't answer. He tossed the directory on a bed and refilled his glass, carrying the bottle to Keely.

"More?"

She held up her glass without looking at him and he filled it.

Later that evening after a dinner Keely barely touched had been cleared, they walked on deck. They could hear music playing somewhere on a lower deck, but Keely preferred the solitude of the warm sea air. The stars were out in profusion, and the two walked slowly around the promenade. When they reached the stern, they stopped to watch the wake trail through the dark water. After a long while, she leaned close and let Jonathan wrap his arm protectively around her.

Early in the morning, Keely lay in bed curled in a tight ball. Jonathan had given her a sedative, but sleep still eluded her. When she had finally decided sleep was impossible, she had slipped quietly out the door so as not to disturb Jonathan sleeping peacefully in the next bed. She admired his ability to compartmentalize all the violence that surrounded him. He seemed to have made peace with himself about his line of work. Something Keely knew she never could do.

Now sitting alone as the first rays of the morning painted the sky, she still could not fully grasp the reality that the chase was over, and it was time to move on.

She didn't hear Jonathan approach until he was only a few feet away. Fully dressed and obviously showered, he carried a tray loaded with coffee and croissants.

"Are you hungry?"

He set down the tray on a small table next to Keely and fixed her a cup. He then fixed one for himself and settled into the chair next to hers, gazing admiringly at the rolling sea.

"Beautiful, isn't it? Never can get enough of the sea. Comes from living on an island."

Keely sipped the strong, black coffee and then set down the cup. "You know I need to go back to Colorado."

Jonathan continued to look straight ahead. "Perhaps I should join you."

"No."

He looked shocked. "You didn't let me finish."

"You were going to say you were thinking of leaving the business. You'll never do it."

Keely sat up in the chair so Jonathan could not avoid looking at her. She reached out and gently touched his face.

"You mean so much to me. More than I want to admit-- can admit. You've saved my life. More importantly, you've taught me who I am. I'm not afraid now to say I love you. I believe in your own way, you love me, although that British reserve of yours just won't let you say it."

She looked into his eyes and held his gaze a moment. "But it's okay. Because I know. And, just as certain as I am of that, I know I can never be part of your life-- this life. Like you said before, this is what you do best. And in a strange way, I do think you are trying to make the world a better place. But I can't do it. And I can't see you walking away from what you do best. It has to be this way. I can't go back to Swift and you can't go with me."

Jonathan started to speak, but the resolve in Keely's eyes indicated that an argument was useless. Instead, he leaned forward and kissed her gently. As he leaned back, he smiled. "I guess you have to have your way, even at the end."

The ship docked in Spain, and Keely and Jonathan disembarked. After passing through customs and onto the bustling sidewalk crowded with tourists and vendors, they stood facing each other, neither knowing how to say goodbye. Keely spoke first.

"You'll have Rhonda forward my stuff. And tell her that if she ever wants to check out the wild west, she has a standing invitation."

"I will. That offer open to me, too?"

Keely didn't answer but wrapped her arms around Jonathan's neck and kissed him deeply. When she released him, she smiled through the tears. "Thank you."

Before he could speak, she turned and walked away.

THE END

ABOUT THE AUTHOR

Dr. Richard Welch, a native of Pittsburgh, retired as a senior lecturer in Journalism and Public Relations at Georgia State University. He has been a college teacher for 32 years in communication, journalism and public relations at the University of Denver, Villanova University in Philadelphia, Kennesaw State University in Atlanta and Mercyhurst College in Erie, PA., and Georgia State University, Atlanta, GA.

He has also worked in nonprofits, as an advertising designer, a public relations & advertising coordinator for a manufacturer and a newspaper reporter.

Dr. Welch spent four years in the USAF as a photo interpreter including a tour in Vietnam and Thailand, where he met his wife, Jill Williams, who was an assistant director of the USO on Udorn Royal Thai Air Force Base.

 Dr. Welch has a bachelor's degree in journalism from Duquesne University in Pittsburgh and a master's in mass communication and Ph.D. in speech communication from the University of Denver.

ABOUT THE AUTHOR

Vallorie Neal Wood grew up in Marietta, Georgia, writing stories as a young school girl. In hopes of pursuing her passion, she earned her Bachelor of Science degree (Magna Cum Laude) from Kennesaw State University and a Master of Art in Film and Video from Georgia State University.

Vallorie taught media production at American InterContinental University (AIU-Atlanta) for many years, as well as broadcast journalism at Kennesaw State in Atlanta.

She and her husband Wayne Wood produced the documentary entitled, *Lithia Springs Medicine Water,* which aired on People TV in Atlanta, Georgia. For over 20 years, she was the director and editor for the variety program "Concrete Jungle" (producer, Wayne Wood).

Three of her scripts have placed as finalists in the California Scriptwriting Competition, Sacramento Film Festival, the Creative World Awards Screenwriting Competition, and Filmmaker International Screenwriting. Vallorie's print articles have appeared in *Southern Screen Report* and *Georgia Magazine.* Her fiction novel, *My Kingdom for a Boy/Letters Unopened* is available on Amazon.com. In collaboration with Dr. Richard Welch, they have written four novels (also available on Amazon) and several screenplays.

Currently, Vallorie lives in North Georgia with her family.

If you can, please leave a review on Amazon.com
It's the best way to connect with readers!

Made in the USA
Columbia, SC
15 August 2021